RISE OF THE VEILBREAKER

MICHAEL SCHUSTEREIT

RISE OF THE
VEILBREAKER

MYSTIC
VAULT
SOCIETY

Library of Congress Control Number: 2025942032

ISBN: 979-8-9991649-0-2 - Paperback
ISBN: 979-8-9991649-1-9 - eBook
ISBN: 979-8-9991649-2-6 - Hardcover

Dedication

This book is dedicated to my grandmother, Ella Mae Higgins, who handed down her love of reading to me.

Acknowledgments

Thank you, Mom, for allowing me to purchase those first science and fantasy fiction books that fueled my imagination.

To my love, Leah, who willingly gave up time with me to allow this novel to see the light of day. My children (Thomas, Patrick, Jason, Haley, Andrew, and Carley) for the encouragement and for listening to my little tales as I tried to get them out of my head onto paper.

To my friends Marlin and Kim, Doug and Tanya, thank you for listening to me drone on about this strange little world of mine. Thanks to my friend and coworker, Vaibhav, for doing the same. To Martin, for his feedback and support.

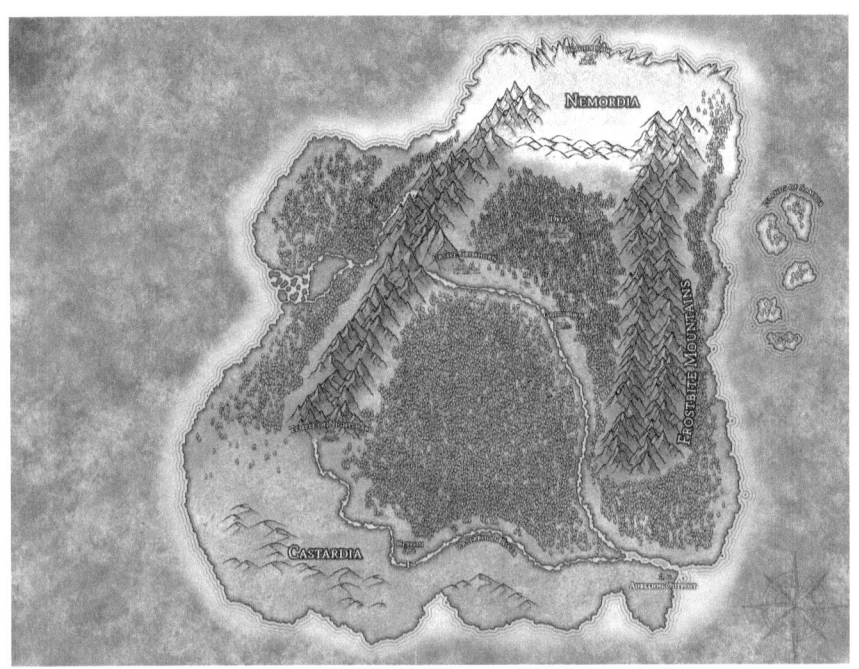

Continent of Binsmuth

created by Andrew Schustereit

CHAPTER

1

Sir Thomas gazed out across the thin strip of plain where the combined armies of the goddess Aleara and kingdom of Zel'Drea waited to advance. To the east stretched the Frostbite Mountains. Tall and forbidding, they formed a barrier against the ever-raging storms that lashed the eastern shore. Like the poorly kept teeth of a commoner, they towered erratically over the land west of them. Few climbed those towering peaks.

Biting wind worked its way through his chainmail into the padded gambeson underneath. This far north, the terrain was inhospitable, rarely rising above freezing. Why the Nemordians chose to live here remained a mystery to him. The relentless cyclones brought the moisture, losing their strength as they washed over the mountains, and it came down as snow. Two months, at the height of summer, most of Zel'Drea had a respite from snowfall, although it was never certain. No one knew why Klydos forced these harsh conditions. It just was.

Worse still, it was now the domain of the frost giants. The first of those the Lord of Tempests called upon to plague this world. Like fleas on a dog, those gargantuan creatures remained on Binsmuth, infesting the frozen peaks, venturing down when their foul master summoned them. To his knowledge, they had not found their way to the Grimhorn Mountains. The place of his birth. He would not call it home.

Two men rode up, cavalry trailing behind them. Unlike his dark hair and deeply brown skin, the two men at the head of the troops were blonde and lighter-skinned, though the older man had lost much of his to grey. A bannerman followed the older paladin, marking him as leader of the army. Pride swelled within Thomas' chest. They were the holy knights of Aleara, the paladins. The man removed his helm, shaking loose his thick, greying hair and a generous mustache that dominated the lower half of his face. The younger paladin saluted, dropping it after the commander returned the gesture.

"Seen any movement?" the elder knight asked.

"No, sir," he replied. "There is at least one family nearby. The frozen pathways are telltale signs."

Sir Silas Morgrave grimaced at his words, looking around to take it in for himself. Neither liked that they were at this forsaken place . Klydos liked waging war here. Open ground was scarce. Deep depressions marked the land, solemn reminders of the icy boulders the giants hurled down from above. Dotting the valley were the graves of Aleara's soldiers. There were many burial sites. A testament to the stakes in their war against the father of their goddess.

Silas gazed at something off in the distance. Misty eyes, unashamedly on display. He was reminded of some battle from the past. From the stories Silas had told him during his years as a squire there were many. Did the elder paladin see some feature that reminded him of those lost years ago? Someone dear to him never returned from these plains. There was no way of knowing. Too many had been fought on this arboreal plain.

Years of campaigning along these mountains had reduced the land nearest the foot of the mountains to plains. In years past, priests of Donegal had been paid to shape the ground, making it easier for cavalry to charge. They were few and far between. Giants trampled everything underfoot, caring nothing for Aleara's creations.

Thomas was still a child at Grimhorn when the last major battle occurred, but Sir Silas had been a newly commissioned paladin then. His commander knew all too well how much precious blood had been shed on this land.

Thomas asked, "Does it look the same?"

"Pretty much," Silas replied. "A few trees have grown back. Not enough for one of those pesky druids to take up residence, but the forest is trying to come back. Any recommendations for where the Grand Commander place her tent?"

Last campaign, Thomas tried to fight a giant solo. Everyone but the Grand Commander could laugh about it. Months of wages spent to replace her command tent. Distracting them from his moment of embarrassment, he pointed to the unnatural swirling of the mist shrouding the peaks of the mountains.

"Fecking trees!"

Silas believed the goddess loved trees above all, and since Aleara sent no signs of displeasure with his comments, it was one of his favorite curses. To the west of the plain began those majestic forests that dotted Versevor, and presumably the other continents of Binsmuth. The other lands were a mystery. Their focus was on the war with Klydos.

Aleara gave them life. Her father wanted to take that away. Harmony with the world was her command. Those who believed adhered. Priests, druids, and paladins enforced her tenets. They did so to protect the balance. A druid might wreck a crop grown on unsanctioned land, then spend the next month helping the farmer reap a better harvest.

There were indeed more trees than humans. More animals also. For whatever reason, civilization was kept in check. There were rebels, living deep within the forest. Most clung to the towns and villages. That allowed them to remain ignorant of the larger struggle.

This was not such a place. Humankind had long ago learned not to settle here. The duchy of Relond, to the south, was one of the closest bastions of humanity, and perhaps the most peaceful. Thomas had never visited there, and unless the minions of Klydos ventured there, he would ignore the place.

Spruce, fir, and pine dominated the forest. Even in the winter cold, he could smell them. Alongside the mighty evergreens were the Frostbloom Trees. Their iridescent leaves were harbingers of the changing of the seasons, and their sap was coveted for its sweet taste and healing properties. Trees were Aleara's presence in this world.

Stunted trees marked the northern boundary of the battle-field. That also marked the border with Nemordia. It was a haven for the believers of Klydos.

Thomas ignored them as well. The northerners were fools, worshiping Klydos, even though the Lord of Tempests craved their death as much as any other human on Binsmuth. Their land had fewer resources, whether due to their failure to worship the goddess or some other twist of fate, was irrelevant. Every so often, they emerged from the icy north to raid or try to gain more of the fertile ground to the south. They might fight the royal guard of Zel'Drea, but they had never joined Klydos in his attempts to sub-due this world. That is what made this battle so different. Klydos had lured the royal army to this place. Then he set his monsters upon them.

The orders of Aleara came to the battle late. Tabards on the corpses testified to that. Klydos had won the first round. More humans dead than anything else. Several of them were Grey Wizards. Their runed robes were easy to spot. Dangerous things, those runes.

Betraying Aleara for the Lord of Tempests was reprehensible. The only good wizard was a dead one. The elder knights referred to them as newcomers to the war against Binsmuth, for they had only become a threat in the last decade. Where they had been and why they joined now might be speculated in the chambers of the Council of Orders, but no one out here cared. All Thomas cared about was sticking his sword through those soft robes and into their flesh, grinning at the thought of it.

Not enough were dead. Off in the distance, their presence was noticeable. Portals opened in the air, spewing forth flying creatures. Where they came from, no one knew. When they died, they turned to stone. Very little was known about them. If Aleara did, she had not shared that information.

The goddess of creation might have created them, but it was hard to discern a purpose for them except destruction. They were formed from the aether to terrorize humanity. Avery thought the idea had merit. According to Aleara all things were created by her. Wolves were created to consume other animals. Were the foul beasts created by their beloved goddess?

That would be a harsh reality, if true. The alternative defied understanding. Klydos was no creator. Only destruction flowed from that being. It was the choice of Sambor, that puzzled him.

In the last five years since being knighted, Thomas had traveled all over northern Zel'Drea. By the age of seventeen, he had traveled farther than most people did in a lifetime or several generations, depending on their place in society. As a knight in the Order of Valor, it was his duty to respond when the god of chaos launched another attack. Small battles and skirmishes occurred frequently. Once upon a time, it had been just foul monsters.

To the west, were the Grimhorn Mountains. Neither as tall, nor were they inhabited by giants. Generations ago, Donegal had convinced some of his followers to follow him under the mountains and never return. As a boy, Thomas imagined hearing pickaxes beneath him as he clambered over rocks in pursuit of his brothers. Snow was just as present there, but not nearly as deep, and there were a couple of months where grass grew without having to push through fresh snowfall.

Thinking about the Grimhorn Mountains made him think of his family. It was not home, just the place of his birth and early childhood. The thirdborn's arrival at Castle Grimhorn was regarded as a failure on his mother's part. In repayment, his father had offered him to the order, hoping that it would lead to knighthood or at least remove him from the political equation.

There were no fond memories of those early years. As much as Thomas hated leaving his home, it had never been a place of happiness for him. His eldest brother had been a tyrant, his middle brother quiet and complacent, leaving Thomas to bear the brunt of his father's ire. When announcing his fate, his father had summarized it bluntly.

Duke Kendrick Grimhorn had said, "Kendrick is heir. James is spare. You are a waste of my seed. It would have been better had you been born a girl."

Not the kind of sentiment that would make someone want to go home. A flush went over his face. Even in the cold chill of the wintery morning, he could feel the heat of his anger. Pulling the helm from his head, he allowed his long black hair to whip about in the wind and stared across the battlefield. There was more to his anger than memory. Somewhere out there on this plain was the army of Duchy Grimhorn. Either his father or brother was leading those troops.

It was unusual for the royal forces to be engaged against those of Klydos, but this fight had started as a mundane war between Nemordia and Zel'Drea. Once Duke Victor Relond realized that there were monsters among his enemies, the call went out to the Council of Orders. As if to reinforce that revelation, lightning streaked across the plain, not from a storm, but from the wizards allied with Klydos.

The younger paladin glanced over at Sir Silas Morgrave. The Knight Commander was not just his ranking officer, he was also his hero and father figure. Silas had taken him under his wing in his second year as a squire. That act got him out of the barracks and the daily fights with his rivals. Thomas often felt that without the guidance of the gentle knight, his time at Godsdown might have been insufferable.

The knight turned, his greying mustache caught the wind, and was plastered against his cheeks. His wizened, brown eyes locked on Thomas. With his free hand, Silas motioned that Thomas should take his cavalry to the left. Then he turned to Caleb, who sat on his destrier nearby, and motioned in the same direction. Thomas welcomed the decision as he and Caleb worked very well together. Quite different from his brother.

The situation that sealed his fate was a recurring memory. Running through the halls of the castle, he, James, and Kendrick Jr. played a running battle, taking turns being stalked by the other two. Wooden swords and shields were their toys. Kendrick had taken a wrong turn, leading them down to the servant's wing. Unlike the royal areas of the castle, the corridors were bare and drabby. These were functional, hardly taller than a fully grown man. They raced along, ducking under trays and around baskets of laundry. When they found themselves at the exit from the kitchen, things had gone from bad to worse.

Thomas remembered it as if it were yesterday and not fifteen years ago. The serving girl pushed through the door just as Kendrick backed into it. The eldest brother was focused on defending against the onslaught that James and Thomas pressed against him. The woman went down. Serving tray toppled, spilling its silver dishes, dumping hot food and gravy on the lordling and servant alike. The woman cried out at first, in horror that her tray had spilled, and then due to Kendrick kicking and bashing her with his sword.

There was little love between him and his eldest sibling. When hauled before their parents, Kendrick had lied, claiming the woman had caused the incident. Thomas remembered how his father had ignored his and James' version of the story. The woman had been punished. The boys had received lashes. Thomas had received extra ones for continuing to claim the woman's innocence. Not much later, his father announced his intention to send him to Godsdown.

The sent an angry boy to the squire's barracks in Godsdown. It had started with a seven-day journey from Castle Grimhorn to Godsdown. The paladins accompanying him from his home were an unusual escort. They had come for the prisoner and not for Thomas. The son was sent along because it was easier than his family taking him to the sacred city. His father could not muster enough caring to make the trip, and his mother would never leave his father's side.

The barracks were hard on a royal boy. When he arrived, the knights had made his former rank known. It was a cruel ploy. There was no rank in the squire barracks, and he found himself fighting the other first years to prevent them from stealing his things. Caleb had treated him fairly. When Silas selected them, it brought a rare smile to Thomas' face.

Their bond had been cemented under the care of Sir Silas. They served in his house, listening to every conversation and taking note of every order, while they went about their duties. When they completed a task, they received praise, and when they slacked off, they faced consequences. The Knight Commander was a tough man, but his toughness never descended into cruelty or anger. Flourishing under that leadership had been easy. When it came to the final test, though, it was all on Thomas.

Either he learned to channel the spirit of Aleara and light the coin, or he would be released. There was no going back to Grimhorn. Enlisting in the royal cavalry was his only other option. That had not happened. The coin had lit, he showed it to his master, and transitioned from squire to knight, blessed with the holy spirit of Aleara.

Jürgen, his second for the day, said, "Thomas, there are trolls amongst the forward troops."

"That is not good," Thomas replied. "We need to be careful. Everyone, light your torches."

His fellow knights nodded in agreement, pulling the long brands from their saddlebags and lighting them. The only way to put down a troll for good was to burn it. Any part that did not get reduced to ash would sprout into a new one. Sir Silas had let him learn that the hard way, allowing him to hack and hack until they surrounded him. It had been a good laugh, though some laughed harder than others.

Across the plain, several wizards emerged from portals. They always arrived in groups of ten. A senior wizard and his nine underlings. In that respect, they did honor nine as the number sacred to Aleara. The junior wizards fanned out. Slowly, more portals blinked into existence. It was not always nine. In some cases, the wizard made a mistake. They were too far away to tell what happened, but in his experience, it was never good for the wizard.

Enough portals opened, allowing the minions of Klydos to begin pouring through. Green-skinned and taller than humans, the trolls emerged, roaring their guttural howls, pounding their war drums, and rattling the necklaces made from the bones of their fallen foes. They swarmed, filling the ground closest to the mountains with more and more warriors. From other portals spilled tall, alien-like figures, similar to humans. These were a combination of a warrior and an aether wielder. This would be no small battle.

Thomas glanced over at Caleb. The other paladin had placed his helm on his head. It was a gaudy affair, with large, swept-back wings decorating it. Opting for something simpler, Thomas chose a one-piece helm. Most of the time, it stayed strapped to his saddlebags. Today, however, he placed it on his head.

"This would be easier," Thomas said, "if Aleara would give us the ability to create fire. Trolls would flee at the sight of us."

Caleb shouted back, "Pray for her holy light."

The paladin said it in jest, but the idea was sound. If Aleara answered, he would see how well it worked.

"Aleara's blessings to you," Thomas said. "Either we shall meet again or we shall return to her this day."

"Do you have to be so gloomy?" asked Caleb.

"You saw the Valkrunians," Thomas said. "Trolls fight like rabid dogs. Those bastards fight with tactics."

He had met a Valkrunian when he was a child. They had talked quite a bit during the journey from the keep at Grimhorn. Thinking back to the night when he had stolen the key from the paladins guarding them was a moment of remorse. Faisel and he had broken away. Despite the pitch black darkness of the woods, they found their way to a clearing, which he now understood to be a druid's grove. In it was a fawn, trapped by a twisting vine. Faisel had stopped him but had become entangled. A man in black armor had appeared. Thomas awoke in the camp, at first thinking it a dream, then saw the chafed flesh of his ankle where the vine had captured him.

Despite his adult interactions with the fearsome Valkrunians, he still remembered how kindly the alien had treated him. Faisel chastised Thomas for his backwoods way of speaking, cajoling him into speaking their language correctly. When Thomas questioned where he had learned their language, Faisel told him of the Grey Wizards of Sambor. Thomas had shared his anger at his parents, and Faisel had cautioned him against judging his mother too harshly, though the alien had no such words for the duke.

Caleb charged forward, pulling him back from his memories. Trolls were rushing across the plain. It was time to bring glory to Aleara. His sword was raised to signal their entry into the battle.

"All glory to Aleara," he shouted. "Make them pay for coming to our world."

His fellow knights errant shouted in response, and they charged forward. They neared the trolls. Thomas glanced up at the mist uncurling from above. The frost giants would send the fog to shroud their approach. They were big and strong, but not especially intelligent. The order had long ago learned the tactic and used the information to counter the gargantuan beasts successfully, but the giants had not realized it. Even though he knew what was coming, their joining the battlefield was a terrible addition.

There was no more time to think about the giants. His combat-trained horse waded into the trolls. Their long claws scraped at its barding. In response, the destrier kicked with its hind legs, crushing the chest of one and sending it careening off to lie still. One of his companions rode up and plunged his torch into the pulped flesh, and it slowly lit up, oily smoke emanating from it. They had learned. The only permanent way to put down a troll was to burn it.

Thomas slashed left and right, then dismounted. His horse would stay close by, fighting its way. Whatever the destrier killed would still need to be put to the torch. A troll broke away and ran toward him. Thomas crouched. When it came close, he drove the blade down, cleaving it where the neck joined the torso. Black blood sprayed out of the gash, covering Thomas in its gory wash. Claws scrabbled at his armor, growing weaker with each pass. The creature fell to the ground, growling in its incomprehensible language. The torch was shoved into its mouth. A prayer to Aleara and the troll burst into flames.

"Thank you, goddess."

Stepping away from the burning troll, he stopped twice to light on fire corpses left behind by his horse. The other knights were moving away, working their way south to where other portals had deposited the foul creatures. Silas would be angry that he got separated again.

Motion caught his eye. One of the trolls had been cut up. The pieces were slowly reassembling. Whoever had forgotten to put this one to the torch deserved extra duties. Hefting his sword, he hurried to it.

Curiosity got the best of Thomas, and he watched morbidly as the green-skinned monster knitted itself back together. The head must have flown a considerable distance, as it was still missing. A new head began to form. That was not good. Praising Aleara, he put the torch to it, then circled in wider and wider loops, trying to find the head. It was getting harder to see. The mist of the frost giants had reached the plain. Lightning flashed, illuminating the fog, and Thomas saw another troll rising from the ground. Worse still, the sounds of fighting were getting farther away by the minute.

CHAPTER

2

Silas was the most influential person in his life with Avery close behind. The ecclesiastical debates with the priest forged his ability to think differently from most of his fellow paladins. It had been a chance meeting in the depths of the library at Gods-down that began their mentorship, then friendship. Banned from the sparring circle for injuring his opponents, Thomas was searching for information to help him achieve his final test. His prowess in the circle was second to none. It was the channeling of Aleara that eluded him. Stumbling onto the priest turned the tide. Avery patiently taught him how to sense Aleara. Though he scoffed at the nature of the paladins, he returned day after day to teach Thomas.

The priest held the paladins in high regard, though he felt they were the most rigid of the orders. Avery had asked the Grand Commander to serve as her liaison to his order, the Order of Jus-tice. In Avery's opinion, they were too consumed with fighting the material forces to search for the divine answers that would end the conflict. It had resulted in many heated debates. When Thomas was given orders to his first battlefield, he learned that while the priest pondered the mystical, he was not afraid to wade in and fight the opposition.

Somewhere on the battlefield, his friend and mentor was min-istering to the wounded while fighting alongside them. The man was a hale companion. Thomas wished he had the priest at his side now. Perhaps Caleb's idea was worth a try.

Aleara, he prayed, please light my sword with holy fire so that I may dispatch these awful beasts. The blade roared alight, though the flame was bluish in tint, not the orangish of a wood-fueled fire. He marched over to the troll to test it.

It howled, spittle flying from its lips as it ran toward him. The sword sank into its chest and Thomas instantly regretted it. Momentum carried it to the crossguard of his blade, and talons raked at him. A lance of pain shot through him as one found a chink in his armor, driving itself into flesh. Flames began to spread across its body, and the attacks changed to desperate attempts to break free. Heat coming off the creature caused Thomas to wince. The slimy green skin started to char. Soon, the troll stopped flailing, and Thomas shoved it off his blade.

The flames resumed as the blade emerged, burning away bits of troll. Thomas was admiring the blade when the lightning struck him from behind. He tumbled into the burning troll and tumbled past it. His armor had heated up, and burns crisscrossed his frame. He rolled over and drew upon the well of energy within him, willing his body to heal. He felt all but the wound from the claw healing. That was a problem to be solved once this latest foe was dispatched.

As he sat up, he realized he was in worse trouble than he had first imagined. It was not a lone foe. Advancing were chaos thralls, the servants of the grey wizards. He drew upon more of Aleara's spirit and bounded to his feet, slashing at the closest one. It howled from multiple mouths as the flaming blade found its body multiple times. He felt a prickle and twisted, pulling the thrall into the path of whatever was coming his way. A black ray hit the beast, withering it until it fell, shriveled, and died.

Two more of the chaos thralls advanced. Without thinking, he dashed between them and whirled his sword in an arc that took the head from the first and buried it in the chest of the second, taller one. Multiple, human-like hands grasped at him. He kicked it, pulling his blade free. Vicious darts of energy hit him, knocking him backwards. The thrall fell upon him, some fluid landing in his eyes. In a panic, he kicked upward, forcing it away, but it fell back onto him.

One or more wizards remained out there, searching for him in the fog. The foul breath of the chaos thrall washed over him, and he gazed directly in its face. It was a tortured caricature of humanity. Wild eyes stared back at him. Its hands threatened to crumple his armor. Entangled with his foe, his sword was useless except to bash against its forehead. He reached down and pulled his dirk, ramming it into the skull. The creature went quiet.

Pushing it off him, he lay in the snow, feeling it slowly turning to liquid from the combined heat of him and the two corpses around him. He heard voices.

"Do you hear the thralls?" one said.

Another replied, "No, surely they bested the fool."

"Don't underestimate the paladin," the first said, "they have an uncanny knack for survival."

The words became unintelligible as they moved away. Before long, they came back. His sword was still enflamed, and soon it would be a beacon for them to follow.

He rolled over and stood, holding the blade low, hoping it would buy him time. He was wrong. That same prickle came to him. He dove for the ground, and more of the missiles flew over him to land harmlessly in the snow behind him. Think, he said to himself. There had to be some way to turn this to his advantage. He crawled to the chaos thrall and retrieved his dagger. He thrust his sword into the thrall, smiling as the flames spread, covering the creature and burning away the fog.

A glimpse of a wizard was enough, and his dirk flashed out, striking the man with a disturbing wet sound. The wizard dropped to the ground. One less to fight in the future. He was confident that one wizard was no match for him up close. He heard curses as the man struggled through the muck to put some distance between them. Pulling his sword free, he willed the flames to disperse.

He ran toward the sounds of the retreating wizard with his sword raised. Slashing down, he cleaved through the woolen robe, ending the life of the wizard. Thomas stood, panting and wincing at the claw wound in his side, which ached despite his earlier healing. Perhaps the talon still was embedded in his flesh. The chirurgeon that aided Aleara's priests would have to take a look at that.

As the burning bodies went out, he fog swirled back in, eliminating what visibility he had. The sounds of battle reminded him that he still had work to do for Aleara. Standing about would not bring glory to his goddess. Lost as he was in the fog, it wasn't easy to discern which way to turn. Giants would be entering the fray. That added a dimension to warfare that he dreaded. He had spent too much energy and time to come out as the loser of this fight.

An ache suffused him. Calling upon Aleara once more, he prayed that the wound in his side would heal. At first, it resisted his attempts, but then the flesh slowly mended. He would have a scar. It was one more to add to this collection. One more visible scar. Others could be felt but not seen.

Thomas whistled, hoping that his horse would be able to find him. When the destrier did not arrive, he resigned himself to finding his way back to the primary battle. Reminded again of Avery, he paused, allowing his senses to aid him in finding his way. He turned, trying to orient himself to the sounds. He wasn't entirely confident but set off anyway. Either he would find members of his order or more foes, fulfilling his service to Aleara as long as he still drew air into his lungs.

The plains were slowly turning from snow-covered to muddy. Aleara's forces were making their mark upon the battlefield. The number of dead now included a significant number of those allied with the Lord of Tempests. A breeze blew overhead, drawing away the fog long enough for him to see icy boulders being hurled from somewhere above. They would be coming from the east, throwing them from above until forced to join the melee.

He turned, sure that he was heading south to the primary battle. It sickened to see mangled horses and fallen paladins. Not an easy fight, given the number of dead trolls around them. They had served Aleara valiantly. Their spirits would return to the goddess, to be used once again to bolster this world against her father and his minions. Some would have families that mourned them. Others would be lost to the annals of time.

Skirting piles of dead, he followed the telltale signs of continued combat. It was reassuring to know that the vanguard still held together. Silas would be somewhere in the thick of it, reminding all around him why the older paladin held the rank he did. Only the Grand Commander, Marla, was even more fearsome on the battlefield, calling upon Aleara in ways that few other paladins could master. Rumor had it that in her earliest days as a paladin, she had considered leaving the order. He thanked Aleara for rekindling her desire to serve.

A half dozen chaos thralls emerged from the fog. At first, they did not detect him, then one caught sight of him, and it screeched, turning the others in his direction. They were all different sizes and shapes. One sprinted ahead of the others, reaching Thomas and falling to his blade without fanfare. He smiled, hoping that Klydos was watching and seeing his servants dispatched. The thought was lost as three descended on him. He fought, using his long sword and dirk together.

One slipped past his guard, and his helm flew from his head, tearing a flap of skin from his cheek. Air rushed over the raw flesh with each breath. There was no time to heal the wound. Both his weapons were necessary to survive this moment.

He struck a scaly black arm from one. In its pain, it turned upon the one next to it. With two of them distracted, Thomas drove both blades into the remaining attacker. The corpse went limp, dropping to the ground. The other chaos thralls approached. He gestured, and moonlight shot down into their path. Flesh sizzled as they entered the beam. A cacophony of noise erupted. Despite their injuries, the two continued forward.

The chaos thrall, which had lost its arm and the contest, lay shredded on the ground. Its foe thrashed about, gnawing on its body. The beast was distracted.

Thomas ignored his cheek and raced over, driving his sword into its neck over and over until it fell on the other. He turned, only to be bowled over by the three other chaos thralls. They sank their teeth and claws into him, some striking armor while others found exposed flesh. Thomas bled from multiple places. He was forced to slam his gauntleted fists into the creatures, using the dagger to inflict injury as he drew back for another round of blows.

One snapped at his leg. When it found purchase on his shin guard, the metal buckled, crushing the leg beneath. He howled in agony. There was nothing to do but continue fighting. Tears filled his eyes at the thought of failing the goddess. With his good leg, he pushed one off him. He drew on the energy within him and plunged his dirk into the eye of the one on his leg. It stilled, jaws remaining locked around his leg.

His vision blurred from the pain. He screamed in agony, fighting through the pain as more of the beasts attacked. Fatigue was setting in, and soon he would be unable to move at all. Every muscle was spent from the day's fighting. Flesh parted, and blood flowed. He abandoned tactics, lashing out at whatever he could reach.

After some time, he noticed that none of them were moving. Lying back on the muddy ground, he felt the cold seeping in. Thomas contemplated letting the injuries take their toll and taking the journey back to Aleara. The pain and loneliness would end. Perhaps next time she would make something genuinely worthy of his spirit. He waited for a sense of peace, instead becoming agitated by his lassitude.

Desperately, he called upon Aleara, hoping for her to grace him with more healing. His wounds were many. Resolve might not be enough to come back from them. She heard his prayer, but it took some time before he was able to push the chaos thralls off him.

With a groan, he rolled and got up on his hands and knees. Mustering enough strength, he stood, then searched for his sword. His leg, despite the healing, ached and refused to flex without extreme effort.

Gasping for breath, he examined the chaos thralls. In death, they resembled humans. Black skin had faded, and the flesh appeared very human. That thought caused him to shiver, exacerbating the coldness of the temperature. The Grey Wizards were worse than the other beings Klydos employed. The Lord of Tempests had found fiendish allies when he joined forces with the men and women of Sambor.

Thomas knew such people existed. His father was one of them. Ruthless and calculating, the Duke of Grimhorn did nothing out of love or caring, only caring for securing more power. Secretly, he feared that one day soon his father would set upon the capital city of Drea. The duke longed to usurp King Cyrus. The fact that the king was his kin would not dull Kendrick's aspirations. Thomas often shared such fears with Avery.

It had been a lively discussion between Thomas and the priest. While Avery sympathized with Thomas concerning his father, he felt it was secondary to the battle Aleara and Donegal waged against their father. Aleara did not concern herself with human politics. As a loyal follower of Aleara, Thomas put aside such concerns and focused on his service. It mattered to the ordinary people. A mortal tyrant was just as terrible as a raging god to them. If the day came when Klydos was not a threat, there would be a reckoning amongst the nobles.

He recalled when Faisel had been captured and brought before his father. The duke grew enraged by the presence of the Valkrunian in his court. Kendrick called the man, Ihuaj, and Thomas learned later that it was a slur that some used to describe the outworlders in their realm. Against the High Priestess's wishes, for Grimhorn was also home to one of Aleara's nine sacred groves of trees, Duke Kendrick had held the Valkrunian within his dungeon rather than turning him over to the Council of Orders. For two years, Faisel had languished in the depths of Grimhorn. It was only after Thomas reached the age of squirehood that Kendrick relented and sent word to the council of the alien's presence.

As he thought of that decision in Grimhorn's audience chamber, Thomas flexed his leg, taking note that the strength was returning to the limb. Fog still roiled the battlefield, and the sound had moved away from him again. Stepping back into his memories, he remembered the silver chains Faisel wore that day. His mother, the Duchess Carina, had explained that silver dampened the ability of Valkrunians to draw upon the aether. He had asked why the Valkrunian was there, and she had turned the conversation to other topics. It was one of many mysteries that plagued him from his childhood. His mother was part of the invisible wounds that continued to plague him.

Greater still was the affliction left behind by his father. Worse than the mystery of Faisel or his mother, Thomas always wondered why his father despised him so much. Perhaps it was because of his growth. He emerged from the womb larger than his siblings, growing slowly but generously. As the youngest, he had grown taller and stouter than either Kendrick Jr. or James. His size had been one of the reasons the eldest brother resorted to deception instead of outright violence. In the years before his being sent to Godsdown, Thomas had fought without holding back, often giving a worse beating to his eldest brother than he received.

He shook his head to rouse himself from wandering in the past. There were more foes to defeat, and getting lost in his childhood trauma was a slight to Aleara. She had taken him in and given him powers that few received. Her gifts to him had allowed him to stop thinking about that childhood trauma. They were there, buried under the scars of adulthood. The fog was dissipating. That meant the giant family, or worse, multiple families, would be descending to enter the battle themselves. Usually, one family unit was enough to occupy a battalion of the paladins. With Valkrunians, trolls, and whatever else had emerged from the portals, it made for a deadly combination.

The few druids sent by the council would not enter the plains, instead lurking in the forest to prevent the army of Klydos from disappearing into there. They had their powers, and while Thomas sometimes wished he could manifest brambles like the wild men could, he was grateful for his place in Aleara's servants.

With the fog losing its masking ability, Thomas saw wizards plying their spells and assumed they were arrayed against the larger forces. He set off at a trot, whistling once again for his horse but resigned to reentering the battle on foot. His shield was still strapped to the animal, and that was a loss in itself. There was a chance that the spells being tossed were Valkrunian and not the Grey Wizards.

More honorable than the human wizards, the Valkrunians would abandon their use of the aether to fight weapon against weapon. The citizens of Sambor would use every advantage the aether gave them. Combat with weapons was against their nature.

Off to his left, fire erupted, and he swiveled to see a wizard, fighting with soldiers liveried in the colors of the royal army. Those men and women would be hard-pressed to find tactics that would counter these unusual foes. He was torn between letting them figure it out on their own and intervening. Finally, he relented and trotted in their direction. It was his derision for the Grey Wizards and not sympathy for the soldiers that swayed his choice. Adding more of them to the spirits being returned to Aleara would bring her glory and find him in her favor. Seeing the look on their faces as he dispatched them was even more enjoyable.

As he approached, the wizard recognized Thomas was the greater threat and left his chaos thralls to dispatch the remaining soldiers. She stared at him with wide eyes. The paladin must have been a sight. Covered in troll and chaos thrall blood, the wizard had to know that the paladin was dangerous. Thomas intended to prove it.

CHAPTER

3

With a deafening roar, bolts of flame arced towards Thomas, the wizard's eyes locked on him as he stalked forward. Thomas crouched down, bracing himself for impact as two bolts struck him with enough force to make him grunt in pain. The heat washed over him like a wave, causing his skin to prickle and his gambeson to cling uncomfortably to his body. He smelled the acrid tang of heated metal and the sharp scent of sweat vaporizing from his clothes. Water puddled where the snow had instantly melted.

Before him stood a horde of chaos thralls. Horrors to behold, their grotesque forms moved closer with each passing second. They resembled giant, melted candles, but with twisted, human-like features contorted in agony. Failure in the order of the Grey Wizards of Sambor meant a gruesome fate. These parodies of humanity were tangible evidence of Sambor's insanity. No vestige of human thought lingered in those maddened eyes.

Closing his eyes, he prayed to his patroness, his skin tingling as her energy surged into him. Shambling forward on uneven legs, one reached him. Its lopsided mouth tried to speak. Thomas lunged forward, slashing left and right to counter its clawed limbs. A blood-curdling howl erupted as flesh split and ichor dripped from where the sword opened up its body. What he first thought were warts turned out to be eyes. Instead of blood, foul chaos energy spewed forth from its nightmarish mouth, threatening to overwhelm Thomas.

He stumbled back, struggling to keep his footing as the creature lashed out at him with its gnarled claws. Thinking fast, Thomas slammed his shield into the creature's face, using its chaotic magic against it. With a screech echoing through the battlefield, its spell tore the beast apart, falling limply to the muddy ground before him.

A second monster lumbered forward, stepping before the wizard and taking the full force of his latest spell. It groaned in pain. Black skin bubbled and sloughed off the creature until it fell into the mud and snow. The face, covered in eyes, leered back at him, even as it fell forward. Thomas pressed ahead. He readied himself for the next onslaught. His dirk, although nicked and dulled, remained steady in his right hand, ready to ward off the next attack.

The melted creature lashed out wildly, swinging an arm dripping with chaos energy. Thomas dodged to the side, driving his blade into its head. A spray of dark liquid splattered onto the ground, sizzling as it hit the mud. The creature screeched, its form flickering as if on the verge of collapsing. He called out to Aleara. Her strength surged into him, and he pulled his sword free. The evil wizard stood behind the grotesque creature, muttering dark words under her breath, and her eyes never strayed from Thomas. Once again, flames erupted from the woman's fingertips.

"No more tricks," Thomas growled.

He swung his sword upward, catching the third creature's malformed head. It stumbled, faltering as the flames shot toward Thomas. He raised his shield arm out of habit, but the heat blistered his arm, causing him to drop to one knee, yet he refused to yield. He struggled to his feet, the sickly-sweet smell of his burning flesh causing him to pause. He either expended energy to recover, or he ended this right now. Only the living experienced pain, and he welcomed the motivation. With the path free of the misshapen underlings, Thomas locked eyes with the wizard, his confidence unshaken.

"You chose the wrong battlefield," he muttered.

He stalked forward, sword readied. The wizard's voice trembled as she fell to her knees, hands raised in a gesture of surrender. Thomas glared, his muscles tense and ready for battle.

"I don't take prisoners," he growled.

The wizard bowed in submission with a flourish. Thomas trusted none of it, expecting sarcasm and treason to flow in the same vein. Formidable in magic that contrasted with her slender frame. She served the Lord of Tempests and had traded away fragments of her soul for immense power. The Grey Wizards acted with fanatical zeal. What damnable reason would they have to betray creation? Traitors to the rest of Binsmuth. In his judgment, the wizard would not walk this world another day, but he gave the final say to Aleara. What is your will, Goddess?

The whoosh of something massive rippled the calm air of the battlefield. A giant ball of fire exploded into the ranks of cavalry. Thomas spotted the familiar banner of Grimhorn in the distance. Despite his reluctance to deal with his father and brother, those lives deserved saving. He uttered a guttural sound when the Grey Wizard gestured to draw upon the aether once again. Evenly matched on the battlefield, but one spell could change its course.

He clenched his jaw and let out a muttered curse. "Of all the moments..."

He glanced at the wizard who bowed before him, contemplating how to handle this enemy of Order. His feet shifted on the slick ground, a testament to the amount of blood spilled around him. Thomas ground his teeth, torn between his pride and his duty. Part of him wanted to let Grimhorn experience a defeat. He could hear Avery repeating the teachings of Aleara in his head, and he cursed. He peered down at the wizard beneath him.

"If I thought a Grey Wizard honorable, I would allow you to retreat from this fight."

"I will retreat," the wizard replied. "I will return to Sambor."

"Go!" Thomas exclaimed.

With a combination of alien words and gestures, the wizard began chanting another spell, and a dark portal materialized. Thomas grasped his long knife, flicking his wrist, and the dagger sailed the precious distance between them. It plunged into the wizard's back, pushing her with its force. Despite being mortally wounded, the wizard stumbled into her portal before it vanished into thin air. Thomas cursed under his breath at losing his prized dagger.

He surveyed the monsters, hating them for what they represented, praying to Aleara to capture their spirits and use them for good. It sickened him to see people perverted into believing the lies of the Lord of Tempests. Memories of past battles gnawed at him, but he refused to let them control him now. Sword in hand, he charged through smoke and fire with his chainmail clanking, announcing his presence.

Fire arced across the distance, taking down one of the knights of his former home. Anger flared inside him, not for the fallen knight, but for the weakness it represented. He pushed himself harder, willing his body to cross the distance and engage with this latest threat. With a roar, Thomas leaped into the fray, determined to show them real strength. He called out to the soldiers of Grimhorn.

"Stand and fight! Grimhorn's people do not falter!"

His father's men turned towards him, some surprised, others relieved by his arrival. But Thomas didn't look back. Each strike meant more than mere survival. It showed those who abandoned him. His prowess invigorated the soldiers, and for a moment, Thomas imagined what might have been if he had led the troops of Grimhorn into battle. The citizens of the Duchy would have less to mourn.

Thomas hacked his way through the last of the wizards and their misshapen minions, every ragged breath a reminder that there were limits to what Aleara provided. Deprived of their misshapened minions, wizards began to fall under the blades of Grimhorn. Losses like these would hamper their efforts in the Lord of Tempests campaign, but their ranks would swell and show up again.

Fresh snow fell, adding to the danger of their already treacherous footing. A foul stench hit his nostrils, one he dreaded. Gnolls! He turned toward the slopes of the foothills leading to the mountain range. First trolls and now these dog-men. Klydos made a determined push to defeat Aleara today.

They poured out from the scattered tree line in droves, and their twisted hyena faces snarled as they closed in on what remained of the duke's forces. Their jagged weapons gleamed in the cold light, and their wild howls echoed through the valley.

"Hold the line!" one of the knights shouted.

Tired and stunned by the otherworldly nature of their enemies, the soldiers of Grimhorn sucked in the air, resigned to another skirmish. This would be a brutal fight. The gnolls were ruthless, perfect servants for the God of Chaos, but they served as harbingers for something worse. The Lord of Tempests employed horrific creatures in his ceaseless battle against his offspring and their creations.

On the snowy ridges above, moving like old titans, the frost giants emerged. In their wake, drifts of snow broke, becoming avalanches behind them. The flow outpaced them, but the giants rose, riding the wave of snow like titanic steeds. Their enormous forms trudged down from the hills, the ground trembling with each step. His eyes widened as frost curled from their mouths, great clouds of icy breath turning the air around them to a freezing mist. Their blue, frozen skin shimmered in the light, their immense bodies towering over even the tallest trees. Each swing of their massive weapons obliterated a squadron in one blow.

"Frost giants," he muttered.

His knuckles whitened around the hilt of his sword. Aleara's healing light, though still with him, seemed fragile in the face of such ancient power. He glanced around, hoping to see the banner of the Order of Valor, but his fellow paladins remained engaged elsewhere. Sir Silas enjoyed fighting giants and would curse at not getting there in time. It was more personal to Thomas. Their presence might be the difference between walking off this field and being carried off.

The gnolls arrived, hurling themselves at the knights of Grimhorn with wild abandon. Their eerie cackling sounds threatened to break the morale of the soldiers. They looked around as if hoping to find some way to flee the field. Retreating to live another day strengthened Klydos' campaign. He committed to marshalling them, using divine energy to augment their courage. It emboldened them, and they turned, preparing to prevail or die. Thomas planted his feet to meet the charge head-on. Wicked claws slashed at his helm, and a spray of blood blinded him, knocking him over.

Flesh bruised and ribs broke as the gnolls trampled him to reach the soldiers and knights behind him. Enraged, Thomas reached out to the goddess, asking her to infuse him with power, and rose. Much like an elemental force of destruction, Thomas attacked from behind, killing several until the cackle of gnolls turned, sensing the greater threat. He stood on a pile of gnolls, beating his chest and cajoling them to attack. They howled and charged, bowling him over. Mailed fist and helm took the place of his sword. He bashed and hit until the soldiers overcame their fear and came to his aid.

Pushing himself free, Thomas found his sword. Smiling at the efforts of Grimhorn's soldiers, he experienced an unusual sense of pride. Even as the gnolls fell, Thomas paid attention to the giants steadily approaching, their breath freezing the air. A harsh wind whipped across the battlefield, biting at his exposed skin. This new threat chilled his companions to the bone. Grimhorn's soldiers faltered, fear spreading as one of the giants reached the base of the hill. Levied from the towns and villages of Zel'Drea, their training prepared them to face other humans. The hideous creatures summoned by the Lord of Tempests were far worse.

It let out a roar, the sound rumbling out like a storm. With a deep inhale, it unleashed a torrent of icy wind, freezing everything in its path. The frozen soldiers crumpled where they stood, their weapons shattering as they hit the earth.

"Get back!" Thomas yelled.

Between his voice failing him and the unnatural wind, the soldiers were unable to hear him. They might not have heard him, but a stray gnoll did and dashed toward him, coming close enough that its foul breath and fetid fur filled his nostrils. Thomas lopped its head off and grimaced as his muscles revolted from the day's work. He frowned, focusing on the towering giants that demanded his attention. The odds were not in their favor. The skills of the soldiers of Grimhorn worried him. They trained to fight armies, not giants. Their typical tactics would have no meaningful effect. Still, better to die trying than to wait in a cottage for them to come.

The giants employed no tactics. Every creature fought for itself. A desperate attempt would be using that independence against them, but it was all they enjoyed at the moment. He heard a horse approaching, and he hoped a scout from his regiment had found him. Paladins would make a difference. He glanced and cursed again. The plumed helm, fancier than any other in sight, caught his eye. Thomas didn't need to look twice to know who wore it. Kendrick, his older brother and heir to Grimhorn. The man rode with the confidence of the highborn. His armor gleamed in the light, untouched by the battle around him. Despite the untested look, Kendrick carried an air of command. To Thomas, it also said, I let the others get dirty while I point and shout.

"Thomas?"

The voice cut through the din of battle, incredulous and tinged with disbelief. His brother, atop a horse looking too well-groomed for the battlefield, regarded him with wide eyes.

"By Aleara's grace... what are you doing here?"

"Last I checked," Thomas said, "this is a battlefield, not a family reunion."

"Father will want to..."

"Your duke can wait," Thomas said. "Right now, we have bigger problems."

"Have you ever faced such beings? What do you think we should do?"

Bitterness overtook him as Kendrick asked his opinion. Their father lavished praise and affection on the eldest. In the mind of the duke, his heir was the smartest and most capable of the boys. Listening to his brother's confused questions made him snort. Kendrick had never reached out in the years since Thomas left Grimhorn. The younger Kendrick had imitated his father in every way. Gone from the keep, Thomas meant nothing to him. He checked his anger. The gnolls swarmed, and the giants closed in. There was no time to focus on the emotional scars of childhood. He needed Kendrick's help, even if it twisted his gut to admit it.

"Listen," Thomas said. "Those things have a hide thicker than your skull. We need fire and lots of it. Distract them, and I will take care of the rest."

"Fire?"

His brother looked skeptical but accepted without debate.

We cannot fight the giants head-on," Thomas said. "They are slow, but their breath will kill us if we are targeted by frost. We need to spread out, force them to move, strike at their legs, or blind them from the side. Their size makes them vulnerable if they are isolated."

Kendrick nodded curtly, his face unreadable. It was a look Thomas remembered well. The short blonde hair that was so different than their mother or him and James. Looking at him was difficult. It was as if Kendrick were a branch carved from his father, maturing into a duplicate. If that were true, then he would bear the same bitter fruit as their sire. They had not seen each other in years, but the old grievances threatened to distract them from the battle before them. The tension was thick between them.

Kendrick said, "Fine. I'll take the right flank. You take the left. We'll keep them off-balance."

"There is no better plan. Trust me," Thomas said.

"This isn't skipping rocks at beavers in the ponds back home."

"I have killed several of these bastards," Thomas replied. "Listen to me or die, I do not care."

Kendrick examined him. The edge in his voice had left no room for argument. And for once, his brother did not choose to oppose him. Without argument, he placed his helm on his head and prepared to gather soldiers for his part of the effort. The plan reeked of recklessness. Sir Silas would say it was typical of Thomas' plans, but it might work. If his brother drew the attention of the leading giant, the foot soldiers could close and take down their foe. Despite his feelings about Kendrick, Thomas called upon Aleara's divine power and blessed him. Kendrick's eyes widened as he felt it wash over him.

"Neat trick. You can do miracles through Aleara?" Kendrick asked.

"Yeah," Thomas said, "otherwise, I would be back there waiting for you to devise a plan. Earning this crest was an honor."

Kendrick didn't reply. Instead, he turned his horse to where Thomas suggested. Thomas frowned, watching as Kendrick spurred his horse away, rallying the men under his command without a second thought. He might act lost around his brother, but would not let it show with the soldiers. Lessons learned from their father, they always stayed in control. His anger cracked, and gratitude took its place. Kendrick tried to make a difference.

He never bothered to come to see Thomas be knighted. Their status as brothers seemed superficial and fake. Thomas shook his head and turned to the left side of the battlefield, shouting orders to the soldiers nearby. A battle remained to be fought, not watching his brother.

"Spread out! Do not let them catch you off guard. Aim for their knees or eyes, anything to slow them down!" he commanded.

The soldiers, desperate and terrified, followed his lead. Someone with a plan required less effort than devising one oneself, and these individuals, whose typical decisions affected their homes, farms, or businesses, fell in line with his commands. He explained it, hoping that the candor would give them confidence. Stealth benefited them. The giants would focus on the larger threat. The behemoths wanted to wage war against hundreds of soldiers, not a small group. This would allow them to be effective. They moved in small teams, using rocks and trees for cover as they flanked the giants. In places, they could not secure cover, but the growing legion at Kendrick's back kept the giants oblivious to them.

Tired of waiting on the humans to charge, one of the giants lumbered forward. Its roar shattered the stillness that had fallen over the battlefield. That icy breath froze the humidity in the air. Snow mixed with the ground, turning the field into a frozen mess. The giants would use any moisture to their advantage if given a chance. A dead soldier lay nearby, twisted by rictus. Beside the woman was an unbroken shaft with a shiny tip on it. Probably the first time the weapon had seen the light of day since its forging. Thomas grabbed the spear from the ground, steadying himself as one of the frost giants lumbered toward him, its icy breath leaving a trail of frozen earth in its wake.

Thomas hurled the weapon, aiming for the giant's leg. The spear struck true, sinking deep into the creature's knee. It let out a thunderous roar, staggering backward as it swung its massive arm. Thomas dodged out of the way, the ground trembling beneath him. It fell backward, crashing into a copse of trees, unfortunately, for the soldiers hiding there. Thomas did not have time to see if any survived. The giant tried to pull the spear from its leg. He ran up, slashing at the hand, only to be bashed by it.

Other soldiers emerged and swarmed over the creature. It wailed as they thrusted, and they took it down with numerous cuts rather than one killing blow. Its blood added to the field, and muck formed around it. Another of them approached, probably one of its family, though it was rare for the giants to organize into larger groups. Not very smart and highly territorial, their infighting kept them from being a greater threat. In his short time as a paladin, he never met more than six together.

Across the battlefield, Kendrick's forces managed to cripple another giant, driving it to its knees with well-placed arrows and spears. Together, they turned the tide of the battle, weakening their monstrous foes. The battle raged on, but the odds improved with each fallen foe. The last giant fell to the combined efforts of Grimhorn's soldiers, collapsing into the snow with a loud crash. Thomas stood, panting and covered in sweat and blood, his chest heaving as the final foe fell. The army fielded by Klydos no longer existed.

Gratefully, he thanked Aleara for the strength she had given them. Exhaustion threatened to overwhelm him. He needed to find his horse, get some food, and rest. In a short amount of time, they would know whether there was another wave of foul creatures descending upon them.

As Thomas turned to leave, the sound of clattering barding and steady hoofbeats caught his attention. He looked up to see a column of paladins riding toward the battlefield, their gleaming armor and white cloaks contrasting sharply with the surrounding carnage. At the head of the group rode Sir Silas, commander of the third regiment of the Order of Valor. Beside him, their father, Duke Kendrick. His heart sank as he recognized Kendrick, the elder. Sixteen years had passed since his father released him to become a squire in the Order of Valor. Time had not been kind to the lord of Grimhorn. His blonde hair was greying. His bearing had lost none of its strength. The man was inspiring, that is, unless you were his child and suffered his displeasure. Like the heir, his armor was highly decorated. Unlike the younger Kendrick, his platemail remained clean.

In the years since his knighting, they had spoken infrequently. The family made a showing at his knighting, sitting in the grandstands but making no attempt to congratulate him themselves.

As the duke dismounted, he glanced briefly at Thomas before settling on the younger Kendrick. No sign of recognition was present in those blue eyes. He did not recognize his offspring. Thomas smirked at the thought. It was true that he was gore-covered and helmed, which might explain his lack of recognition. However, Thomas believed the duke only cared for his heir.

"Well done," the duke said.

He clapped the younger Kendrick on the shoulder with a broad smile. He lavished praise on his eldest son, causing Kendrick to blush.

"This is a great day for the armies of Grimhorn and Zel'Drea. We have met the forces of Klydos, and they have found us to be deadly. My son has acquitted himself well as an heir should. All hail the line of Grimhorn."

Soldiers of the royal army cheered, but the paladins remained stoic on their steeds. It did not stop the heir from basking in it. Men and women who had helped them dispatch the giants came up and bent the knee to their lord and his heir. Thomas snorted and shook his head. No paladin would ever ingratiate himself the way these people did. His brother looked his way, and Thomas cursed Klydos in frustration. No matter what he did, he would always be overlooked by their father. He started to walk away, and then the younger Kendrick spoke.

"Thank you, Father. I was proud to have led our valiant soldiers against our first giants. I have brought glory to our house. Next time I see the king, Uncle Cyrus will have to listen to quite a tale. We wouldn't have succeeded without teamwork, of course," he said.

The words had elicited a nod from their father. It was clear he was not truly listening. Anger grew within him. Thomas fought hard not to say anything. He looked over at Sir Silas, where the knight stood shaking his head. It was a knowing look. It served to help Thomas swallow his frustration. Whenever he thought he put his childhood behind him, it reared up from some hidden recess. The ache of old wounds twisted inside him, but he kept his face neutral. He proved himself today, even if the duke did not know it. Aleara knew it and loved him for his service to her. That was enough.

"Sir Silas," the duke said, "thank you for coming to help us see this through. Aleara must have sent you in our hour of need."

The Knight Commander surveyed the battlefield, his eyes briefly locking again with the younger knight's eyes. Silas showed no tension, but his eyebrows betrayed the seething impatience within. Where Kendrick was tall, Silas was shorter and stockier. He held the gaze with Thomas, then his attention turned back to the duke and Kendrick. The man dismounted, his eyes now un-readable. He walked over and grasped the proffered hand of the duke. Though he had to look up at him, Silas gripped the duke's hand until the man pulled away. Thomas smiled at the subtle show of power between the two men.

"We are here to aid in the name of Aleara, Your Grace," he replied, "not to rescue you. Had the entire army of Zel'Drea lay dead on this plain, we would have done our duty to Aleara. The Order of Valor fights where there are threats to creation, and the frost giants are an ancient blight upon this land. Luckily, most of you were still living. I'm honored to fight alongside you and your sons on the battlefield."

"Yes, yes," the elder Kendrick said, "my namesake did an amazing job. King Cyrus' armies need to whet their swords. There was no need for the holy warriors to get all the glory."

"You may rest assured, the Council of Orders will convey to King Cyrus the valor displayed today against the forces of the Lord of Tempests. My knights and priests will tend the wounded and drive back any lingering threats."

Again, Kendrick nodded vacuously, comprehending only the vagaries of the compliment and not the subtle sarcasm lurking underneath.

"Of course. We are grateful for your intervention nonetheless."

His father glanced over at him again. He stopped, lingering. Confusion, then recognition quickly followed by surprise. It was the merest of emotions passing across that face, before the man resumed his controlled countenance. Damn. Thomas wished he had walked away instead of risking being recognized.

"Thomas!" the duke said. "My son! Holy warrior of Aleara."

"Hello, Father," Thomas said. "I assumed Kendrick would have told you I fought alongside him."

"Never got a chance," the heir said. "Your commander jumped in with his speech. Father, what he says is true. It was Thomas who devised the plan to rout the giants. I carried it out with perfection, but his idea made the difference."

Their father smiled and said, "Look at you. Covered in blood and gore like a hill tribe savage. You must have fought well, by the look of it. It's been a long time. I don't think I've seen you since your knighting."

Thomas met his father's gaze for a moment, the words hanging in the air between them. His anger grew as much from the near compliment as the thought of having to reconnect with the man who abandoned him. Words came to mind. It would not go well, but Thomas refused to be cowed or bullied. Not trusting himself, he nodded curtly, offering no words in return. The duke's face flushed with embarrassment and anger. The paladin did not care. Fighting wore him down, and anything he said would dishonor Aleara. Besides, soldiers lay injured nearby, and his duty to Aleara required that he heal them. He turned away to find them.

"Thomas!"

Thomas got as far away from his father as the battlefield allowed him. After repeatedly whistling and cursing the destrier, it found him. He thanked Aleara that it was safe and continued his sweep on horseback. There were plenty of reasons to do that. Around him, soldiers were doing the mundane work that took place after each fight. The dead were collected or buried where they fell. Weapons and animals corralled. Valuables, though rare, were taken from the corpses of the enemy.

It was the cries of the living that he sought, sweeping the battlefield for wounded soldiers. In the third year of his service as a squire, he had found himself on a much different battlefield. Nearly a thousand paladins had journeyed to Castardia at the behest of a nomad warlord. Two-thirds did not return to Godsdown. Sir Silas had to conduct the formalities with the warlord, which left Thomas to keep himself busy. It was on walks with Avery that he learned how important it was to look for the wounded and pray over the dead. The priest solemnly blessed them each time, ensuring their spirits returned to Aleara and were not drawn to Klydos. He made his way to an area that had not been checked yet, stumbling upon Sir Silas and his retinue.

The Knight Commander was speaking to the scavengers. These men and women disgusted Thomas almost as much as those in service to Klydos. Unofficially, they followed the soldiers of Aleara to the battlefields, remaining behind to conduct the grisly work of dismantling the corpses. He had stayed behind after a previous battle and had been deeply affected by what these men and women had done. They hacked the flesh from the corpses of the monsters, liberating the bones and carrying them away to sell. In some villages, skeletons were ground down and used for various purposes. He had no reason to engage with those who profited from the strife Klydos visited upon this realm.

Realizing he was in no mood to be civil to them, he angled away, only to be hailed by the Knight Commander. The man shook hands with the woman he was negotiating with, probably reminding the scavengers of their strict instructions. The elder knight's warhorse cut across, blocking his path to force the conversation. The two warhorses slammed their necks together, whinnying and gnashing their teeth at each other. Silas smacked the other horse with his mailed fist, and it rocked back, threatening to rest on its haunches. Thomas brought the horse to a standstill and launched a salute. Sir Silas frowned at the grandiose gesture. He ignored the salute, giving Thomas a stern look and silent disapproval.

"Sir Thomas," he said, "a word. Don't you dare ignore me, boy."

When Silas called him by his title, he meant to chastise. They had spent many a day together. If the man decided he needed a dressing down, Thomas would listen to every word. As his pseudo-father figure, Silas calmed the tumultuous storm that usually raged within the younger knight. Thomas frowned but stopped, allowing Sir Silas to dismount. The elder knight landed in the muck and cursed. Any other time, Thomas would have laughed despite the difference in rank. Silas gave him a look, and the thought dissipated. He joined his leader in the mud. The commander kept his tone neutral, but his voice radiated authority.

"You fought well," Silas said, "but you allowed yourself to be separated from the rest of the order during the battle. You're one of Aleara's, and we fight as one. You cannot act alone when the goddess guides us all."

Thomas blushed with embarrassment and anger at the reminder of his duty. Being admonished after pulling off the salvation of the Grimhorn forces grated on his nerves. His love for the Knight Commander held him in check. He explained his actions and how they led to their victory. The look on the commander's face suggested it fell on deaf ears. He took a deep breath to calm himself.

"I did not choose to be separated," he replied. "The battle unfolded too fast and overwhelmed the duke's soldiers."

Silas squinted, hardening his gaze. "Don't lie to me, son. You were separated from us long before you found those soldiers from Grimhorn. That's no excuse. Caleb fought at your side, and he returned to the vanguard. We are the fists of Aleara, and we move as one. A finger is not as strong as a fist. Your place is with us, Thomas, not striking out alone. You risk more than yourself when you go rogue."

Thomas forced himself to stay calm. He hated disappointing Silas. Thomas spent most of his years in the service of Aleara under the Knight Commander. The words stung because they touched on something more profound. No matter what he did, isolation reigned, even amongst those who valued him. He ground his teeth in frustration.

"I will keep that in mind, sir," he said.

Silas studied him for a moment, his expression softening slightly.

"You're a capable warrior, Thomas, and blessed by Aleara, but don't let your anger cloud your judgment. The paladins of the Order of Valor don't fight for personal glory. We fight so Aleara's creation will prevail over the Lord of Tempests' chaos. You're stronger when you remember that."

"I care nothing for personal glory," Thomas replied. "All I want to do is serve Aleara faithfully. It's the only thing I have."

Sir Silas said, "If you want to take my place someday, you must learn that serving means sacrifice. One of those sacrifices may be that you do not always get to serve however you want."

"As long as I do not have to spend my days in Godsdown," Thomas said, "I will serve Aleara however she wants."

"Keep that in mind," Sir Silas said. "The Grand Commander would not have you serve anywhere close to her. She still remembers the avalanche right over there on those blasted mountains."

"I will take digging out the camp over being bashed by a frost giant," Thomas replied.

They laughed at the memory of that battle. His attempts to blame the destruction on the frost giants had fallen on deaf ears. Thomas had been remorseful over the ruin of her command tent, but stood by his decision to remove the giants from the equation. He had prayed to Aleara many times, hoping that the head of his order would see past that decision, seeing the value of his actions. Until that time, he could not formally command troops, only serve as an informal lead over other knights waiting to be added to the ranks of the battalions.

"The Grand Commander has a long memory," Silas said.

Thomas nodded. It was true. Unfortunately for him, no one else was rash enough to do anything to take his transgressions from the top of her mind.

"I have told her I was sorry," Thomas said. "Many times."

"Apologies mean little to Marla. If you knew her like I do, you would realize that only actions will absolve you with her."

Thomas said, "Help me then. Tell me how to make amends. What do you know of her early life?"

"I'll not tell her story. If she wants you to know, then she will tell you. Just know that her trust isn't given easily but can be quickly lost."

"I know that all too well," Thomas replied.

The commander clapped him on the shoulder, adding a genuine smile to reassure the paladin. Despite the difficult conversation, Thomas admired the leadership Silas provided. They exchanged promises to dine together, and Silas made his way to the command pavilion to prepare their next steps, leaving the younger knight to survey the battlefield.

He walked around, taking note of the number of trolls, Valkrunians, and wizards dead on the battlefield. The trolls seemed endless, but fewer and fewer of the latter came to battle recently for the Lord of Tempests. It was not without losses for Aleara's forces. Many men and women had returned to Aleara this day. He muttered a quiet prayer, hoping for guidance on how to process what he felt was senseless death. That was the one benefit of the human scavengers. They would bury the dead. There had to be some way to placate the god of chaos without continuing to lose more and more people.

He could mourn the dead later. The wounded cried for help. Either paladins who had reached the limits of their powers or members of the royal army with no such resources. Thomas found some men trying to bind the wound of one of their fellow soldiers, and he bent down to see what the wound looked like. Something wickedly sharp and deadly opened her abdomen, and they did their best to keep her insides from becoming outsides.

"May I offer some assistance?" Thomas asked.

"Yes, sir," one of the men responded. "She's not doing too well."

"I can help."

The men stepped back. He scooted closer to the woman. She looked like many of the peasant women of Grimhorn. She was stocky and built to live in a harsh land. The torn chain mail shirt outlined the jagged wound. Blood pulsed from the torn flesh. Thomas pressed his hands against her abdomen.

"Aleara," he said aloud. "You created us and gave us this world. Please help this woman. She served you faithfully, and saving her life will do more for your creation than her spirit returning to your fold. Work through me and heal her."

Soft, silvery light spilled from his hands into her wound, slowing the blood at first, knitting the flesh back together. Her skin began to take on color. The woman's eyes fluttered open and focused on Thomas. She sighed and closed her eyes again in relief. The soldiers around her praised Aleara and the paladin who brought the healing to their comrade. Thomas rocked backward and stood, allowing her companions to help her.

"Thank you, milord," the woman said.

"You are welcome," Thomas replied.

At that moment, the men and the woman jerked to attention, their gaze switching to someone behind Thomas. He turned slightly, looking over his shoulder, and cursed, seeing his father behind him. From the look of it, their last conversation had left him angry and ready for another confrontation. For a tense moment, the two of them stood there staring at each other. The injured soldier dispelled the impasse, requiring help to her feet. The soldiers saluted, steadied their friend, and bolted. Thomas grinned, seeing their weapons lying on the ground. He used it to delay the inevitable, bending down to pick up the spears and taking time to wipe the mud away from the embossed stag on the blades. They would regret the hasty retreat during their next formation.

"Son, I'll not have you disrespect me in front of other people."

"Did I?" Thomas asked.

"Speak to me like that again, and I will have you disciplined," the duke said. "I am both your father and the lord of Grimhorn. You will show me respect."

"I am no longer part of Grimhorn. Your royal desires carry no weight here. You want respect, earn it!"

"I was fighting for Zel'Drea long before your birth," Kendrick said. "You think of me as less than you. I command thousands. Don't dare to stand up to me."

Thomas bristled at the words. He remembered all too well that his father loved the lash and the cane.

"Try it. I am no little boy. Raise your arm, and I will burn you in the light of Aleara. She will sear the truth of you from your bones."

"I'm not afraid of what the goddess might see. The goddess cannot judge the living. Aleara's symbol is not an excuse for how you behave."

"No one is hiding behind it. I am right here. Father."

"I'll not degrade myself by fighting with you in front of these people. You deserve it, though. Angry at me for not letting you become a dandy. At least this way, you are useful to someone. It was never going to be Grimhorn."

"Thank you, milord," Thomas replied, "for allowing me to spend my years as a child under the care of knights and priests instead of my family."

"Is that how you see it?" the duke asked.

The words elicited a hurt response. The duke looked up at him, a mournful look on his face. If anyone heard them, it would seem Thomas was the one in the wrong. However, he did not believe any of it. Everything his father did was a calculated move in some game where only he held the rules and how to keep score. Instead of answering, he handed the spears to his father. They clattered to the ground. The duke would order new ones forged rather than carry them back to his soldiers.

Thomas said, "It is a moot point."

"Not really," his father said. "I could make you useful. Abandon this holy folly, and you can lead our army into Castardia. I'll name you baron over whatever territory you can hold."

"Is that the will of Aleara? Is that what King Cyrus wants? Or is that your aspirations to a bigger throne? I do not want your pity," Thomas said. "Chance brought us together on this battlefield and nothing more. Do not concern yourself with my life, I am blessed, and you are happy with yours."

"You don't seem happy," the duke said, "you sound like I robbed you of something and gave you something lesser in exchange. You never said anything about wanting to come home."

"I did not want to leave home! Nobody asked me what I wanted, but it is behind us. I will not give away the one thing bringing light into my life," Thomas said. "I passed the test and trials to wear the badge of the order. I won't forsake them just because you want to make up for past years. Nothing changed since you sent me away."

His chest tightened as anger walled him away from his father's words. Aleara, please give me a way out of this, he prayed. Waited impatiently, then cursed when nothing came from her.

Aloud, he said, "There is nothing to resolve. Knighthood is my path. A paladin serving Aleara. Thank you for the words, but I must return to my duty."

"Would you consider coming to visit? Not for me, Thomas, but for your mother. She would love to see you for more than an hour."

"Yes, milord."

The duke walked away, leaving Thomas alone with his prayers. Such an attitude was unbecoming, and he knew that if the goddess had observed his actions, he would need her forgiveness. Still, Aleara left him without peace. Anger over his stolen childhood wedged between her spirit and him, but he was not ready to let it go. He could hear the priest chastising him for childish sentiments. Avery would say he liked to stew in his self-pity because it was a warm and comfortable place to be.

Rather than imagine the words, he went off in search of the priest. Besides Sir Silas, Avery was the one person who could help Thomas escape the hurricane of anger and bitterness that formed when his father came to mind. Worse still, seeing his eldest brother showed that the bloodline was further tainted and that the son was a mirror image of the man Thomas loathed. He thanked Aleara for giving him different burdens to carry. During his prayers, he asked her to send him to Avery so that the priest might hear him out and dissipate his feelings.

He went from wounded to wounded, aiding those he could and keeping watch for the priest. It took some time, but he eventually found the man. Despite the carnage around him, Avery looked fresh and composed. Neither bloodstain nor sweat sullied his robes. The smooth-shaven priest showed signs of exhaustion, though, and his voice strained as he prayed over the man bleeding out before him.

"Only you could face Klydos and look like you just stepped out from breakfast," Thomas said.

"You are covered in enough blood for both of us," Avery replied. "Did you wash yourself in their blood?"

"My father is here."

"Is that meant to explain the blood?" Avery asked. "Seems strange that you would shift from one line of questioning to talk about Duke Kendrick being here."

"I got separated from my cohort. Fought most of the morning by myself."

"That doesn't surprise me," Avery said. "Why you persist in such heroics is beyond me?"

"Did you hear me say my father is here?"

"I am a learned man, young paladin. I surmised as much when I saw the banners flying over the battlefield. You know that the Grand Marshall called up the troops of House Grimhorn to fight Nemordia. Why you're surprised is the real shocker."

Thomas did not rise to the sarcasm. He expected it from the priest.

"Should I presume that your irritation is more than just the presence of your father on this battlefield?"

"I fought alongside my brother. It was not planned, just happened by chance. It was my tactics that allowed us to prevail over the giants, but Kendrick took credit for it with our father. Worse than that, my father did not even recognize me the first time he saw me."

"Did you look like this, or was this bathing in blood something that happened later?"

The priest was still bent over the wounded man. He must have spent all of his energy as he was applying bandages to the wounds that remained unhealed. For a moment, Thomas considered stomping away. Avery was doing nothing to simmer the anger he felt. Recognizing the pause in the conversation, Avery looked. Thomas stared into those eyes.

"I am sorry," he said. "I do not mean to take it out on you."

"Don't apologize to me. I know how deeply the rift between you and the duke affects you. Did you bring glory to Aleara with your actions?"

Thomas was unsure whether the priest was referring to the battlefield or the conversation with his father. He chose to believe he meant the battle. In his mind, he thought that Aleara was proud of him. However, his conversation with Sir Silas cast some doubt on that.

"Aleara was glorified this day," Thomas answered.

"Then all is right on Binsmuth. How did you leave it with your father?"

"I threatened to burn him with the holy light of Aleara."

"Probably not your finest moment then," Avery replied.

Thomas laughed. The priest was right. He appealed to the goddess, asking her forgiveness for being rash and ungrateful. It was true that being sent to the Order of Valor had felt like a betrayal by his family. Over the years, he was thankful for that decision, even if it had been due to a callous ploy by his father.

The priest finished his ministrations and stood. He made as if to clap the larger man on the shoulder, then stopped. Thomas laughed again. He would need to find one of Sir Silas' squires and have them begin cleaning his armor. There was no need to remain covered in gore. This battle was over.

Somewhere in the argument with his father, his horse had wandered away again. It had the same temperament as its owner and the same amount of patience. He and Avery wandered around looking for his horse. Thomas repeated the whistled command until he finally heard a whinny and the thunder of hooves. The black gelding trotted up and snorted at him. Rubbing slowly with his fingers, Thomas brushed through the soft velvet between its eyes. The animal ceased its protestations, stood still, its ears twitching forward, its eyes half-lidded in contentment. He traced the long jaw. The horse gave a low, satisfied snort and then pushed against his face. It was mollified, though Thomas suspected the steed had been angry at being left on its own.

Avery said, "I don't think he was amused by your antics today."

"Seems to be the consistent response. I assure you, there was no intention to go solo. Things just happened."

The horse snorted and pushed at him again. He envied the druids of Aleara and their ability to communicate with animals. It would make some situations easier, although getting chastised by his mount was not one of them. Avery chuckled again.

"I've got to check in at the hospital wagons," Avery said. "Go wash up. I'll meet you near Silas' command tent for a meal."

Thomas said, "Do not expect an extravagant meal. This is a battlefield."

"I'll expect a standard ration of stale bread and cheese," was the priest's reply.

It was the knight's turn to laugh. That was a favorite slur hurled at them. Although the orders did sometimes find themselves longing for a good meal, they often ate better than the peasants did.

After they parted ways, he made his way to the tent Sir Silas occupied. The Knight Commander was giving orders to his junior officers so that, once they reached Godsdown, the army would disassemble and rest, ready for the next call to duty. He watched as the man efficiently doled out a rotation so that each paladin would have time to have a break from service.

Thomas let Silas finish his work, instead seeking someone to give an order to for the evening. As a knight errant, he had no squire, but he would cajole either Reed or Janelle into helping him get out of his armor. He spotted the boy first. Thomas gestured to the straps, and the squire groaned but followed him back to where his equipment sat under a tree.

Reed said, "You could have asked Sir Silas for a tent and a squire of your own."

"And let you get away with doing nothing?"

"Nothing," Reed said. "I've been all over this battlefield. Delivering orders and taking back word from the scouts. I nearly had to fight a troll."

"Nearly?"

"Yeah, one of Caleb's paladins killed it before I got the chance."

"Quit making all those groaning sounds," Thomas said. "It makes the job all more difficult."

"Caleb finds out I helped you, and I'll be helping him next," Reed said.

"Janelle is probably done getting him out of his armor. Caleb is washing up, and a clean set of clothes is waiting for him."

Reed groaned and said, "She was helping Sir Silas. Caleb probably asked another knight to help him."

He let the squire finish freeing him from his armor, then released him, tossing a coin at him as thanks for taking on the extra duty. Sir Silas might question the lad about where he was, but after a long battle like today, he would expect that his squires were engaged in multiple tasks. Still, Thomas would explain that he was the reason for Reed's absence.

Exhaustion was taking hold of him. Despite the divine healing of the day, his body knew the truth. He was torn between going to sleep and waiting for Avery so that they could eat together. That was the truth of his service to Aleara. She gave him strength in battle, but afterwards, his exhaustion reminded him that he was just a mortal vessel for her power. Drowsiness threatened to take control. It became a moot point when the priest arrived, chuckling at the sight of Thomas sitting on the ground.

"It never ceases to amaze me the depths of your stubbornness. You should have brought a tent. Let's get something to eat. I'm starving."

Thomas replied, "How do you get hungry? All you do is talk or pray. I burned more energy getting out of my armor than you do all day."

"This mind is always at work," Avery replied, tapping his forehead. "My head is more than a helm holder."

With a wry smile, the priest held out an arm, gesturing for Thomas to lead the way. Thomas playfully rubbed the bald priest's pate. They walked over to the serving tent. The cooks and servers were followers of Aleara but not members of any order. Each time Thomas held out his plate, he would receive food and a blessing. These men and women were among the few who understood the purpose of the orders, which protected their world.

"Any words of wisdom for me?"

"This battle was odd. More a distraction than anything critical," Avery scoffed. "Damned few Valkrunians today. A token force suggests they are mustering elsewhere. That worried me."

"Have your conversations with Faisel gone anywhere?" Thomas asked.

Avery said, "The man is quite the trove of knowledge. Thankfully, he offered it early on. It has been the only thing that has kept him alive all these years. Better silver chains and a generous room than the dungeon of Grimhorn."

"I am sure he is grateful for the generous hospitality."

"He will only speak to me after I share your latest exploits," Avery said. "There are some days I have to make up something interesting just to get him to talk. He will only talk about their world and the times before Klydos came."

"You have been speaking to him for a decade," Thomas said. "Have you learned anything useful?"

The priest looked across the table with a mouthful of food. Thomas hated goading Avery, but it was sometimes the only way to get him to speak candidly. When he finished swallowing, the priest shared what he had learned.

"I know the hierarchy of their armies and the various types of martial weapons they use. The most interesting thing I have learned is that they, too, worshiped a nature goddess. Except for their goddess allowing them to manipulate the aether directly, their society might be a mirror image of ours."

"Do you think it could be our Aleara?" asked Thomas.

"I believe so," Avery replied. "There's no direct correlation with Donegal, but it seems as if our creator populated more than Binsmuth."

"I do not understand."

"I've questioned him many times, thinking they might be from another continent. With our constant strife with Klydos, we have never ventured out across the seas to know what's out there. Only the pirates who attacked years ago gave us any clue that there were any other lands. His people had lived peacefully for thousands of years. They were explorers. Our continent did not exist in their world."

"What if he is lying to keep you from true knowledge?"

Avery pondered that, rubbing his fingers across his scalp. A patch of hair seemed to trouble him. As a squire, the priest had often convinced the boy to shave that head, though it was not one of his official duties. Thomas shoveled more stew in his mouth as he waited for the priest to stop fussing.

"He would no more tell me lies than I would make up something you did. Alien, he may be, but he is an honest man, and he fears losing touch with you."

"The man cares a lot for a boy who shared one journey with him. Even when I tried to help him escape, it backfired on us. Nonetheless, I did value his company on that trip and my subsequent visits to his cell. Will you take him a letter from me?"

"If you write it, I will make sure it gets to him."

With their meal finished, Avery and Thomas parted ways for the night. Even though he longed for sleep, the paladin took the time to write to Faisel. Sharing his exploits over the last few years had been a small joy, knowing that someone might care about news about him. Long ago, he stopped sending such letters to Grimhorn, as no one ever bothered to answer.

He awoke, leaning against a tree near the edge of camp. Not the best sleep, but better than some. Training under Sir Silas, Thomas had learned to sleep in the saddle. Sometimes it was the only rest one could get. It was why he traveled light. Without a squire, dismantling a tent, maintaining baggage animals, and the additional cost were unnecessary things in his mind.

The scavengers were hard at work. They had an enemy of their own. The crows and vultures were making quick work of the dead. Even now, the smell of death hung heavily over the camp and the surrounding plain where the battle took place. Sir Silas would have paladins roaming amongst them, ensuring that they buried those of Aleara and did not add them to their gruesome payload.

Compared to some of their battlefields, this one was relatively close to Godsdown. It was as if Klydos sought to get a foothold near the place where Aleara and Donegal had created the world that infuriated him. Given past campaigns, it would be some time before the god of Chaos brought more of his minions. One thing was sure, though. He would try again.

They would return to Godsdown and refit. Preparing for where Klydos would emerge again. It was inevitable. Defeat only served to ignite further incursions. Thomas knew that whatever time they had until the call came again would be less than needed. He would have to spend some of his time getting his armor repaired and spending time with the worshipers of Donegal to ensure it was ready for whatever came next. While he did not understand the men and women who preferred the god of the land to their creator, Aleara, he valued what they were able to do with steel.

He allowed his destrier to follow the others ahead of him, turning his thoughts to the lessons he had learned that day. The ability to imbue his sword with holy fire showed growth in his abilities. Others had manifested tricks and skills with each battle. He would share his knowledge freely, hoping it would give other paladins an edge over their enemies. They were fearsome warriors individually, but when they fought together, it was a truly awe-inspiring sight. Aleara had truly blessed the people of Binsmuth through the Order of Valor. Admittedly, the other orders had their place in her glory as well.

Even his brother James, serving in the grove at Grimhorn, glorified Aleara. Those sacred glades were otherworldly places. He had not truly understood their magnificence as a child. Even at his knighting ceremony in the grove at Godsdown, his comprehension of their importance had grown, but it was not truly clear to him what purpose they served.

The Order of Valor formed up. Groups of nine paladins marched behind their leader, forming a long line of cavalry ready to return home and rest. Some groups had dead paladins strapped across the backs of their horses. They would receive a funeral with honors once they made their way to Godsdown.

He looked ahead of him, taking in the sight of the knights and their retainers. Villagers along the road to Godsdown would honor them by standing and watching them pass through. Some might even see one of their family members now serving the goddess. Weary though happy, the men and women of his order knew their place in the scheme of things, taking nothing for granted. Each gratefully thanked the goddess for the gifts she had given them.

He gazed at them in awe, even after all the years of service to Aleara. It was terrific to see how mighty the regiment was. The long line of paladins and squires was impressive. Janelle and Reed came alongside him. The third-year squires still experienced the adrenaline of battle, and their giddiness betrayed nerves stretched taut as they witnessed the sheer might of their foes. Thomas remembered those days.

The first time Silas had taken him to the field with Caleb was a fond memory. The monsters they had fought frightened him. Seeing his master face them, that fear dwindled. He remembered planting his long spear alongside Sir Silas, sitting on his horse, and feeling the violent thud as the winged creature impaled itself upon the broad blade. Some might question exposing children to such horrors, but this was a world that faced them, so they might as well learn the truth of it early.

"Sir Thomas," Janelle said. "I overheard Sir Silas say you took down a frost giant today. Was he a big one?"

"Big and blue," Thomas said. "Like a ripened berry. Even his snot was frozen on that ugly face."

"Any other good battles?" Reed asked.

Thomas looked at the squire and his companion. They had come through the battle well, seeing what was possible as a paladin. He only hoped that they would grow to adulthood and not die before they had taken their vows. Many did not make it. Some battlefields were littered with the bodies of young people. It was hard to find a way to reconcile it. Their lives should be filled with joy and not war. Even worse were the children of villagers, starved from endless raids that killed their crops or robbed them of loving parents. They waited for him to share more.

"A gaggle of Grey Wizards and their hunchbacked minions."

He recounted the story, delighting in the oohs and aahs from the squires. He envied the way they shrugged off the grim truth, still young enough to be excited by the prospect of taking their place in the ranks of paladins. They would be less happy once the task of cleaning armor started. It would be a long night for them. Sir Silas slowed down, easing his destrier alongside the younger knight, and shooed the squires away. The commander's permanently solemn face was grim as he motioned for Thomas to move their mounts to the side of the vanguard.

"I owe you an apology," Thomas said.

"No," Sir Silas said, "I know when the Duke of Grimhorn comes around to expect a bad mood from you. One day, when it doesn't matter, I'm going to tell him what I think of his parenting skills."

Thomas laughed, though he imagined it would be far more grave than humorous. The old paladin had never married. The squires and knights were his family. Thomas was more than thankful for them.

"A druid came to visit us during the battle," Silas said. "Says he comes on the orders of the Council."

"Must be important if they sent him to an active battlefield. What news did he bring?"

"Something dangerous is brewing in the eastern forest. Please work with the druid. See if what he told the Council is true," Silas said. "If it is, we shall discuss it at Godsdown."

"Discuss it," Thomas said. "Is that Aleara's will, or should I take care of the situation?"

"Not the way the druid tells it," Silas replied. "It won't be just the two of you going on this journey. You have a good rapport with my squires. Which of those two ruffians is ready to be paired with a knight?"

Thomas thought about the merits of both of the squires. Reed was more mature. It would be a short amount of time before he passed the test and became a paladin. His behavior was very typical of their order. The girl was more like himself. Although she talked more than he wanted, she would make a better companion, even on a short adventure like this. He cared not for the responsibility, but had learned that when Sir Silas spoke, it was not meant for discussion. It was meant to be followed.

"Janelle," Thomas replied. "She knows she is not physically strong and makes up for it with her prayers and tactics."

Silas nodded, a sign of their maturing relationship. Thomas knew the Knight Commander had great hopes for him, respecting his prowess on the battlefield. Not every paladin had the makings of a leader. Some were almost as solitary as the forest-loving druids.

"When we stop to water the horses, I'll convey her to you as your squire. You can take her with you and the druid."

That was not what he expected. The commander valued his opinion, but Thomas believed that it was to be a squire for Caleb or someone else within Silas's command. Arguments would be useless, but the words came out anyway.

"I am not ready for a squire."

"Nonsense," Silas said. "You've been a full-fledged knight for five years. Seen plenty of battles. It's high time you started to work on your leadership skills."

"But..."

"No buts," Silas said. "Thank me and salute, and do as I tell you."

"Can I take Avery with me?"

"No," Sir Silas said, "the priest will be needed on funeral duty. We lost many good people today. This is but a scouting mission. If the druid is correct, once you return, we will dispatch a full battalion to address the threat. Do your job and return. You will be reunited with the priest soon enough."

"To do what?"

"I will approach the Grand Commander about giving you a command. Taking on a squire is the first step."

That revelation took away the last of the sting from his confrontation with his father. His pride swelled at the acknowledgment of his growing abilities. It would cement his place in the order. He thanked the Knight Commander and went to find Janelle. When they camped, he would begin explaining to the young woman how they would carry out their mission. He intended to make the most of the upcoming mission.

CHAPTER

6

S oft sunlight bathed the eastern forest as the three horses left the main road. Snow fell through the taller trees. In his mind, warm summer days were few and far between in this harsh world. Marveling at how these woods differed from those of his homeland, Thomas took in the forest and the canopy above them. The giant conifers rose like the trees of Aleara's groves, blotting out most of the daylight.

A light snow fell on them, growing from flurries at first to a stronger storm. After some time, the trail itself disappeared, becoming a shallow depression of white surrounded by an even whiter landscape. Before long, most of the undergrowth was covered in the ever-present white powder, making it difficult to discern a rock from a bush.

Smaller trees sprang up in the shade of those giants, straining to take in whatever sunlight trickled down to them. Wilderness dominated Aleara's world. Given more to nature than to humanity. It was a wild and unfettered beauty. He regretted his companions keeping him from enjoying it in peace. All hopes of serenity were shattered when they encountered the devastation of the forest.

The first signs of withering brought their incessant chatter to a halt. Even Janelle could find nothing cheery to say after seeing the blighted woods. The druid had warned them about this, but his description fell short of doing it justice. After recovering from his shock, Brontë hastily checked a hand-drawn map, muttering about how much the blight spread. Thomas half-listened, sickened by the sight of the beautiful trees laid to waste. Blackened leaves dotted the snow. Rotted trunks dripped black ichor, staining the ground around their base. He took offense on behalf of the goddess, knowing this sickened her. The deeper they went down the trail, the worse it got.

"This is worse than when I left," Brontë said. "We should leave."

"I thought you were committed to protecting this land?" asked Thomas. "Aleara has given you the power. Embrace it."

Janelle said, "We should go back. The Council needs to know."

"Know what?" Thomas asked. "Sir Silas already knows this much. He needs better information. Find your courage, squire. Aleara blesses us."

Janelle gulped and accepted his orders. Thomas doubted it would keep her quiet for long. She spent the first half of the day alternating between sadness at leaving Reed behind and feeling grateful for his choice. If it had been Avery, he would have welcomed the conversation as the man often had some new quandary to air out on their rides. Janelle was no such philosopher.

The priest had been dismayed that Thomas was going out without him. Freed from service to the Grand Commander, he constantly found reasons to avoid being assigned a church or missionary work. The priest was content to haunt the library at Godsdown or accompany Thomas wherever Silas sent him. For some reason, the Knight Commander had resisted attempts to bring Avery along. He had said he consulted Aleara, but Thomas had his doubts. Instead, he was forced to endure Janelle's rambling and constant twisting in the saddle, expecting gnolls to leap from hiding or some other imagined danger.

Numerous chores would distract her from her nervousness. He had switched to his plate mail at the beginning of their trip, leaving behind the muddied and bloodstained chainmail shirt. Polishing his armor would tire her out. Between erecting the tent, polishing his armor, and tending to the horses, she would find little time to talk. Janelle reminded him of the ones he had avoided during his training.

Depressions in the ground caught his eye. Melted snow and muddy depressions betrayed the footprints. Even the falling snow melted as it touched them. Something recently passed this way. Thomas held up his hand, drawing his sword as Janelle and the druid fell silent. The squire followed suit, years of training overcoming her nervousness. Brontë, less attuned to the tension, furrowed his brow and tried to follow where the paladin pointed but failed to detect the clue. The paladin was focused on the faint footprints, deep, uneven impressions in the mud. His gut tightened. These weren't from ordinary travelers. He cursed Klydos under his breath. Minions of the Grey Wizards of Sambor made those tracks.

"Fucking chaos thralls," Thomas muttered.

The wild-eyed stares of his companions echoed his feelings. The wizards created numerous horrors, but none so sickening as what they did with their own failed apprentices. Aleara's squires conjured light to pass. Apprentices to the Grey Wizards of Sambor tried to channel raw aether to prove themselves, sometimes becoming Chaos Thralls when they failed. None looked the same. Despite them being uniquely warped by their failed attempts at magic, their presence stained Aleara's beloved flora.

The path itself began to warp, corrupted by whatever creature passed over it. Motioning for his companions to remain still, Thomas dismounted, careful to keep his armor from making too much noise. It seemed impossible to move without making noise, and he proved it as a faint clink of metal echoed in the air. A sharp crack from the underbrush to his left drew his attention. He turned, only to be knocked over by the hideous creature rushing from its cover. The grotesque creature turned to look at them with its three heads. One remained slack and lifeless, but the other two snarled, their teeth gnashing as they clawed at his armor, trying to find a vulnerable spot.

"Aleara, give me strength," he whispered.

In response, a cold, silvery light sprang up on his sword. He thrust his sword into it, pricking at the creature, causing it to veer away from him. It angled toward their mounts, spooking his squire's horse, causing her to push off the saddle and land awkwardly. Thomas yelled, and the creature halted, turning back to look at him with its two working heads. Janelle took advantage of the distraction and maneuvered to join him. It padded toward him. Janelle stepped forward, thrusting at its slimy flesh to give Thomas time to recover. Brontë reacted more slowly, but his incantation sprang from the snowy ground as twisting vines, entangling the creature. It let out a blood-curdling screech. Despite having encountered them many times, the sound made Thomas shiver.

Janelle slashed at the horror. These abominations devoured peasants with abandon. The poor common people could not prepare for the atrocities Klydos and his followers unleashed. He looked around for others. Where one showed, usually many more followed, with at least one wizard guiding them. Hot balls of flame arced from the depths of the woods, providing at least one answer. Sharp wooden spikes flashed past Thomas and Janelle in response, ending in surprised grunts from somewhere in the underbrush.

"Janelle, keep your distance!" Thomas said.

The squire nodded in understanding. More shadows shifted among the trees. They weren't alone. Another creature burst from the foliage, charging straight at Brontë. Chaos energy radiated off the Chaos Thrall, emanating from its twisted hands. The druid reacted with little time to spare, thrusting his staff forward causing roots to surge from the earth, blocking its path. It leaped over the writhing vines and crashed into Brontë, sending him sprawling backward into the mud.

"Brontë!" Thomas cried out.

He started toward the druid only to find another creature blocked his way. It roared a deep, bone-chilling sound, rattling Thomas to his core. An odd thought crossed his mind. He wondered if his brother would have the stomach to fight such a being. The wizard emerged, bloodied but headed nearer with an angry snarl on his face. The man cast another spell. A spray emerged, arcing toward Thomas. It landed on his armor, sizzling. He started forward, realizing the acid affected his armor, burning through the padding and his skin beneath.

More of the melted human minions came from the woods. Despite their origins, their remaining intelligence did not make them very tactical. They converged on the nearest thing, focusing on Janelle. She cried out to him, not daring to look away from their horrible visage. With their lurching movements, she could escape, but fear prevented her from making a choice. Thomas experienced similar feelings during his first battle. His sword had shaken in his hands. Any thought of prayer to Aleara was forgotten in that moment. Sir Silas had pulled him out of the way of an armored steed while he stood stammering a prayer. Several battles occurred before he thought without being distracted by his opponents and their actions.

"We can't hold them off!" she shouted.

Panic showed in her voice. Mind racing, Thomas gauged the odds. Janelle's assessment of their situation was correct. Despite their ability to outmaneuver their opponents, the numbers favored the chaos thralls and their wizard. The ferocity of these chaos thralls was a new experience. Bless us with courage, he thought, and rejoiced when Aleara's spirit spread out, emboldening Janelle, driving away her fear. Where there was flagging courage, his aura provided some. He reminded her to stay close, to stay within Aleara's protection.

The largest of the chaos thralls was almost upon her. He charged at it, ignoring the wizard for the moment. The thing swung its massive claws at him. Thomas ducked low, rolling beneath its attack and driving his blade into its exposed side. The creature howled in pain, sounding far too human for comfort, staggering back as black, foul-smelling blood poured from the wound. There was no time to savor the victory as more were coming.

Janelle was fighting valiantly beside him, sword weaving a wall between her and the advancing creatures, but she was tiring. Their claws snagged at her armor, and she was freely bleeding in multiple places. His aura was helping, keeping her from focusing on her injuries. Instead, she dealt wounds to whatever came near her. She was running on adrenaline, and it was wearing off. Her movements slowed, and her breath was ragged gasps. He spared a glance at the druid. Brontë struggled, fending off the beast attacking him with desperate bursts of woodland magic.

As he turned back to his foes, another wizard emerged from the woods, wearing ornate robes with gold embroidery. It was not a good sign. The paladin recognized the markings of a High Warlock. This one raised his staff, and a black globe flew toward Janelle. The aether slammed into her. Thomas flinched as her screams echoed throughout the forest. Heart pounding in his chest, Thomas searched for a tactic to help them. Their position was untenable.

"Fall back!" he shouted.

He motioned for the small mound off to their side. If they got to higher ground, they stood a chance. The druid could protect their flanks, allowing them to narrow the possible attacks. They began to retreat, followed by the wizard's minions. It appeared the High Warlock was using chaos to focus their efforts. Thomas noted it with mixed feelings. He was not casting spells. Instead, he somehow directed his minions with his mind, giving them greater determination.

One of the smaller beasts lunged at Janelle, knocking her off balance. She fell with a cry, her sword slipping from her hand as the thing pinned her down, its teeth snapping dangerously close to her throat. Thomas rushed forward to help her. The monster injured itself, trying to bat away his blade, leaving its arms dangling uselessly. He sliced into the neck, and his sharp blade took the head off cleanly. Gouts of black blood squirted from the stump of the neck. The body slumped to the ground, twitching as its life drained away.

A blast hit Thomas from behind, the flames burning the skin on his back. He grimaced and pushed his squire ahead of him. She fell. Stumbling, he reached down, and grabbed Janelle's arm, pulling her to her feet.

"Keep moving!"

Brontë struggled toward them, blood running down his temple from a gash on his forehead.

"There's no end to them," he said.

The druid raised his staff, and it flared with light. Vines surged from the ground. They were ineffective and did little to slow the pursuit. Both the druid and the squire were spent from their efforts. They were not alone. With each passing moment, his armor weighed heavier on his body. Aleara's strength flowed through him, but his body failed even though the divine did not. The wizards and their minions were closing, their numbers seemingly endless. The air was thick with the coppery scent of blood and the musty smell of decay.

Thomas whirled on instinct as a massive beast, more hideous than the others, emerged from the trees. Its dagger-length claws and spindly limbs came at him with terrifying speed, ready to strike. He reacted as best he could. The creature's weight slammed into him, knocking him back into the mud. His sword flew from his hand, landing several feet away. The beast snapped at him, trying to slip a claw through his armor into soft flesh, digging into his sides as it pressed down on him.

"Aleara, give me strength," Thomas whispered.

When renewed strength did not come, Thomas realized he was at the limits of his ability. The light of the goddess faded, and his body weakened under the relentless attack. His vision blurred as pain shot through him, muscles screaming in protest. Just as the creature's teeth closed in, something shifted. A sudden burst of energy surged through Thomas, flooding his body with one final wave of strength. With a roar, Thomas shoved the creature off him, rolling to his feet and grabbing his sword from the mud. He swung wildly, his blade catching the creature in the thigh. It howled in pain as the limb buckled, taking it to the ground, but it was not enough. The falling creature lunged again. The world spun as Thomas hit the ground again, head slamming into the mud. Darkness fought the light in his vision, and strength faded with consciousness. He heard Janelle screaming, the sounds going quiet as he succumbed to the blow.

Thomas awakened, his head pounding, his body aching. The sticky and thick mud beneath him clung to his armor. For a moment, he lay there, disoriented, the world around him a blur. It all came back to him. He recalled the battle, the creatures, and the overwhelming sense of helplessness. Blinking until his vision clearing, he pushed himself up onto his elbows. Brontë lay motionless in the mud a few feet away. His staff lay broken at his feet, and his body was still. Groaning in despair, the paladin felt hope leaving him.

He tried to heal himself, but his body was on the verge of total collapse, and prayers resulted in no noticeable improvement. Crawling to the druid, he checked. The man was dead. Not just dead but gnawed on by their horrific foes. Janelle was beyond him. Her sword was still clutched in her hand. Though limber, her body twisted in impossible positions. She, too, was lifeless.

Getting to his fee was a struggle to stand amidst the lifeless clearing. Failure pressed on him like a millstone. The air was still, heavy with the scent of the rotting woods around him. Janelle and Brontë's bodies were pulled from the muck on the side of the trail. Aleara would guide them back to her. Tears were his admission of failure. They streamed from his eyes, blurring the two bodies before him. A low whistle sounded off in the woods, and Thomas scrambled to find his sword. He spun about as he took it up, imagining new enemies were about to fall upon him. When his panic subsided, his eyes focused on the ground, where his shield lay in the dirt, its once-bright emblem of Aleara fractured, a jagged crack where her holy sigil had split in two. Like him, the shield, a symbol of her power, now lay broken.

"Aleara," he said, "please guide me! Tell me what you would have me do."

There was no answer. Silence a testament to his failure. For the first time in years, no inner response came from the goddess. Like his shield the connection to his goddess was broken, because of his failure as a paladin. Without another thought, Thomas snatched up the shattered shield. He held it tight despite having lost its blessing. He had failed his companions, causing them to lose their lives.

With a grunt, he drove the shield's edge into the soft earth. The ground was loose, but the effort required was more than physical. His body ached, skin tightening over the unhealed burns, but it was nothing compared to the heaviness in his heart. He pushed the shield down repeatedly, the jagged metal scraping the dirt, digging a shallow, crude grave.

He glanced at their bodies, stiffened into a caricature of their dying moments causing his stomach to ache. It was his weakness that caused this. Sir Silas taught him to think more than swing, yet in the heat of the moment, his arrogance led him to believe he could fight through and win. A good leader listens to those around him. Both of his companions had suggested they leave, and he had ignored them. They deserved better. Each thrust of the broken shield was a confirmation of that damning thought.

After the first grave was deep enough, Thomas wiped the sweat from his brow and dragged Janelle's body to the pit. She had trusted and followed him loyally, believing in his wisdom and connection to their goddess. Shaky hands lowered her into the grave. Tears spilled onto her stiffened body. He covered everything but her face, giving her one last chance to be in Aleara's light before returning to her bosom. Thomas shied away from her face, afraid that in death it might judge him unworthy of her loyalty and faith.

Hacking into the ground, he made another grave for the druid. Loyal to Aleara and this forest, Brontë had asked for help. The Order of Valor had sent Thomas. He failed. Lifting Brontë, he placed him in the grave next to Janelle. The soil slid from his hands as he pushed it back into the grave, covering the two people who followed him to their deaths. He used his shield one last time to pack the dirt over them, the broken symbol of Aleara almost invisible beneath the blood and grime.

Thomas knelt in front of the graves, his heart pounding in his chest, his thoughts darker than the clouds hanging overhead. He stared at the mounds, unable to move. Why he had survived escaped him. He should be lying next to them. It was strange that the chaos thralls did not finish him off. He would have preferred death rather than staring into the lifeless eyes of his companions. Who would entrust him with any more lives? What right did he have to continue, to claim some divine purpose when he failed in the simplest things? Now Aleara, knowing he was inadequate, left his prayers unanswered, severing their connection. Snow began to fall, settling on his hot skin and melting, running into the burns, but Thomas did not move. Instead, he stared at the graves. How long since that fateful day?

The sun dipped below the horizon, casting long shadows over the twisted, dying trees. Blood seeped from the deep wounds to his body, and the blistering skin on his back matted to his gambeson through a mixture of pus and blood. They were oozing with infection. His body trembled from the fever, and he struggled to draw breath into his chest. He collapsed to the ground, his broken shield falling from his hand. The world spun around him, darkness creeping in at the edges of his sight. With a final shudder, his consciousness slipped away like water through his fingers.

At first, there was only a deep, all-encompassing void, but Thomas heard faint voices in the distance.

"He's not strong enough," one voice murmured.

It was a woman's voice, soft yet filled with an ancient weight. Who stumbled upon him in this out-of-the-way location? He thought it was the voice of someone he had heard once before but was unable to identify them. The voice was melodic and other-worldly. It had to be his goddess, Aleara. Hearing and seeing her brought him some relief. Perhaps he was not cut off from her.

"Look at him now, holding on to a thread. Is it right to demand more of him?"

Another voice answered with a low, almost imperceptible bass coming from beyond the very fabric of reality.

"Thomas must endure," the voice replied, calm and detached. "The Lord of Tempests will not be stopped through half-measures. We will lose if we try to fight force with force. Your father can muster many more resources than you and Donegal can."

Aleara's voice softened, but there was a note of sorrow in it. "He is dejected from his losses. His faith, his companions, his very sense of self. What more can we ask? Can we honor my creations and justify this, knowing his path is filled with struggles?"

A sharp pain lanced through his side, pulling him deeper into a fevered state. His breathing quickened, shallow and ragged. He wanted to speak, to ask them to stop, but his mouth failed to form the words. No, he wanted Aleara to embrace him, take his life force, and use it again. Make him into something new. Something that gave her a chance not to fail.

"The choice is his," the hidden figure said. "To stand against the darkness and understand the cost. He can turn back. It is the world that will suffer."

Aleara hesitated, her voice heavy with emotion. "But is this the path bringing him to the Threshold? Or are we merely breaking him, using him as a pawn in this war? He is slipping from us."

There was a long silence, broken only by the sounds of his labored breathing. His mind swirled with images of his father's stern face, Kendrick's laughter, Janelle's lifeless body, and Brontë's hollow eyes staring into nothingness.

The hidden figure spoke again, "He will reach it, or he will fall. Either way, the storm will come. He is the one we have chosen, Aleara. And now, you must either choose to intercede in this world and risk your father doing the same or let this one face the storm. I will not take a more direct role."

Thomas wanted to scream, reach for Aleara, and beg her not to leave him. His body convulsed as the fever raged through him, and the voices faded, swallowed by the darkness.

He awoke again, hearing voices and smelling smoke from a fire. He tried to recall the voices from earlier, but the memory faded, leaving him with only the memory of Aleara speaking. That brought him joy. He sat up and looked around at his surroundings. His plate mail sat in the tent, clean and arranged next to him. He wore a loose-fitting woolen robe that replaced his undergarments and gambeson. His weapons were nowhere to be found, and it worried him the most. Even though they had some-how healed him of his injuries, Thomas was unsure whether he was among friendly people or not. If this were to be the end of him, he would not go down without a fight. He would bring glory to Aleara. In death, he might erase the stain of failure.

Wielding an impromptu cudgel from the nearby stack of fire-wood, Thomas went to determine whether he faced a friend or foe. Edging forward until he stood inside the tent's flaps, he tried to listen to whoever was outside. The voices stopped. Thomas de-cided to wait to see if someone would come and investigate, as-suming the conversation had stopped because of some noise he had made.

"Are you going to stand there all day, lad?" a gravelly voice said.

He did not recognize the voice, but it was sufficiently human that he took a chance. Stepping through the flaps, Thomas took in the sight before him. Two men sat around a campfire. One wore a robe almost identical to the one he now wore, and the other wore a robe, but it was better kept and dyed white. He recognized the priest. It was Avery, his longtime mentor.

"He's going to bash us," the first man said, chuckling as if he found it funny.

"Did Aleara send you to me?" Thomas asked.

"Sir Silas did," Jaxxon replied, "so pretty much the same thing. I'm Jaxxon, druid of the Order of Nature."

"How long have I been here?"

"By my estimate," Avery said, "three days. You gave a good ac-counting against your foes. I counted six of those chaos thralls dead. Proud of you, Thomas."

"Avery, I failed them. I have to avenge their deaths. Was there any sign of dead wizards?" Thomas asked.

"No."

"Then they are still out there," Thomas replied. "Is the forest still wilted?"

"No," Jaxxon said, "but I talked to a few of the local animals, and they said it resembled a forest fire without the fire. You'll see in the morning. The trees have recovered."

"We cannot wait for the morning," Thomas said. "Where are my weapons? I have to find their trail and avenge Janelle and Brontë."

Avery sighed. "They reside with Aleara now, Thomas. Vengeance is not going to make them come back."

Thomas stared incomprehensibly at the man. Even though the burns and wounds had healed, weakness persisted. Logic said to run off into the woods after the wizards was folly. Instead of continuing to look for his sword, he sat down by the fire. The pain went, but his scars were more than physical. Reuniting with Avery was a reminder that he was more than brute force, and he thanked Aleara for keeping the priest from being a part of Thomas's failure. He needed to think more than fight, choosing to engage in combat only after he understood the battlefield and his opponents.

He would have to change, or he would continue to fail the goddess. Something about failing her sparked a memory of the dream, but the images were distant, and he did not recall enough to make sense of the situation. Something told him that if he did not change his brash ways, he would face even tougher lessons.

CHAPTER

7

The three men slowly made their way back to Godsdown on foot. Thomas bemoaned the loss of his destrier almost as much as the druid and squire. The druid did his best to keep Thomas from thinking too much about the events of that day. Despite his garrulous nature, Jaxxon quickly built a friendship with the paladin, though it was different from the relationship between Thomas and Avery. The priest was pious and rulebound, while Jaxxon refused to follow rules out of habit. Adding the druid to their philosophical musings often brought Thomas to fits of laughter. For Avery, less often.

Avery had taught him the importance of politeness and respect. Jaxxon taught him boldness. They provided much-needed balance as he recovered from the ordeal in the woods. He was glad to have the time on the road. It was short-lived as the walls of Godsdown soon came into sight. When they arrived, Thomas prepared himself for the worst. He expected to be dismissed by the leaders of his order. Whatever happened, he would not go back to Grimhorn.

It was not the punishment he imagined, though it was just as humiliating. The Council of Orders had chastised him, then let him stew on their remarks before bringing him back to let him know his future. He was thankful that he remained a paladin, but they had relegated him to scouting duty. Unspoken was the sentence. He was not worthy of being around the valiant members of his order. His orders meant he wouldn't have to see them very often.

Shattered by the separation from the host, he berated himself. He knew there were members of the orders that had missions like that. Often, they were barely members, having failed Aleara much like he had. It was a half-existence. Most died alone at the hands of monsters.

He was shocked even more when his companions were informed of the same orders. Jaxxon didn't care. His disdain for Godsdown was evident, though Thomas had learned that the man had grown up within these walls. Though Avery looked as if the decision rocked his world, he dutifully bowed his head in acceptance. Thomas had spoken up for the priest, but Grand Commander Marla had silenced him with a withering glare. He had stolen several tomes from the library in hopes that they would brighten Avery's spirits.

Embarassment was the only thing the young paladin could think about as the words were said and they were released to provision themselves for their meandering exile. Thomas kept his head down until they exited the chamber, fearful of catching Sir Silas' gaze. It could have gone much worse. While he was grateful, it did not sit as well with the druid. Avery grumbled at their assignment, looking over at the druid for support. Jaxxon smiled and shrugged.

The trio made the best of it. With no real orders, it left them to wander the edges of the world, looking for signs that the Lord of Tempests was readied for another attempt on their world. They fell into a routine. Deep religious discussions, bawdy tales of their encounters at roadside inns, and tactical planning dominated their downtime. It did not erase his dwelling on his failure, but did help to pass the days. At first, Thomas longed for the presence of other paladins but grew to enjoy their travels.

Better still was the random coin that fell into their hands as they crossed paths with those needing the aid of warriors. Ostracized by his order, they took on jobs for anyone willing to pay. Finer drinks and better companionship always availed themselves when there was a clink of coins in their belt pouches. Avery despaired that they had offended Aleara by taking money for executing her will. It didn't stop him from taking his share or frolicking with the tavern wenches.

The best part of their assignment was submitting their findings to the nearest garrison and continuing, never having to spend any real time in Godsdown. Having no real home, they wandered the continent. Neither the border guards in Nemordia nor Castardia cared about them crossing into their countries. They steered clear of the narrow strip of the mainland Sambor claimed as its own. Thomas had tangled with his fair share of the Grey Wizards in the past and hoped never to cross paths with them again.

A summons to Godsdown ruined their happy adventuring. With a heavy heart, the three companions turned their steeds to the North. The note was plain. Return at once. They passed through the great forests of the South, crossing the plains and their tall golden grasses to come at last to the seat of the Orders. Godsdown, the ancient and imposing seat of the barony of Thistlewilde, stood tall and proud amidst the undulating hills and lush green meadows.

Like his home of Grimhorn, it was near the mountain range and the river Congryr, which roared out of the mountains and became wide and navigable at Godsdown. Its stone walls rose high into the sky, a symbol of strength and power for those worshipping Aleara. Godsdown was legendary as the place where Aleara and Donegal came together, stealing the stuff of chaos to form their world. Every time someone mentioned it, Jaxxon quickly pointed out it was the last peaceful day the gods enjoyed.

Currently, a border pass to the North created strife with Nemordia. When not under attack by Klydos and his minions, human lords quickly grew bored and tried to serve as alternates to celestial terrors. Baron Gaslon, who ruled over Thistlewilde Duchy, served in King Cyrus' place at the head of the royal armies. Thomas could almost hear his father ranting about their king sitting in Drea while another defended his honor. The people of Godsdown spoke proudly of their leader, but Thomas detected unease in their comments. The Zel'Drean military differed from the forces of Aleara. Most remained oblivious to the horrors Klydos visited upon this realm.

Still, the absence of many fathers, brothers, and sisters gave the city a forlorn mood. Pilgrims, seeking joy and a spiritual experience, found the city's people unenjoyable. Though many stopped coming, some still walked about, spotted by their oohs and aahs at the carvings on the council house or gawking up at the trees of the grove. The disposition of sellers and innkeepers contrasted with that of their visitors.

Worse still, gossip flew from stall to stall, changing and worsening as it went. The companions heard all the rumors. In truth, hill tribes warred with Zel'Drea for Nemordia. Limited in resources, up in their icy abodes, the hill tribes took in the weapons and armor and used them to harass caravans. Thomas doubted the hill tribes fought for Nemordia. They gave allegiance to no one. If giants came down from the mountain peaks, they served as their foot soldiers. If Nemordians fed them during the deep winter, they rained rocks and arrows on the heads of Zel'Dreans. The monstrous frost giants used the hill tribes in many ways. Sometimes, it was for food.

Pilgrims and locals alike listened to these tales. Some shivered in their beds after hearing all the rumors. Klydos gave Binsmuth frost giants as an early gift to counter the works of Aleara and Donegal. Campaigns to wrest them from their lofty lairs failed time and again. Humans could not fight in the frigid altitudes the giants occupied. The Council of Orders only responded to news of frost giants when they marched down the slopes. Tiring of the stories, the men paid their bills and made ready to face the council.

They traversed the main road, passing by the sacred grove on their way there. Thomas grinned with nostalgia as they passed by the barracks. The cycle of fresh squire to knighthood continued. He could tell from the sounds that they were busy sparring, some probably getting injured for the first time. Somewhere within those walls was a squire determined to light their coin. Also, within those walls were those who would never earn the badge. Some, like Janelle, would fall in honor, while others would walk out the gate and have to choose what else to do with their lives.

He rocked back in his saddle to stretch and stared up at the towering trees of the grove. The trees were unnaturally tall, something he never thought of until the priest mentioned it. Avery pondered such things, and Thomas often found himself numb from the discussions. When the priest began rambling about the nature of Aleara, Donegal, and Klydos, it was time for him and Jaxxon to find something more interesting to do.

He looked down and groaned. Ahead, with its ornately carved walls, was the Council of Orders. The building brought back bad memories. Its grand facade was carved with intricate scenes of forests, farms, and children playing with various animals. Inside was judgment. He would never forget retelling the story of how Janelle and Bronte fell in battle.

"It has been a long time since I have set foot in this place," he said.

Avery replied, "I'm sure they still remember you."

Thomas ignored the priest. Part of his duty meant answering when summoned, though it engendered no fond memories of the place. Despite his past ill feelings, he hoped this trip would be more than a waste of time. It had been years since the three of them felt more than an afterthought by any of their orders. They halted at the open gate and dismounted. Two squires came from within, grabbing the reins of the two horses and the mule. Avery refused to ride a horse. The furry ears of his steed swiveled with curiosity when led away.

Thomas held his helm in his left arm. It was the protocol that they passed through by invitation only. The female squire bowed to them and stood waiting for her companion to return from stabling their animals. When he returned, one of them would invite them in. Thomas looked at the girl while they waited. She was fit and well-suited for battle. She was from one of the few plains settlements. Women from his part of the world were stockier.

"What is your name?" he asked.

"Elisa, sir," she replied.

"Well met, Elisa," Thomas said. "Who do you squire for?"

"Sir Victor of Relond," Elisa answered. "I am in my second year."

He nodded, noting her calloused hands. A second-year squire would not accompany their knight on a journey. Victor must be on a mission, most likely with another squire who was about to receive their commission. Despite the many years that had passed since his own time there, Thomas remembered the excitement and nerves of his commissioning day. That caused him to think of Janelle and her bravery in the face of the wizards. Buried on a trail, forgotten and replaced. He sighed, looking away not to show emotion before the squire. When he stilled his feelings, he looked at her again.

"How did you come to be chosen?"

Elisa said, "My parents died in a hill tribe ambush. My little brother, sister, and I were the only ones who managed to escape.

They took my brother and me for squires while my sister chose to marry a knight."

"I'm sorry that happened to you," said Thomas. "Study Victor's every move so when your moment arrives, you are prepared before he even asks. Have you submitted yourself to Aleara?"

"Not yet, sir," Elisa replied, "but Donald here has and can already make the light shine on a coin."

The other squire arrived from the stables, nearly stumbling as he tried to bow before coming to a complete stop. Donald came over at the mention of his name, and Thomas tousled the boy's hair. He remembered those days. Separated from family and unsure of expectations, it had been an actual test of faith. Elisa had no option but to take to the streets. The other orders remained a mystery, but he did know the Order of Valor. None stayed in the barracks if the coin did not light up. For those with nowhere else to go, that was heartbreaking.

"Sir," she said, "the council invites you and your companions to join them."

He motioned for the two squires to lead the way. Torches whipped back and forth when the inner doors opened, their flames almost lifting off the sponge and its oil-filled cavities. Thomas counted the clinks of his soles upon the stone floor to occupy his mind. Elisa and Donald opened another set of double doors, taking their position next to them. The chamber they entered was imposing, a circular room with high ceilings where banners representing the four orders of Aleara's chosen hung with silent authority. The large, round table at the center of the room, hewn from ancient oak, reflected the soft glow of the candles illuminating the room.

"Welcome, brothers," an older priest said.

He rose to greet them. His deep and resonant voice echoed slightly in the spacious chamber, and his richly embroidered robes whispered against the stone floor as he moved. Thomas saluted out of respect, and Jaxxon bowed his head. It was Avery who struggled to maintain his composure.

"High Priest Edogir," Avery said.

Three others occupied the round table. Thomas grimaced at seeing Sir Silas sitting there next to Grand Commander Marla. The Grand Druid, David, was there as well. Ringing the wall of the chamber were the other senior members of the Orders. This conclave was unexpected. This many called from their duties suggested war or censure.

Thomas hesitated. They did nothing to deserve punishment. In the five years since the deaths of the squire and druid, Thomas complied with every order, exercising caution rather than running into situations without understanding them. He did not always like it, but he did it anyway.

"We have heard much of your deeds in the north," Edogir said. "Nasty business with those giants up there."

"Many brave men and women lost their lives," Thomas said.

Since Janelle and Brontë, he kept a tally of all those lost alongside him, battling against the Lord of Tempests. Many rejoined Aleara too early due to the conflict with her father, Klydos. Edogir patted him on the shoulder.

"I know. Not too long ago, I stood on the shores of the Rangir Ocean, fighting the sea creatures raised by the Lord of Tempests. Be as it may, the council sought Aleara's wisdom and received direction. You have been chosen to aid us in a dire situation."

Avery leaned forward in his chair, his curiosity piqued. The priest ran his hand through his hair. Thomas sighed and shook his head. His companion did not hide his emotions very well. Avery spoke up, proving Thomas correct.

"What kind of situation are we talking about?"

Before Edogir responded, a sharp voice interrupted, saying, "Aid us? Or lead us to ruin?"

An older woman with sharp features rose from her seat. Her short hair was a rich red, glinting even in the dim candlelight. Thomas sighed. The Grand Commander was not a supporter of him. Sir Silas owed many in this room favors for the votes needed to counter her original sentence. Despite his opposition, he somehow now sat at the table. Marla made for an impressive figure, dressed in full plate mail as a show of power. Sitting in the plate mail for any length of time was irritating.

"I still find it hard to believe the goddess would choose these three for a holy mission."

Thomas met her gaze calmly. He respected the Grand Commander. She was a strong paladin and an even better tactician. Jaxxon spoke of her with an unusual fondness that was reserved for woodland creatures. The paladin's only disappointment was her dismissive attitude about the other orders. He learned that five years ago, she would berate anyone who said a kind word in his favor. A murmur rose from the assembled members of the various orders. Conversations broke out amongst the attendees. Despite originating from their goddess, the members of this assembly exhibited contention.

Edogir said, "Commander Marla, I understand your concerns, but you, too, said Aleara came to you via a dream and said their names. They are who the goddess wants, so their skill is what we need."

"My faith in Aleara is the only reason this audience is even happening," Marla said. "I am witness to what she can do in the face of terrible odds."

Thomas remembered her arguments well. It was true he lacked discipline that day in the forest. He should have listened to the squire and backed out. The knowledge of the blighted woods alone would have sent a full complement of paladins to investigate. His brashness had led to deaths. She lashed him with her words during his censure, stinging far worse than the lash at home. He deserved every one of those blows.

That man was no more. In the years since losing his squire and the druid, Thomas had learned much, treading the world with his two companions. Although none of them claimed rank over the others, he had assumed the tactical leadership. He was pleased when others remarked on how well they coordinated their various skills into a deadly combination. Throughout their time together, they refined their tactics to near perfection. Avery had surprised him the most, transitioning from researcher to adventurer without much effort.

The priest laughed, which startled Thomas. It was unlike the man to disrespect anyone. However, Avery had served under Marla before her promotion to the council and was familiar with her. Thomas looked over at the priest, staring at the Grand Commander. Avery respected her leadership, but his current disdain for her attitude was evident. Luckily for Avery, his attitude was out of her control. Edogir commanded the priest, not her. Thomas would find himself wearing leather armor, trying to dig minions of Klydos out of their nasty nests.

"You think you know better than the Council, priest," Marla said. "Perhaps you can explain to this assembly why Aleara chooses you and these other two ruffians. Why would your names come to me in a vision from Aleara?"

Avery said, "I am not privy to the mind of Aleara. Like you, I am called to serve. If she named us, who am I to question it?"

The Grand Commander held her tongue. She looked over at Jaxxon, but Thomas saw no noticeable response from the man. The redness on her face betrayed her true feelings. Thomas wondered if they would be able to exit this place on their own. Pushing her was possible, but she would push back harder. Loud conversations erupted again. The priest's words found others who shared his opinion. All of the men and women in this chamber served Aleara. Marla was not the speaker for their goddess. He stepped forward, hoping to change the tone of the conversation.

"A contrite knight came before this assembly," Thomas said, "broken and shattered by my failure. If stripped of my badge, I would have walked away. I failed them."

"You did!"

"I am not that man anymore," Thomas said. "You placed wise and careful men around me. We have done whatever has been asked. If Aleara asks us to do something, we are ready to answer."

Marla slammed her gauntleted hand on the table. The Grand Commander had voted alone to strip Thomas of his knighthood after he lost his companions in the blighted forest. To this day, he still believed her judgment to be proper. However, Aleara forgave him, and that was more important than the leader of his order. He would sacrifice his own life to repay the goddess for trusting him again. A murmur ran through the council members, some nodding in agreement, others looking uncertain. The council navigated between making decisions and waiting for Aleara's guidance. Thomas discussed this many times with Sir Silas. In tactical matters, they would decide and pray for clarity. Since the council's formation, it had never let them down.

"Marla, we cannot afford to be so rigid. The Lord of Tempests' forces grow stronger with every incursion. Aleara sees these men as part of her plan."

"I don't expect you to understand, Grand Druid," Marla said, "the Order of Nature is a disorganized collective of misfits whose purpose is lost to me. They lost their way when Grand Druid Holly was taken back to Aleara. Your order has caused me nothing but pain."

"We all know your history with the druidic order, Grand Commander. Luckily," David, the Grand Druid, replied, "I serve at Aleara's will, not yours."

Edogir nodded in agreement.

"Indeed. We serve Aleara, and she determined these men to be the tip of the spear. We are merely the messengers. Act with haste. You are to go to the city of Ceylon. Reports have come in of increased activity in the surrounding areas. Villages are being razed, and people have disappeared. We believe the Lord of Tempests' influence is spreading."

Thomas glanced at Jaxxon, whose brow furrowed in thought. It was within the duchy of his family. A backwater southern province that existed to guard the border. There were very few reasons to go there. Klydos always came down from the mountains with his hordes. This was a feint, a ploy to divide their forces.

"Ceylon? That's a far journey and not some place we know very well," Jaxxon said. "Grand Commander, you know what is down there."

Marla's head swiveled to glare at the druid. Thomas was unsure what was happening between the two of them.

"That is the wisdom of Aleara's plan," Edogir said. "You three can move nimbly. Without knowledge of the lands you are entering, you will be cautious, which is what this mission calls for. We cannot send an army. They would be spotted. You will do it under the guise of supporting the King of Zel'Drea."

Marla scoffed, folding her arms and saying, "We are not in league with any kingdom. This has been the case since the inception of the Orders. We cannot ask them to give fealty to Zel'Drea."

Edogir sighed, saying, "Your predecessor served as Grand Commander for Nemordia during the war with the corsairs from across the ocean."

"Aleara herself anointed Harold," Marla said. "These misfits received no such ordination."

Jaxxon's eyes narrowed, his usual easygoing demeanor slipping.

"You think of us less than you in Aleara's eyes. You can doubt our choices of service, but we do not turn tail and run. We fight every battle bathed in her spirit."

The druid transformed as he spoke. His body stretched and grew, sprouting claws, feathers, and a beak. Where the man once stood, a giant owlbear towered over those at the table. The Grand Commander stepped back, gasping as she did so. She never attempted to reach for her sword, though it was at her side. Only Aleara might know the outcome of that decision. Instead, she held out her hands, speaking quietly, seeking to calm the transformed druid.

"I fight," Jaxxon growled, "blessed with the light of Aleara. My father does the same. Do not dishonor him with your casual remarks."

The druid emphasized his words by smashing his giant paws against the massive oak table. It surprised Thomas, as he had never seen the druid transform into an owlbear, much less speak in a new animal form. Jaxxon talked about the creatures often. Marla gripped the table, poised to vault over it into Jaxxon's path. Aleara sent a message in the transformation. She imbued them with favor.

"Enough," Edogir said. "The Council made its decision. We honor the wishes of the goddess. You will go to Ceylon. The rest is not up for debate."

Marla opened her mouth to argue, but a look from Edogir silenced her. Thomas stood in stunned silence, thinking back to the censure he had received. It was deja vu. The Grand Commander alone against the rest of the Council leaders. Angry shouts echoed across the chambers as opinions lobbed from one faction to another. He did not question Aleara's will. He would go to Ceylon. Council members exchanged glances, some still wary, but they understood the message from their goddess, and it was up to the companions to carry it out. Jaxxon growled and shifted back into his human form.

"Mothers," Jaxxon said cryptically.

As they left the council chamber, the weight of their mission settled over them. Largely ignored for the last five years, they had allowed events to dictate their actions. With the order from the Council, those days were over. Commissioned by Aleara herself, the city of Ceylon awaited. The three men walked in silence. Thomas was still absorbing what had taken place there in the council chamber. He was interrupted from his thoughts by someone clearing their throat. A squire wearing the livery of the Order of Valor stood waiting for them outside the building.

"The Lord Commander would like to speak to you, sir," the young man said to Thomas. "He asks that you dine with him in his quarters before you depart."

"I assume you mean Silas. Let your master know I will see him this evening," Thomas said.

The squire replied with a grin, "Sir Silas says you found a way not to have to trudge ass-deep through the snow this campaign."

Thomas laughed. Gordie was a waif who had found his way to squire for the Lord Commander much in the same way Thomas had. He tousled the boy's hair playfully.

Thomas replied, "I have a feeling I am going to wish I were trudging through the snow with you before this is all over. Just because we are going south does not mean there will not be snow. It snows everywhere in this forsaken kingdom."

"I'll let Sir Silas know you are coming. See you this evening," Gordie said. "Good day, gentlemen."

The boy sprinted away, off to whatever chore awaited him next. Silas always had a full day's work for his squires. He remembered countless days polishing anything metal and dusting everything else. What that had to do with battling Klydos still eluded him, but he understood the value of hard work. He looked at his companions. They did not seem amused by his invitation.

"Kind of crappy, Silas didn't invite us," Jaxxon said.

"I should be the one offended, unlike you. If I recall," Avery said, "you pooped in his helm."

"It was deer poop," Jaxxon quipped, "and it was a day old when he found it."

"Ah," Avery replied, "So true. I have no idea why the man would hold a grudge."

Jaxxon turned to Thomas and said, "Please give the Lord Commander my apologies. Let him know I will make it up to him someday."

Thomas rolled his eyes and let out a sigh. It was no wonder Marla considered them a poor choice. He was tempted to ask the druid about his comment in the council chambers. Over the previous five years, Jaxxon had spoken little about his life before becoming a druid. He decided there would be plenty of time during their journey to Ceylon to unravel that mystery.

"Tell Cassidy to put your food and drink on my tab," he said to the two men. "And Avery, tell her you are off on a grand adventure and need some motivation for the ride."

"Good idea. I'm friends with you for a reason. Aren't you going to join us?" Avery asked. "It's too early to show up at Silas' door."

Thomas hesitated. He did not want his friends to know his fear that they were being set up to fail, not because of the situation, but because Thomas was not sure he was ready to bear the weight of this mission.

"Saddlemaker," Thomas said as he walked away. "I'm going to check on the saddle I ordered."

"When did you order a saddle?" Avery asked.

Thomas ignored the priest and walked away. He hated lying to the man. It had been years, and he took the opportunity to reacquaint himself with the streets of Godsdown. The city had grown since his last visit, with new buildings rising where old ones once stood. Yet, the heart of the town remained the same, a bustling center of commerce, faith, and whispers of power. The cobblestones beneath his feet echoed with memories of his time wandering the city as a child, but today, they carried him forward with purpose. He needed to unravel the council's strange command.

He wandered at first, his general track leading him to the home of Sir Silas. The common folk worried. An uprising in the north, unrest among the tribes, and Aleara's forces were struggling. Those furtive glances were sure signs of the toll taken on Godsdown, which wore its people thin. They, more than any town on the continent, lost members of their community. During the last war, people from Godsdown demanded an audience with Aleara, begging her to seek peace with her father. Their audience went unanswered. Many blamed the warlike orders for the ongoing struggle. Those sentiments now reared their ugly heads.

He did not know how many people inhabited Zel'Drea. There were hundreds of druids, thousands of priests. In the Order of Valor, there were over seven thousand paladins. What the villagers and townspeople rarely saw was the horrible reality that necessitated the forces Aleara marshalled. When they did, they were quick to call upon Aleara for deliverance from those monsters. Still, they quickly forgot, and there were periods when paladins had been pelted by fruit as they rode through areas where peace and stability were maintained.

Conversations stopped when he approached the booths of the sellers. Furtive glances suggested his status as a paladin failed to enthuse those around him. Those conversations that continued told the truth of the matter. King Cyrus demanded reinforcements, and soon it would be the older folk who answered. These were dire tidings. Zel'Drea was at war. Aleara's servants were always fighting the minions of Klydos. It only served to add weight to the mission before him. If the mission was a distraction and the uprising was in the north, he needed to assure the council of Ceylon's insignificance in the battle against Klydos.

There was the chance that the Grand Commander sensed his fortunes were improving in the eyes of their goddess and meant to keep him from any real glory. As soon as he thought it, he regretted that and asked Aleara to forgive him for being petty. He had deserved his separation from the host. It had given him time to mature and reflect on what service to her meant. Who was he to question the Grand Commander?

Time passed, and as the sun began to dip below the horizon, Thomas made his way to a small villa on the quieter side of town. His old friend, Lieutenant Commander Silas Morgrave, lived here. Thomas entered the gate into the private garden and knocked on the door. A servant, limping like a former soldier, answered and ushered him inside. Thomas handed the man his trench coat and followed him to the study, where Silas sat, poring over maps and making hasty notes. Silas was a man of medium height, but what he lacked in stature, he more than made up for in presence. The blonde hair Thomas remembered was completely grey now, tied back in a neat ponytail. The paladin had aged in the years since Thomas left, but his sharp eyes were alert, taking in every detail around him.

Approaching the table, Thomas smiled, breaking through his intense mood. He extended his hand to the man, foregoing the traditional salute. Anyone but Sir Silas would have reprimanded him, but the man was as much a father as anything else to the lad. Silas grasped Thomas' hand in a firm handshake. He gestured with his free hand, scarred and callused, and Thomas complied, taking a seat. He took up residence in the large, overstuffed wing-back chair next to the desk.

The Lord Commander was one of the finest tactical minds in the order. A fact that kept him near the Grand Commander. Thomas had seen the man stripped down to his loincloth and knew that the knight had paid dearly for every experience that shaped his understanding of warfare. A shallow depression in his abdomen marked the spot where a gnoll gnawed on him as Silas choked the life out of it. This was no theoretical leader. He had proven himself in countless battles.

A squire entered, bringing over a pitcher of ale and two mugs. The aroma of a strong drink was a welcome thing to Thomas. His reflection on the events left him with more questions than answers. The girl filled their mug and left. Silas lifted his mug, and Thomas clanged his against it in honor of the ritual of the toast. Paladins toasted in gratitude to those who came before them, those who lost their lives in the never-ending war against the God of Chaos. Silas began, setting his mug down with a thud.

"Marla's going to be pissed for weeks. That damnable Jaxxon made quite a show of it in there."

"He made a point."

"If you only knew. That druid is probably the weakest spot in Marla's otherwise impenetrable armor."

"Why do you say that?" asked Thomas.

"It's not my story to tell," Silas replied. "Ask your friend. If he wishes to share, it will be a tale you will never forget. As much as the bastard pisses me off sometimes, he may have saved your assignment."

"She hates me. That much I know."

The elder paladin nodded in agreement. It was not very comfortable to see the man admit that truth. To hide his embarrassment, Thomas examined the maps on the desk. By the sheer number of troops denoted on the map, Marla had a lot going on in the north. Nearly half of the ordained paladins were on the move. Silas pushed it closer, so Thomas took the full breadth of it in. It was a significant campaign. Thomas had studied engagements of this magnitude, but none of them ever occurred in his lifetime. It was a surge. The god of chaos tended to wax and wane in his irritation with the existence of Binsmuth. Avery suggested it was the nature of the god to be fickle, though why he opposed his children was a mystery.

"Word on the streets suggests an uprising," Thomas said.

"The people grow weary of the endless attacks. I think they question whether we are making a difference or making things worse. They act as if we enjoy going out and fighting and dying, although I would not trade places with a farmer for any amount of peace."

"What will you do when we finally defeat Klydos?"

"I loved fishing as a boy," Silas said. "Might ask to settle on the western shore, so I can spend my final days doing that. That is, once you are the duke of Grimhorn."

"Keep dreaming, then. We have a chance at defeating Klydos, but I have no chance of being the lord of anything."

Silas grimaced, taking another long drink of his ale. He pointed a finger at the notations. Hill tribes. Whether goaded by Nemordia or the Lord of Tempests was irrelevant. They took to the field against Zel'Drea and joined with the forces of Chaos. Not as primitive as the nomads of the south, but with less moral fortitude, they typically annoyed the royal army more than the forces of Aleara. Silas treated the hill tribes like wildlife fleeing a forest fire. If they ran past without engaging, they were not something the old paladin worried about. What they did once they were past the paladins was the problem of the royal army.

"The field generals, they are trying their best, but the army is fractured," Silas said, "Too long we have been skirmishing, and now a true battlefield is before us. We are herding cats out of a barn on fire."

"Marla seems frustrated," Thomas said. "I did not realize it was this bad."

Silas leaned back in his chair, his eyes narrowing as he considered the knight's words.

"Frustrated does not begin to cover it. She has been butting heads with her generals and the other council leaders for months now. They don't listen to her."

Bluntly said, though he expected as much from Silas. He was surprised by the revelation of discord among his brethren. Strife within the orders concerned Thomas. Avery often spoke of a great schism in which the Orders turned on each other, much to the delight of Klydos. It started with a similar situation. The Grey Wizards of Sambor appeared, guiding monsters from their side of the mountains and uniting the Orders once again. Each time there was strife, each order was convinced it was they who heard Aleara's voice.

"I know you to be an honorable and pious man, sir," Thomas said. "If you believe we are waiting for answers that are not coming. Why not press forward?"

Silas shook his head. "Lad, there is something foul in our midst."

What did that mean? Did corruption exist in the ranks of Aleara's chosen? Avery would consider it fodder for a lengthy discussion about Aleara's lack of omniscience, so deception of her own was a possibility. He called it omniscience. With all the outside threats, Thomas failed to envision how much disruption an internal struggle would cause.

Silas said, "Whatever you do on this mission, trust no one. I fear the Lord of Tempests has spies within the army. No, not spies but traitors. Those who have lost their way believe that destroying this world will lead to something better. We who have looked into the eyes of those serving the Lord of Tempests know better."

The younger paladin nodded at the advice.

"Some days," Silas said, "I wish you were still my squire. Simple. The banners are switching directions on us, and a foul breeze is about to blow harder."

Those words sent a shiver down his spine. This was no simple skirmish. It was a full-blown crisis, one threatening to unravel the very fabric of the world.

"What can I do to help?" he asked.

Silas met his gaze, his expression serious. "For now, keep your head down and do what you came here to do. Marla's got enough on her plate without worrying about you making trouble. But Thomas, keep your ears open. Things are changing, and not for the better. Wherever they are sending you is dangerous."

It would be dangerous. Ceylon was part of Grimhorn's holdings and a border town with Castardia. Most of Castardia lived a no-madic existence, opting to view the river as an obstacle to prove their transition to adulthood rather than a line of demarcation. There was always strife down there. On the bright side, the weather was usually better than in the north.

CHAPTER

9

S now pelted the group as their steeds trudged through the drifts, struggling to find the road before them. Distant thunder warned of worse weather. Thomas cursed himself for thinking the weather would be better as they moved south, affecting all their moods.

Jaxxon displayed it through his constant grumbling, which echoed the rumbles from the sky. The druid was usually easygoing, though gruff, and Thomas was unsure whether the weather contributed to his ire or the lingering hangover. He scanned the sky, cursing the weather and the Lord of Tempests.

The sailors of Castardia called this the Kiss of Klydos, like a jaded lover giving a kiss before sliding a blade between ribs. Harsh conditions were a constant reality in their line of work, resulting in many nights when a cold tent was their reward for their service. Still, Thomas hoped their moods would improve. It was a long trip, made worse by the dark conversation that dominated their time on the road.

"I still don't understand why the existence of Valkrunians doesn't bother you more," Avery said.

Thomas shrugged and said, "The goddess does not have a problem with assimilating the minions of Klydos into our ecosystem. As long as they honor her tenets."

"You're a priest," Jaxxon replied. "You should know whether Aleara said we were her only creations."

"The scriptures do not speak of such things. Is the absence of explanation sufficient? Why would she lead us to believe that this is the only world?"

Thomas snorted and said, "The Order of Valor does not concern itself with such matters. Aleara has called us to defend this world. Perhaps if we are ever successful in thwarting Klydos, she will ask us to do the same somewhere else."

"I wasn't expecting your lot to think on such matters," Avery replied. "It's deceptive. Ignorance of the truth is not an excuse. I've taught you to think deeper than that."

"Aleara will provide us with the answers when she feels it is necessary."

"All I care about is getting out of this damned weather," Jaxxon said. "That would be something beneficial. Stupid orders compounded by the shittiest of weather is a bad omen."

"All you care about is your next meal. Use your mind. That is all I'm asking."

Ahead lay the road to Ceylon, stretching through ancient and deep forests, a gift from Aleara to this world. It was not only Jaxxon unsettling Thomas. The priest had spent time in prayer, trying to discern what Aleara planned for them to no avail. Despite Avery's apparent calm, Thomas sensed his friend's unease, an undercurrent of tension mirroring the storm's gathering force. It was unlike the priest to rise to the quips of the druid. The two men argued about their mission and its meaning. Recalling the words of Silas, Thomas kept the fears of traitors within their ranks to himself. That bit of intrigue would fuel the fire of debate.

The sky transitioned from a dull, lifeless gray to a menacing palette, signaling the storm's imminent arrival. The wind picked up, becoming more than a nuisance as it whipped at the companions' cloaks and tested their resolve. It whistled through the needles and leaves of the forest. A nearby Frostbloom Tree showed deep blue leaves, a sure sign that the weather was worsening.

"Jaxxon is right. We should find shelter soon," Avery said. "We won't make the next village without getting covered in snow."

Thomas turned, assessing their surroundings and the increasingly volatile sky. He doubted they would make the village. They would need an alternative and soon.

"Look for anything that can provide shelter. Jaxxon, can you scout ahead?" he said.

Jaxxon, shivering in the biting wind, transformed into a wolf, darting into the trees without hesitation. Snow swirled behind him, cloaking the road and his tracks in endless white. Thomas and Avery struggled to keep him in their sight, and the horses began to stumble on the icy road. The biting wind found every crevice to take away what little warmth Thomas still had.

"It looks like more than flurries are on the horizon," Thomas said, pointing at the telltale blue leaves.

Avery's reply came laced with sarcasm, reflecting his mounting frustration. He had been in a bad mood since the council session, and their evening in the tavern had done nothing to improve it. Customarily, the priest ranted about trivial inconsistencies. However, this was an exceptional situation in which they found themselves. Aleara herself ordered them to Ceylon. Who were they to disobey?

"This trip keeps on providing us with blessings," Avery said.

The previous night's events lingered between them, a source of unspoken tension. The altercation at the tavern, instigated by Jaxxon's indiscretions, left Avery with more than a physical reminder. Thomas needed them to be ready for whatever was to come, and it did not bode well if the trio was at odds with each other. He attempted to lighten the mood, referring to the barmaid's confrontation with Avery.

"She had a nasty right hook," Thomas said.

"I was a perfect gentleman," Avery insisted, the indignation evident in his voice. "Jaxxon set me up."

Thomas couldn't help but laugh, recalling the late-night disturbances.

"Very true. Although I did hear knocking on your door later in the night."

"I'm under no vow of chastity. That would be a foolish request for the goddess to make. Anyway, it's none of your business," Avery said. "Perhaps that intelligence of yours would be better suited for finding us some shelter."

Pointing down the road to where Jaxxon loped, Thomas shrugged and gave the priest a sheepish smile. Avery responded with curses and commentary on Jaxxon's lack of focus. The paladin worried about relying on the fickle druid. He released his inner beast in these circumstances. He kept his reply to himself. It would be of no use to add to the priest's irritation.

"Sending a moron off to find us someplace safe to stay is not the best example of leadership I have ever seen," he grumbled.

"I am not in charge," Thomas said. "Aleara called on each of us."

Avery snorted, saying, "Well, somebody has to keep him in line. Can't very well send a note to Godsdown asking for more money after we had to pay for broken tables, sullied reputations, and a cask of ale."

"True," Thomas said. "Although Grand Druid David would approve just to see Grand Commander Marla turn that funny shade of red."

"I'm still confused about all of it," Avery said. "If it was a big issue, why would Aleara tell the Council to send the three of us? Why are we being called out instead of any number of order members?"

"I choose not to question Aleara's will," Thomas said.

He fidgeted with the reins at the hollowness of those words. The warning from Sir Silas worried him. If there was any truth to those things, they might not be following Aleara's plan. He started to share the conversation with the Knight Commander but never got the chance. Wolf-Jaxxon bounded toward them, leapt into the air and came down in human form, one knee touching the ground. The flourish broke the men of their sour mood, filling the frosty air with their laughter. He pointed behind him, and there was a wolf again.

Without a word, the transformed druid turned and sprinted away. Thomas and Avery spurred their steeds into motion. They struggled to keep up and called after the druid to no avail. It had been easy for a wolf to traverse, but not so much for the mule and horse. For an hour, they trudged through knee-deep snow, the storm howling louder with each step. Just when Thomas thought his legs would give out, Jaxxon shifted back into human form, pointing to an oak grove nestled in the shadow of a hill.

"There," Jaxxon said.

They pulled under the towering tree and dismounted. With trembling hands, Jaxxon called upon Aleara's power. Tender green shoots sprang from the earth around them and their steeds. They grew thicker, roots and brambles weaving together into a dense boma. Inch-long thorns belied the protective nature of his conjuring. The wind still whistled through the gaps in the hedge, but the snow was piling up against the new brambles. It would provide little respite from the bitter cold until the snow piled up enough to block out the wind.

Avery staggered and cursed the Lord of Tempests. The priest defaulted to praying, even though Aleara had no control over the weather. The snow was falling so heavily that it was hard to see anything. He held his prayer beads tightly, seeking Aleara's protection, but the biting wind cared not. Thomas joined Avery and Jaxxon in prayer for warmth, a bit of sunlight within them to fight the bitter cold. Despite the weather, the real tempest was the mood of the group.

The sky roared with thunder, the storm almost taking on a life of its own, as if it were an observer, watching their every move. Thomas caught Avery murmuring about the Lord of Tempests' intentions, linking the ferocity of their current predicament with the recent assault on Binsmuth.

They settled into making the best of the situation. Thomas moved with difficulty, hemmed in by his icy armor. He struggled to draw the chain shirt from his body, resorting to getting assistance from Avery.

"We're never going to make it to Ceylon," Avery said. "Here lies Avery. Dead from the council's folly."

"We'll make it," Jaxxon said.

Thomas agreed with the druid. This was a storm, not a troll uprising. They would need to be patient. That seemed to be their dilemma for the day.

"What is wrong with you?"

Avery turned on him, his uncharacteristic anger showing in his look. A bolt of lightning punctuated the moment, striking nearby and drowning out Avery's angry retort. It was clear he disagreed with why they were in their current predicament. Thomas heard some of what the priest was saying. It was uncharacteristic of the priest to have doubt. The man rankled at the thought of Aleara speaking to others about them, rather than to them. As devout as he was, Thomas agreed that Avery should have received a vision from Aleara. He and Jaxxon, on the other hand, were blunt instruments of the goddess and far less likely to be graced by such clarity.

"Since when do we ignore our goddess?" Thomas asked.

Avery waggled his finger at Thomas. "Don't you dare preach to me!"

"I am not preaching. I want to understand why you have such dire thoughts on this mission."

A fierce wind silenced their conversation. The gust doused them with snow, drawing more curses. The cold bit at them all, its teeth sharp with the wind's chill. Outside their modest shelter, the storm raged, the clouds swirling ominously. Unease crept over him, sensing an unknown force within the tempest. If there were spies or traitors, this could be the work of minions of the Lord of Tempests.

When the wind died down, Avery said, "Something isn't right about this adventure. Aleara doesn't act this overtly about the locations of Klydos' armies."

"Does not mean it is a deception."

"What if it is part of a larger deception?" Avery asked. "I want confirmation from Aleara, not the council."

Jaxxon shook his head in disappointment. It was rare for him to voice his opinion. Thomas waited for the man to speak his mind. When Jaxxon did, it resonated with feelings the paladin already had about it.

"Aleara will confirm our path in Ceylon. That is what they told us. Simple."

"Can we hold out here?" Thomas asked.

"It's permanent enough," Jaxxon responded. "The brambles will hold for about four hours. Either the storm will have blown over, or we'll be inside a massive bank of snow."

"That's good enough," Thomas said. "We've been through worse."

Yet, despite his words, Thomas sensed this storm was different. Its intensity was unmatched, not boding well for their trip. This was the southern part of Zel'Drea, immune to the intense winter storms besieging the north. As another howl of wind swept through, Thomas shivered. He alternated blowing on his hands and praying.

They huddled together, seeking warmth as the storm continued its assault. Creases lined Avery's eyes, the thought of being mere pawns in a grander scheme weighing heavily on him. A strange whisper seemed to ride on the wind. Would his doubts abate once they had confirmation from Aleara? If they got confirmation from Aleara. While the council ordered them to the grove in Ceylon, this did not mean Aleara would deign to speak to them.

"Did you hear something?" Avery asked.

"No," Thomas answered. "It is the wind."

"I've never doubted her like this," Avery said. "Even in the worst battles, my confidence in the goddess remained, but I don't in this."

Avery went on to speak of the scrolls Kynan left behind. The wise druid was one of the few people documenting the rift between the orders and the chaos it allowed. In addition to strife within the followers of Aleara, a group of Donegal's priests also confronted the druids. There were precious metals in the ground in contention. However, there was also a two-hundred-year-old fir tree. Kynan wrote a disturbing passage that ate at Avery. Donegal's priest was attacked. Those priests had been instructed to retrieve it at any cost. Kynan had been the only one to escape. In his opinion, Donegal cared nothing for Aleara's creations and used his worshippers to reveal the treasures buried in the ground. During his recounting, the Council of Orders reprimanded Kynan for speaking harshly of Donegal's priests. Avery repeated this often, betrayed by a century-old story.

Thomas listened to the priest while he gathered firewood inside their shelter. It wasn't reassuring, but they had more pressing concerns to attend to for the moment. He attempted to light a fire, and with Avery's whispered prayer, the flames took hold. The horse and the mule stamped nervously but quieted down. As the fire brought additional warmth to their hasty lodging, so did their mood.

"Thanks," he said.

"You're welcome," Avery replied. "Cup of tea, anyone?"

Both Thomas and Jaxxon welcomed the offer with a nod, finding solace in the simple gesture. Avery set about brewing tea amidst the storm's fury. There was some comfort in being able to do mundane things to distract the mind. Nonetheless, the priest was deep in thought. He and the companions all agreed there was a stark contrast between Marla's objections and the mission ahead of them.

The storm seemed to be only the first of many obstacles. If he and his friends failed to make it through this without being at each other's throats, the mission was in jeopardy. Was the task ahead truly within their abilities? He agonized over whether the council voiced Aleara's desires or steered them into mortal treachery. He took comfort in Jaxxon's miraculous transformation. Surely, that came from the goddess. Despite his doubts, he intended to prove himself, adding one more victory to his successes.

Thinking of failures brought him to the Grey Wizards of Sambor. They would be capable of altering the weather in this fashion. Infusing chaos into the storm had been a tactic they had employed in the past. It served them well when used in conjunction with the mighty frost giants. He despised the wizards, having seen too many good people fall to their magics. Even though he failed to remember the faces of the wizards who murdered Janelle and Brontë, he imagined himself plunging his sword into them and exacting retribution.

"Thomas!"

Avery's voice pulled him back from his thoughts. He apologized and passed Avery three cups, their thin metal rims frosted from the moisture of their last washing. Avery placed them near the fire. The ice turned to liquid, each drop sizzling as it struck the flames. Avery produced some herbs from a pouch and doled them out into the cups, adding water to draw out the nutrients within. The smell elicited a grumble from their stomachs.

"Sorry," Thomas said. "I was thinking about the Grey Wizards of Sambor. They have not been a factor in recent years since... Janelle and Brontë died."

Avery replied, "You can't blame yourself for that situation. The Council sent you on a fool's mission. Sending three people..."

"It's idiotic," Jaxxon said. "Just like sending us to Ceylon is idiotic. I'm highly suspicious of this whole adventure."

"What scares me even more is they are listening to Aleara," Avery replied.

Thomas looked over at the priest. His words bordered on apostasy, and it was uncharacteristic of Avery to say such things. He constantly challenged the written word, suggesting fallible men and women could not swear to the accuracy of what they proclaimed, but this struck a different vein. To believe Aleara led her creations astray. It was inconceivable. He looked over at Jaxxon, hoping the druid did not take it the same way, but the look on his face reflected his thoughts. Avery tried to explain his misgivings.

"I've seen what the goddess can do," Avery said, "but I can't help but feel like a pawn in a game where I don't know the rules."

The word triggered a memory of a dream in which someone called him a pawn. He tried hard, but he could not recall it. The coincidence left him shaken. If this mission ended up like the one where his squire died, he did not know if he would heal again. To this day, he refused to take on another squire, though Sir Silas often chided him for depriving someone of a mentor. Suffering in the cold, his brain struggled to function. It wasn't very clear. Thomas prayed to the goddess for understanding, although she seldom answered that prayer.

Jaxxon said, "Don't go down that path, not tonight. Let's head to Ceylon and make sure everything is in order. We reassure them, and we can go back for a real assignment from the damned council. Or better still, we can go off in the deep woods and serve Aleara by ourselves."

Avery sighed and said, "Jaxxon has a point. We need to find out what Aleara plans for Ceylon. It may be nothing, or it may be a great adventure. Either way, we serve Aleara."

"I do not mind going to Ceylon," Thomas said. "I am afraid of dragging you down with me. I may be cursed to face failure again."

"It doesn't matter," Jaxxon said. "We are in this together."

"Maybe it is time to find myself a church somewhere," Avery said.

Jaxxon pointed at the priest and said, "Tell the lad we are in it with him."

"Yes," Avery said. "We are in it with you. Even if it takes us to Aleara's bosom."

Outside, the storm's intensity increased, with the brambles bending inward under the pressure of the snow building against them. Smoke twisted in the branches above before being whisked away by the wind. He envied the druid's ability to transform into things better suited for such harsh conditions.

"Bet that bear form is nice and cozy," Thomas remarked, trying to lighten the mood.

Jaxxon laughed and said, "It is. Plenty of fat to keep me warm."

"You're fat in any form," Avery replied, although the corners of his mouth turned up, threatening a smile.

That broke the tension, and the three friends shared a hearty laugh at the druid's expense. It was needed. Their time at the last inn was full of strife. Jaxxon blamed Thomas for the misunderstanding with a local woman, shouting and pointing out his resemblance to the duke, which caused quite a stir. Despite the protests raised by him and his companions and the assertion that he was not royalty, the banter continued.

"I don't want to steer us back into doom and gloom," Jaxxon said moments later, "but I ran out of coin at the last inn."

Avery shook his head and said, "You do this every time. I'm not covering for you this time."

"Fine. I don't want to stay in that nasty city anyway," Jaxxon replied. "Might be a good time to head off and find my father. He'll put up with a human intrusion for a couple of days."

"Can you transform into a donkey?" Thomas asked.

Jaxxon snapped his fingers. "As easy as that."

"I'll pay you to carry my plate mail then," Thomas said.

"Finally," Avery said, "we get to spend time with Jaxxon in his true form. That of the mighty ass."

That drew another laugh, although Jaxxon did not seem as amused as the other two men. They continued small talk but focused on staying warm. Jaxxon shifted to bear form, and the other two men huddled around him to take advantage of the heat coming off the larger body. During the remaining hours, Thomas awoke and threw wood on the fire. It melted the snow closest to the briars, and as the temperature dropped, it froze back, creating a near-solid enclosure for them. It was still not warm, but it was better than being outside. Twice, Thomas and Jaxxon awakened to Avery screaming in the night, talking to someone in his dream. Even in the frigid temperatures of their shelter, the priest was sweating, worrying the paladin.

CHAPTER

10

The nonstop snow left drifts on either side of the road leading to the walled city of Ceylon. The mud and the wagon wheel ruts were annoying. Even worse, they had to wait in line to enter. Thomas heard the frustrated stomp of a hoof from behind him. Jaxxon transformed into a mule like the one Avery rode to avoid paying the entry fee. Thomas was not sure which mule expressed its frustration, but he guessed it was Jaxxon. Whether this was normal in Ceylon, Thomas did not know. From the way people grumbled in the line, he suspected it was a recent change.

As the wait dragged on, the crowd began to bunch up. Everyone wanted out of the mud and onto the cobbled stretch of road nearest the gates. His horse protested as well, nipping at anyone who got close enough to its muzzle. Soon, Thomas had a clear area around him until a man dressed in a soldier's livery stopped, fumbling around with the straps on the large bag strapped to the spare mule. The paladin drew his blade and backed up to slap the man with the flat of his blade. The soldier bristled and drew his sword.

"I wouldn't do that," Avery said. "That is a paladin, a holy knight of Aleara. Have you ever met one of those?"

"Never have," the man said. "Don't care either."

"Luckily for you," Avery said. "I happen to be a priest serving Aleara."

"What do I care?" the soldier asked.

"Because I will hurt you," Thomas interjected. "He might be able to put you back together, depending on how I do it."

"I'm following orders," the man said.

Thomas replied, "Go follow orders elsewhere, but if you touch my polished armor, I will make it painful."

The mule heehawed until the man backed away. The man spat on the ground in spite, but moved on, taking out his frustrations on the wagon behind them. To Thomas's dismay, he discovered that other people were poking and prodding the goods and packs of the crowd. Something was afoot. While not at war with Castardia, Ceylon was beginning to look like a city of unease. Like Godsdown, the constant threat of Klydos and the kingdom's dynamics trickled down to the general populace. A greater struggle loomed with rising tensions.

"Why don't you announce who we are?" Avery asked.

"I do not recall the council telling us to ride in proclaiming who we are," Thomas replied.

The line edged forward, but not enough to bring them near the gate. Thomas twisted his free hand on the pommel of his saddle. It was his right to demand privileged access, but he was loath to do so. He did not want to be the cause of additional strife between the common people and their rulers. The crowd surged in around them, memories of his horse snapping at them momentarily forgotten. His horse protested, causing space to open around the paladin.

"Are you going to sit there and wait like everybody else?" Avery said.

"I am looking for the sign saying official church business this way," Thomas replied.

"Pull rank," Avery said. "Tell them your father sent you to talk to the baron."

RISE OF THE VEILBREAKER

Thomas glared at the priest. They were all ready to be inside the city, but the priest's jab hurt him to the core. Avery, sensing he pushed too far, shrugged his shoulders, angering the paladin even more. Relying on his father was not going to make this visit any easier, even if the barony was part of Grimhorn.

"Why would you suggest it?"

"Because I'm tired of sitting here waiting for them to let people in," Avery said. "We've been on the road for ten days."

"Ten wonderful days," the mule said.

"Keep quiet," Thomas replied. "You are supposed to be an animal, Jaxxon."

"He is an animal," Avery said. "He shit on the roadway."

"Show me a horse, mule, or ox not relieving themselves while waiting in this line," Jaxxon said.

It was fair to say tensions were running high for the trio. It had been a long journey, exacerbated by the questions revolving around the mission to Celyon. Thomas, days before, grew tired of the endless philosophical debates, refusing to participate. Speaking with Aleara in the grove would confirm or deny their mission. They needed it because their relationship was strained to a breaking point.

Avery had all but outright blamed the goddess for every predicament on the road, whether it was snow, mud, or bandits. It didn't help that Jaxxon aggravated him at every turn with his nonchalance about what they were heading into.

Thomas vacillated between his two partners' viewpoints, concerned about what lay ahead but realizing no matter what Aleara brought him to, she would see him through it. His inability to save Janelle and Brontë nagged at him, breaking his otherwise optimistic disposition. The line moved. It was about time. Their turn came only to end in crossed spears blocking their entrance. Thomas held the reins tight to prevent the animal from lashing out.

"One kingdom gold or two foreign gold per person," the soldier said.

Thomas took Avery's proffered coin and added one of his own.

It would be easier if you asked the men searching people's stuff to collect the coins so we can enter."

"What do you mean?" the soldier asked. "We don't have anybody searching stuff."

"So you idiots are letting thieves rummage through people's things," Thomas said.

"You look like a capable lad," the soldier said. "If you're so concerned with thieves, go back and bring them to us. We'll take it from there."

"I'm not some spear-toting lackey," Thomas replied. "This is your town. Do your job!"

The soldier cursed at Thomas, grabbing his spear from where it leaned against the wall.

"If you don't mind your damn business, I'm going to do my job."

"You move that spear again, and the next thing you'll see is Aleara," Thomas replied.

The soldier bristled at the retort. He pointed his spear at the paladin, and Thomas batted it away with his blade. The other soldier spoke to his companion. For a tense moment, the spear remained poised, and then the man tilted it away. Anger brewed within the paladin, and the guards would bear the brunt of his frustration. This was the kind of useless bureaucracy that frustrated him. However, the guard thought the better of it and waved them onward. Thomas centered himself, apologized for being rude, and thanked the soldier for helping them.

"Would it hurt you to be nice?" Avery asked.

"Aleara does not call me to be nice," Thomas said. "Piety and niceness are two different things altogether."

"Welcome to Ceylon," Jaxxon said. "Home to pious assholes."

Although it was confounding, there were valid reasons for trying to intercept troublemakers at the gate. Ceylon was the southernmost city of Zel'Drea, and as such, it was as much a fortress as it was a part of their civilization. Out of the south gate was a road leading to the bridge over the Castardian River, with the river serving as the border between the peaceful kingdoms. It was not always the case, as Castardia wavered between those who wanted peace and the religious zealots who interpreted the word of Klydos' priests as saying the Lord of Tempests wanted all but Castardians to perish.

Entering the gates gave them a view of the city itself. This was not like the castle at Drea, home of King Cyrus. That was a gilded parody of Ceylon. This was a city prepared to close its gates and rain destruction on whoever tried to invade. Catapults and ballistae were visible, ready to aim at a foe.

Inside the curtain wall, a vast stretch of greenery extended from the outer wall to the road circling the city's perimeter. Today, the road was congested with hawkers using stalls, wagons, or whatever they found to showcase their goods. Thomas weaved through the crowd until he realized Avery was nowhere to be seen.

He backtracked and found the priest standing at the edge of a booth, staring at a potted plant.

"I thought we wanted entrance to the grove," Thomas said.

"True, but look at this," Avery said. "It's a Strangler Tree."

"That's nice. Why is it worth stopping to see?" asked Thomas.

Avery launched a rant about the corruption of the flora, a tactic of the Grey Wizards of Sambor. He was long accustomed to the diatribes Avery would go into about the most esoteric of subjects. Thomas ignored most of the lessons on their magic, wanting to know as little as necessary about the minions of the Lord of Tempests. When his patience failed, he stopped Avery's tirade.

"All I want to know is how to kill the grey bastards. Please make a point, Avery," Thomas said.

"It should not exist," Avery replied, "but because Aleara forbids the eradication of any creature, it continues to exist. Her doctrine says all creatures are her domain. We recite, 'All creatures are precious to Aleara.' The High Priests interpret that to mean Strangler Trees and other abominations as long as they are not in conflict with Aleara's creations. Doesn't make sense."

"You should pray about that in the grove," Thomas said. "Perhaps there, your philosophical questions will be answered."

"It concerns me that we have these contradictions, yet no one tries to resolve them."

"Yes," Thomas said. "This is why the owlbear still exists."

"Love me some owlbear," mule-Jaxxon joined in.

It was a topic of debate. However, he wanted answers to their more immediate problems. Eliminating loose ends in Aleara's recorded religious directives was not as important as eliminating those who sought to destroy her creations. As he looked at the potted plant, with its strange green dangling branches, he struggled to understand why it captivated Avery so much. The priest concerned himself with the why of their pantheon, and Thomas cared little for it.

" We need to move on," Thomas said.

Avery frowned but climbed back on his mule. As they rode away, he cast an illusion of a bird flying toward the Strangler Tree, and the plant came to life, trying to capture the bird as it flew into the tree and disappeared. The ropy tentacles flailed for a moment before dropping down, becoming placid again. Thomas altered his assessment. It would be a deadly encounter once it matured.

Thomas considered the conundrum of a magically created creature being not one of Aleara's creatures but deserving of her protection as a living thing. Inherently, Aleara wanted life to prosper, and Thomas thought it magnanimous of her to include something not of her making as long as it was not at odds with her creations. There was a lesson to be learned, but it eluded him as he navigated his destrier past passersby on the streets.

Several times, he had to restrain the horse from biting someone who came too close. This only served as a reminder that they were out of their element in the city and should proceed with caution. The horse's steel-shod hooves echoed on the cobblestone street.

The buildings were sturdy and functional, made of cut stone, and served as a secondary defense in case the outer wall was breached. Workers in the warehouses loaded and unloaded various goods and raw materials. There were workshops of all sorts of craftspeople, and Thomas heard the steady clanking of blacksmiths hard at work. Carts in various laden states passed them by, and the constant hum of trade was evident in this part of the city.

Beyond the city changed again. The homes and inns of the ordinary folks spread out before them. Neat rows of streets headed off to the east and west of the main road into the heart of Ceylon. The health of the city was evident by the children laughing and playing in the streets, weaving in and out of the traffic. The air carried the scent of meals being cooked, alternating between the aroma of baking bread and the spices wafting from a meat or stew. Ceylon was not flashy. Its homes were modest and functional. There were places where repairs had been made. He assumed some prior conflict caused the damage.

Ahead, the second wall appeared. It was lower, older, and unmanned, its gates standing wide open in welcome. This marked a change from the older border town that grew into Ceylon. Some long-distant relative of his must have decided this is where the people of Grimhorn would protect their claim to the north side of the river. Some warriors, like himself, carved out a place in the wild, blessed by Aleara to clear the land and let people flourish.

Beyond these gates, the streets were quieter and more refined. A small park lay at the heart of this inner circle, where trees taller than naturally possible rose above the walls, dwarfing everything around them. This was one of the nine magical groves Aleara placed around the world, serving to unite her believers. Here, like Godsdown, true worshippers come as close to Aleara as they would while living. Avatars of the goddess came to some, and they walked away blessed.

Sitting at the center of it all, near the grove, was the keep, home of the current baron, Baron Eldric. It was in sharp contrast to the greenery of the grove. A stern, square fortress pockmarked with evidence of battles from long ago. It was a reminder that, despite the beauty within the city walls, Ceylon was still ready for war. He recognized some of the same architectural traits as those his parents kept at Grimhorn.

He steered the warhorse toward the grove, stopping outside its ring of gigantic trees and dismounting. He pulled his armor from the mule, and once Jaxxon was free of his burden, he transformed and thanked the knight.

"I have a greater appreciation for our beasts of burden after this trip," Jaxxon said. "Aleara bless them for being what they are."

An acolyte walked from the grove, her yellow robes denoting the initial stages of education as a priestess. She gave them a slight bow.

"Good day, gentlemen," she said. "Do you have a request for the High Priestess?"

"We are here at the directive of the Council of Orders. Who is your High Priestess?" Thomas asked.

"Lady Jane," replied the acolyte.

"Please let her know Sir Thomas of the Order of Valor, Avery of the Order of Justice, and Jaxxon of the Order of Nature are here and seek audience with the goddess."

"I will. Please wait here," the acolyte replied.

Thoms hesitated to try to enter on his own. Despite their service to Aleara, the groves were an otherworldly place, bridging the gap between the mortal world and Aleara herself. Only those granted access by the High Priestess breached the ring of trees. In recorded history, none had been able to do otherwise. When the acolyte returned, she bowed and waved them into the grove.

Each of the massive trees predated human civilization. Their bark was weathered and etched with symbols that only the most learned druids and priests could decipher. Thomas said a prayer, and his companions echoed the words as they crossed into the grove.

"Think they'll let us take a leaf home as a souvenir? Maybe, hide it in a hat?" Jaxxon asked.

Thomas gave the druid a stern look.

Avery said, "I don't know if I would try it. Might end up with a tree growing from your head."

Thomas shook his head as the druid laughed, nodding in agreement. The grove was no place for antics. Thomas drew a sharp breath as they entered. The barrier washed over them. Instead of the ring of trees, he found himself in a massive, enchanted forest. This was a place transcending the laws of nature. Unlike the city air, this air was rich with the scents of pine, earth, and flowers, mingled with the sweet fragrance of honey and the freshness of rain. Gentle sunlight beamed down, with shafts of golden light filtering through the dense canopy, casting a warm glow that bathed him in Aleara's essence.

Jaxxon inspected the mighty oaks, intertwined with moss, that hung down from their strong branches.

"Now that's what I call landscaping," Jaxxon said.

The words failed to express their awe. Even Thomas had to acknowledge the beauty of the grove. Their teachings said that from the nine sacred groves, Aleara manifested all flora and fauna of this world. They were the conduits that purified raw chaos and turned it into the stuff of order. At the beginning of Binsmuth, new creatures emerged from the groves and spread across the world.

Willows dipped their branches into a gently flowing brook that found its way to a pool at the center of the forest. The sunlight faded there, becoming silvery like moonlight. Trees of every kind dotted the forest floor, forming a protective embrace over them. Thick undergrowth with vibrant ferns, moss-covered stones, and flowers in endless varieties of colors.

All kinds of woodland creatures roamed freely within the grove, unafraid and at peace. Majestic stags with antlers that seemed to be made of woven branches roamed like sentinels, their eyes reflecting the wisdom of ages. Squirrels darted among the tree branches, and badgers and foxes darted about. There were birds of many species, perhaps all. Huge flocks rose into the air, darkening the sky. Instead of a cacophony of noise, it was a blending of sounds that resulted in a natural symphony playing around them. Jaxxon grinned.

The druid said, "I think I just heard a bird sing off-key. Must be a rookie."

"Perhaps it is new here," Avery replied. "Maybe this place has us all in more tune with nature. I bet you might even find an owl to cozy up to in this place."

It was good to hear his companions finally putting aside the differences of the trip and engaging in lighthearted banter. They would need to come together to identify whatever peril lay in wait in Ceylon.

"I do need to work on my landings still," Jaxxon replied with a grin.

Thomas stood there in silence with his companions, taking in the tranquility of the grove. He had to admit that the place had a healing effect, for some of his fears and aspersions seemed dulled or dispelled. His eyes continually darted from one wonder to another, then fell back to the moonlit pool off in the distance. A peacock flew by, landing before him and spreading its beautiful plumage. The bird walked toward them, transforming into a blonde woman dressed in a simple green dress adorned with the symbol of Aleara. Power emanated from her, a testament to her communion with the goddess. The three men bowed to the High Priestess.

"We are blessed to be in your presence," Thomas said.

"Blessings be to Aleara," Avery added.

"Thank you for allowing us to be here," Jaxxon said.

"Greetings, gentlemen," she said. "The goddess told me you would be coming, although I heard it from Edogir first. Do you need anything, or would you like to speak with her first?"

Thomas looked at his companions. Seeing no objection, he said, "We are ready to speak with Aleara. Lead the way."

"The pool awaits you," Jane said.

With no further fanfare, she led them to the edge of the water. Its beauty stunned Thomas. The pool was like a mirror, its silvery surface like molten steel. Her presence emanated from the water, even more present than in this magical forest itself. He had been inside the grove at Godsdown twice, but never this close. The first time was when he became a squire at ten years old, and the second was at eighteen when Sir Silas elevated him to the rank of knight.

Thomas walked to the pool in silence. The priestess moved with a grace that seemed almost celestial, her every step light as if she floated just above the ground. She neared the pool, undid the clasp at her shoulder, letting the dress slide to the ground, and slipped naked into the silvery waters. He shed his clothes and walked in behind her, hearing the sounds of his companions doing the same. She turned to face them, her eyes warm and wise, reflecting the light of the grove, and her smile carried the peace of someone deeply in tune with the goddess she served.

Thomas prayed out loud for the strength to be the soldier Aleara needed, giving his past failures to her and asking forgiveness for his doubts. He heard Avery praying for forgiveness, apologizing for questioning things he did not understand, and asking Aleara to help him see her plan. Jaxxon's prayer was to ask that Aleara bless more people with the experience of her groves.

Once his prayer was done, he opened his eyes, and Jane held out a hand to him and Jaxxon. He grasped her hand and reached for Avery's, as did Jaxxon. His spirit lifted from his body. His mortal form floated there in the pool as his consciousness flew upwards above the grove, looking out over Southern Zel'Drea. The view was broad at first, showcasing the majesty and harmony of the city of Ceylon nestled within the surrounding forest and fields. Then it focused, and just to the south of Ceylon were dark spots, places of blight. He flinched at the memory of the place where Janelle and Brontë lost their lives, but a peace settled on him, causing him to relax and see it for what it was.

He witnessed an atrocity. The trees of the blighted woods blackened, much as if a flame had burned them. The few remaining green trees looked stunted, as if a giant finger had crushed them. From this perspective, it was clear that the Lord of Tempests utilized the destructive effects of chaos to harm what his daughter had created. It angered Thomas that Klydos would take such beauty and reduce it to uselessness.

When he emerged from the vision, the expressions on his companions' faces suggested a similar experience, if not the same. Avery was visibly distraught. Jaxxon's silence was telling. Jane climbed out of the pool and went to a spot where the moonlight danced about. The light glowed brighter until it was impossible to see the woman. Emerging from the moonlight, she retrieved a staff, a shield, and the pelt of a lion. She spoke a soft prayer to Aleara, and the moonlight subsided.

"Gifts for each of you. May they give you an advantage over whatever foe seeks to injure Aleara's children and be a reminder that the goddess loves each of you."

Thomas looked at the shield. It was similar to the one he broke five years ago. He took it and examined it, realizing that it had a blemish that looked like the place where it had sheared in two. This was his shield, restored to him by the goddess. It was a sign. He often wondered if she had regained faith in him, and this was the answer he had been seeking.

Jane said, "The weld symbolizes how your faith is now stronger due to the trials you have faced."

Thomas nodded and looked over at Avery. The priest was examining his gift, a staff covered in runes and pictograms. It resembled the staves that the high clergy of the groves carried with them, which were carved from a limb of one of the groves. These were potent conduits as well.

The druid cast a spell, and the pelt melded with his body, transforming him into a massive lion. Jaxxon roared and then transformed back, his ability to become a creature of the forest enhanced by this gift. That was his true calling, serving as a protector of the great forests. Thomas regretted that Jaxxon had been tasked with keeping him on the right path.

While they examined their gifts, Jane donned her dress and watched them with slight amusement. He thanked her for her assistance and found his clothes. Once they were all dressed, they walked from the pool back to the forest around it.

"High Priestess..." he started to say.

"Jane," she said, interrupting him.

"Jane, we now know what we face," Thomas said. "What would Aleara have us do?"

"Edogir is one of my oldest friends," Jane said. "He loves the politics of the kingdoms almost as much as he loves Aleara. He provided you with a ruse to keep the spies of the Lord of Tempests from being aware of your activities, at least for now."

"Did he tell you of the opposition to our coming here?" asked Thomas.

Jane said, "No, but that is not surprising. I do not like politics. That is why I serve here."

"The groves are true places of beauty," Avery said. "I wonder why Aleara does not just have us live here."

"That would not leave room for those who worship Donegal," Jane said. "Those who love the plowed field and the ring of the hammer onto hot steel need a place to live as well."

"But they would not exist without Aleara," Avery said, his voice taking on that harsh tone of recent days.

"True," Jane said. "Aleara protects them as well."

"I can see protecting those who worship her brother, but she shouldn't be protecting those buggering bastards that worship Klydos," Jaxxon said.

"It's like that Strangler Tree in the market earlier," Avery said. "An abomination, but allowed to exist. It must make the worshippers of the Lord of Tempests think Aleara is weak."

The conversation was taking a dark turn. As much as he valued continued education, he needed a break from his companions. He stepped away from the others and prayed, thanking Aleara again for the clarity of his gift. Even if it was just his shield that was repaired, it was a boost to his faith and commitment. If it had been more, then it would have been a true blessing from the goddess. He heard Avery raising his voice and shook himself free of his private thoughts.

"You're telling me that Aleara would let gnolls live on Binsmuth?" Avery asked.

Jane sighed and said, "Yes. Life is precious, not its origin."

"You've never fought a gnoll," Avery said.

Bitterness and disappointment dripped from those words. Thomas walked over and placed a hand on Avery's shoulder. The priest shrugged him off and glared at Jane, who, despite the difference in their status with the goddess, seemed open to the discussion. Thomas sighed, his exhaustion at the forefront of his mind. The journey had been long and stressful. He was ready for a whole night of sleep.

"High Priestess," he said. "I am exhausted. Is it possible for us to rest here in the Grove? We will follow Edogir's lead in the morning."

He looked over at Avery, who remained red-faced and ready to argue his point. Thomas implored the priest to drop the matter. Avery finally took the hint.

"Forgive me," the priest said. "It has been a long journey."

"There's nothing to forgive," Jane said. "Yes, please sleep wherever you would like. In the morning, I can introduce you to Harold, the Minister of Finance. I will have Katya retrieve your horse and mule and have them picketed inside."

Thomas thanked her again for the hospitality. She responded with a warm smile. Left to their own devices, Thomas and his friends walked around. Together, they took in the wonders of the magical grove. Their wandering led them to another brook feeding into the pool, and they bedded down, plucking ripe berries from nearby plants to quench their hunger. It would have been good to have a solid ale to mark the end of their journey to Ceylon, but Thomas would not complain about sleeping in the presence of the goddess.

"I still don't understand why Aleara prevents people from entering here at will," Avery said.

Jaxxon said, "I don't know either, but for those that can enter, it is such a blessing."

"Enough of that," Thomas said. "What did you see in the vision?"

"A blight on the forest," Avery said. "It was sobering."

"Yeah," Jaxxon said. "No animals to be seen in that place. I am hoping that Aleara will give us the power to heal it."

"First, we have to remove whatever presence is causing it," Thomas said. "Good night, my friends. Rest up, for adventure awaits us tomorrow."

CHAPTER

11

Thomas enjoyed the touch of the warm sun on his face and opened his eyes. He sprang up, expecting to see snow and forgetting that he was within the grove. He stripped down to a linen shirt and pants, looking over to see an acolyte dressed in her yellow robes watching him. He spent the night tossing and turning, plagued by dreams that haunted him, despite his inability to remember what had happened. Jaxxon and Avery snored away without a care. They awoke with gentle shakes on the shoulder. Years ago, he learned the hard way that Jaxxon could switch forms straight from sleep. Badger teeth scars proved the point.

For the first time in weeks, they greeted him with good humor. It was worth his lack of rest to see that they were in a better mood. Thomas grinned at the druid, whose hair was sticking out in multiple directions, looking like a small child waking from a nap. He donned his plate mail with Katya's assistance and then waited for Jane and his companions at the grove's edge.

Jane's good mood proved infectious. The grove appeared to have the effect. Acolytes walked amongst the trees with smiles on their faces. He longed to stay and find that same inner peace. Jane dispelled any notion by sharing information about Ceylon.

"The baron is a difficult man," she said. "He's not very spiritual and craves more recognition."

"He's a bit far out in the backwaters of Zel'Drea for that," Jaxxon said. "Don't you think?"

"The baron is under pressure," Jane said. "The king pressures Duke Kendrick to bring in more revenue, as do the other lords. This passes down from Kendrick to Eldric, and it does not sit well. The church of Aleara is the final arbiter of whether additional land may be cleared, which irritates Eldric."

"We all are responsible for adhering to the balance that Aleara seeks between civilization and the wilds," Avery said. "Does the Baron understand that?"

"In his way," she said, "he does. But he is a vassal, and telling his duke that expansion is not the answer does not sit well in Drea. If he asks your opinion on the clearing of additional forest, defer to me."

"Whether the baron's request is relevant or not," Thomas said, "that is not what we are here for. Aleara showed us what must be done. We must root out the corruption of the Lord of Tempests."

"I agree," Jane said. "Be careful, though, who you speak with about this. There are agents in the city that serve the Lord of Tempests. And you will find that your allies come from unlikely places."

"Unlikely allies," Avery said. "Can you be more specific?"

"Aleara gave me a vision of you being aided, but there was no clarity around who it was," Jane said. "I will tell you that this mission has world-altering consequences. Aleara chose you three to make an impact against the Lord of Tempests. I will help in any way I can, but my role is to protect the grove here at Ceylon. It will be a place to rest and reflect when needed."

"Nothing like an ominous-sounding message from a High Priestess to start your day," Jaxxon said.

Thomas glared at the druid. He and Avery generally ignored the flippant nature of the druid, but she might report them to the Council. They would heed the advice of the High Priestess and exercise caution in their dealings. Together, they emerged from the grove, passing through the veil, and Thomas sensed his contact with the goddess somehow lessened. Looking at his companions reinforced that sensation. He did not like that. The oppressive energy of the fortified city compounded it. Jane led them across the park toward the keep. Thomas took note of the fresh snow settling on his boots as they strode through the greenbelt. As they neared the keep, the fresh scents of the forest gave way to those of city living.

Thomas smelled the oil, applied to their blades to ease their work, as the gate guards took a sharpening stone to them while idling away their duty hours. His boots clattered against the cobblestones, the spurs clicking in time with their pace. They were approaching the grim monolith of grey stone that loomed over the city like a guardian from a forgotten age. These were walls built for defense and not decoration. Ivy struggled to climb the stone. Its green tendrils dulled as if contact with the stone was leeching the life out of it. The green, tinged with snow, was a stark contrast to the grey of the stone.

The gate itself was a marvel of engineering, rising high enough to dwarf the tallest man, its iron-bound wood darkened by age and use. Four guards, clad in chain mail with tabards bearing the baron's crest, stood vigilant on either side. They continued sharpening their blades until they realized Jane walked with the men and then stood in rapt attention.

"Good morning, High Priestess and gentlemen," one guard said as they approached. "What business do you have in the keep today?"

Thomas started to speak, but Jane put a hand on his chest and said, "I've brought them here to see Harold, the Master of Finance."

"May we announce your presence?" the guard asked.

"Certainly," Jane said. "Please let him know that the gentle-men from Godsdown are here."

"Geoffrey," the guard said, and one of the other guards pre-sented himself and saluted. "Announce them to Master Harold."

"Yes, sergeant," the guard said. He nodded at the group and then started through the gate.

Thomas said, "Thank you for the introduction and for letting us stay in the grove. It was a spiritual experience."

"You're welcome. I sense that you are about to walk a danger-ous road," Jane said. "Be wary of paths that are too well-lit."

Thomas stood near the gates, eyes scanning the city streets, anxious for Geoffrey's return. The quiet hum of activity on the streets near the keep kept him entertained, but he felt trapped, impatient to be away from the city. Though he respected the High Priestess, he was ready to move beyond the political posturing and root out the problem that brought them to Southern Zel'Drea.

When Geoffrey returned, Thomas pushed Avery and Jaxxon to follow the man. His companions followed him. They moved to join Geoffrey, who led them into the keep's dark corridors. The air inside was cool and stale, and the walls were devoid of decora-tion and uniformly grey. Halls stretched in all directions, making every turn look the same. The plain, undecorated walls reminded Thomas of Grimhorn. He had not thought of those memories in years, of him and James running wild through the corridors of Grimhorn, seeking out mischief.

He soon lost his way, distracted by thoughts of how this day might unfold. The air was damper now, suggesting they were be-low ground. Vague memories from his childhood nagged at him, implying that the person should be closer to the baron. Geoffrey continued in silence. Torches became fewer and fewer, until Ge-offrey eventually grabbed one off the wall and carried it with him. His senses, augmented by the spirit of Aleara, caused him to hang back. Something that opposed Aleara lurked in these halls, but it dissipated.

He twisted and turned, trying to make sense of their path in case they had to find their way out. Something caught his attention out of the corner of his eye. There was a glint of steel in the shadows behind them. His confusion turned to distrust. His mind went back to the caution of Sir Silas. There might be traitors amongst them. He cursed himself for not paying more attention from the beginning. He grimaced and pulled his long knife from his belt. If treachery were afoot, there would be no room for a sword in this hallway. Tactically, they were in the wrong order. If the enemy were ahead, it would be fine, but having to face an enemy in a physical fight was not ideal for Avery. He glanced over his shoulder. Nothing revealed itself.

Thomas slowed his steps and allowed Jaxxon and Avery to catch up, then pass him. He turned and crept backward as his senses told him that something was coming up behind them. He squinted, trying to distinguish anything down the poorly lit corridor behind them. The hallway was darker for a moment, as if a dark shadow passed across it and into the wall. Aleara, could you help me see what is there? His eyesight changed, and humanoid shapes blended with the walls. He didn't know for sure, but he feared that there were minions of the Lord of Tempests within the Ceylon keep.

Further down the hall, a diminutive figure emerged, hooded but with blonde hair spilling from the collar. The figure held up a dagger, motioning for Thomas to stay where he was. The telltale, inky color of the shadow emerging from the wall into the hallway blocked his view of the other person. He contemplated flooding the hallway with light, but the other party intrigued him. He did not trust the caution they suggested. His desire to capture this mysterious figure and eliminate their supernatural allies held him in check. The darkness started toward him. Please invest your spirit in this blade, for I fear that mundane steel will have little effect. His blade flared with silvery moonlight, and he thrust forward into the shadow.

The shadow shrieked and then winked from existence in a flash of light. Another advanced, but more importantly, the other figure became clearer. What he had first taken for a child was a very short woman, moving with the grace of someone accustomed to living in the shadows. She struck with her two blades, and there was another shriek. Thomas heard the pounding of feet and assumed that Avery and Jaxxon had turned back to see what the ruckus was about.

The remaining shadow rushed toward Thomas, and he raised his blade to strike, but a black ray shot out from the creature, and Thomas groaned as his arm weakened; the knife tumbled from his grasp. He raised his other arm to block the creature. It went through him, and an icy chill sprang up as their bodies combined for a moment. The woman ran forward, intoning some spell, and the creature pulled back, then dissipated. He reached down with his good arm and plucked the knife from the floor. If she were coming for him, she would find a foe ready for her.

Avery got to her first. The moonbeam shot past him and knocked the woman backward, her blades flying away from her. Aleara, please send me healing so that I might defeat your enemies. Divine energy poured into him, but he failed to shake the effects of the shadow's attack. Not trusting his weakened arm, Thomas advanced, ready to put the woman down for good if she made a move. She held up her blades and then placed them on the floor. The woman held her arms above her head. He kicked the knives away from her and held his in her face.

"Who are you?" he demanded.

"Who am I? I was trying to save your lives," she said. "Some thanks that was. I think you've broken my leg."

Thomas said, "Saving our lives? It looked like you were following your minions to us."

"Thomas," she said, "if I were going to kill you, I would not have announced myself before doing it."

"How do you know my name?" he asked.

"My master sent me to watch over you," she said.

"Master?" Avery asked.

"Master Harold," she said. "He sent me to fetch you. I got to the gate to find you gone."

Thomas looked back. "Where's Geoffrey?"

"Damn," Jaxxon said. "I thought he was behind us."

Thomas looked at the woman, torn between trusting what she said and believing that she was part of the plot to attack them. He pondered the exchange between the sergeant and the guard, Geoffrey. The sergeant ordered Geoffrey to announce them, not escort them. Thomas, in his haste to complete this part of the mission, followed the guard.

"Why did you come for us?" he asked.

"The High Priestess of Aleara requested you speak with Master Harold," she said. "Kind of hard to ignore that request. I'm his undersecretary, so I used it as an excuse to leave my desk."

"A clerk with fighting skills," Jaxxon said. "Doesn't make sense."

"Master Harold can answer for himself," Thomas said.

He reached out to help her to her feet. The woman grabbed his hand and stood on one leg, wincing as she tried to keep the other leg from moving. Thomas motioned to Avery, and the priest stepped forward, praying to Aleara as he helped the woman knit her leg back together. The woman murmured alien words as well, and Thomas tensed as the familiar prickle, letting him know the aether was being used, rose within him. As she wiped the sweat from her forehead, her hood fell backward, and Thomas gasped, drawing his blade again.

She was Ihuaj. They were vicious members of the army of the Lord of Tempests, and the companions frequently faced them. Plucked from some other realm and dropped in Binsmuth, they fought with a frenzy that would frighten lesser people. He placed the knife against her throat. She was diminutive but proven deadly.

"You seek to deceive us?" he asked. "Foul creature. Tell us the truth."

She leaned away from the knife before answering.

"I am Fada, that is true," she said. "My family escaped from the Lord of Tempests with others and came to Ceylon before my birth. I have never served the God of Chaos."

"Lies," Avery said. "Jane would never allow a rat's nest of evil to infest Ceylon. The grove is at stake."

"Thomas. Avery," Jaxxon said. Thomas turned to look at the druid. "This will go nowhere. Let's find Harold and sort this out. I think the lass realizes that you have her at a disadvantage."

Thomas agreed, and after tying the woman's hands, he pushed her ahead of him, having her guide them to her supposed master. She led them back some ways and into a wider corridor, this one well-lit with sconces and tapestries hanging on the walls. Several people walking toward them gave the group strange glances but did not intervene. Thomas looked at the door she stopped in front of, hoping nothing was lurking on the other side.

"Knock," she said. "It's common courtesy in most places to let someone know that you are about to enter."

"Do not speak to me like that," Thomas said. "I am one smart remark from cutting your damned throat."

She paled at his remark, her bravado slipping away. He knocked on the door and pushed it open. An older man looked up from his desk, smiling at first and then jumping up to reach where the woman stood.

"What happened?" he asked.

"They were following someone when I got to the gate, and I chased them down only to find some kind of living shadow about to attack," she said.

"So, why are you tied up?" he asked.

"Ask these dumbasses," she said.

"I am Sir Thomas, paladin of the Order of Valor," Thomas said. "High Priestess Jane wanted us to meet with you."

The man said, "I doubt her recommendation included attacking one of the people who work for me."

"She's Ihuaj," Avery sputtered.

"Thank Aleara for your presence," the man replied. "I would have never known otherwise."

Thomas pushed the woman through the door, forcing the man back into the office. Avery and Jaxxon entered and closed the door behind them. There was a tense moment of staring.

"Master Harold," the woman said. "Your guests have arrived."

Thomas found no humor in her remark, but it did not stop Jaxxon from laughing. He would give the druid a look to silence him, but that would only encourage worse behavior. Instead, he cut the cord he used to bind her and pushed her away from him in case there was more treachery afoot.

"Scherie," Harold said. "I am sorry. I am so comfortable around you and your people that I forgot how narrow-minded my fellow humans can be."

Thomas bristled at the insinuation. Ihuaj were not common. Few people besides the forces of Aleara had ever encountered them. For this man to imply otherwise went against everything Thomas had experienced. The paladin looked down at the man, and Harold stared back at him. Harold finally sighed, walking back to his desk and sitting behind it.

"Please, let me explain," Harold said.

"There is a guard," Thomas said. "We need to find him first."

"Scherie," Harold said, "can you find this guard? He's either returned to the gate, or the sergeant will be looking for him. Don't tarry. They expected them. We might have more trouble before long."

He reluctantly accepted the Fada to be the best choice. He and his companions would soon be lost within the strange castle.

"What if she is with them?" he asked.

"Then we are all undone," Harold replied. "I've employed Scherie for years. Everything, or at least most of it, she knows. If you don't trust her, go or send one of your companions."

"I'll go with her," Jaxxon said.

"Be careful," Avery said.

Jaxxon nodded and said, "All creatures are precious to Aleara. I'm going to let the goddess guide me on this one. If she turns out to be what we suspect, I'll kill her before she even knows it's happening."

Thomas looked at the druid, agreeing with his strategy. The woman held out her hands, and Thomas pulled her blades from his belt. She took them, slipping them into her sleeves. Jaxxon and Scherie exited the office before Thomas turned his attention back to Harold.

"This is Avery," Thomas said. "He is a priest with the Order of Justice. That was Jaxxon. A druid with the Order of Nature."

"Not a typical paladin, are you?" Harold asked. "Usually, you knights are solemn and level-headed."

"I can be solemn when I need to," Thomas replied. "Level-headed, not so much. I pray to Aleara to give me more patience, but she gives me things that piss me off."

Avery said, "I've told you, she is giving you opportunities to improve. It is Aleara's fault you don't take them."

Harold laughed and then said, "You have questions. I'll answer them, but I expect the explanation will cause more questions."

And Harold did explain, but it was politics to Thomas. Deserters from the Lord of Tempests' army found their way to the Southern forests and hid until found. Thomas had to work hard to piece the timeline together, but it appeared that this occurred during the reign of his grandfather. There was no trust then, and these ihuaj, the Fada as they called themselves, became slaves to the humans of Ceylon, trading one servitude for another.

Duke Kendrick's ascension changed that, allowing them to build businesses or farms. With a lifespan greater than humans, they didn't have children as often. As a result, Scherie was the first generation of Fada born in this realm, but she was not the only one. This occurred before the ascension of King Cyrus to the throne. His father granted the Fada of Ceylon full rights. Pockets of prejudice still existed, but since most people did not have the experience that Aleara's soldiers had, it was stereotyping and jealousy.

"They are hard workers," Harold said. "Devout followers of Aleara."

"Why wouldn't Jane have said anything?" Avery said.

Harold shrugged. "The High Priestess may not have expected such a reaction. She came here before me but has always been a supporter of the Fada."

This made Thomas anxious, trying to understand the web of deception that seemed so prevalent here in southern Zel'Drea. The Council of Orders was fighting Ihuaj in the North along with every revolting creature that the Lord of Tempests could conjure, and here they were, living as bakers or clerks. Aleara, is this why we are here? To end the corruption of this city? He waited but received no indication that the Goddess corroborated the prayer.

The door opened, and Scherie walked in, followed by Jaxxon. The two were laughing like old friends. The paladin could only shake his head in disbelief. Jaxxon was not much for people unless it was a member of the opposite sex. Thomas waited for them to share what they learned.

"Fled," Jaxxon said.

"He's been a guard since he reached adulthood," Scherie said. "The sergeant has never had a bit of trouble out of him until today."

Geoffrey was on the loose. Whoever was behind his actions and summoned the shadow creatures was now aware of their plot's failure. This meant they would remain watchful, but it was a twist to their supposed brief stay in Ceylon. If the Council wanted a quick assessment, Thomas was about to let them down.

"We cannot trust the guards," he said. "No offense, Master Harold or Scherie, but I do not entirely trust either of you. Since Jane led us here, I have to question her allegiance as well. We might have to go to the baron ourselves."

"Wait," Harold said. "I can accept that you might have questions, but I am not part of Ceylon. I am here on the orders of King Cyrus. My allegiance is to the kingdom of Zel'Drea. Born and raised in Drea, right outside the keep walls."

"That is all well and good," Thomas said, "but we have things trying to kill us."

"The baron does not care about your problems," Harold said. "He cares about power and position. If you walk into his throne room and raise doubts, it will only serve to enflame his quest to become more than he is."

"How would that serve him?" Thomas asked.

"You may think this trip of yours went unnoticed," Harold said, "but the baron knows about every person that comes through those gates. If he can use your group's arrival to his advantage, he will profit from it. It is not a matter of good versus evil, but rather the great game of politics. Even here in the backwoods of the kingdom, schemes of importance happen."

"Is the baron faithful to Aleara?" Avery asked.

"Dutiful, yes," Harold replied. "Are all his aspirations known to the goddess? I would think not. I'm not saying he is a bad man, just one whose motivations are driven by a desire for power and influence."

They must find Geoffrey. His intentionally leading them into a trap meant his loyalty was suspect. Once they extracted the information from the guard, they would find a way to the true culprit. He politely declined Scherie's offer to help. The fewer people who knew their business, the better. It was bad enough that they were on the trail of someone. He hoped it would not lead back to this office. They made their way back to the gate.

Thomas scoured the streets for anyone taking more than a casual interest in their presence. Jaxxon, in the form of a hound dog, was busy sniffing the ground, following the scent of Geoffrey. They got lucky and paid the sergeant a coin to allow them to search the bunkhouse for Geoffrey. After a quick sniff of Geoffrey's bed put Jaxxon on the trail, they proceeded out of the keep into the town. Around them, people went about their day oblivious that creatures of the Lord of Tempests were within their walls. Their struggles were those of the everyday world.

The trail led them to a warehouse. Thomas identified the windows and exits Geoffrey might attempt to use if cornered. He nodded to Jaxxon, and the druid resumed following the scent, leading them inside. Several men were unloading a wagon, and they stopped their work to stare at two armed men and a hound dog in their place of business. One started toward them, but Thomas held up his mailed fist and pointed back to the wagon. The man got the gist of the gesture and went back, but they stared as the companions worked their way to the back. Jaxxon alerted to a room and then transformed.

Thomas laughed as the men decided the shape-changing druid was enough to vacate the place and return later. He motioned to Avery to stand in front of the door, ready to cast a prayer and inflict damage. He and Jaxxon stood on either side of the door. Thomas gave Jaxxon the signal to open the door and expressed disappointment in finding nothing but crates stacked floor to ceiling with an aisle running down the middle.

"Can you transform again?" Thomas asked.

"I can," Jaxxon said, "but my brain is already getting a little fuzzy. Too much more, and I'll be taking a risk."

"Do what you can," Thomas said.

Jaxxon transformed back and picked up the scent again, stopping before a crate somewhere near the back left of the room. He transformed back.

"Won't be doing that again for a while," Jaxxon said. "I'm worn out."

"Rest. You have gotten us this close," Thomas said. "Thank you. Now, let us find this bastard."

Prying on the crate revealed it was empty, and an opening in the floor led to a ladder plunging into the darkness below. Thomas invoked Aleara, and his shield burst into light, golden sunlight shining out from its surface. He fingered the scar of the repaired shield, thinking of his failure to save the squire and druid. He held the shield for Avery and Jaxxon to descend, then handed it down before descending behind them.

The hidden passage was roughly cut, but it was passable. It stayed level, then descended, coming to a landing where an underground stream flowed past lazily. Thomas didn't need the senses of a hound dog to realize that unless they followed the stream's flow, Geoffrey's trail would elude them. He stuck his sword in the water, measuring the depth. It was shallow and square-cut, revealing that it was not a natural cave.

"Is this going South?" Thomas asked.

"I think so," Jaxxon said.

"If this runs to the river, then it must run for miles."

Avery asked, "Think our friend Geoffrey is fleeing to Castardia?"

"Perhaps," Thomas said. "Or maybe just getting to the border and then backtracking to where the minions of the Lord of Tempests are camped."

It was useless to stand here debating where Geoffrey went. It put Thomas at a crossroads with his trust issues. He did not want to separate from his companions, but they would need someone to watch the warehouse for Geoffrey in case he returned. It was unlikely but still necessary to watch for him. The Council either was unaware of the Lord of Tempests' widespread influence in Ceylon, or they withheld that information from him and his companions. The last was unlikely, but at each turn, Thomas questioned more and accepted less.

An agent of the Lord of Tempests was on the loose inside the city. Worse, he had to contend with the idea that the rot of the forest mirrored the rot within the walls. The presence of the Fada woman and the revelation that a contingent of them lived as citizens of Ceylon did not help to assuage his fears. He would have to keep a close eye on her and the Master of Finance. Aleara was not all-seeing. Their deception could be hiding right in plain sight.

He pondered this as they made their way back to the grove. Thomas discussed it with his companions. While he tended to speak for them, he valued their perspectives, and they provided a calming force when his volatile temper overcame his training. When they suggested that the grove was the safest and most trustworthy place, he went along with it.

CHAPTER

12

Thomas rested in a seat made of living branches woven through the magic of the grove's druids. From where he sat, a stream wound down to the pool in the center of the grove, the water reflecting the sunlight that filtered through the canopy. The air here was fresh, filled with hints of damp earth and pine needles, contrasting the stony reality of Ceylon just beyond the magical barrier of the grove. Where winter dominated Binsmuth, the groves were bathed in an eternal springtime.

The acolytes of the grove were keeping a careful watch on the warehouse, but there was no sign of Geoffrey yet. Stranger still was that no one else inquired about him or his two companions. The paladin found it hard to believe that the one skirmish foiled the plot of the Lord of Tempests. A deity sworn to devour the world wasn't likely to be thrown off course by one minor setback.

He glanced up as a giant owl, the transformed druid Jaxxon, crashed through the branches overhead before righting itself and soaring onward. Jaxxon was making good use of his time, as was Avery, who engaged in a lively debate with several junior clergy. Even amid the peaceful grove, Thomas was restless, his mind circling unanswered questions.

He spent hours in prayer, seeking Aleara's guidance. Thomas was hoping for a revelation that would help uncover the figure or figures plotting with Klydos. He was having trouble finding answers. Jane's initial anger when they questioned her loyalty still lingered in his mind. She was powerful, perhaps as much as any member of the Council of Orders, and her restraint had only increased his distrust. He wanted to trust her, but that trust would have to be earned. Too many things didn't make sense. It was difficult to separate the individual from their bloody history.

Jane had been coy about the Fada. When he and Jaxxon talked, the druid suggested that it might be a test from Aleara. This left him unsettled. Was the test to see beyond their race and let go of his suspicions? Did Aleara want him to investigate the truth about the Fada? They had been one of the races serving the Lord of Tempests in all of recorded history. The fact that this enclave broke away and the strange things happening in Ceylon suggested that there was more to their presence than was being told.

At least he could eliminate Jane from his list of immediate threats. Harold was still an enigma. The Master of Finance was more than he appeared, with his deadly Fada lieutenant raising more questions than answers. Thomas found it hard to believe that Harold's ambitions were limited to managing revenue. The political posturing of Baron Eldric did not surprise him. If Duke Kendrick could cast out his son without a second thought, surely a vassal with aspirations would not fare any better. That thought stirred old wounds, but it made him respect his father a little more. Kendrick never allowed doubt to fester.

They would not be able to stay as the Council expected action and response. He could imagine Grand Commander Marla beating her fists on the table every extra day that she did not receive word from them. There was nothing to report. Speculation, much of it. The shadow creatures were the only tangible evidence that the Lord of Tempests even acted in Ceylon, and that was a trifling thing. Drea, the beautiful capital city of the kingdom, had hedge wizards and failed Grey Wizards in its back alleys. Thomas needed something more substantial to go on before he sent word to the Council of Orders.

The wind rustled through the grove, carrying with it the scent of pine. Thomas sighed and stood, his hand resting reassuringly on the hilt of his sword as he caught movement at the edge of his peaceful space. Avery joined him, rolling an apple between his palms. The wind was an unnatural thing in the grove, and they quickly learned it signified that someone or something was outside the perimeter of the trees.

"Someone's coming," Thomas said.

They walked together to the edge of the grove, where the magical barrier shimmered faintly. No matter where one entered, they always arrived in the same place, a minor mystery of the grove. Thomas growled with dismay at the figures emerging from the barrier. Harold and Scherie. The two approached, waving like old friends, but Thomas was suspicious. There was something they weren't saying.

Before he could say anything, Jane arrived in her typical flourish, dropping from the sky as a dove before transforming into her human form. The display, though not unexpected, was a potent reminder of the tangible power Aleara granted her mortal servants. The transformation was too druid-like, and Thomas did not recall this being a particular skill of priests, although he was certainly no expert on priesthood or being a paladin either. He embraced the gifts Aleara gave him, seldom questioning why.

"Welcome," Jane said.

Jane hugged Harold and Scherie in turn. Thomas noted how Harold accepted the embrace. The group adjourned to a quiet glade where chairs and a table had already been arranged as if by magic. Thomas wondered whether the grove anticipated their needs or if it was simply the work of well-prepared acolytes.

Thank you for the welcome," Harold said, "but I fear after I share my news, you may wish we had not come."

"Nonsense," Jane said. "Please share what you have learned."

Thomas leaned in as the man smoothed out the map, a detailed rendering of Southern Grimhorn and Northern Castardia. New markings dotted the map, perhaps sightings. The paladin studied it with interest but also suspicion. Why would the Master of Finance be gathering tactical intelligence like this? He hesitated to express his doubts. Instead, he let the man continue explaining the map. The incongruency of this man and his knowledge of events transpiring around Ceylon only furthered concerns about whether he was trustworthy.

Thomas glanced at Avery. The priest remained distracted. The paladin worried about his friend and this new indifference to the plotting of Klydos. Something shook him in Godsdown. Thomas wanted answers, but he would not give them to these strangers.

"And what does this have to do with the Lord of Tempests?" Thomas asked. "Is this about protecting the king's coin?"

Harold met his gaze. A moment of silence passed between them. Neither man broke his stare at the other. Besides Jane, the others seemed oblivious to the tension rising in the exchange. Harold placed his hands in his lap.

"It's about securing the future of the kingdom," he said. "And if we don't act soon, the Lord of Tempests will make sure there is nothing left to protect."

Thomas held Harold's stare, the seriousness of the statement and unspoken truths hanging between them. There was more to this man than he let on, and Thomas intended to find out what it was. He grunted at the obviousness of the statement.

"All these secrets are not helping us focus on the core problem," Thomas said.

Thomas looked over at Jane. The High Priestess was visibly nervous. He let the silence continue. Someone would break. There was too much at stake not to understand who he was allying himself with. He was a man of action. However, he understood that information was a powerful weapon in its own right. Jane fidgeted with her dress, sighing repeatedly.

"There's something else you need to know," she said.

Thomas shifted his gaze to her, ready for whatever treachery was about to rear its ugly head. He did not like the tone of her voice. She was High Priestess, one of ten voices who spoke for Aleara. Why would she hesitate? Her actions increased his suspicions.

"What is it?" he asked.

Jane took a deep breath and leaned into the table, where the map still lay open. Her fingers lightly traced over the parchment as if to give her time to compose her thoughts. He glanced at Jaxxon and Avery. The druid was useless, preferring to flirt with Scherie. Avery looked around, lost somewhere in his thoughts. Jane cleared her throat.

"It's about Baroness Lyrei," she said. "She's going to surprise you, perhaps worse than Scherie."

"Explain," he demanded.

Jane met his gaze. "Baroness Lyrei is Valkrunian."

The word hit Thomas like a blow. The grove seemed to tilt around him. Valkrunian! The word itself carried a weight of memories he would rather remain buried. Thomas fought them before on the frozen plains North of Grimhorn. Like the Fada, the Valkrunians were Ihuaj, an otherworldly race enslaved by the Lord of Tempests and conscripted to fight in his ceaseless wars. They were formidable, as adept in the chaos magic as the Grey Wizards of Sambor.

"No," Thomas said. "Are you telling me the baroness, who has the ear of the baron, is Valkrunian? A creature of the Lord of Tempests?"

Jane nodded. "She's not a slave anymore. She broke free of Klydos' control years ago, long before she came to Ceylon. She keeps her identity hidden. She had to, given her past."

The past. A past of fighting for the very god they were trying to stop. The air around Thomas cooled, or maybe it was just the heat from his anger. His pulse hammered at his temples, and his mind raced with the implications. Valkrunians were dangerous. Powerful fighters imbued with the chaos magic of their master. They had no mercy, no hesitation, and Thomas dreaded every battle with them. They fought like cornered animals because they were. Trapped between a mercurial god and those who were trying to save their world.

"You expect me to believe that?" Thomas asked. "That she just escaped the Lord of Tempests? That she is not one of His?"

His temper was getting the better of him, and he let it take over. Jane held her ground, though the friction was breaking her usually calm demeanor.

"She risked everything to break free, Thomas. Those loyal to her among her people fled with her. Like the Fada, they came to find peace and be part of this world. She's an ally, not an enemy. Imagine if we shared these things with the Council, and that was the information you focused on when arriving in Ceylon. We need you to see with your own eyes and judge what is real."

He stood and walked away, running a hand through his hair as a flood of old memories rushed back. Memories of Valkrunian blades cutting down his comrades, of their terrifying, unnatural strength. He survived those encounters, though they were difficult. How could he trust one of them now, let alone someone who held so much influence in Ceylon? He circled back, realizing that he needed the information regardless of what it uncovered.

"You fought against them, Thomas," Jane said. "You know what they are, but not all of them sold their souls to Klydos. Baroness Lyrei has her people and ours to look out for. She is trying to stop him, just as we are."

"But why keep it a secret?" Thomas asked. "If she is on our side, why hide who she is? The information she could share with the generals would make a difference on the battlefield. Expose the weaknesses of her people so we can reduce their effect. If she is free from the Lord of Tempests, why deceive anyone?"

"You ignore Aleara's secrets, yet question that of someone trying to survive in a hostile place?" asked Avery.

Jane's gaze flickered to Harold and Scherie, who remained silent throughout the revelation, watching the exchange with great interest.

"Because the world isn't as forgiving as you think, Thomas. You've seen how people reacted to the Fada and what happened to them when they first arrived in Ceylon. She would be executed without a second thought."

Thomas struggled to process this new information. It wasn't just about trusting Lyrei. It was about the precarious balance they were already walking. Ceylon was vulnerable enough as it was with the looming threat of the Lord of Tempests. If it got out that one of His leaders had once served the enemy, it could cause panic, and the Lord of Tempests thrived on chaos.

"You should have told us sooner," Thomas said. "You should have told me the moment we arrived."

Jane didn't flinch from his anger. This revelation might explain the significance of this backwater city. Fada and Valkrunians running free within the town was a sure sign that all was not well within Ceylon.

"I didn't know if you would be able to accept it. We needed you focused on the real enemy, Klydos, not Lyrei or Scherie."

"The real enemy?" Thomas asked. "The real enemy is standing right next to us, manipulating everything behind the scenes while we are left behind to catch up."

He turned to Harold, his eyes dark with suspicion. The man kept his face neutral.

"And you? Did you know? Is this why you've been so interested in gathering intelligence on the Lord of Tempests's movements? Because you're protecting one of his former slaves?"

Harold's expression did not change, though his voice was intentional when he finally spoke.

"When I first arrived here, I did not know the truth either. I've been aware of the baroness for some time, though. I've seen firsthand the lengths she's gone to in order to protect her diaspora from detection by the Lord of Tempests. She's not our enemy, Sir Thomas. She's one of our strongest allies."

Thomas didn't trust Harold's calm demeanor. It was too smooth, too practiced. Something about the man still didn't sit right with him, and this revelation only deepened his suspicions.

"We don't need enemies when our alliances are built on lies," Thomas said.

A silence fell over the group. The peaceful sounds of the grove, the rustling leaves, and the distant trickle of water all seemed at odds with the turmoil he felt. Instincts and his blade were suitable to carve a path through the madness of war, but this was something else, something more insidious. Trust, betrayal, and secrets all shaped a battlefield in ways that a sword could not cut through.

Avery, who had been quiet for too long, finally spoke.

"This changes things, Thomas, but it doesn't change our goal. The Lord of Tempests is still our enemy, and his forces are near Ceylon, perhaps inside as well. If Lyrei has knowledge that will help us stop Klydos, we need her."

Thomas didn't respond immediately. Avery was right, but it didn't make this revelation any easier. Trusting a former minion of Klydos meant stepping into a trap with his eyes wide open, but what choice did they have? The wind whispered through the trees again, carrying with it the imperceptible scent of burnt wood.

Aleara, speaking through the grove, was letting them know that darkness was closing in and they were running out of time.

"Fine," he said, at last, his voice hard. "I want to speak to her. I want Avery and Jaxxon to weigh in on this. I am sorry, but until I have some peace of mind about this situation, I will have to verify everything you say. I will try to be open-minded, but you have to stop assuming that I will act without understanding the truth."

"I'll arrange for the baroness to come here," Jane said.

Harold said. "The forces are on the move, and we must act or lose our chance altogether. I will arrange for our audience with the baron for the morning."

Harold and Scherie thanked them and left the grove. Jane tried to explain, but Thomas heard enough from her for the moment. The evening light filtered through the canopy, casting long shadows as Thomas, Avery, and Jaxxon made their way back to a secluded spot within the grove to talk in private. His mind still raced from the revelation that Baroness Lyrei was Valkrunian. It unsettled him on many levels. Thoughts materialized and then were swept away by that troubling truth.

Jaxxon plopped down on a moss-covered rock, his usual carefree smile in place, but concern lurked below that attitude. The druid stretched his legs out, crossing them, preparing for a lengthy discussion.

"It makes me sorry I was doing other things," he said. "A Valkrunian, of all things. I never predicted that."

Thomas didn't respond immediately. His gaze drifted to the pool in the center of the grove. Deception was occurring all around this sacred place, and he feared for its safety. As daylight waned, the pool took on a silvery hue, its waters darkening as the sun sank lower. The priest, already lost in his thoughts, paced in a circle, muttering under his breath.

"We should have known," Avery finally said. "It fits. The timing and her influence on the city. If Klydos learns of this, we might be facing something worse."

Jaxxon raised an eyebrow. The druid poked at Avery's arguments as much for fun as to delve deeper into the argument.

"You know, for someone who's supposed to be offering wisdom, you're leaning into the doom and gloom here. How about we state the fact that she's not under the influence of the Lord of Tempests' control anymore?"

Avery looked to Thomas for support. Thomas shrugged his shoulders in exasperation. This served to irritate the priest. Avery stood and paced around the other two men. It usually preceded his preaching to them, and this was a clear sign that Avery was about to give them something to ponder.

The priest said, "You're missing the point. She may be free now, but the fact that she once bowed to the Lord of Tempests complicates everything. It raises questions about her, about us, about how far His reach extends..."

"Relax, brother," Jaxxon interrupted. "You're getting all twisted. We can deal with this. We dealt with that necromancer and his exploding sheep. We can deal with this."

Thomas said, "This is different. The Valkrunians are dangerous. You know how they fight. They do not fight like men. Klydos does more than control them. They are broken and remade with a singular purpose. To kill."

He clenched his fists, the memory of those battles rising unbidden. He recalled his ride from Grimhorn to Godsdown and the carefree nature of Faisel. Imprisoned and surely facing interrogation by the Council of Orders, the man was unfazed by his situation. Who could trust beings with so much indifference in their everyday actions?

"If Lyrei was one of them, if she's still that dangerous, how can we trust her?"

Jaxxon rubbed his chin thoughtfully, his cheerful disposition fading for a moment. "I understand. We've seen them at their worst, but I've also seen people come back from some pretty dark places. People can change, Thomas. Ihuaj can change too. Maybe Lyrei's fighting for redemption, same as the rest of us."

Avery, who had been muttering to himself again, suddenly stopped and turned to the others.

"But what if that's the problem? What if this whole thing, Lyrei, the Fada, all of it, is a test from Aleara? Or worse, what if we're walking into a trap, one we're too blind to see because we're so focused on Klydos?"

"Or," Jaxxon said with a grin, "maybe you're just thinking too much, as usual. Not everything is a divine test, Avery. Sometimes it's just...life."

Avery frowned. "I'm serious. We could be missing something. What if Lyrei's presence here is a sign that the lines between allies and enemies are blurring, that the real danger isn't the Lord of Tempests himself but the way his influence corrupts everything it touches? Even those we think we can trust."

Jaxxon chuckled. "You're overthinking it again. If the baroness were still in league with Klydos, we'd all be dead by now, or at least in chains. The fact that we're not says something, doesn't it?"

Thomas was not so sure. He learned long ago that trust was fragile, easily shattered, and not so easy to mend. Doubt can erode a person's resolve and cloud their judgment. He could not afford that now.

"We have to be cautious," Thomas said. "We cannot take anything as it appears. Not Harold, not Scherie, and especially not Lyrei."

Jaxxon shrugged. "Fair enough. Maybe we should try not to assume everyone's out to stab us in the back, yeah? Makes for a much more pleasant ambiance."

Avery gave him a perturbed look. "You do realize we're dealing with Ihuaj, right? Deception is their thing."

Jaxxon waved him off. "Details."

Before Thomas could respond, a soft rustling in the trees caught their attention. Harold emerged from the shadows, his face looking tense. Whatever news he brought, it wasn't good.

"Sir Thomas," Harold began, then paused to catch his breath. "You need to come to the keep. Now."

"What is it?"

Harold said, "Your mother is here."

The words hit Thomas like a mace. His mother? Here? At the keep?

"Are you sure?" he asked.

His mind raced, trying to make sense of it. His mother never traveled without his father, staying in Grimhorn unless pressed, content to live out her days far from the turmoil of the kingdom.

Harold nodded. "She arrived unexpectedly, requesting to see you immediately. Threw the entire castle into a frenzy. She's waiting in the baron's hall."

Thomas arrived at the keep. He played out the various scenarios that would lead his mother to come to Ceylon. Though the memories were vague, he could not recall his mother ever taking a trip without his father. He looked back at Harold, urging the man to keep up. The moon lit their way, casting silvery light onto the cobblestone and the sturdy walls of the keep.

"Halt," the guard said.

The two men at the guard post brandished their spears. Thomas laughed at how feeble their attempt to look menacing was. He started forward, intending to push his way through or fight them if he must, but he heard Harold panting and trying to speak through his labored breathing. He paused and meditated, keeping his first impatient intentions from besting his training. The bureaucrat caught up, and the guards straightened, recognizing the Master of Finance.

"He's with me," Harold said. "Has the Duchess of Grimhorn arrived?"

Thomas turned to look at the man. He came with the news of her arrival. Why was he now uncertain whether she was inside or not? He started to say something, but Harold held up his hands, signaling for him to be patient. The paladin bit his lip rather than respond. He hated being told what to do just slightly less than being patient.

"Yes, sir," the guard replied. "Her carriage and attendees are just inside the gate."

"Then move," Harold said. "This man must see the duchess immediately."

The guard knocked and the inset door opened. Thomas bolted through, Harold close behind him. He examined the carriage, noting the soldiers arrayed around it. They came to attention, readying their weapons to block his attempt.

"Stand down," he said. "All I want to do is see my mother."

The soldier laughed, "There are no whores here, son. Best be on your way."

Thomas cuffed the soldier, dropping him with a single blow. As three more advanced, he summoned divine energy, blinding light bursting from him and sending them sprawling.

"Mother," he said.

The veiled woman looked at him, recognition dawning on her, and she ran toward him. She raced past her remaining soldiers and threw her arms around Thomas. Though he towered over her, her embrace was fierce, tightening around him like a memory he had not dared hold onto. He inhaled deeply, the scent of lavender filling his lungs, a distant echo of childhood.

"It is true," she said. "When they said it at court, I knew it was true."

More soldiers poured out of the keep, ready to counter whatever was causing the commotion. He glanced at the soldiers on the ground, and his rage subsided. What have I done? Aleara, please help me make it right. He knelt and poured divine strength into the man at his feet. When he stood, his mother grasped him, clinging to him as if he were a raft in a hurricane. His mother clung to him as he walked her along, and he apologized. He took the time to make right his impetuous actions. After checking on everyone, including Harold, he focused on his mother.

"What are you doing here?" he asked.

"We need to talk, Thomas," she said. "I am afraid for your life. There are things you need to know."

"Don't be," he said. "I'm not your weak little boy anymore."

He looked up. By their clothing, he assumed the baron and baroness joined them from the keep. When they arrived at the duchess, the baron knelt and kissed her hand, while the baroness curtsied. Thomas couldn't care less about the baron, but the baroness was his concern. Her raven-colored hair shimmered in the moonlight, every strand in place, as though even the elements obeyed her. The stillness of her expression hinted at secrets, her eyes watching Thomas with quiet calculation.

"Do I know you?" Baroness Lyrei asked.

He gave her a puzzled look. Not knowing what to say, Thomas knelt, slower than he might for any other lord, and held out his sword with his arm. Respect was due, but not freely given.

"Stand up, young man," the baron ordered. "Whoever you are, you should explain yourself on your feet."

"Milord," he said, "I am Sir Thomas. I am a knight errant of the Order of Valor."

"This is a strange night indeed," the baron said. "First, my liege's wife arrived unannounced, and now I learn that the goddess sent one of her brave paladins to grace our city as well."

"Eldric," Duchess Carina said, "this is my son. He is third behind Kendrick and James."

Baron Eldric turned to Lyrei and said, "Do you remember him from our wedding?"

Anger rose in Thomas. His brothers were always there before him, even when they were absent.

"We are not here together, milord."

"Stop calling him milord," his mother snapped uncharacteristically.

"I stopped being a noble when I was twelve," Thomas replied, trying to keep the anger out of his voice. Too much was at stake for him to mess this up.

"Lady Carina," the baroness said. "You've had a long ride. Would you like me to take you to your rooms so you can freshen up?"

"I need a minute with my son," Carina said.

The baroness exhibited nothing but concern, maintaining the deferential poise due to the duchess. The Valkrunians served a deceptive god. The former queen surely learned a lesson or two at his feet. For his part, the baron nodded and waved away his soldiers.

"My Lady," he said. "We will wait for you inside and will await your direction."

"Thank you," Carina said.

Her attendees and the rest of her retinue moved away, leaving Thomas alone with his mother for the first time in eighteen years.

"We don't have much time," she said. "Have you heard of a sword called Nightshard?"

Thomas paused. The name stirred a long-buried memory of his father telling a story to his sons in a slow and serious voice, speaking of a weapon that could be held but not controlled.

"It is just a legend," he said.

"No, it's not," she said sharply. "Your father is looking for it. You must find it before he does."

"Why?"

"Join me in my quarters once I have pacified Eldric and Lyrei," she said. "Please, Thomas. I know you think little of me, but I need you to hear me out."

"Eldric is going to ask how you learned I was here," Thomas said. "Best not let on that father trusts him so little that he has spies in the barony."

"Should I ask him when he is going to recall his spies from Grimhorn?" his mother asked.

Thomas realized he was seeing a new side to his mother. He believed her to be meek and subservient, but this was a shrewd mind at work and he was happily surprised to see that she had a more authoritarian streak within her. Something prompted her visit to Ceylon, and while he wanted to believe it was to reconnect with her son, he suspected there was more to it than that.

"I'll see you in an hour," he said. "Enjoy taunting the vassals."

"Thomas," she said. "I am just here to visit my son. So close to home."

She hugged him again and turned to the keep. She motioned for her retainers to join her and then proceeded into the keep. Harold sidled up to him as she departed.

"You've got a dangerous temper, boy," Harold said. "One day, it will cost you more than a bruised soldier."

"My apologies, Master Harold," Thomas said. "I have tried to change, but some memories, some wounds, they make it hard to keep control."

"Did she say why she was here?" Harold asked.

"To visit her son," Thomas said.

They stood in silence, the air heavy between them. Thomas stared at the keep's looming shadow and the candles in the third-story room. Perhaps it was his mother wiping the dust from her face after traveling this way. Was she here to warn him or play her part in the game? Thomas stayed lost in thought, trying to remember the legend of Nightshard. Harold cleared his throat, shaking the paladin from his thoughts. He refocused on the courtyard.

"Sir Thomas," Harold said, "the baron and baroness request an audience with you. It seems they have matters to settle before you meet with your mother."

Thomas furrowed his brows at the request. He had no time for pleasantries or small talk with nobles who were beholden to his father. Yet something in Harold's voice suggested that this was more than a formality. With a nod, he followed Harold into the inner chambers of the keep, the sword at his side a reminder that should he face enemies, he would be ready.

Inside the grand hall, Baron Eldric and Baroness Lyrei stood waiting. Eldric, still dressed in formal attire, looked ready for bed, kept awake by the unexpected arrival of the duchess. Lyrei stood calm and poised, her raven hair cascading down her shoulders. Her presence unnerved him earlier, and now, seeing her so composed in the candlelight, it became harder to ignore the nagging suspicion in his mind.

"Baron. Baroness," Thomas said. "What may I do for you?"

Eldric was first to speak, his voice slow and measured.

"It is not often that we have the honor of hosting a knight of the Order of Valor. Now, we have seen two in less than a month. Ceylon must be in peril. It seems the goddess keeps sending us her soldiers at opportune times."

"Forgive me, milord," Thomas said. "I am unaware that one of my brethren visited you."

Thomas studied the baron's face, concern etched upon it.

"The Council of Orders said nothing about Ceylon being in trouble, only that we needed to commune with the goddess at this grove. It is a mere coincidence that my mother is here."

"She said captured bandits told a tale of being accosted on the road by a knight fitting your description," Eldric said.

"Yes, milord. My companions and I did encounter bandits," Thomas said.

"Of course," Eldric replied, "but Ceylon is your mother's city too. Although I am surprised that she rode out with so few soldiers and without your father."

"Again, I am not sure of what to say," Thomas said. "I left home when I was nine. I am not sure how my mother and father decide such things."

"Dangers lurk in the forests. Dangers that threaten her and all of us," the baron said. "Harold, perhaps you should explain."

Harold, who had been standing nearby, stepped forward.

"I've talked to them, milord. I intend to solve two problems at once with the help of this brave trio that came to Ceylon."

Thomas half-listened to the exchange between the baron and the Master of Finance. This would indeed make King Cyrus happy. Thomas and his companions would serve as tax collectors, focusing on taxing the minions of Klydos in the forests beyond Ceylon. This would lessen the danger to the people of the barony, and it would give King Cyrus the tithe he so adamantly demanded.

Eldric said, "I have reservations about throwing you into this, Sir Thomas. These creatures are many, and my soldiers often fight bravely but accomplish little. Klydos' servants are not easily vanquished."

"I am sorry, milord," Thomas said. "In Godsdown, there has never been a word spoken of a contingent of the Lord of Tempests harrying the people of Ceylon."

"I did not request assistance."

Thomas didn't respond immediately. His mind raced, torn between the mission Harold proposed and the warning from his mother. Something else lurked behind this, something Lyrei had yet to reveal. He turned his gaze to the baroness, whose eyes never left him.

"And what do you say, baroness? You're quiet, but I imagine you have your thoughts about me and my friends chasing down Klydos' filth."

The corners of her mouth twitched slightly as if amused by his question. He was taunting her, hoping to gauge her response. Perhaps to reveal her true alliance.

"I say you are more perceptive than most, Sir Thomas," she replied. "But there are truths best left for more private conversations."

Thomas said, "Like the fact that you are a Valkrunian?"

The words hung in the air. Harold said nothing, but both he and Baron Eldric became white, their faces drained of color. Lyrei remained still, her gaze piercing into him. Her hands remained at her side, but Thomas kept them in the periphery of his vision in case she tried to cast something.

"So," she said, "you know."

"Not until Jane told me today," Thomas admitted. "In my short time here, there have been many half-truths and lies. I would have seen it myself. Your aura. The way you move. They betray you."

"I thought you meant something else. Interestingly, my glamour does not affect you," Lyrei said.

Eldric tried to speak, but Lyrei silenced him with a glance. The room rippled as she cast something. It was almost imperceptible, but the effect on Eldric and Harold was noticeable. The two men relaxed and gazed at her with rapt attention.

"You are tired," the baroness said. "It has been a long day. You have done your duty to the kingdom. Go and rest. Tomorrow will be an important day for Ceylon. The people will be graced by their duchess. There will be many things to plan. Sleep well."

The words had a magical effect on the two men. Harold and Eldric both reacted like marionettes, turning according to her manipulation and leaving the room. The Valkrunian woman was demonstrating her hold over Ceylon. She turned and walked to another door. When he did not follow, she turned back to him.

"This is not a matter to discuss here, Sir Thomas," Lyrei said. "Let me show you something."

He followed her, unsure at first if it was his own volition or whether he, too, was under her spell. He stopped to test the theory, and she turned back to smile at him.

"You have already proven that you are immune to my charm," she said. "I tried in the courtyard. You do not have to trust me, but I need you to see something."

She turned, and he followed. She led him to a smaller room, which looked like a library. In the center of the room, a table depicted Ceylon, but in a large version. He looked at it, shrugged, and waited for her to explain.

"Innocent enough," Lyrei said. "Aspirations do not make a man evil. However, Jane has already told Eldric that Aleara will not allow the forest to be cut down to enlarge his fiefdom."

"This means nothing," Thomas said. "This could be your room. A place where you contemplate a Valkrunian resurgence."

"Do you know how I came to be the baroness here? Do you remember me? Give me something that will help me feel as if I am not falling into madness."

"It would seem that you showed me earlier," Thomas said. "And no, I do not think I was at your wedding. My father had already sent me to serve Aleara."

Lyrei sighed. Thomas sensed a frustration in her. It was as if she wanted to warm to him, but he had no idea why. She took down a scroll from one of the shelves and spread it out before him on the table. Thomas read and then reread its contents. He looked from the words to the baroness and back again in disbelief. He had never imagined that it would occur in Grimhorn. His father was a stern man, but this was tantamount to apostasy. She pulled her dress away from her chest and exposed the magical rune inscribed on her left breast.

She was a captive. If it had stopped at Eldric, it would have been devastating enough, but to see his father's seal on the document was damning. Duke Kendrick's agreement to use a Grey Wizard to chain Lyrei to Ceylon magically shone a new light on the cruel machinations of his father. He struggled with the knowledge, and it certainly engendered no new feelings for the man. Thomas hoped his mother was unaware of this travesty.

"Who are you?" she asked. "Do you know?"

Thomas regarded her strangely. She sounded insane. She continued to speak to him as if he were an old acquaintance. The prickle of his skin alerted him to the aether. Lyrei moved her hands as if beginning a conjuration. He drew his blade, preparing for the treachery that he suspected.

"I mean you no harm, Veilbreaker," Lyrei said. "I just need to understand what is going on."

"Veilbreaker?"

She ignored his question and completed her ritual. When she looked at him, tears streamed from her eyes.

"What did you see?" he asked.

"If you would like, I can explain as we walk. You have been kept from your mother long enough. She wanted the three of us to talk alone."

Thomas was unsure whether he trusted her. Despite his misgivings, he needed answers. The way she spoke about his mother also nagged at him. He gestured at the door.

"Lead the way," he said.

They walked in silence through the dim corridors of the keep, candlelight flickering and casting long, undulating shadows on the stone walls. He did not like the closed-in nature of the place, preferring the open outdoors. Their footsteps on the flagstone floor were the only break in the silence. Hers was the soft scrape of leather, and his accentuated by the steel-shod heel and toe of his boots. Lyrei glanced at him from the corner of her eye, her face impassive, though her posture grew more rigid.

"We all have our secrets. I know what you must think of my people, but it is only one side of the story. You would have more compassion if your mother revealed her secrets to you."

"I do not know. Merciless killers with chaos-fed powers tell a pretty complete tale," Thomas said. "What do you mean about my mother's secrets?"

The remark landed, erasing her careful composure. His surprise was that it left her looking saddened. He girded himself for deception, calling on the goddess to help him see through her lies. Aleara, bless me with clarity, for my thoughts are jumbled. Please guide me.

"Chaos consumed my realm," she said. "I bowed before that fearsome god, not because I wanted to become part of His endless armies, but because I wanted my people to live. I suspect you wanted my people to live as well."

"Do not presume to understand me. Your realm?" Thomas asked.

"I am not merely a Valkrunian," Lyrei said. "I was the queen of the Valkrunians for hundreds of your years."

Thomas took a step back at the revelation. He did not accept that as truth, but he could not fathom how the queen of a people would find herself in such a predicament.

"I would have fought until my dying breath," Thomas said. "Bowing to the Lord of Tempests surely was a last resort? You sold yourself and every one of your people to the God of Chaos. Did you expect a brighter future? This is simply a lie intended to evoke sympathy. I'll not trust a being that would gladly end another's life to preserve theirs."

"Is it not what you do?" Lyrei asked.

Thomas bristled at the implication. He turned her to him and got in her face. The baroness held her ground, but she looked frightened.

"I am defending my realm," Thomas said. "You came here. If you had not come, no one would have had to die. I have to bear the burden of those deaths, which is true, but I did it to protect Aleara and her creations. How could you expect me to trust you?"

"I kept my people alive in hopes of finding a way to escape," she said. "I found it here. Do you remember that? Centuries have gone by in this realm without falling to him. Some fall in days."

She pulled away and continued down the hall. Lyrei's lips pressed into a thin line as they turned a corner, the air in the corridor growing cooler.

"I never asked for your trust, but in the matter of your mother, I have no ill intent. Beyond her, I only intend to protect the small part of Binsmuth that allows ihuaj to coexist peacefully. You are right to be wary of those who serve Klydos, but it is not me. Soon, you will understand."

They ascended a narrow flight of stairs, the torches on the wall flickering erratically, casting eerie shapes on the walls. Shadows seemed to twist and writhe as they passed. Someone was using chaos magic nearby.

"I know who I am wary of," Thomas said. "You claim to have no ill intent, but why do I detect the aether in the air?"

"You think I do not feel it?" Lyrei asked. "Ceylon is under siege, though few know it. We must hurry. Something is wrong with your mother."

The words served to cement his fear that the situation was a trap and he was being led into it. She was a mix of contradictions, and her visible concern for his mother added another layer to what he suspected was deception.

"What is wrong with my mother? You speak as if you know Klydos' plans," Thomas said. "How close are you to his agents?"

Lyrei stopped abruptly in front of a large arched door. She turned, her expression neutral, though Thomas thought fear lurked beneath that polished gaze.

"You want me to be the enemy. Nevertheless, I am not his ally," she said, "but I can sense his magic. I cannot sense it on you like I did before."

"What do you mean by before?" Thomas asked. "We have never met."

"I... I don't understand," Lyrei said. "I am here because of you or someone like you."

Thomas asked, "Are you trying to confuse me to distract me from the evil you are unleashing?"

"No," she said with a frustrated gasp. "I'm trying to explain that I came to Ceylon..."

She stopped, turning her head as if trying to pinpoint something.

"That will have to wait. The air is thick with chaos. Prepare yourself, paladin. We may be doomed."

They stood there in silence for a moment, the weight of her words hanging there. Thomas called upon the divine energy within him, a reminder of Aleara's gifts to him, but it was as if the creeping darkness of chaos was dimming her presence. Lyrei said a prayer to Aleara, and that caught him off guard. Aleara imbuing this Valkrunian with divine spirit shattered his worldview.

"Then why bring me here?" he asked. "Why not deal with this yourself? What are you not telling me?"

Lyrei's expression softened, and her hand touched his face. Either she was cold, or he was feverish, for her touch chilled him.

"There are things even I cannot fight alone. You will need to be stronger than you think, Sir Thomas. Be the man you once were. Not just for your mother, but for what is coming."

She reached for the door, pausing for a moment before pushing it open. The creak of the hinges echoed down the hall, a sound that stretched into the night. Thomas hesitated, the fire in his stomach causing him to tense. Something was wrong. There it was again, a prickle at the back of his neck, dread intensifying with each passing second.

"Lyrei," he said, "if anything happens to her..."

"I know," she said, "I'll answer for it."

The door swung wide, and the stench of flesh burning came on a gust of wind. His heart stopped as his eyes fell on the figure crumpled on the floor. It was his mother, her body lying on the floor, and the faint glow of aether swirling in the air.

"Mother!" he said, rushing to her side.

CHAPTER

14

He held the book he had stolen from the library at Castle Grimhorn. He thumbed through its worn pages and stopped at a picture. It depicted a man holding a bluish blade, about to strike at the foe lying at the man's feet. This was the story of Nightshard. A weapon that, if the legend were true, fell from the sky after Aleara and Donegal worked together to create Binsmuth from chaos itself. It passed through the hands of early warlords who consolidated the lands that would become Castardia, Zel'Drea, and Nemordia.

The book speculated on the origin, powers, and location of the sword. He caressed the worn pages of the book, the archaic wording of its passages echoing like thunder off the mountain range next to Grimhorn. Thomas imagined that his father stared at these pages in much the same way, lusting after the power that the sword offered. He cursed angrily, drawing the attention of his companions around the fire. He took his eyes off the page and stared into the fire, trying to recall the dim memories of his father reading to him and his brothers. This story came up often, and while Thomas wanted to believe that it had been a favorite of theirs, it was most likely their father reading it obsessively, trying to find the clues to where Nightshard lay hidden.

The intricate layers of his father's schemes were like a complex web. Each thread spun to lead Thomas down a path that served the duke's selfish desires. Thomas refused to be a pawn in his game. He seethed with anger at the thought of his mother's death, a casualty in his father's quest for power and control. The days he lost with her would haunt him forever, stolen by those manipulative ways. Her last words haunted him. Find Faisel.

With a burning desire for revenge, Thomas planned to thwart his father's plans and retrieve the weapon first, showing Duke Kendrick that his greed would not prevail. His mother was a gentle soul, unlike him at this moment. Thomas plotted destruction against everything his father held dear, even if it meant destroying the keep and all its valuables, including the sword itself.

His loyal friends, Jaxxon and Avery, were like family to him, standing by his side through thick and thin. Even they could not understand the turmoil and pain Thomas endured. They urged him to rest and meditate in the grove, but every moment spent away from their mission was another opportunity for Grimhorn's lord to triumph.

As he discussed their plan of attack, Jaxxon brought up the conversation Thomas had with his mother before she passed away. The memory twisted inside him like a dagger, but he pushed it away, not wanting to burden his friends with his grief. They were grieving for him, too, offering their support and loyalty without question. Deep down, Thomas needed more than just their words. He needed proof of his father's guilt before he could confront him and take the sword Nightshard for himself. With it, he would confront his father and put an end to the forces of the Lord of Tempests.

As he stoked the fire for warmth and light, Thomas buried himself in the book of Nightshard. One passage caught his eye: "The tail of the mighty dragon points the way to the entrance." It was a metaphor, he realized. Dragons were mythical creatures, and if they did exist, paladins would have hunted them down. But what did it mean in this context? Thoughts churned like the waves of the ocean, each one crashing against his mind with fierce determination. He had to unravel the mystery. It could be the key to unlocking his father's plans and defeating him.

"Tail of the dragon," he said.

"What dragon?" Jaxxon asked.

"It is a sentence in this story," Thomas said, "but I cannot make sense of it."

"The mountain range where Grimhorn Peak is," Avery replied. "Cartographers said it resembled a dragon with one mighty horn reaching to the sky."

Thomas tried to picture the map. The range ran roughly down the westernmost reaches of Zel'Drea. It had been the original border of the Duchy of Grimhorn until his grandfather crossed the mountains and conquered the coast. In his mind, he traced it. The tail of the dragon would end roughly fifty miles west of Ceylon.

"Damn," he said. "She led us right there."

"Right, where?"

"Ceylon," Thomas said. "Aleara led us there, and now I know why."

"Why?" Avery asked.

"Nothing," Thomas replied. "We are headed to where we are meant to be. That I am sure."

He was also sure that his mother's funeral was the last time his father would speak to him that way. He thought back to standing in the grove at Grimhorn. It was as mystical as the one in Ceylon, but the pyre on which his mother lay in display ruined its beauty for him. He stood next to his brothers and the two sisters who had been born after his leaving home. The two girls sniffled, holding back the tears.

Thomas had reached out and put his hand on his brother's shoulders. James exchanged a sad look with him, while Kendrick pushed his hand away. When the High Priest uttered the prayers, the elder Kendrick walked to the pyre and lit it. He turned and walked back. Thomas hoped for some sign of emotion. He found none. Instead, his father doled out blame.

"This is your fault," Duke Kendrick said. "She chased after you and got herself killed."

Thomas held his tongue, instead watching the flames rise into the canopy, magically wicked away without causing damage. His mother's ashes would be spread around the grove, and her spirit would return to Aleara for the goddess to use for her purpose. He clenched and unclenched his fists. Rain, uncharacteristic for the grove, began to fall, and the mourners scurried away, leaving the duke and his three sons alone.

"You can leave, paladin," the younger Kendrick said.

"Ken," James said, "we've only just now given Mother back to Aleara. Do you have to turn it into a fight?"

The eldest son turned on James, his imperious look suggesting that the middle son was not needed. Thomas fumed at the eldest brother's disregard for the emotions of others. James ignored his brother and turned to his father, but the duke remained silent. Without their mother to temper his mood, the duke looked as if he were the thunder and lightning in the clouds above.

"Thomas," James said, "please visit it with me before you leave."

"I shall do that," Thomas said, embracing him.

James hugged Thomas and walked away. He called this grove home. Neither the duke nor Kendrick would interfere with him going about those duties. Thomas, however, stood there expecting the worst from them. If it came from his brother, Kendrick would learn that Thomas was no small boy to be bullied about. But it was the duke who took the first blow.

"Why did you ask her to come see you?"

"I did no such thing," Thomas said. "She heard it from your spies."

"Nonsense."

"Be warned that I will not have you call me a liar, no matter who you are," Thomas said.

"If father calls you a liar, you are one," Kendrick said.

His anger was rising, its usual fever pitch hastened by grief. Thomas wanted to smack his brother, but this was a place sacred to Aleara, and he would not bring dishonor to his goddess. Instead, he laughed at the jibe. The irony of these two traitors calling him a liar, especially here in this place sacred to the very goddess they sought to betray, was not lost on the paladin.

"You wrote us off," Kendrick said.

"Yes," Thomas said, "I, a boy, sent for men to collect me and take me somewhere. I had to fight to earn my place, prove myself worthy to keep my place, and then go out into the world to protect other people's places."

"Your mother cried at night when you rejected her," Kendrick said.

"Our mother lied to me," Thomas said.

The duke slapped Thomas, causing him to stumble and catch himself so that he would not fall into the lush grass around them.

"Your mother worried for you every moment after you left. I should have kept you at Grimhorn and put you in charge of something trivial. You have been a disappointment since your gender became known."

Thomas ignored the jab. It was an attempt to goad him. It would not work. He had plans. Soon, his father would pay the toll for allowing Klydos to kill his mother.

"Then why not visit?" Thomas asked.

"I told her to prioritize the family that would make a difference," the duke said. "It wasn't until we realized you were strong enough to become a paladin that I thought that included you. Even then, I was wrong about that. Your values are misplaced. Family should come first."

Thomas bit his lip at the slight. Kendrick grinned at his discomfort. They understood nothing of his trials as a man. The horrors they witnessed once fighting alongside the holy forces of Aleara were but a glimpse into the things that Klydos rained upon this realm. Their disdain and mockery meant nothing to him. Without another word, the duke turned to leave, and Kendrick followed. That left Thomas alone to watch as the wind and rain took away the last remnants of his mother's body.

What had her life accomplished? He remembered her loyalty to her husband and her motherly obligations, which she fulfilled secondary to the duke's needs. Beyond that, there was not much to his mother. She lived and died without doing much more than birthing children. Her most significant contribution now would be a greater wedge between him and his father. Find Faisel, he remembered again.

***

Sleep came to Thomas, but it was far from restful. He dreamed of that place between places, the Threshold. It was surreal, watching the building crumble as he walked away and form as he drew closer to them. He hid behind a pillar when he heard voices coming from ahead. The landscape continued to shift, becoming more real as the beings approached. A tall table formed, and then she came into view. It was Aleara. She was as solid-looking as Thomas. With her was what he imagined Donegal, her brother, might look like. He could hear their words, but they warped and twisted in the intervening distance, leaving him with random noises to try to interpret.

Another joined them, and even from this distance, Thomas shivered at the cold radiating off this being. This was Klydos, the Lord of Tempests. As this terrible deity walked up, he dropped dice on the table. Thomas imagined Him to be a monster, but Klydos was a handsome man, tall and raven-haired. Other, less-formed beings emerged and stood next to the three. Klydos spoke, and Thomas realized that he had to take a chance of getting caught. He crept forward, more obstacles springing up and giving him cover as he advanced. He crept forward until he was able to hear them.

"Cast them for Ryfal," Donegal said to Aleara. "Father will let the realm live on as a lifeless place if you lose. I will have my minerals and mountains to play with either way."

Aleara took up the dice and rolled. Thomas could not see what she cast, but when Klydos took his turn, her face told the story. Doom would befall Ryfal. Whatever creations she had on it would be consumed by chaos. It was strange, though. Donegal exhibited more joy than Klydos. One of the vague figures winked from existence. He was not sure what that indicated, but it was concerning. He jumped at the sight of a hooded figure coming toward him. The creature approached confidently, heading directly for Thomas.

"Tricky stuff," the hooded figure said, "deciding the fate of uncountable flora and fauna on the roll of the dice."

"This is not real," Thomas said. "Aleara would never decide such things that way. She pours too much into creation."

"Judge for yourself, champion," the hooded figure said.

Thomas looked at Klydos. He looked human, although his bluish-black skin was a tone that Thomas had never encountered. He wore no armor, only bracers and a leather kilt adorned with bronze plates. His long, wavy mane was inky black with splotches of grey dotting it. Thomas grew up fearing the titan. He created Aleara and Donegal, but for some reason, he came to hate everything they did with his gifts. It seemed absurd, except Thomas himself was living proof of the lengths a father would go to erase a child from existence.

"Roll for Cranthor," Klydos said, a deep, resounding voice that echoed across the Threshold.

Donegal held up his hands. "Would you spare this world, too?"

Aleara looked at her brother, rolling her eyes and grunting in exasperation. Thomas, too, felt betrayed by the god. What good was a lifeless place except to be the private playground of some immature god? Was this why the clergy and warriors of Donegal rarely engaged in the fight against the Lord of Tempests? A deal cut by their deity that would leave them dead alongside those who worshipped Aleara.

"I will spare the world," Klydos said.

"Roll, sister," Donegal said. "Life depends on you."

She rolled. Klydos rolled. Another figure vanished.

"This is a sick game," Thomas said to the hidden figure.

"But one with hope," the being said, and he pointed to where the figure that Thomas thought had gone lingered but in a diminished state.

Klydos' voice boomed across the space again.

"Roll for Binsmuth. Do not ask, Donegal. I will not grant you this one."

Donegal picked up the dice and rolled. Aleara picked up the dice and rolled. Klydos laughed.

"This shall be good," the Lord of Tempests said. "I expect nothing but your best. I hoped you would have learned to craft something that lasts, but eons have passed, and you still beg me to allow your imperfections to exist."

Thomas considered lunging forward and attacking Klydos. It was impossible, but part of him wanted to end his agony in this futile manner. If it were all a game, living was for naught. The hand of the hidden figure tugged on his arm, and he looked at the being.

"They have won the toss three times over your realm," the hidden figure said. "Perhaps Klydos has less animosity for Binsmuth than other places."

"Should I go back and tell people that?" Thomas asked. "Live your lives. The Lord of Tempests sees fit to wage endless war on Binsmuth. We are the lucky ones!"

"I don't picture you as the prophet type," the hidden figure said. "Find Nightshard. It will give you a chance to tip the dice in your favor."

"Who are you?" Thomas asked.

"I'm someone who wants you to succeed," the hidden figure said. "To give Binsmuth freedom from celestial strife and let you get on with living your lives."

Thomas laughed and said, "I am to believe that you are the benevolent one. Should I abandon Aleara and follow you?"

"I care," the hidden figure said. "Your life is not a game to me. Wake up! You are about to have a fight on your hands."

Thomas awoke with a jolt, the dream leaving him sweating even with the chill of the winter night. He burst from the tent to see the campfire, once a comforting glow, now flickering weakly, casting long, dancing shadows twisting against the backdrop of light. A hissing sound cut through the silence, sharp and menacing. He flexed his arm, comforted by the sword in his hand. Something was wrong. Avery had been on watch, but there was no sign of him.

The first shape emerged from the dark. It resembled a giant snake, but the upper part bore a resemblance to a human torso with scales. It undulated, slithering closer. The face was a mix of reptilian and human features twisted in a mockery of the beautiful creations of Aleara. This abomination must be a creation of the Grey Wizards of Sambor. They used their chaos magic to combine captives with reptiles, and the result was a creature with a single-minded purpose. More of the creatures followed, their movements quick and deadly, cutting through the underbrush with ease. Thomas smelled them, like something that wallowed in a stagnant pond.

"Jaxxon!" Thomas shouted.

The druid was already up, transformed into an owlbear, claws extended as he rushed toward the closest Serpent Man. Jaxxon's swing arced toward the creature, but the thing twisted away, its body far too fast and too fluid. Jaxxon snarled, swinging again, dodging a lunge, and escaping the pair of fangs that snapped at his paw.

The camp was a chaotic scene. Another Serpent Man lunged toward Thomas, a rusted blade in its clawed hand. Thomas blocked just in time, the jarring impact sending a shock down his arm. The creature had tremendous strength, and the force of the blow sent him stumbling back. His boots slipped on a patch of ice hidden beneath the snow, and fear overcame him, not a natural one, but a magical aura emanating from the creatures trying to break through his concentration. He mumbled a prayer, and it dissipated, going from an icy death to disgust after dispelling it.

He slashed wildly, connecting with the arm of the creature. Sluggish, hot blood spurted from the wound, covering Thomas in gore. The creature recoiled, its elongated tongue darting out to aid its other senses. It lunged again, a nerve-wracking screech coming from its warped mouth, and Thomas ducked. The blade whooshed by, skimming the top of his helm.

A scream tore through the night. It sounded like Avery. The priest was nowhere to be seen. He heard a wet choking sound, then nothing. The paladin tried to run in the direction of the noise, but a Serpent Man caught his ankle in its coiling tail, pulling him down into the muck. The earth sucked him down, soaked in melted snow and the enemy's bile. He struggled, panic mounting as he tried to shake loose to reach his friend. He stared at the serpent man. Behind the fangs dripping with venom were needle-like teeth, and at that moment, Thomas could not even remember to pray. The horror coming closer held him in place, stunned by its alluring gaze. The green and black scales wove an intricate pattern that both mesmerized and terrified Thomas simultaneously.

This was not like him, he thought. I've fought all sorts of monsters. Why hesitate around them?

Jaxxon came down hard on the creature's skull. The slimy skin split open with a sickening crunch. Blood spattered over Thomas and the ground around him, mixing into the snow and dirt. This broke the trance he found himself under. Thomas extricated himself from the coiled tail and stood. Jaxxon did not wait to see if Thomas was okay, but sprang away into the darkness to find other opponents. And there was no lack of them.

It was a grim scene. For every horror that they killed, two more emerged from the darkness. They slithered forward relentlessly. The numbers were overwhelming, and somewhere in the darkness, Avery lay injured or dead. An unwilling moan escaped his lips as he thought about his mentor and friend falling prey to these creatures. He looked about, trying to determine which direction to take to find Avery.

Thomas caught his breath just before a new figure came into view. It wore blue-black plate mail, the armor dulled and scarred from countless battles, each dent a testament to his skill and brutality. The Serpent Men parted for him. Like dogs that cornered their prey, they parted so the foul knight could make the kill. The warrior stepped forward, prepared for battle. Realizing this was the true threat, Thomas focused, bringing his sword to bear on the man.

Etched along the armor were runes that faintly glowed, causing Thomas to have to look away from the terrible things written there. He realized chaos energy infused the armor. The knight's helm resembled a snarling beast, with jagged fangs and eyes that glowed an eerie blue. His sword also crackled with blue energy. He held onto the collar of Avery's robe with his other hand, dragging the poor priest behind him. Avery fought for freedom to no avail. The knight smacked him with the flat of his sword.

The air sizzled when the blade made contact, and Avery screamed as the chaos energy washed over him. The priest raised his staff with its symbol of Aleara in a defensive stance. The knight did not speak but swung his sword around, and it connected with the staff. The force of the blow sent Avery flying backward, shattering the staff and sending pieces flying. The holy symbol landed in the snow and sunk from sight. Avery landed on the ground, air forced out of his lungs, leaving him breathing with ragged gasps. Thomas sagged as blood pooled from beneath Avery, dark against the muddy ground, spreading into the snow and melting it.

"Avery!" Thomas said.

He scrambled to the priest. Avery was in bad shape. He bled from several puncture wounds. His body convulsed as the poison continued to work its way through his system. His face burned and melted from contact with the chaos energy. The priest was trying to say something, but his mouth did not respond as he intended. Thomas tried to intone a healing prayer, but black entered his peripheral vision.

The knight moved forward as well, heavy boots leaving deep imprints on the muddy battlefield. Thomas stood, sword raised, but the knight ignored him. Instead, he kicked Avery's body aside and then looked upward, seeing the new threat of the paladin. A cry of rage escaped Thomas' lips as he launched himself toward the knight. At every turn, the Lord of Tempests was taking those he loved from him. Unfettered from restraint, Thomas poured every ounce of energy he had into defeating the other warrior. One of them would not leave this battleground.

He swung his sword relentlessly, blows ringing out without end. Muscles burned from the exertion. Thomas buckled as the other's sword hit him squarely in the abdomen, opening up a deep wound. He backed away, circling and using the strength of Aleara to cause the wound to close. He would not be able to do that many more times. He had to find a way to best his foe.

The knight moved with unnatural speed, advancing on the paladin. His free hand began to glow with sorcerous intent. Thomas glanced at Avery, whose labored breaths were getting weaker. He could not lose someone else, not so soon after losing his mother. He had to end this and save the priest. The knight spoke, rattling Thomas with its words.

"You never did understand your place, Thomas."

The voice was familiar. No! It could not be. It crushed Thomas as recognition dawned on him. He froze mid-step, the sword slipping slightly in his grasp. His chest tightened. He tried to speak, but his throat was dry.

"What?" he said.

The knight laughed again, a cold sound that echoed in the paladin's head. The knight raised a gauntleted hand and lifted the visor of his helm. Beneath, staring back with hard, pitiless eyes, was Kendrick, his older brother.

"Kendrick," Thomas said.

The name was more vile than the poison of the Serpent Men. Kendrick sneered, his face twisted in cruelty.

"You have always been your own worst enemy. Stumbling. Failing. This has to be a new low in the chronicles of the third-born. Half-breed. Piece of shit!"

Thomas shook his head in disbelief, his fear contrasting with the rage that consumed him. "Why? Why are you doing this?"

Kendrick stepped closer.

"Do you think Father thought of you as more than a nuisance? A disappointment? Carina's death only proved it."

The words cut deeper than the wound in his abdomen had. Thomas remembered his father's words.

"If you had done what I told you, boy," the duke said. "She would still be here."

Thomas opened his mouth to speak, but the words died in his throat. He would have saved her if Lyrei had not distracted him with her tale. He got there too late to save her, only enough time to hear her dying words. The memory faded, but the guilt remained. He grappled with his brother's betrayal.

"You do not know what you are talking about," Thomas said. "I loved her."

"Carina never felt that," Kendrick said. "You were too busy blaming everyone else for what was happening to you. In the end, it was you who let her die! You robbed me of a future lay."

Kendrick roared, slamming down his sword onto the blade of the paladin. The impact broke the long sword, vibrating up through his arms, leaving him to stare at his broken blade.

"Kendrick, please," Thomas said, "we are brothers."

"We aren't brothers. Or rather, we are half-brothers," Kendrick said, malice in his eyes. "You chose the wrong side. One of many bad choices in your life."

Thomas staggered under the weight of Kendrick's blows, reeling from the words. He slipped and slid on the muddy and bloody ground around Avery. While his shield was holding up, his broken long sword looked worse and worse after each one. This wasn't just an enemy. This was the boy he admired as a child. The one who now sought to end his life. His betrayal and sadness gave way to fury. Whether the words were true or not, Kendrick revealed himself to be the enemy. Thomas ground his teeth and gripped his sword and shield until he thought his bones would snap.

"You betrayed us," Thomas growled. "You betrayed your mother!"

"I did what my duty as heir," Kendrick said. "Carina would have been part of my inheritance. Maybe I'll take one of your little sisters as a plaything."

"Just because Father disagrees with King Cyrus doesn't mean destroying the world."

Kendrick rained down more blows. One struck Thomas in the head. Splotches of light flashed in his eyes. He was close to passing out. Close to it ending. He could not let it happen this way. Thomas prayed to Aleara for strength. Avery had always been the one who questioned things. Right now, Thomas questioned his sanity.

He faltered, his vision blurring. Something tugged at his consciousness, drawing him away from the battle. The world around him dimmed, and he found himself in the Threshold. Was this happening to signal his imminent death? In the distance, the three figures were still at the table, casting dice. Aleara, radiant and beautiful, cast a warm glow over her part of the table. On the other side, Klydos cast a shadow as if stopping the light from expanding further. The dice rolled. Another realm's fate hung in the balance. Aleara looked across the distance, meeting his gaze.

"This is how it must be."

Klydos laughed, the sound reverberating like thunder on the horizon.

"Every realm ends this way. Until you learn your craft, all things will return to chaos."

A presence appeared at his side. It was the hidden figure, its voice a tempting murmur.

"You see, Thomas? The gods play with your lives, with your realm. They always have. Do you see lines of good and evil drawn over there? This will not be the last time those die are cast. If your realm does not prevail, it will be consumed. Erased."

Thomas returned to reality with his brother's blade pressed to his throat. Avery lay motionless in the dirt, his blood pooling around him. Jaxxon fought on in the distance, fending off the Serpent Men, but he could not hold them off forever. Kendrick's blade pressed closer.

"This is the end for you, half-breed," Kendrick said.

Before Kendrick could cut his throat, the hidden figure appeared once more, its voice echoing in his head.

"Let me save him. Let me save Avery. I can give you the power to defeat Klydos, your brother, and the chaos that plagues your realm. I can help you find Nightshard. All you have to do is take my hand."

Thomas looked at Avery, desperation fueling the decision before him. Was this the only way?

CHAPTER

15

What is faith if it does not aid someone in the worst moments? It was at that moment that Thomas realized that availing himself of the help offered by the hidden figure was tantamount to losing his faith. Aleara brought him this far. He would either live through her help or return to her bosom with his honor and faith intact. Faisel and his kin had bowed to another god, but he would not. He ignored the voice in his head and cried out to Aleara. She answered in ways he had not dreamed. Avery cast one last spell, healing the bruises and cuts crisscrossing his body, then fell backward with some finality to it.

Healing given, Thomas prayed that Aleara allow him to take vengeance for Avery. A beam of sunlight brightened the area around him, filling him with energy. It burst from his body, blasting Kendrick and pushing him back. Thomas hefted his broken blade. Moonlight ran from his arm into the hilt, turning the broken blade into a blinding sliver. When the glare died down, his blade formed anew, silver light replacing the missing parts. Kendrick stepped back, shock on his face as Thomas received the full blessing of the goddess.

In response, Kendrick lowered his helm and drew on chaos, forming a blueish-black energy around him. From where he stood, Thomas sensed it, anathema to the light of his blade. He glanced over at Avery, knowing that he had little time to dispatch

Kendrick and give his friend a chance to live. Kendrick roared, motioning for Thomas to engage with him. When he was a boy, he feared Kendrick. Now, he recognized that it was Kendrick's turn to be afraid. He was facing a holy fist of Aleara. Thomas hesitated for a moment, thinking through his strategy. He would not give in to recklessness. Too much was at stake. Klydos be damned. He was going to claw this world back from chaos, starting with Kendrick.

He advanced, catching the first blow and pushing it aside. Kendrick formed a globe of inky black energy and threw it. Thomas screamed as the globe expanded, enveloping him in its burning touch. His flesh melted, and the chainmail shirt only served to spread the heat across his entire torso. Thomas flexed, drawing upon Aleara once again, and light filled him, cracking the orb until it burst and disappeared. He looked, but Kendrick was nowhere to be seen.

Somehow, the knight escaped while Thomas fought off the attack. He backtracked to where his friend lay and circled the area around Avery, watching for trickery. He looked for some sign that the knight was still near but found none. In the end, Kendrick ran away rather than face that Thomas was a more powerful warrior. Once satisfied that Kendrick was not lurking in the shadows, Thomas turned his focus on Avery, picking his way over to him. The priest was horrifically mutilated, his face warped beyond recognition. No breath came from his misshapened lips. There was no rise and fall of his chest. His exposed skin blackened from the poison of the Serpent Men. His face was locked in a cry for help. Thomas laid his forehead on Avery's. Hot tears ran down his face onto his friend. A shudder swept across his body, ending with a mournful cry.

The priest was dead, sacrificing himself to save his friends. Hot tears blurred his vision as he searched for a way to change the outcome. Thomas kept touching his friend, wailing and caressing him, praying for healing or some sign from Aleara. His heart was broken by the events of the day, but none more so than seeing his mentor and friend dead before him. Where his mother had been a distant part of his life, Avery had been there from childhood to now. He bellowed to Aleara, offering anything to bring Avery back. Nothing happened.

He wept over the man until he heard lumbering footsteps and turned, ready to do battle once more. Instead of an enemy, it was Jaxxon, over ten feet tall in owlbear form. As the druid drew closer, he transformed. Feather retreated into the skin. His head rippled as the beak transformed into lips, his eyes shrinking, and his head rearranging to become human again. His body morphed as well. Bones bent awkwardly to take on their human shape. It looked painful, though it took mere seconds to leave the druid human. His chest heaved from the exertion. Thomas started to say something, but stopped at the sight of Jaxxon catching sight of Avery.

The druid howled in grief, joining Thomas in mourning. When they were too exhausted to yell anymore, they wept together. The battle had been but minutes. However, Thomas felt he had spent a lifetime staring at his dead friend. He was afraid to look away, fearing some movement or sign that this was an injury rather than death.

"What happened?" asked Jaxxon.

"I do not know. I woke up when you did," Thomas said, "and Avery was not by the campfire."

"The serpent men ambushed us, and I transformed," Jaxxon said. "Who was the knight?"

Thomas hesitated to say anything. He was still reeling from the revelation, which shattered his sense of sanity. The only thing keeping him from giving in was the knowledge that Nightshard was out there, and he would find it. Once he had that weapon, he intended to storm every keep and root out those who worshiped

Klydos. When Thomas didn't respond, Jaxxon gave him a shove. Thomas looked up at the druid, agony prolonging his response.

"Thomas," Jaxxon said, "I've got no patience for your brooding. Did you see who the knight was?"

He looked over at Jaxxon, realizing he would not escape giving an answer.

"It was," Thomas said, "Kendrick."

Jaxxon stood, pulling away from the paladin. Thomas reached up. It was a silent plea for understanding. From the look he gave, Thomas realized that Jaxxon had no empathy left in him at that moment. Thomas understood. He had no words for the druid either. His guilt and remorse over the deaths of his mother and Avery, mixed with the faces from the past that haunted him. As much as he berated himself, Thomas kept coming back to the fact that the cause was Klydos.

Recovering Nightshard and defeating the Lord of Tempests was the only way to prevent this from happening again. Jaxxon shook his shaggy head.

"You're not thinking straight. We need to find a way to bring Avery back. Perhaps Jane can help us or the Valkrunian bitch."

"They were not able to help my mother," Thomas said.

Jaxxon sank back to the ground with a hoarse moan escaping his lips. Their time together had forged a friendship, which then evolved into a brotherhood. Losing Avery hurt him worse than losing his mother. She had been but a distant memory for many years, while Avery had been a tangible part of his very being. Together, they prayed, hoping to beseech Aleara to bring Avery back. It was of no use. The priest had sacrificed himself to allow Jaxxon and Thomas to continue the fight.

"No, goddess, no," Jaxxon cried out.

The druid was shifting without thinking. Talons raked the ground as he cursed and pleaded for any reality but the one staring lifelessly back at them. With each moment, the druid was growing closer to losing control over his human form. There was no telling what he would do if he transformed in his gried. Thomas placed a hand on his friend, not caring if the man lashed out at him. Anything to prevent what Thomas feared happening.

"Jaxxon," Thomas said. "We have to remain calm. We have enemies all around us. Avery is dead."

"I don't care anymore," Jaxxon said. "I couldn't care less about what humans do to each other."

Thomas said, "We still have each other. I need you, and you need me, too."

"What I need," Jaxxon said, his body shifting as he spoke, "is to make those serpent men pay. If I find your brother, he will also pay. No, I will find him first. They are not to blame. It is your cursed family that has done this."

Jaxxon's body grew, taking on more muscle, and his hair became the fur of a bear, tinged with the orangish feathers of an owl. A pained growl escaped Jaxxon's lips as his lips changed to a beak. The large eyes of its owl head looked down at Avery one last time before he looked up and roared at his enemies. Thomas wept as the druid's grief manifested as anger. Jaxxon sprinted away, leaving Thomas alone to face this latest failure.

He looked down at Avery and stroked his face. This was his true brother, a man who stood beside him in doubt and faith. The look on Kendrick's face burned in his mind. That was not a brother. That was the enemy. He didn't know the exact way, but somehow, Kendrick and maybe his father conspired and killed his mother. They would pay, as would anyone aligned with Klydos, the Lord of Tempests.

Kendrick called her Carina, not mother. He had called Thomas a half-breed, not a brother. He threatened to take their sisters as concubines. There was no logic to their actions. Jaxxon was right about that. If his family had bent the knee to the god of chaos, they were cursed. Insanity ruled over those who worshipped the Lord of Tempests. That much was evident to Thomas.

He waited for a few minutes, then sobered to the idea that Jaxxon might not come back any time soon. Cursing the druid for leaving him with the worst duty of all, Thomas addressed the reality of his situation. The mule Avery rode was nowhere to be seen. His horse was nearby, but with a day and a half ride left before they reached Ceylon, there was no way he could carry Avery with it. Though he despaired of the idea, Thomas would have to bury Avery here in the forest temporarily.

He found his blade and began digging into the ground. His heart wrenched as the memories of burying Janelle and Brontë came rushing back to him. The muddy ground had not yet frozen over. He threw handfuls of mud, stopping to throw up at the sight of the dirt mingled with snow and Avery's blood. This was no final resting place for the priest, but it would have to do for now. Jaxxon was in a maddened frenzy, heightening the risk that he would succumb to the primal nature of the owlbear and lose himself within.

Once he was done with that dreadful task, he set off to bring Jaxxon back. It was not hard to find the trail of the druid, marked as it was by corpses or pieces of serpent men. Without Kendrick to force them to hunt, the vile creatures fled without regard for where they went. It was no use, for Jaxxon was relentless in his pursuit. The carnage he was leaving behind suggested that the druid was recklessly attacking. Feathers mingled among the bodies, suggesting that Jaxxon was being wounded in his attempts.

Jaxxon fought a much longer battle here. Thomas struggled to find a clear path from this place, his confusion aided by the trampled ground. There were trees all around, and it was possible that Jaxxon climbed one during his pursuit and came down further away. Circling the latest kill, Thomas could not tell which direction to take.

He dismounted from his horse, stiff muscles rebelling against the movement. Seeing nothing obvious, he remounted. Thomas let the horse wander for a moment while he prayed for additional healing. Aleara, I need you. It came, but the strain left him with a headache, trading his bruised body for pain in his head.

A roar sounded in the distance. Thomas goaded the horse into a trot. Waiting gained him nothing. Wasted time would limit how much he could reason with the humanity left in the owlbear. He steeled himself for the chance that he could lose both of his friends tonight. He half-hoped Jaxxon would find the heir of Grimhorn, as Thomas remained enraged by his brother's deceptions. No, not brother. He would not call Kendrick that.

Once, Thomas and his brothers wandered away from the family procession during a visit to the grove inside Grimhorn Keep, stumbling across a family of rabbits. Without hesitation, Kendrick grabbed a stone and bashed the closest one. The boy looked at his brothers. Both Thomas and James looked at the dead rabbit in horror. The other rabbits returned, sitting and looking at their fallen kin. The older boy chased them away and threw the dead rabbit into a nearby pool. Kendrick's actions then foretold what kind of man he would become. Thomas should have recognized it. Easier to blame their father than to acknowledge that both Kendrick's viewed the world in the same way.

The duke's constant pandering to his heir only served to worsen him, and if, underneath all that manipulation, there had been service to Klydos, it was a small wonder that either James or Thomas survived their childhood. That was the lingering doubt in his mind. Why would the elder Kendrick allow two of his sons to enter service to Aleara if he were a vassal of the Lord of Tempests?

A roar brought him back to the present, and he spurred the horse on. He called upon Aleara, lighting his shield and using it to direct his steed to where the noise was coming from. It was dangerous in the dark, but light might draw Jaxxon to him, and Thomas wanted to control the search for the maddened druid. It would do him no good to be killed by his last friend and ally. Suddenly, thrashing became evident, and Thomas stopped the horse. He would continue on foot to prevent the destrier from becoming part of this latest tragedy.

He emerged into a clearing, and there was Jaxxon, still an owlbear stuck in a leg trap. The maddened druid clawed and pecked at the trapped leg, making the wound worse. The chewed-on torso of a serpent man was nearby, likely the distraction that led him not to see the trap. Either that or his humanity gave way to the primal nature of the owlbear.

Thomas approached. He could tell that the exertion was wearing Jaxxon out, but approaching and frightening him was the last thing Thomas wanted to do. Thomas waited. Though time was of the essence, he was more concerned with having the best chance to save his friend. It was near sunrise when Jaxxon finally collapsed from exhaustion. The paladin worked his way closer and pried the leg trap free, then healed his friend while he slept.

Dozing, he woke to the mighty beak of the owlbear in his face. Carrion breath washed over him. An apex predator loomed over him. Thomas expected pain and likely death until he focused on his eyes. Tears formed in them, and Jaxxon brushed his face with a shaggy paw, somehow gentle at that moment. The paladin responded, trying in vain to hold the giant limb. Jaxxon let it linger for a moment, then shrugged him off. He turned, bellowing to the sky and running off deeper into the woods.

Calling after him, Thomas pleaded for him to return, but Jaxxon never looked back. His mighty form disappeared into the thick underbrush. Those human-like eyes reflected grief, anger, and a desire for vengeance. He pounded the ground around him with his fists, each blow a reminder that failure followed him like a specter. Kendrick thought Thomas had the problem. As his mailed fists pounded the snow into the frozen earth beneath it, he reluctantly agreed with his brother.

He retrieved his warhorse and debated what to do next. He could chase Jaxxon, but there was much more at stake. The battle revealed Kendrick's true allegiance, and no one in the Duchy was safe if its rulers paid fealty to Chaos. Despondent and unsure of who to turn to, Thomas wandered back on horseback until he reached the road that led from Grimhorn to Ceylon. The horse turned toward Ceylon. Locked in his head, Thomas cared not.

He was a sight to see. Covered in dried blood and gore. A caravan came along, and the wagon master ordered one of his workers to grab the reins. Thomas left his delirium, ready to fight. They calmed him with food and drink. His tale of serpent men, a raging owlbear, and the sinister actions of Grimhorn's heir caused the wagon master to ask for his help in guarding their cargo. He agreed, pausing his introspection to guard their return to Ceylon. They passed through the gates without hesitation, and Thomas breathed in relief.

After getting the name of the caravan master and thanking him for his kindness, Thomas slipped away. He boarded the destrier at one tavern and then sought a room in another. After a hot bath and the purchase of some fresh clothes, he slipped out the window and went to retrieve his horse. Ceylon was a vast place, but it was also rife with spies. He meandered until coming at last to the perimeter of the grove. Once inside, the protective magic of the grove would prevent most from entering. He would have to assume that those who had access would be worthy of trust. Surely, Aleara could help him that much.

He chastised himself for such thoughts. It was not the goddess who was at fault. He was the weak link. Avery died because of his frail faith, and temptation from the hidden figure slowed his attempts at prayer. He would beg her forgiveness.

He suspected everyone passing by. Another part of him hoped that Jaxxon would return. Every prayer included that request. In reality, he believed Jaxxon would find peace in the deep forest, far from civilization. If they failed to counter the Lord of Tempests, it would make no difference either way. At least in the forest, Jaxxon would be surrounded by things he loved.

He hesitated for a moment before approaching the grove. If he were wrong, he was announcing himself to his foes. Despite his reservations, he had to trust someone. He snuck to the grove, trusting Aleara and High Priestess Jane to help him recover and plan what to do next. It was but a moment before an acolyte ushered him within its barriers. Here, he could recover and make the plans he would need to bring down Duke Kendrick. Also, he needed to make sense of the last few days.

CHAPTER

16

S imple tasks freed his mind to think, and Thomas was grateful for those distractions. With each scrape of the whetstone against his new sword, he renewed his desire for revenge. There was no impending battle, but Sir Silas taught him that preparation was just as necessary as the actual battle. More importantly, it was an essential distraction from the turmoil in his mind as he plotted his next move.

He returned to the grove somber and sullen, refusing to discuss the prior events. Jane gave him space and provided him with care and resources, but he couldn't shake the regret of not having sought retribution against Kendrick and the duke immediately. He needed this time to strategize, but the pressure was mounting with each passing day. Worse still was the reality that he was hiding within the grove. Did he deserve to be a paladin if he could not charge out and confront those who conspired against Aleara?

Even after confiding in Jane, who scolded him for doubting himself, he still struggled to form a solid plan. He remembered how Sir Silas would break down the opposing armies to place strength against weakness, using the skills of the various orders to maximum effectiveness. He worked on a strategy to match, but struggled with his strengths. Even though it was eluding him, he had to trust in the goddess. He thought of the events in the Threshold. Unlike past trips to that mystical place, he recalled everything he witnessed there. He could reconcile the fickle nature of the gods, but he was sure that there was no turning away from this fight. His very world depended on it.

Aleara chose him for a reason, but he questioned whether he was capable of fulfilling her demands. He confided in the High Priestess, sharing the events that had transpired at the Threshold. Thomas recognized her shocked look and expected her to chastise him for his apostasy. Instead, Aleara shared little about the source of the conflict between Klydos and his children. Within those gaps might exist the possibilities he described. She agreed to pray and consult with those more knowledgeable in such matters.

While Jane continued her research, searching for hidden figures or influences, Thomas did the same. His lessons with Avery taught him to question everything until it made sense. The world believed Aleara, Donegal, and Klydos to be the only gods, but the Threshold dispelled that notion for him. He shared his thoughts with Jane. She tried to ease his mind about it, but he kept his feelings guarded. He doubted his ability to trust. It had never been one of his traits, and recent events had only served to diminish it even more.

Ceylon reflected his gloominess. A dark and foreboding mood settled over the baron after the duchess' death, taking an even worse turn around the time Kendrick slew Avery. The flow of pilgrims remained steady, but their reception in the city underwent a change. Monsters rampaged in the forests and on the roads, causing destruction. In the days since Thomas returned to the city, fewer and fewer made it in from the road. The common folk bore the brunt of that, helpless against the aggression they faced. They turned on their ruler, clogging the audience chamber and demanding protection. Baron Eldric responded by ceasing to grant audiences to those seeking help with attacks.

Thomas was in anguish with every tale he heard. His duty tugged at him, and he struggled not to venture out and fight those creatures. He failed to understand why Eldric would not send out patrols to counter this rising tide of violence. Upon hearing another pilgrim's story, he left the group and took a walk, fearing what he might say if he stayed. Deep in prayer, he paced through the never-ending grove, hoping for some guidance from Aleara. Without any support from the barony, they might have to reach out to Godsdown for assistance. The chance that the corruption would spread all the way there kept him from doing so.

Instead, he paced and plotted, hoping for a plan to surface or Aleara to speak. Jane found him wandering the grove, a caravan of woodland creatures following in his wake. Lost in his trauma, the sight of the creatures startled him. Why would they follow him within the grove? The goddess was trying to tell him something, but he was missing it, stewing in his petulant walk. When pressed about his disappearance, Thomas confessed to feeling frustrated and angry. At that moment, an elk trumpeted. Was it a sign from Aleara?

Jane thought so. She invited him to meditate and pray with her. They spent hours together for the next nine days, asking Aleara for clarity, but their pleas went unanswered. While Jane accepted this stoically, Thomas struggled with not getting an answer. Years of living as a cast-off child made him sensitive to the lack of clarity. He wanted answers despite believing that he deserved none.

"Your childhood scars do not define you," Jane reminded him. "You are the warrior chosen by Aleara."

"I do not know how to move past them. Maybe if Sir Silas were here," Thomas said. "He always finds a way."

"You don't need anyone else's support. You need faith. When you doubt yourself, have faith in Aleara," Jane said.

"I'll try," Thomas said.

The marketplace stood half-empty, stalls abandoned as merchants fretted over how to feed their families. A woman in a tattered shawl entered the grove, clutching at her hands as she told Jane that the baron no longer sat on his throne. Jane nodded in understanding. As things worsened, an increasing number of people sought refuge within the grove. Pilgrims hesitated to journey to Ceylon. Jane provided the lone beacon of hope, her presence keeping the city from unraveling. She opened the grove to the people.

The ordinary people turned out in droves, hoping for divine intervention. While the soldiers could expect their pay to be steady, merchants and innkeepers were seeing little to no income reach them. Their prayers to Aleara had a tinge of desperation. His swollen eyes and fidgety look reinforced his belief that the townspeople were not safe behind their walls and now stood on the frontline of this cosmic struggle. Jane preached patience and faith. It would not feed the families of the merchants.

Thomas, lost in his thoughts, could not focus on Jane's urgent explanation of the dire situation. The memory of his mother's death weighed heavily on him, and he struggled to push it aside as he listened to the events unfolding in Grimhorn Keep. The guilt of not being able to save his mother was still fresh and raw. A sudden rustling of leaves snapped him back to reality. His heart raced as Lyrei emerged from the trees, her once beautiful dress now tattered and dirty. Enchanted silver shackles clung tightly to her wrists, causing her skin to bruise and bleed. Despite her disheveled appearance, Lyrei exuded an air of power and knowledge. His eyes stung from crying, but he raised them and looked into hers. Her eyes sparkled, defiant despite the cruel conditions she was enduring.

"Baroness Lyrei," Thomas said.

She curtsied gracefully, causing the silver chains to clatter together. Unsure of what to say or how to act, he sat quietly.

Thomas couldn't focus on her gestures or words. His exhaustion left him with little physical or mental strength. Doubts about the battle occupied his mind during the day. At night, his dreams replayed the fight, ending with him looking at Avery's dead face. Kendrick's shocking revelations couldn't compare to the weight of that loss. Jaxxon's anger and anguish had only added to the chaos that surrounded them all.

Everywhere he turned, those he thought he could trust betrayed him. Those he relied upon paid the price. He feared for anyone who got close to him. As for the baroness, he was reluctant to speak with her. Her Valkrunian heritage still had him on edge. Despite her assurances, she could still be in service to the God of Chaos. Betrayal and death combined to frustrate him. The plaintive look on her face softened his thoughts. She was already cast down from her lofty position. What danger could she pose?

The mention of the Serpent-Men and the knight in black armor sent shivers down Lyrei's spine. Silent tears streamed down her dirtied face, leaving streaks of clean flesh in their wake. She pulled her sleeve up and showed him fang marks. She, too, knew the dangers of the Serpent Men. They were part of the force that stormed her world.

"They are evil," she said. "Their venom causes madness. I only escaped it because my retainers jumped in quickly. I owe them pain."

Those last words came as a shout. If he took her words as truth, he understood them all too well. Their actions caused Avery's death.

"I owe them that debt as well," Thomas replied.

She took his hands in hers, promising him she would aid him in achieving that. He admired her spirit. Here she was in chains, facing a man who should be her enemy, and she was trying to give him hope. Or was she luring him into a trap? If she were part of her husband's scheming, trusting her would put a snake in the middle of his camp long before facing the Serpent Men again.

Lyrei's answers only added to his inner conflict. He wanted her to help him, to give him the information he sought about their common enemy. Silence fell over them, and Thomas waited as she worked up the courage to speak again. The days since Avery's death oppressed her as well. Baron Eldric's initial responses failed to appease his subjects. He blamed Lyrei, outing her as Valkrunian to shift the anger from himself. It worked. Peasants and guards alike forced him to act, placing her in chains for her supposed crimes against Ceylon. Her normally coifed hair and formal gown suffered in the dungeon. Before him was a broken version of the formerly regal baroness.

Unfortunately, without her calming presence and the news of Kendrick's flight from the battle with Thomas, the baron showed his true colors. He took it out on everyone. Though proud of their royalty, it did not take long for them to realize he cared nothing for them. She explained how the servants turned against the baron and sided with her despite her true identity as Ihuaj. And now, with her in chains, Eldric was free to reveal his allegiance to the duke over the King. Even as she spoke, Thomas could sense her hesitation and conflicting loyalties. A surge of anger rose for his family, considering their part in this betrayal. She sighed at his vehemence and promised to revisit him the next day.

True to her word, she arrived the next day. His retinue of animals parted at her entrance. Surely Aleara would prevent a foul creature from spoiling her pristine grove if she were an ally of Klydos. He hoped it was true. There were too many things that dragged against his ability to continue. She engaged him in small talk. It was refreshing to have something to discuss besides treachery, but his mind wandered back to what brought him back to Ceylon.

"They may be my brother and father by blood," he said, "but they are not my family."

Lyrei leaned forward, her shackles clinking ominously. "At last, the truth begins to dawn on you. Kendrick has been groomed for this, molded by forces older than Zel'Drea itself."

She paused, her gaze locking with his. "But I can help you stop him and end this madness."

"At what price?" Thomas asked. The cost was likely more than he was willing to pay.

Her smile widened. "My freedom. Yes, I am in chains, but you know what holds me within Ceylon. Free me from that, Thomas, and I will give you an army."

Thomas did indeed understand what she asked of him. He was not able to cope with Avery's death alone, and upon his return to pray with the High Priestess, he confided that to her. She gasped at the thought of Lyrei being under a spell to keep her within Ceylon. It was dark magic to bind someone in such a way, and that rattled the High Priestess. The layers of deception that surrounded her and the precious grove left her shocked. Together, they sought answers from Aleara, and the goddess confirmed that another heir of Grimhorn could break the spell.

Despite his reservations, Jane suggested that he take Lyrei's offer and free her from the spell. It felt wrong, and he shared his reservations with the High Priestess. Her counterarguments were sound, though they seemed more pragmatic than emotional. This was a harsh world, and Lyrei, though not of it, faced it without flinching. In the end, he gave in to the logic of the idea. Although he had no issues with the decision, he feared an entanglement that might skew his ability to mete out justice. Staying with Jane revealed much, but he was confident in her loyalty to Aleara. She might be taking the odd coin from a believer to help them receive their prayer requests, but Jane was a steadfast and devout worshipper of the goddess.

She invited Lyrei back to the grove. The Valkrunian woman stood before him, her youthful appearance at odds with the years and wisdom she had accumulated. She agreed to share all that transpired during her time in Ceylon. And as if these were not enough reasons to seal the deal, she had also been a powerful general in the army of the Lord of Tempests, making her insights invaluable. However, love was not mentioned by either party. This union was of convenience, an alliance forged by a common enemy.

"Jane says to trust you," Thomas said.

"If you do this, I am bound to you. You can dictate where I can go," she said.

Thomas looked at her. Her body suggested she was speaking the truth. He could see her eyes sparkling with hope. It was unsettling to believe that she would trade obedience to one lord for another. One whose future was not as certain. He thought about the conditions she endured and realized there was a strength to her. Like a strong willow branch, culled and cut to become a stave, she could bend and not break. He could learn much from her.

"Take me as yours," she said, stepping closer to him, "and I will lead you to an army of Valkrunians. Our ancient magics overcame his shackles once. We can do it again. With our kin at your side, no mortal army can stand in your way."

Thomas frowned, his mind filled with thoughts of loss and betrayal. He had already lost so much because of Kendrick and the duke. Lyrei might be strong and wise, but her motivations were still questionable. He had few allies, and their bond would prevent all but the most devious of plots. He hesitated in putting faith in anyone. However, Jane trusted Lyrei, and Thomas trusted Jane.

"What do you mean by our kin?" Thomas asked.

"Your mother, Carina, was Valkrunian," Lyrei said.

"Lies," Thomas growled.

"She was like me. Ensorceled to be bound to the duke."

"If she is bound to him, how did she make it to Ceylon?"

The binding was not impossible to overcome, but it took great strength. Lyrei explained that Carina would have fought each step, forcing herself not to turn back and not face the pain that separation from his father caused. Her body would have been wracked with pain. Lyrei fled once, and with each step, a fire threatened to consume her from the inside. Knowing this caused Thomas to weep. He had often cursed his mother for her weakness. He realized now that it was not true. The thought of his mother suffering to reach him overwhelmed the paladin, and it brought forward a torrent of grief that had been held back. He looked at Lyrei, his heart flooded by those terrible thoughts.

"How did this happen?" Thomas asked.

"Your grandfather was a noble and just man," Lyrei said. "He granted us a village to call our own, for which I served as payment to the line of barons at Ceylon for our new home."

Years passed. Human lives were fleeting compared to her people. Kendrick took over as ruler, while Eldric became the new baron. Lyrei, once a mere servant, had been elevated to a position of importance after the younger Kendrick's birth. However, it was not a happy occasion. The duke's wife had died in childbirth, leaving behind a newborn son. Lyrei recalled how Eldric had been summoned to Grimhorn and ordered to bring her with him.

"Your mother was nursing your brother at the time," Lyrei explained.

"James?" Thomas asked.

"No," Lyrei replied, "It would be easier if that were true. But the truth is far more tragic. Kendrick had ordered her newborn to be killed, and then he bound Carina to his side, placing Kendrick on her breast even as she cried for her child."

Carina suffered in silence, bearing whatever pain the duke inflicted. In letters to Lyrei, the duchess confided that the younger

Kendrick was free of her malice. She treated him like a son, despite how he had come into her life. While she embraced the situation, the duke rained down his temper upon her at every chance. Thomas clenched his fists at the thought of his mother enduring such suffering while he and James stayed behind during Kendrick's campaigns. He couldn't help but regret the harsh words he had said to his mother in the past.

Lyrei and Carina joined forces to cast a powerful spell that made the people forget about her death and believe that Carina was now Kendrick's wife. This deception was necessary for their safety and survival in Grimhorn's dangerous court. Lyrei's shocking revelation ignited a fiery rage within Thomas. Kendrick had manipulated everyone in his path to fulfill his sinister plans. Thomas vowed to bring them all down. None would be spared, not the Grey Wizards, the duke, his heir, and anyone who dared stand in his way. And then he would topple Klydos. He struggled to contain his fury.

"If what you say is true..." Thomas said.

"It is," Lyrei said. "Test it however you must."

Thomas sighed, overwhelmed by the weight of this new information.

"I need time to process all of this. Can we speak tomorrow?"

Lyrei nodded understandingly and assured him that she could easily sneak away from her controlling servants. As she departed, she urged him not to wait too long, as every day was another opportunity for Kendrick to continue his scheming. The revelations only served to fuel his resolve. Somehow, the duke believed in the myth of Nightshard and spent years learning everything he could about its possible location. The fact that it was not in his possession gave Thomas additional hope.

Alone with his thoughts, Thomas gazed out at the water, trying to make sense of everything. Lyrei left him with one sliver of hope. Faisel was his uncle. If he could find a way to free the

Valkrunian from the dungeon at Godsdown, Thomas would finally have some semblance of family again. With renewed determination, he sought out Jane. She, too, found these revelations stunning as Thomas recounted the events. He observed her expression shift from one of disbelief to one of awe as she took in all the evidence. It also explained the animosity between him and the elder Kendrick. He smiled, grateful that his hatred had an origin and was not just the pettiness of a younger brother. Jane interrupted his thoughts, asking if something amused him.

"The duke believed that sending me to the Order of Valor would result in my failure and eventual recruitment into the royal army."

"He does seem to be a master manipulator," Jane said. "I often wonder why the Council of Orders tolerates the monarchy. We name these lands as if they belong to us. Our lives are too fleeting to claim anything."

"Because fighting humans is beneath the orders," Thomas replied. "Those unworthy of Aleara's service plot those schemes."

As they contemplated their next move, they both agreed that seeking Aleara's guidance was their best course of action. Together, they shed their clothes and waded into Aleara's pool, spending time in prayer and meditation. Thomas hoped for clarity. He needed to know what to do about Lyrei. He communed with the goddess, torn between two worlds. That of his human lineage with Kendrick and that of the Valkrunians. He couldn't help but wonder what Avery would have thought about all of this. Lost in his thoughts, Thomas was suddenly brought back to reality by a tear slipping down his cheek and landing in Aleara's sacred pool.

The water flared where his tear landed. A sign from Aleara? That should have brought him peace, but the decision ahead weighed heavily on his thoughts. There was only one true answer, and he hated being forced to do anything. He exited the pool, leaving Jane to her prayers. She looked up and waded out next to him. They dressed and took a walk to speak openly.

Conflicting thoughts troubled him as he walked through the sacred grove of Aleara, with the High Priestess Jane by his side. The will of the goddess was clear. Thomas and Lyrei should join forces, freeing the former Valkrunian queen from the evil curse that bound her to Ceylon. Jane sighed in relief when he shared his decision. She dispatched an acolyte to retrieve the former baroness.

The acolyte returned, informing them that Lyrei was not far behind. A sick pain rumbled around in his stomach. He was an honorable man and knew that in making this decision, he was linking their future as well as their fates. Jane veered off the path. Thomas followed, knowing that she led him to the Valkrunian woman. A pang of guilt stabbed at him as he approached the glade where Lyrei awaited. Despite the necessity of their action, it felt like manipulation. Yet, as they neared Lyrei, he was hard-pressed to deny the pull toward her.

Lyrei looked worn from her captivity. The people respected her, but the guards feared the baron's return. Grime soiled the hem of her dress. A frown crossed her face, realizing he had taken in her state of disarray. Thomas did not care at all. This would free her from the conditions she suffered.

She had been a queen, and that still emanated from her despite her garments. Her eyes met his, and the spark within them reinforced his commitment. His heart sank as he thought of how his mother must have faced a similar moment. From what Lyrei said, Carina faced her situation with dignity and hoped that it would lead to a better future for her kind.

He stood next to Lyrei. Jane walked around and stood in front of them. She held a branch, broken in two before her. This would serve as a symbol of their union. Jane held out the branch and prayed. The words of the priestess wove a connection, becoming physical as the spirit of Aleara took form. Tendrils of green emerged from each broken half, weaving together until it was whole again. A knot at the place of joining was a visible reminder that though they were now one, it was not an easy undertaking. She blessed each of them. Before retreating, she caused brambles to grow around them, providing them with some peace as they came to terms with this new connection.

Lyrei turned to him. She held the branch Jane used across her palms. Thomas took it into his own hands as well.

"I am not one for symbols," he said.

He unlocked the silver chains and let them fall to the ground. Lyrei flexed her wrists and rubbed where the manacles chafed her skin. Thomas gently grasped her wrists, and healing energy flowed unspoken from him to her. She gasped as the skin returned to its normal color. Another sign that the goddess blessed this union. He was a servant of Aleara, and this was her gift to them. He prayed that his patroness would reveal any deception.

"I never contemplated marriage," Thomas said.

"Thomas, you are a good man," Lyrei replied. "You may be the best of both of our races. Stay true to that. I will not be a burden."

He looked at her, taking in the woman who was now bound to him, both by the silver rune on her breast and by their joining in marriage. It was a marriage of convenience. However, she was strong and proud, traits Thomas admired. He did not know how she came to be queen. She caught his gaze, a strange look on her face, and not the first one she gave him. There was a connection, though he did not know why. It frightened him. On the battlefield, he would have to make choices. He could not skew them to protect her alone. His duty was to Aleara and to the world of Binsmuth.

Lyrei touched his chest, her palm hot against the linen shirt. It was good to feel her touch. He had been deprived of that since childhood, never seeking it, but saddened by its absence. She drew closer.

She said, "Traditionally, we seal a marriage vow with a kiss. Would my Veilbreaker object to a kiss?"

Thomas could only nod his head. She leaned in and kissed him. It started gently, but passion grew from it, and she was soon in his arms. His heart was already heavy, knowing that he could easily fall for her, and that would cloud his judgment. He started to pull away, but his ability to resist faded as her lips caressed his. The brambles isolated them from the outside world. Here inside this space, Thomas forgot about all of his duties, and they became one. They were inept. She, the virgin queen, and he, the stoic knight. Despite that, Thomas feared that the sounds of their consummation alerted those within the grove.

He traced where the rune once marked her chest. Now that she was fully his wife, that curse dissipated. As she snuggled against him, he wondered if the mark had moved to him as he experienced strange emotions. For the first time in his adult life, he committed to someone besides Aleara.

"You have called me Veilbreaker twice. Why?"

"You remind me of someone. A warrior whose honor allowed me and my people to have a place in this world," she said. "It is folly, though, because you were not even born then, much less a grown man."

Jealousy. He laughed at the thought of it. This woman had just given herself to him, and he fretted about someone from decades ago. She told him of that warrior from long ago, though he drifted in and out of sleep. He awoke and found her asleep on his chest. Her dark hair cascaded down over him. He traced the scars that crisscrossed her body. Each was a reminder that he married a proven warrior, not a soft castle dweller. She moaned in her sleep. Perhaps his touch triggered a memory of one of those scars.

CHAPTER

17

News coming in from outside Ceylon presented a bleaker and bleaker picture. The minions of Klydos were ravaging the people of the Southern lands. Though they needed to turn their thoughts to Nightshard and begin their opposition to the Lord of Tempests, Thomas could not move on without retrieving Jaxxon. He feared it was too late, but said nothing to his companions. Scherie, and to his surprise, Harold agreed to join them in the search. Lyrei delighted in being able to leave Ceylon for the first time as a free woman.

Thomas considered the possibility that she tricked him into freeing her. Her actions suggested otherwise. However, he knew that deception never showed itself clearly. He watched her as they rode. For her part, Lyrei enjoyed the freedom. She caught his glance and blew him a kiss. Such a simple gesture, but it dissolved some of his doubts.

The forest echoed with the sound of their two horses traveling down the hard-packed road leading North toward Castle Grimhorn. It was but a day's ride to where Jaxxon went wild. Harold and Scherie would leave behind them, hoping to cause whatever spies lurking within the walls to question their intentions.

He recalled their journey from the grove to the city gates. Townspeople gathered along their route and cheered the couple on. The news of their beloved baroness marrying the paladin brought joy back to them. No one knew his connection to the ruler of Grimhorn. It was simply that they believed him to be a better match for their lovely baroness. Even when she dropped her glamour and revealed her Valkyrian heritage, it did not diminish the fervor of her adopted people.

The steel-shod hooves turned the dirt, and Thomas took in the scent of damp soil mingling with the leafy smell of the forest. An early break in the snow boded well for the trip, though the weather was as fickle as the Lord of Tempests. The hard-packed and unforgiving dirt road stretched out before them. He glanced over at Lyrei. She rode with a smile. A light chain shirt and stout riding boots replaced her bedraggled prison attire. She carried a thin sword, and an unstrung bow lay flat against her back.

From their planning days, he knew that these were not for show. She was an expert marksman, and though her swordplay was archaic, it was deadly. She taught him several unique maneuvers that he intended to master. Better still was his Valkrunian education. His education in the order portrayed them as bloodthirsty savages, but from her tales, he realized that, in many ways, humans were the savages.

In her world, the Valkrunians lived in peace and harmony with the land. Their version of Aleara's avatar was male, and Lyrei's predecessors enjoyed a more direct connection to him. She believed that had been their downfall. In turn, Thomas described his trips into the Threshold and the words of Klydos. It rattled her to hear that the gods wagered on worlds like pouches of coins.

Those moments gave Thomas some of his greatest joy, and it was only the lingering need to recover Jaxxon that spurred him to learn more about his bride. What started as an alliance blossomed into a true romance. He also realized how balanced they were as partners. She studied his tactics, and they worked together to become even more deadly as a pair. Free of the binding, Lyrei taught him how she harnessed the raw chaos around them to cast spells.

As he considered the bargain, it reminded him of the proposition put forth by the cloaked figure. He suspected that, like his agreement with Lyrei, engaging in a deal with that being would come at a price. The price of their marriage was selfishly wanting to protect her from danger. He forced down such thoughts, reminding himself that she survived many battles without his presence. The mysterious deity was an altogether different issue. Despite knowing that, Thomas was willing to make whatever sacrifices were necessary to end the conflict with Klydos. As they rode, he reflected on that and other tasks he needed to accomplish.

His marriage altered his perspective in many ways. Being quick to judge was foremost. Before they left, he apologized to Scherie for his initial judgment of her, learning that appearances alone did not define a person. Looks could be deceiving, as in the case of Jaxxon, the owlbear. There was no telling how much humanity remained in him.

Worse still, finding him meant going back to where Avery lay buried. His lonely grave was an insult to his service to Aleara. Thomas resolved to give him a better place to rest, although he knew the spirit of Avery was safely within Aleara's bosom or perhaps already back in some form on Binsmuth. Every length they passed raised his dread. His mind already replayed the incident, internally berating himself for perceived mistakes. His frown was infectious, and Lyrei's joy began to fade. She asked no questions, for which he was grateful. To make matters worse, the weather turned, and light snow began to fall on the road.

It was a perfect grey and damp day to visit a grave. The persistent snowfall only added to the sense of foreboding. It was a place unfit for the pious man that Avery had been. Thomas could not help but think that another loss was imminent as they ventured deeper into the woods, nearing the area marking the rise into the Grimhorn mountains.

He slowed and then saw the marks left behind, allowing him to return to Avery. Lyrei turned about in her saddle.

"Is this the place?"

"Yes," he replied. "We can wait on the road for the other two."

He heard the crackle of limbs moving and then saw Scherie's blond ponytail as she hopped from a snowbank. Harold popped up behind her. Thomas laughed at the distress on the man's face. He was out of his element. Scherie saw the surprise on his face and held up her arms, stamping the snow in a victory dance. That caused everyone to smile. Thomas was glad for the break in his brooding.

"Scherie, Harold," Thomas said, "Do I want to know how you beat us here?"

"The old man couldn't sleep, so we snuck out before dawn."

Harold grinned, saying, "Couldn't let you have all the fun, could we? We took a look around. Jaxxon stayed busy finding serpent men in the woods."

"Must have been quite a few of them to last all these weeks," Thomas said.

Scherie led them back to where they had steered their mounts off the road. Thomas cursed at missing the sight of the narrow trail and hoofprints. He pounded a mailed fist against the pommel of his saddle, causing his horse to startle, and he struggled to get it under control. His face revealed his inner turmoil. Lyrei came over and asked if he was okay. He kissed her forehead in response.

Walking the horses in, Thomas saw the first signs that Harold mentioned. Skeletons were everywhere, still held together by sinew and skin. Further in, corpses, some of them partially devoured, littered the forest floor. In other areas, scattered bones remained for scavengers to finish off. Jaxxon ruled in this forest, and the grisly displays visually depicted the fury spent on his enemies.

Thomas and Scherie took the lead, identifying clues and tracks to piece together a picture of the events that had occurred here. Trees bore the marks of Jaxxon's claws, alerting other predators of his claim to this territory. They retreated closer to the road before darkness fell. It would not do for them to be too deep into those woods. If Jaxxon went feral, he would be a danger to them as well. Two caravans stopped in their proximity and set up camp on the road. Rather than have their scouts discover people in the woods, they made their presence known. It was well received.

Since Avery's death, Jaxxon's presence in this part of the forest had quickly become a legend. In addition to tales of the owlbear, they shared news from the kingdom. Some information pertained to Grimhorn, but most centered on the giant owlbear that prowled this road. Caravans considered him a guardian and left the haunches of deer or live animals as a sign of thanks.

The news about Jaxxon was disappointing. Worse still was the news of Grimhorn. The seat of the Duchy was preparing for war, though no one knew who threatened the duke. Thomas did, and it brought a wry smile to his face as he thought about his father's discomfort. He hoped Kendrick admitted to how hard-fought his escape had been.

They reflected on the words of the caravan masters. If Kendrick was marching to Ceylon, they were unprepared to resist. Thomas also cursed, for his secondary goal of retrieving Nightshard would have to be put on hold. He thought of options and finally spoke.

"You should go back to Ceylon and prepare for an attack. Lyrei and I will find Jaxxon."

"You're headed toward more trouble," Scherie said. "You're going to need our help."

She curtsied respectfully to Lyrei. "Baroness."

"Not baroness anymore," Lyrei said, "Elara, Elara Grimhorn."

Thomas winced at the reminder of his familial name. The embarrassment of that mingled with the pride from her joy in pronouncing it. Scherie maintained a neutral look on her face, but Harold raised an eyebrow in surprise. The diminutive woman managed to sneak in a crude gesture, causing Thomas to blush again. He didn't have time to explain his recent bargain or his complicated family history. Not yet. He ignored the unspoken request to clarify.

"For now, our focus is on the druid," Thomas said. "He is not himself."

Druids could maintain their animal shape indefinitely, but there were risks. Thomas shared what he knew, mainly because Jaxxon had told him of the perils. It could be better, and it could be worse. Druids were not strong on theory. They tended to learn things the hard way. Thomas had porcupine quill scars to prove that. He spoke to Jane before their departure about the endeavor, and she told him that it was impossible to know whether Jaxxon had gone feral or not. Thomas disagreed. Getting attacked by an owlbear would be a clear sign. He hoped it would not come to that.

"He seemed half-mad on a good day," Scherie said. "This is dangerous if you ask me."

Thomas knew the odds were against him. Knowing that Kendrick was prepared to march on Ceylon made this expedition dangerous. Selfish reasons guided this trip, and he vented his frustration on Scherie.

"I can not just leave him like that. He is lost. I have to try to bring him back."

Scherie bristled at his retort. Harold placed a comforting arm on the diminutive woman. Hot tears melted the snow in front of her, and she scolded Thomas for acting as if he alone might be losing someone. The Fada woman made him ashamed. Knowing that she saw something in his friend reminded him that his narrow view of the world prevented him from seeing others in a different light.

Lyrei stepped forward, her presence radiating calmness like a soft breeze at dusk. The words were gentle yet confident. Thomas tensed, expecting her to use chaos to bring their emotions in check, but they were just kind words.

"Jaxxon's spirit is fractured, torn between the human world and his inner rage. But I believe Thomas, as someone he trusts, can guide him back. It won't be an easy task, though. If we are going after him, we must act. This mission is threefold. Secondly, we need to reach Brindall and utilize its resources. Lastly, Thomas believes he knows where Nightshard is located."

Harold's puzzled expression caught the attention of the paladin.

"What is it?"

"Isn't Brindall where the remaining Valkrunians are settled?" Harold asked.

Lyrei confirmed with a nod, "Yes, my people have made their home in an abandoned village once occupied by miners. With the right leadership, they may be persuaded to join our cause."

Thomas saw hesitation in Harold's eyes and understood his concerns. An army of Valkrunians would benefit them against their enemies, especially with the treachery around them. However, it was also risky to reveal the existence of Valkrunians living among humans. Many viewed them as mythical creatures. Thomas agonized over revealing their existence. Worse still, if the Duke of Grimhorn found out about their alliance with the Valkrunians, Thomas would not live long enough to see this plan through. His father would never allow it.

The weight of this alliance and the consequences it could bring weighed heavily on his shoulders. He trusted Lyrei's bond and promise to help them, but years of betrayal taught him not to trust easily. He could not shake the lingering doubt that she was still playing her own game deep down. The stakes were high, and Thomas knew this was a delicate alliance. In their tent, he expressed his fears.

"I know I have to trust you, but my experience has taught me to do anything but that."

Lyrei sighed but thanked him for being honest with her. She said no more. They both knew that the path to full trust lay in actions that validated it.

Despite her vague advice on the druid, Jane's suggestion to establish a search pattern proved effective. The next morning, they split up, each taking a different direction to cover as much ground as possible. This also allowed them to check in with each other along the way, as their paths intersected and created a network of search efforts. Jane suggested using a freshly killed animal as bait to lure the druid out of hiding. Thomas hoped they could find something large enough to draw the elusive creature to them. Jaxxon, now an apex predator, would consume anything within his chosen territory with voracious hunger. From the recent stories they heard, it seemed that the druid was constantly moving along the road between Ceylon and Grimhorn. The extent of his range into the forest was still unknown, causing frustration and uncertainty in their search.

As they regrouped at the end of the second day, they set up camp under a massive oak tree. Scherie and Harold were saddle sore from all the riding. They gratefully pitched their tents and leaned back against the saddles to rest their legs. For her part, Lyrei looked as fresh as in the morning. Thomas smiled at his companions. Their search grid took them deep into the forest. Tomorrow would be more of the same.

"Any ideas on where he might be?" Harold asked.

"As far away from humans as possible."

Jaxxon had been a reluctant companion at first. It was only through Grand Druid David's insistence that the druid agreed to join forces with Avery and Thomas. They bonded through their shared adventures. It was Avery and Jaxxon who were close. Where Thomas could chide either of them, he could not match their exchanges and theological musings. He could only imagine the internal struggle and turmoil that the druid must be facing. While Thomas didn't have extensive knowledge about druids, he was aware of the difficulty in maintaining their animal form. He hoped that Jaxxon was reverting to his human form frequently, giving them a better chance at finding him.

While the group settled in for the night, Thomas watched as Lyrei tended to the fire with a smile on her face. Despite the mundane task, she seemed to be genuinely enjoying herself. When she caught him staring, she gave him a small curtsy before returning to her duties. Even with his mind consumed by worry for Jaxxon, her positive energy was infectious. When Scherie returned with rabbits for dinner, even she seemed to be in higher spirits than usual. As they ate and shared stories around the fire, Thomas couldn't help but feel grateful for these moments of calm amidst their chaotic mission.

As they were about to turn in for the night, Harold emerged from the forest and joined Thomas by the fire. The man poked around in the fire, wanting to say something.

"Has Lyrei told you anything about the Valkrunian village?" he asked.

Thomas shook his head. He knew very little about the situation. The village, a former mining town left behind by Donegal's followers, existed in isolation. It had been some years since they had any direct contact with anyone. They left their contribution to the barony in the middle of the night, fearing contact with those who thought them enemies. Always correct and with no fanfare. It had been on Harold's list of places to research, but events prevented him from doing so.

Harold portrayed them as loyal but standoffish. Even with Lyrei riding with them, there was no certainty as to the response from its citizens. She felt otherwise. Thomas wondered if her optimism would be rewarded. They operated every day knowing that Kendrick sought to retake Ceylon. It anguished him to risk the future of many to save one.

"This is why Lyrei wants to gain support from the Valkrunians," Harold said. "Once we find Jaxxon and have them on our side, I should make my way to Drea and inform the king of everything that's happened."

"That would be wise," Thomas replied, "as Master of Finance."

Harold chuckled and then turned serious. "By now, I'm sure you've figured out that I am more than just a humble bookkeeper."

Thomas raised an eyebrow in question.

"I am one of the spymasters who serve the king in maintaining control over his vast lands," Harold revealed.

Thomas went through a mix of surprise, admiration, and betrayal.

"Was it all a lie?" he asked.

Harold shook his head. "The best lies are those bathed in truth. I am a devout believer in Aleara, sent to Ceylon as a Master of Finance. But I also have been working for the Council of Orders."

"The ones behind all of this," Thomas said.

"Yes," Harold said, "but I can assure you that Grand Commander Marla's words were genuine and not just staged. She has strong feelings about you, Thomas Grimhorn."

Thomas looked up, his head throbbing from the overload of new information. Scherie looked at him. Absentmindedly, she pulled the skin from the rabbits she had caught, focusing on

Harold and Thomas. She made some hand signs, none of which Thomas recognized as spellcasting. Astonishingly, Harold made signs back to her.

"She's worried about you," Harold said. "And she has a bit of a crush on your druid friend, so she asked if you were considering abandoning him."

"We will search so that it leads us close to Brindall. If we reach the village without finding him, we will have to accept the reality of it."

Dinner was uneventful. The forest was tranquil. Snow stopped falling to everyone's relief. No wind whispered through the trees. Everything was still, as if poised for the next event to occur. Scherie took the first watch. Thomas lay on their pallet, his mind drifting back to the Valkrunian village and the truth of who Harold was. Lyrei slept blissfully. He ran his fingers through her raven locks, causing her to snuggle tighter to him. He heard Scherie wake Harold. The hours were slipping away, and his mind was turning in circles, solving nothing yet preventing sleep from setting in. When Harold came to wake Lyrei, Thomas let her sleep and took both their watches. He watched the dawn, wondering how many more he would live to see.

They moved swiftly through the forest, Scherie scouting ahead with her keen Fada instincts. Today, they would stay closer together. It looked like another dead end until they came upon the first serpent man. Fresh bodies were sure signs that the owlbear was in the vicinity, though Thomas doubted Jaxxon would remain nearby. Everyone had instructions to keep Jaxxon's attention if they found him. They spent most of the morning circling in larger and larger swaths around the fresh kills. If he were near, this was their best chance.

A shuffling sound alerted Thomas to something nearby. Snuffling sounds and then the clatter of a beak buoyed his spirits. Thomas' skin prickled at the sound of it, his body preparing itself to face what was likely the remnants of Jaxxon's shattered mind, supported by the body of the giant beast. Hopefully, the others would hear him and orient themselves to the sounds.

"Jaxxon!" he said.

There was no response. He pushed through a thick wall of brambles, emerging into a clearing bathed in sunlight. Jaxxon stood at the center, his owlbear form even larger than it had been previously. The druid clawed at the dirt, eyes wild with fury and grief. The ground around him had been torn asunder, vines and roots twisted chaotically as though the forest itself mirrored his pain. Somewhere within the primitive brain was a signal telling the druid that he needed a burrow to hibernate and await the spring thaw.

He was massive. He had a thick, shaggy coat, feathers sprouting from the back of his arms, becoming fuller at the shoulders. Where the bear's head should be, it was the head of an owl, large and predatorial-looking. The feathers interspersed across its bear-like torso bristled, displaying its response to a threat. The large eyes swiveled in their sockets, and his head turned at impossible angles to seek out what lurked nearby. Jaxxon caught sight of Thomas, letting out a roar of challenge to the intruder. The paladin raised his arms, showing Jaxxon he was unarmed. Hopefully, the man inside the beast would recognize that.

"Jaxxon, stop!" Thomas shouted.

The massive head snapped up, eyes flaring. Jaxxon turned, eyes widening at the sight of the horse. The beak clattered together, sending a chill down his spine. The owlbear only saw prey. His horse whinnied, sensing the same thing, but Thomas knew the destrier would be no match for Jaxxon. It would be a good fight, but there was too much at stake, so he commanded the horse to retreat. The warhorse snorted as if to suggest it should stay, but Thomas sent it away. He could not chance either of them injuring the other.

As the horse sped from the clearing, Thomas sat on the ground. He heard a low whistle and realized at least one of his companions had found them. Without taking his eyes off Jaxxon, Thomas motioned for them to wait.

The owlbear faced him on all fours, ready to charge. Thomas called to him, hoping his name might stir some memory of who he was. He told stories of their time together, reminding Jaxxon of his bravery and the comical things that he had done. The bird-like head cocked to the side as he mentioned Avery. Thomas finished in tears, his desire to recover his friend in every word he spoke.

"You're not alone in this," Thomas said.

The head swiveled, an unnatural angle for a human, but one that the owlbear easily managed. The tufted ears pricked up, picking up some sound only Jaxxon could hear. The beast backed away from Thomas. Feathers prickled along its body. A mighty roar came from the south, and Thomas turned just as another owlbear broke through the brush into the clearing.

Jaxxon was large for owlbears. This creature was gigantic. Its height towered over Jaxxon. Significant scars crisscrossed its body, signs of past battles. Burns and puckered scars competed with the fur and feathers. It was an ancient specimen, and Jaxxon surely intruded upon its territory. Its beak, like the broken halves of a canoe, gnashed together. Thomas was irrelevant. The two owlbears focused on each other.

Quietly, Thomas slid his sword from its sheath. He invoked the goddess, sending a blessing to Jaxxon in hopes that the spiritual forces would provide additional armor against the larger beast. A glimmer enfolded Jaxxon, a sure sign that Aleara had answered the prayer. Grateful, Thomas readied himself to help his friend in whatever way he could.

The other owlbear roared again, raising its mighty paws. At the end of those paws were long and sharp claws, easily the length of a dirk or maybe more. Jaxxon responded with a roar of his own and charged. A fearsome swipe from the other owlbear sent Jaxxon crashing into the brush. Before his friend could rise, he was trapped in the beak of the other creature. Snarls of pain came from Jaxxon as it crushed him.

Thomas moved, hoping to land a decisive blow that would get the owlbear to release Jaxxon. Arrows flashed past him. Everyone knew the situation was dire. Jaxxon was in danger. As Thomas approached, the enormous head swiveled around, and a paw backhanded him. Shield came up, but it was smashed into him. The paladin flew backwards, landing in a tumble, and jumping up to charge back in.

The hair on the back of his neck rose. Lyrei was preparing something. Black light erupted from behind Thomas, striking the owlbear. It threw back its head, releasing Jaxxon and crying out from the spell. Thomas did not know what she did, but the owlbear looked weakened. Off to the side, Jaxxon was on all fours, trying to push himself up from the ground. Blood streamed from the slashes left by that massive beak.

"Aleara," Thomas shouted, "please heal Jaxxon."

Silvery light flowed over his friend. Some of the wounds closed. However, many more still leaked blood. It was enough, though, to get Jaxxon on his feet. His friend turned and pounced on the other owlbear, gripping one muscled arm in his beak. The two owlbears fell and rolled. Each pummeled the other. Bits of fur and feathers flew. However, it was not clear who had the upper hand. The gyrating motions of the two made it impossible for anyone to take a shot. Thomas held back. Approaching them meant he took the risk of getting trampled.

They disappeared into the brush. Thomas stepped forward and then jumped back. The larger owlbear emerged from the brush, cradling Jaxxon's unconscious form. The paladin called upon the goddess and ran forward, slashing at the larger owlbear. It took a look at him and dropped the other beast. Jaxxon did not move. It held up its paws in supplication.

"You," it said. "I have waited for your return."

"What?" Thomas asked.

The owlbear looked to the heavens. It did not speak, but it remained passive. The mighty head looked down.

"Who is this?"

"That," Thomas said, "is my friend Jaxxon."

The owlbear roared again. It was a distraught sound, unlike anything Thomas had ever heard. The beast dropped down and hovered over the injured druid, sniffing him.

"I did not recognize my kin," the owlbear said. "I am forever cursed. Heal him, Veilbreaker. I will owe you one last favor if you do."

Thomas flinched at the mention of that name. Too many times, it had been said around him that it was a coincidence. Still, he inched forward, careful of treachery, and touched Jaxxon. He was close to death. Healing energy flowed from Aleara through Thomas into the druid. Slowly, wounds closed. As Thomas worked on his friend, the other owlbear stood and backed away.

"One last favor," the owlbear reminded him.

"Who are you?" Thomas asked.

The creature's eyes rolled crazily. It flexed its mighty front legs and rocked back and forth. Thomas wondered if he had pushed the beast too far.

"Once," the beast said, "my name was Selvus. It doesn't matter. I owe you. Once my debt is repaid, Oldiren can kiss my furry ass."

"I don't understand. Who is Oldiren?"

"I stand here before you because of a bargain I made with that bastard," the owlbear said. "So that my son would have a chance to live. The irony that I might be the one to take his life is not lost on my feeble brain. Thinking is becoming easier, but it will be fleeting. Give me your hand."

Thomas stopped his ministrations and held out his hand. A lone claw flicked out, and the owlbear scribed something onto the gauntlet. It flared with light for a moment and then faded into the steel.

"Use that to call me," Selvus said.

The creature turned and dropped down, sprinting away from them toward the south. Thomas placed his hands on his face, trying to understand all that had just happened. Was there no end to the games the gods played with Binsmuth? Thomas closed his eyes and prayed. Goddess, please guide me in this situation. I am your champion. I am committed to that. Help me bring Jaxxon back. I need him as much as you need me. He waited, eyes closed, hoping and praying.

He looked at Jaxxon, slowly rising to his feet. The giant beak neared his face. It took every ounce of his faith to remain still as hot breath washed over his face. There was a sudden movement, and the owlbear bounded away. Thomas opened his eyes, tears streaming down his face. He was too exhausted by the moment to move, so he just sat there. This was not a lack of faith. Aleara found that Jaxxon was better suited to be a creature of the wild than a companion.

He heard another sound and looked for Lyrei, Harold, or Scherie. Instead, the owlbear came back through the thick bramble. It sat down on its haunches in front of Thomas, towering over the paladin. Thomas smiled. All was not lost. Every bit of him ached to reconnect with his friend. Together, they could mourn Avery one last time and set out to prevent Kendrick from harming anyone else.

"I need you, Jaxxon," Thomas said. "Aleara places a heavy burden on us. If you need me to, I will carry it for you and Avery. I understand."

The owlbear turned, and hope sank. It started to take a step, then its head swiveled back, and its eyes blinked incessantly.

Jaxxon let out a low growl, but there was a different sound to it. He stayed still, watching the mighty paws with their dagger-like claws clenched and unclenched. The druid trembled as if fighting an internal battle. He rose to his full height.

"You think you're the only one who lost someone?" Thomas asked, "Avery is gone, but if we let our pain control us, we fail him. Do not let your grief destroy everything he died for."

A twig snapped, and the owlbear swiveled his head, seeking the source. His companions crouched nearby, letting it play out, though they were ready should things turn bad. Thomas rejected any real danger. He held his hand up for them to hold. No matter how it went, this would not be resolved with weapons. He would rather let Jaxxon slip away and be absorbed by the owlbear than put a blade on his friend. He would only defend himself.

The owlbear began to breathe in ragged gasps, its body shaking. Thomas prayed, hoping Aleara was aiding that shattered mind. When Jaxxon spoke, the words were hesitant and foreign-sounding, coming from the owlbear's beak.

"It should have been me," he rasped, "not him."

Thomas crawled closer, holding out his empty hand to the owlbear. He stared into the owlbear's eyes. Jaxxon was part of his chosen family. It was agony waiting to see if he would lose another. The owlbear stood frozen, then it sank to its knees, and Thomas watched the druid transform. Feathers withdrew, the body shrank, and bones cracked as they returned to human form. The process looked painful to the knight, ending when Jaxxon slumped to the ground. The earth beneath him calmed. The vines retreated. Thomas dropped to the ground next to his friend, and they hugged in silence.

"It's doubtful we can win," Jaxxon said. "I couldn't even defeat my father."

"What? You knew who that owlbear was?"

"My mother brought me to see him many times as a child, probably why she hates to see me transform into one."

"You only mastered it recently. When have you had time to see your mother?"

Jaxxon laughed and said, "I've never told anyone this. My mother is Grand Commander Marla."

The paladin was again shocked by a new revelation. He could only laugh. Falling back onto the ground, he laughed until tears flowed from his eyes. If he were not so exhausted, he would try to assemble all the information into something intelligent, but he held on by a thread. The stress of missing his friend and the past few minutes had mentally drained him.

"I'm no use to you," Jaxxon said.

Thomas ignored the words. He disagreed, though at this moment, he did not care. They clung to each other. Each man was unwilling to let go of the other. They held on, embracing their shared memories of the priest as much as each other. As long as they held on, they could pretend Avery was not dead.

The other members of the search party emerged from the bramble and joined them. Lyrei touched his shoulder. Reluctantly, he let go and pushed back to smile at the druid's shaggy head. Thomas took in every feature of that face, committing it to memory. No matter what, he would not forget either of the men who tempered his hot temper and helped forge him into the man he was today.

"We should get out of here," Scherie said. "Whatever you've stirred up, it's going to come for us soon."

Thomas nodded. Exhaustion threatened to topple him over, and he imagined Jaxxon exhausted as well, but they borrowed against their future in this gamble to restore him, and every minute counted. Somewhere out there, his father and Kendrick were searching, hoping to eliminate Thomas and continue with their plans.

"We count Valkrunians as allies? How long have I been gone?" Jaxxon asked.

"It's a long story," Thomas said. "Hopefully, they have ale in Brindall."

Harold stepped forward. "Brindall's not far. If we leave now, we can make it by morning."

Thomas helped Jaxxon to his feet.

"We're going to make this right. For Avery."

"I blamed you, lad," Jaxxon said. "Forgive me."

"We know who is at fault. They are going to pay. What is this?"

Jaxxon looked at the leather cord in his hand. At the end of the cord was a symbol, a strangler tree.

CHAPTER

18

The path to Brindall was treacherous, winding through the craggy foothills and darkened woods. Jaxxon could not remember if his hunts had brought him this far, so he was no help. They talked as they rode, filling Jaxxon in on the events he missed.

Soon, the woods took on a darker tone, and words seemed out of place. It was the silence that unnerved Thomas the most. He preferred the chaotic sounds of battle to the quiet. Silence usually ushered in a buildup to something worse.

The air was thick with the scent of burning wood and charred earth. The occasional gust of wind stirred the snow. As they crested the final rise, Brindall sprawled out below, ghostly with few signs of life. Smoke curled from several rooftops, and scattered fires lit the horizon like the dying embers of a funeral pyre. Thomas pulled his cloak tighter around his neck to ward off the cold.

From this vantage, the town looked like a shadow of what it once was. Its stone structures hugged the ground, some blackened and worn by years of neglect, others still sturdy. It was a testament to the worshippers of Donegal and their love of craftsmanship. New additions caught his eye. The alien design suggested that the ihuaj were responsible. Spirals carved into beams, intricate lattices of wood weaving into patterns foreign to his eyes. He was more impressed with the martial bent of their designs. It was clear that the Valkrunians had modified the town, expecting war to find them. Even their preparations had a light and airy look, a contrast to the grim, functional stone. They were like flowers growing from a crypt.

This was irrelevant as the town was under siege. Even from the ridge, Thomas saw hulking shapes battering at the town defenses. Ironically, the snowfall's silence muted the sounds of destruction in the distance. He heard the cracking of wood, the low, guttural shouts of ogres, and the occasional scream lost in the wind. Thomas led the group forward, avoiding the ogres until they had no choice. Flakes landed softly on the bodies that littered the outskirts of the town, blending them into the frozen landscape.

"Too many," Jaxxon muttered.

Since returning from his primal state, he had been distant, and the devastation before them soured his mood even further. Thomas knew that anger was simmering below the thin veneer of civility Jaxxon managed. It had been weeks since Thomas mourned. Jaxxon was essentially grieving as a human for the first time.

"How many are left?" Scherie asked.

She sat in the saddle in front of Jaxxon and, due to necessity, became privileged in their conversations. Thomas found her to be jittery in such times. Not nervous, but ready for action. Her hands strayed to her daggers as if playing out various strategies in her head. If the scene ahead were less grim, he might find some humor in her preparations.

Not enough was the obvious answer. Crude symbols adorned the shattered outer walls of Brindall, with similar marks on the crude armor of the ogres. Each one bore the twisted form of a strangler tree, a grotesque design of roots and vines wrapped around themselves, suffocating the life they touched. He stared, seeing another detail hidden in the twisted vines. He focused and saw a faint "A" carved into the bark of the tree, just visible.

"The strangler tree? Why use that as their symbol?" Thomas asked.

"What do you see?" Lyrei asked.

"An 'A,'" Thomas said, pointing to the marks. "It is hidden, but it is there."

Jaxxon followed his gaze, his expression unreadable. Harold rode forward to get a better look at it.

"A? Could they be taunting us about Avery?" Harold asked. "Or is it something worse?"

They would have to ponder its meaning later, for there were people to aid. Another crash echoed from below as one of the ogres ripped a gate free from its hinges. The beasts roared, a deep, primitive sound that echoed up the valley walls, sending birds scattering from the treetops where they had been waiting out the snow. The time for talk was over.

A fresh burst of snow whipped through the air as the most enormous ogre yet stepped through the broken gates of Brindall. Thick pelts draped its massive frame, but even from here, the creature's crimson eyes gleamed in the light from the fires like molten coals. It wielded a club, a tree whose canopy had been ripped off.

From its war horn came a basslike, mournful bellow that echoed across the snow-covered ground. More ogres appeared from the edges of the town, drawn by the sound, their lumbering forms converging on the heart of Brindall.

Thomas looked at Lyrei, then Harold. The man looked pale, more suited to lurking in the shadows than attacking head-on. Jaxxon was silent, but his fists spoke volumes, indicating he was ready. Scherie was already moving ahead, trying to find the best approach for them. Thomas kept her in his sight in case she ran into trouble.

"We need to end this," Thomas said. "Whatever this symbol means, I will wait until after we save Brindall."

Thomas and the group descended upon the town, the snow swirling around them in thickening sheets. The town was near ruination, and flames were growing larger as they swept toward the ogres. Even with the snow coming down, the fires persisted.

They went halfway down the ridge when an ogre barreled through the remnants of a stone house, its hulking form nearly lost in the whiteout. The beast let out a roar that shattered the frozen silence, its twisted club crashing down with enough force to fracture the stone around it. Harold raised his sword only to be struck by debris. It sent him flying from his horse through the snow. He landed with a wet plop.

Thomas wheeled his horse around, jumping from the saddle to tend to the man. Harold didn't rise. Blood stained the snow where his body landed, pooling around him, the red contrasting with the snow. His breath came in shallow gasps, eyes glassy with pain.

Jaxxon let out a primal snarl, his druidic power bursting forth like the fury of a storm. He tore past Thomas, shifting mid-stride into a monstrous wolf, a blur of fangs and claws that crashed into the ogre with terrifying speed. The beast didn't stand a chance. Jaxxon's jaws clamped on its throat, tearing through the thick hide as if it were parchment. The ogre crumpled to the ground, gurgling its last breath. Jaxxon sprinted off after his next foe. He would have no lack of them. Ogres poured through the ruined gate. Luck favored them with a respite from the snowfall.

Lyrei joined him at Harold's side. Thomas could feel the chaotic energy, but she channeled it differently than he had witnessed other mages do. She was using the aether to have a positive effect. With her providing healing, he could engage. He raised his sword and stood in front of Lyrei, bracing himself for the next wave of ogres. He watched the ogres closing in and took measured breaths to prepare for the fight. The odds were not good. However, Thomas was spoiling for a fight.

Scherie appeared at his side. Blood dripped from her daggers, and icy breath billowed away as she panted from her efforts. Her skill with those tiny blades impressed him. If any ogres saw her in action, they would respect the small woman. The first two ogres went down, hamstrung, and then throat cut.

"We can't hold them off forever," she said. "What is the plan?"

"If I were Jaxxon," Thomas said, "I would say, do not die. There is no plan."

He didn't wait for her remark. Instead, he swung his sword, meeting the first ogre that charged. The impact of metal against flesh sent a jolt up his arm. He pressed forward, forcing the beast back. Two more stepped forward as it fell, and Thomas whirled around, invoking Aleara, using the energy to cleave through both his opponents. They lost, and Thomas saw something strange.

"What the hell is that?" Scherie asked, seeing the figure also.

Thomas started to respond. Another ogre lunged at them, cutting him off from the other. Scherie darted away, her dagger flashing out as she moved. Thomas was not quick enough and took the brunt of the blow. The creature's meaty fist connected with his chest, sending him spiraling into the snow. The cold bit into his exposed skin as he hit the ground hard, his sword flying from his grip. Dazed, Thomas looked up just in time to see the armored figure raising a hand, fingers splayed. Dark energy crackled from its palm, arcing through the air toward him.

"Thomas," Lyrei screamed.

But it was too late. The energy struck him, coursing through his veins like fire. Agony tore through him as he writhed in the snow, his muscles in rictus, blackness creeping at the edges of his vision. Through the pain, he saw that symbol again. The armored being had the strangler tree emblazoned on its helm. A realization struck him like a cold blade. It was a message.

Thomas struggled to his feet, his body aching and battered from the fierce battle. Valkrunians streamed out of the town, rushing toward the ogres in a frenzied rush. Thomas rose up on one elbow. His broken ribs throbbed with every movement, sending sharp spikes of pain through his chest. The armored being strode forward. It held out its empty hands, but a sickly green ray emitted from its palms, striking down any Valkrunians in its path. A burst of energy surged towards Thomas, and he closed his eyes resignedly, bracing himself for the impact.

Something unexpected happened. Another burst of energy, this time yellow and seemingly protective, clashed with the green one. Thomas opened his eyes to see Lyrei standing nearby. Her face contorted with strain as she maintained the shield cast to protect him. Thomas fought through the pain to rise and close the distance between him and their powerful enemy.

It shifted its focus onto Lyrei, casting yet another spell that sent five small arrow-like blasts of energy hurtling toward her. Her shield sprang up, deflecting the missiles harmlessly away. With a growl of determination, Thomas launched himself at the armored being. It reacted by opening a portal in his path. The paladin threw himself to the side and rolled past the portal as it closed. The armored being was nowhere to be found. Perhaps it had used the portal itself.

Thomas struggled to regain his balance, cursing under his breath. Frantic glances around the other parts of the battlefield revealed nothing of their whereabouts. Lyrei was still tending to Harold. At least he managed to keep the being from injuring any more of his friends. His thoughts kept straying back to the strangler tree emblem and the letter hidden within it. He needed answers, but the ogres would have none. Grunts were the best they could do.

A deafening roar cut through the air, and Thomas turned to see Jaxxon, still in his monstrous wolf form, tearing through a group of ogres. Blood and gore matted the fur of the druid, and his eyes were wild with rage. Attempts to get the druid's attention went unnoticed. It was no surprise. The battlefield was a chaotic mix of Jaxxon and the Valkrunians lashing out at the remaining ogres. His repeated shouts to retreat to the town fell on deaf ears.

Finally, Jaxxon seemed to hear him. The massive wolf form turned, yellow eyes locking onto Thomas. For a moment, the paladin feared his friend was too far gone again. However, Jaxxon bounded over, shifting back to his human form as he approached.

"What's the plan?" Jaxxon asked.

"That armored figure is controlling this attack somehow," Thomas said. "We need to find them."

Lyrei nodded in agreement. "Its magic is powerful. We'll need to work together to bring it down."

Thomas scanned the battlefield, searching for any sign of the armored figure amidst the chaos. The snow swirled around them, obscuring visibility and muffling sounds. He could hear the clashing of steel and screams of the wounded, but couldn't pinpoint the source of the chaos magic.

His bride looked as well. She shouted, and he turned to where she was pointing. Through a break in the snowfall, Thomas caught a glimpse of the armored figure standing atop a partially collapsed building. It raised its arms, and sickly green energy began to swirl around its form.

"We need to stop whatever spell it is casting," Thomas said. "Jaxxon, can you clear us a path?"

The druid nodded, his body already beginning to shift and grow. Within moments, a massive bear stood where Jaxxon had been. Jaxxon roared in anger and charged into the fray.

They were not alone. Valkrunian villagers were using the few weapons they had and having some success. By the time they made it to the town, the residents dispatched the remaining ogres. Thomas winced as he looked at the long, curved blades being wielded by a few of the Valkrunians. His mind vividly recalled how the nimble and mighty wizard warriors combined their might to augment the brutish creatures amassed by Klydos. Unlike his kind, they fluidly used sorcery and melee in a powerful combination.

The armored being had somehow disappeared. With its support troops decimated, the creature must have fled to regroup elsewhere. Having no other enemies to dispatch, the people of the town took notice of the newcomers. Recognition was visible on a few faces, but most held wary stances, afraid of more destruction. It would not come from Thomas or his companions. Harold slumped to the ground, and he was their sole concern.

The townspeople drew closer. Lyrei worked desperately to find whatever wound still beleaguered the man. She looked over at Thomas. He leaned in and drew upon Aleara once more, channeling healing energy into the man. Thomas did not know, but Aleara's power would find the damage and piece the man back together.

Lyrei stood and pulled her helm from her head, scratching and looking at the people around her. Thomas knew this moment was pivotal, and he feared it for many reasons. Once Harold's breathing became regular, he rose and stood next to her. She wrapped her arm around his and waited.

"Queen Lyrei," one of the Valkrunians said.

The speaker was tall and gaunt, his skin pale, and his hair fell past his shoulders in thick braids. "You've returned?"

"Yes, Kemith," she said. "I have come back to you, my people."

A mixture of conversations passed through the gathered diaspora. Did they know the reason for her absence? Some were angry, while others were relieved, and a few stood there, waiting to learn more. He noticed no children amongst them and realized that he had never asked her about Valkrunian children. Was his mixed heritage a clue to how their children matured? Or were he and his siblings anomalies?

"How were you able to escape?" Kemith asked. "Why is this the first time in over fifty years that you grace us with your presence?"

Lyrei chided the man for his tone. He bowed respectfully. She was their rightful queen. Thomas assumed that in her kingdom, explaining things to those she ruled was her choice. He was pleasantly surprised when she regaled them with the conditions of their freedom, which had been bought at her and Carina's expense. Though she endured much, Carina suffered even greater indignity at the whim of her husband.

This united the Valkrunians. Carina was lowborn but a gifted warrior and sorceress. Many fought beside her, and anger was visible on their faces. He smiled, once again amazed at how little he knew of his mother. Hopefully, he would find time to learn more from those who knew her well.

"And these humans?" Kemith asked.

"Sir Thomas freed me from the spell which bound me to Ceylon," Lyrei said. "He is your kin. Thomas is the half-human son of Carina."

The gathered Valkrunians looked shocked. They may have thought it was not possible to produce offspring with a human. They would have never considered the idea. They looked at him much in the same way he studied his first maps. They tried to make sense of what they saw. Kemith stepped forward, his eyes never leaving Thomas.

"Your word is not questioned," Kemith said. "What use is he to us? He does not know our struggles."

A human finding them did not sit well with the Valkrunians. Angry faces and muttering betrayed their thoughts. They were contemplating what to do with them. If he were in their place, the thoughts would be the same. Their location was not truly a secret.

They knew that too. He started to speak, but Lyrei put a hand on his chest, and he kept his thoughts to himself.

"Have faith in me," she said. "I led you from the burning mountain to here. Thomas is worthy of our trust."

Kemith bowed his head, then said, "We owe you our lives, milady. That much is true. Can he influence the aether?"

Lyrei explained his status as a paladin of Aleara. This calmed the crowd, and a few praised Aleara aloud. He was unsure of what the aether was, but the Valkrunians were content with her answer. She looked at him and smiled. Thomas would get an explanation from her later.

"Aleara blesses him," she said. "Let us bless him, too."

A line formed to greet them. The tall Valkrunians towered over Harold. Scherie came to their waist. Thomas greeted them as equals, shaking hands and embracing those who chose to do so. After the introductions, some left and returned with their children. Thomas smiled at the sight of such normalcy. He walked around memorizing as many names as he could. A taller-than-normal Valkrunian pulled him aside and whispered in his ear.

"You must protect her," the woman said. "Together, you and Lyrei can make this realm whole again."

"What do you mean?" Thomas asked.

"If General Caelis knows she is free, he will come for her," she said. "He knows that many of his followers will flock to Lyrei once they know she is alive."

He started to ask more questions about General Caelis, but others pushed her aside to greet him. When he looked up again, she was nowhere in sight. All who wanted to kiss Lyrei's hand came through, and Thomas was sagging, the effects of the battle fever leaving him exhausted. He said as much to Lyrei. She asked Kemith to find them someplace to stay.

"As you wish, my queen," Kemith said. "You'll find little here but ruin, my lady. We've held on, but not much more. Let me show you what we have made."

They followed the village leader. He described the last fifty years as if they were but a moment. Thomas realized that to these beings, that was very true. If anything, the Valkrunians were humble about their attempts to rebuild the village. Thomas could not help but be impressed by their work. From the starting point of the old mining town, they added their flair, mixing wood with stone and infusing their architectural style with that of the human masons. Even the old inn looked impressive, and he was thankful for the kind reception. He was ready for some sleep.

Thomas closed his eyes, and the familiar mist of the Threshold surrounded him. It billowed out, obscuring most of the objects in the distance. Close by, buildings, both ancient and modern, loomed over him. He crept forward, and the nearest brick building behind him began to break down. He turned, curious to see the change occurring. When he stopped, the destruction stopped. He walked back toward the building, and it reformed. He was sure that if he stepped inside, it would be as real as his room in Gods-down. It was as if the place were becoming stable as he neared it.

It was a curious place. Off in the distance, he spotted a ship jutting from the earth. It must have been a trick of the mists, but Thomas swore it was bobbing like it was sitting in a harbor and not buried in the dirt. Her rails and bulwarks were ornate, reminding him of the work done at Brindall. Something about the ship suggested that it was waiting to set sail somewhere.

Unlike the landscape around him, it remained unchanged, seemingly unaffected by the chaotic nature of the buildings. Was it an effect of the place, or was he affecting the place?

He shook himself from his distraction and turned back to his original destination. Before him stood his patroness, her brother, and the mysterious hooded figure. They towered over him, easily the height of a frost giant. Aleara motioned to something on the giant table in front of them and said his name. Donegal responded, suggesting she was putting too much faith in Thomas. He was about to call out and tell them what he thought of their crappy plans when he felt a hand on his arm. He looked, and the hooded figure was next to him. Looking up, he saw that he was also there.

"They can't see you," the hooded figure said.

"How is any of this possible?" Thomas asked.

"I snuck you in," the hooded figure said. "I wanted you to see the truth. To them, you are a shield or a sword. Have you ever included your shield in making a decision?"

Thomas listened intently, hoping to find the answers he needed to reach Nightshard. It sounded like siblings bickering over the last pastry. They talked of Binsmuth as if they needed to have it before their father could enjoy it. There was no compassion for the animals or plants. They were bargaining to see who might have whatever remained after Klydos did the inevitable. If this was no dream, then Thomas was beside himself with how little Aleara cared for her creations.

"She does not care," Thomas said.

The hooded figure snorted, saying, "She's lost too many times. She cares, but something must change for her to have hope."

"Am I that hope?" Thomas asked.

The hooded figure shrugged.

"The possibility exists, but you have to be the right version of you to make that happen. You need to find Nightshard," the hooded figure said.

The statement confused Thomas. The creature spoke vaguely, and Thomas had neither the patience nor the gift to untangle those words. He needed Avery's help to understand the concept. What did the being mean by the correct version of himself? Was there a wrong version?

"Can I bring my friend Avery back from the dead?" asked Thomas.

"Shh," the hooded figure said, "be careful of the things you ask for in this place. The Threshold manifests things. Not always in the way we want them to be. Find the sword."

"But I do not know where it is," Thomas said.

The hooded figure let out a deep laugh, causing Aleara and Donegal to turn and look at it. Thomas looked up and saw that the giant version of the hooded figure had disappeared, leaving only the one next to him.

"You know where it is," the being said.

"What do I do when I find it?"

"You will have to make a choice," the hooded figure said. "I hope you make the right one."

The hooded figure's words hung heavy in the air. They echoed across the Threshold, which Thomas found foreboding. He looked up at the two gods. They exchanged worried glances as they looked at Thomas and the being hidden in the robes. Thomas looked back at his companion, unsure of their nature. The hidden figure held a sword, its blue-black blade pulsing with an other-worldly energy. It seemed to be calling out to Thomas, drawing him closer.

Cryptic words spilled from its unseen mouth, though Thomas could not make sense of what was being said. It twirled the sword above its head, and a faint keening noise began to rise. A powerful force emanated from it. Over the ever-increasing wail, Thomas heard his name. It was his and had always been his. Thomas could almost feel the pommel in his hand. Greater still, he could sense its destructive potential. This fearsome weapon must be Nightshard.

Reality bent around him as he reached out towards the weapon. The vast power dwarfed anything he could comprehend. Visions of him seizing it and reshaping Binsmuth played in his head. Thomas saw himself sitting on a throne, ruling over everything. That vision replaced one where he stood looking out over a burning husk of a world. His mind saw other visions appearing in rapid succession. However, they came and went without him recalling them. He reached for the scythe. The hidden figure disappeared, reappearing next to the gods.

"If you have it, give it to me," Thomas said.

Aleara and Donegal's eyes narrowed as they watched the hidden figure step back from the tiny human. The mysterious being spoke in a language Thomas couldn't understand, but he could sense the tension between them all. It was clear that the two Gods were not pleased with this other entity. They argued for a moment, then the hidden figure looked at Thomas.

"I cannot do it," the hidden figure said. "This is but an illusion. We dare not bring Nightshard unsheathed into the Threshold. You must make the choice, and this is not the place for such a decision."

"I need that weapon," Thomas exclaimed, his frustration bubbling over.

"Yes, my child," Aleara replied solemnly. "You do. But I fear for your safety."

Her answering him rattled Thomas. She heard him. The goddess had spoken to him. Donegal looked at his sister, concern etched on his face. He crouched down to be at eye level with Thomas.

"I hope you are worth all of this risk we are taking."

"What risk?" Thomas questioned. "Your followers are not dying to save this world. Only hers!"

"Don't be so arrogant," Donegal retorted. "Life can still thrive in a world even amid chaos."

"Easy for you to say," Thomas said. "But what about those whom the Lord of Tempests destroys?"

He awoke with a start, momentarily startled by the presence of the woman lying next to him. He then remembered Lyrei joining him in his room, offering to mend him so that he might conserve his strength. What started as soothing quickly turned to passion. He held her tightly, remembering the chilling words of the Valkrunian woman.

Thomas extricated himself from her grasp and stood. He took a moment to look at his wife. She was tall and graceful, her body perfectly sculpted with gentle curves and sleek lines. Her skin, a pale ivory color, seemed to radiate an otherworldly glow. She was like a finely crafted weapon. Beautiful but deadly. Thomas listened to stories about her as he ate his meal, reinforcing his belief that Lyrei had a strong military mind and genuine compassion. He remembered his dream of the Threshold. His prayers would have additional questions for Aleara.

"It's cold outside," Lyrei mumbled, still keeping her eyes closed. "Come warm me up."

"There is no need to pander to me. You are free now," Thomas said. "A queen amongst her people."

"But you took my maidenhood," Lyrei replied with a stretch and a mischievous smile. "And I am powerless against your charms. I think I am in love with you."

"You, a virgin?" Thomas said.

"That is all you heard. Such offense," Lyrei replied.

"As much as I want to know how a centuries-old queen could remain a virgin, we have things to do. If we are to continue our journey to find Nightshard," Thomas said, "we must be on our way."

He confided in her as to the contents of the dream. Those revelations caused her to shiver. He prepared himself. That was all they could do. Lyrei agreed. If the gods started speaking directly to him, the situation must be dire.

CHAPTER

19

The mountains of the Grimhorn Range were Donegal's finest work. Steep and foreboding, their eastern slopes were snow-covered year-round. Traversing the slopes in the dead of winter was dangerous. The drifts piled up and threatened to collapse, spreading their snow into the treeline below. Icy winds howled through the passes higher up in the range.

Thomas let Jaxxon lead the way. The druid proved himself a competent tracker during their campaigns against the frost giants. He steered them clear of many a path that led others to their doom. Thomas recalled the horrifying sounds of the avalanche, the terrified screams of soldiers, and the plaintive whinnies of their mounts. Though he was anxious to know whether Night-shard was here, he would not let impatience cause their deaths.

The companions wound their way through, cursing the Lord of Tempests as they went. Jaxxon found a well-trodden trail, although it seemed very narrow. Soon, it became clear from the hoofprints that a recent herd of goats built this path, but only Lyrei and Scherie could navigate it without causing snow to fall from the narrow trail. It had been many a year since a human trod these paths. Thomas liked that, hoping it meant the fabled weapon that escaped would-be robbers. Looting was rare, but it was possible. He hoped the difficult location prevented that.

As they drew nearer, the once magnificent structure came into view, now reduced to ruins. Years of perpetual cold covered the face of the temple with icy formations resembling the teeth of a giant beast. This winter added fresh piles of snow, and icicles hung from carvings on its surface. The temple had been carved from the hill itself. It was ancient. Time and weather conspired to eliminate it. The intricate carvings that adorned its walls were now worn down and faded, but Scherie's keen eyes caught sight of one scene that seemed surprisingly well-preserved, and she pulled Thomas over to inspect it.

Thomas gasped as he took in the carving. It depicted the weapon falling from the sky, with the twin gods Aleara and Donegal standing below, possibly creating the world. Not only did it depict the scythe, but it also depicted the moment when the grove at Godsdown came into being. This was the beginning. These carvings validated the myths of his religion.

The realization sent a surge of excitement through him. He cheered at the thought that this could be the answer to their search. He couldn't shake off the idea that this was no mere coincidence. Aleara led them here. Thomas knew that he had to make a choice.

The entrance was foreboding, with darkness extending right up to it. His companions pulled back the vines, but they still obscured the entrance to no avail. Natural light refused to shine within. Thomas called upon the goddess, and she responded by shining light from the face of his shield. As they entered, they were being watched, but he could not discern the source.

Whoever carved this temple took great care in documenting the formation of this world. He stopped as they passed a carving that brought back a memory from his dreams. It was Aleara and Donegal, carved to suggest they were pleading with their father, Klydos. The rock, striated with color, glimmered as the light washed over it. Thomas recognized other figures in the carving, standing as if in an arena, watching the events unfold.

"Are we stopping?" Jaxxon asked.

"No," Thomas said. "I thought I saw something, but it was nothing."

He ventured deeper into the temple and sneezed as thick layers of dust billowed up from the floor. A musty scent hung in the air, carrying with it the weight of centuries past. This place was old. The shadows cast by his shield danced eerily on the crumbling walls, revealing more scenes of long-forgotten legends and battles. Thomas tensed as Jaxxon jumped back slightly.

"What is it?" Thomas asked.

"This place is steeped in old magic," Jaxxon said. "And not all of it feels friendly."

Lyrei nodded in agreement, her black hair catching glints of light from the glow off the shield. Like the Threshold, there was a sense that they were not in their plane of existence.

Despite their caution, they pushed on, navigating through fallen debris and avoiding patches of poisonous-looking fungi. He examined the debris. Someone carved intricate designs into wooden chandeliers, but time and decay left them unrecognizable. This was an ancient place. It may have dated back to the beginning of time. Perhaps it was the resting place of Nightshard.

With each step, an urgency he couldn't explain grew greater. He did not want the weapon to be here. He knew it was here. It was as if the very essence of Nightshard itself was calling out to him, guiding him towards it. His hand was beginning to ache from the intensity of holding his sword. He desperately wanted to take Nightshard in his hand. There were debts to collect, and the mystical weapon would give him the power to do that.

The temple itself appeared to resist their intrusion into its dusty hallways. Venturing deeper into the temple's winding corridors, the air grew thick and heavy, almost suffocating. The hair on his skin stood on end in response to the charged atmosphere. It was as if lightning was about to strike nearby. His companions looked at him. Their wild eyes reflected their internal unease. Chaos energy seemed to emanate from the very walls, pulsing with an eerie blue light that guided them toward the heart of the ancient structure. Thomas could not see the light of his shield, and it was bright.

A pull in his chest tugged him forward. His companions followed closely behind, their footsteps echoing loudly in the vast cavernous space. Jaxxon groaned with the exertion, panting like an animal. Despite his companion's admonitions to slow down, Thomas plunged ahead, praying for Aleara to calm them and allow them to reach their goal.

Breathless, they emerged into a massive circular chamber. Towering pillars loomed overhead, casting deep shadows and filling the air with an imposing and mystical atmosphere. In the center of it all stood a raised dais. Carved of a bluish crystalline material, it pulsed with energy. Upon it rested a weapon unlike any he had ever seen.

Nightshard.

The blade shimmered and glowed with an unearthly radiance, seeming to drink in the surrounding light. It pulsed in harmony with the dais it lay upon. Intricate runes adorned the shaft, shifting and changing before his very eyes. They appeared and then cascaded down the blade like snow blown down a stony path. It was a different style of blade from his own. Thomas took a hesitant step forward towards the weapon, both drawn to it and wary of its power. He could feel the energy emanating from it.

He looked away from the weapon, hoping to stem the temptation so he could make an intelligent choice. It took effort to turn away from it. Aleara, help me to know what is right to do. She granted him some relief from the tug of the weapon. This drew his eyes to the room itself. It was a stone, unlike any other, polished white, with streaks of blue within. The streaks glowed. He was unsure whether they reflected the energy emanating from Nightshard or were generating chaos energy themselves.

The surface of the walls was not flat. Carvings covered the circular room. Scenes carved in the wall depicted the beginning of Binsmuth. Though it was similar to the one outside the temple, this one was free of erosion, showing greater detail. The carving depicted Aleara and Donegal, standing in what would become known as Godsdown, with trees and mountains in the background, depicting their shaping of chaos into order. At the top of the panel, Nightshard was falling to the ground. Next to that panel was Aleara, who created the first humans and gifted some of them to Donegal. It went on and on, echoing what Thomas had been taught from childhood. Thomas and his companions moved about the chamber, looking at the interesting carvings.

Not everything was as he remembered it. One of the panels depicted Donegal taking his humans into the heart of the mountains. This was unfamiliar to Thomas, who knew very little about those who served Donegal. He knew that stonemasons, blacksmiths, and farmers worshipped Donegal, but the carving suggested something else. He pondered it for a minute and then set it aside. He wanted to know more about Nightshard. Everything else was irrelevant.

He continued his circuit around the chamber, looking for an indication of the Threshold. He half-believed that it was his overactive imagination and nothing more. Avery had often chided him for his belief that he would prove himself by doing something fantastic. Was this the culmination of his terrible childhood? He knew the weapon was behind him, and he wondered if his desire for it was to do something good for the world or to prove that he was worthwhile.

He found himself standing before a panel where Aleara and Donegal were facing their father. He hoped to have a similar chance reckoning with his sire. To defeat him and Klydos. He laughed at the exaggerated muscles of the Lord of Tempests, which were so unlike how Thomas saw him in his dreams.

Thomas wanted to solve another puzzle. He wanted to know the truth behind the trickster in the Threshold. He looked for carvings that would reveal the hidden figure, but could not find any. The paladin knew that the being was significant, frustrated by its absence from the most comprehensive depiction of Binsmuth and its immortal overlords. As if drawn to the search for him, the figure hidden in robes appeared, crawling from a carving as a large rat and then transforming. Its face remained cast in the shadows of the hood.

Jaxxon turned at the change, seeing the being. The druid's surprise turned to action. He responded with a transformation of his own, becoming his massive owlbear form. Bright orange and white feathers bristled on its shoulders and neck. The druid hissed at the being. Scherie and Lyrei turned at the sound and readied themselves for battle. Thomas held up his hands for them to stand down. He looked at his friends and back at the robed figure.

"I take it that you can see him?" Thomas asked.

"They can see me," the hidden figure said.

He looked at his companions. Their faces reflected the fear of this experience. He regretted not being more open with them about what he encountered in the Threshold. By the look on their faces, it might not have made a difference. Standing before a deity stripped them of their abilities and courage. Harold looked ready to bolt from the room. *Aleara, please give them courage.* The goddess responded to his prayer, and the energy flowed out from him, encircling his companions. He saw them relax, infused with his aura.

His prayer was not the only magical activity, though. Thomas recognized the aether in play. He looked about the chamber searching for its source. Motioning to his companions, they looked about, ready to face some new threat. An annoying buzz filled the air, which was strange in itself, given the wintry conditions. Thomas then realized the absence of a chill. It was comfortable within the chamber.

The buzzing increased. Thomas looked at the top of the chamber. An ever-growing mass of flies buzzed overhead by the sound of it. He peered into the shadows and then saw them descend from somewhere in the darkness above. The swarm of flies swirled around the room. They flew an intricate dance around the companions and then buzzed over Nightshard, coming close but not touching it. Thomas frowned. This was nonsense. He strode over to take up the sword.

"Be warned. Nightshard comes with a price," the hidden figure said.

Thomas knew the ominous tone of those words. Whatever the price, it had to be less than Klydos's destruction of their world. The hidden figure asked him again if he was willing to pay the price. Though he had not explained the price, Lyrei, Harold, and Scherie looked frightened. Jaxxon stayed in his owlbear form, ready to attack. Thomas looked from one person to another, trying to make up his mind. The hidden figure said he would need to become the best version of himself, and he was trying to determine what that meant.

"Thomas," Lyrei said, "don't do it. We can find another way."

She was wrong. There was no other way. He knew that. That was the message delivered in the Threshold. Klydos would bide his time until the dice rolled in his favor. Binsmuth had been lucky, although Thomas could not fathom why. Aleara and Donegal never changed their strategy. He was the other way. Something different for the Lord of Tempests to contend with. Thomas had been born into a family of bullies, taunted by the older squires, and pushed around by the Council of Orders. He knew that the only way to win was to stand up for himself. For the world.

"Choose someone you love," the hidden figure said. "They must die by Nightshard for it to become yours."

Thomas pondered the statement. The price was now laid out before him. It was no small wonder that the weapon lay shrouded in dust and darkness. Few could follow through. He loved Avery and his mother. He loved Aleara. Jaxxon was his surrogate uncle. Two were already dead, one a deity and the other his last anchor to sanity. Lyrei looked at him, and he knew that she did not understand.

"I have lost almost everyone I love," Thomas said. "I believe I have already counted the cost."

"There has to be another way," Jaxxon said. "I'll not die for you, lad."

Thomas smiled, knowing the druid strained to make the words come out of his beaked mouth. They were afraid, just as he should be, but he was not.

"I can feel its power," Thomas said. "I can change the course of this endless war."

Jaxxon said, "Not this way. Forget this weapon, and we will win without it."

"I cannot take that chance," he said to the druid. "I saw Aleara, Jaxxon. She needs me to do this."

The room darkened when he said the name of the goddess as if pushing back her light. It was another sign that Nightshard would have an impact. The aether grew, palpable in the air. On cue with the darkness, the flies resumed their buzzing, hindering conversation. They flew in and out, obstructing the companions, and then swirled up into his face. He gave up trying to explain about Nightshard and swatted at the flies. They avoided his attempts and swirled around the weapon.

They moved in conjunction and then landed on the floor. Thomas drew his blade. Chaos energy raged around them as the flies stretched and grew. Ear-splitting screams came from the flies as they morphed into two knights in black armor. They raised their helms, revealing Baron Eldric and his brother Kendrick.

"You're not going to win," Kendrick said. "Join us and share in the power of Klydos."

"You can even have that traitorous bitch," Eldric said. "since you've sullied her to set her free."

"Join us in the promise Klydos made to us," Kendrick said.

"Promises from the Lord of Tempests," the hidden figure said, "are fickle things. More like options than guarantees."

Thomas saw the baron eyeing Nightshard, his hand twitching in anticipation of grasping it. Thomas suddenly grew afraid. What if he came all this way only to watch Kendrick or Eldric take up Nightshard? He could not let that happen. He saw Eldric tensing, and he knew the moment was at hand. Either he took up the weapon, or he would watch it destroy his world.

Eldric and Thomas both reached for it. Kendrick did as well. There was a blinding light, and when Thomas saw again, his mind teetered on the brink of insanity. He could not believe his eyes. Thomas and the other two men found themselves within the gem on Nightshard. Through its blue tint, Thomas saw his companions staring at the weapon. While his mind grappled with the impossibility of what was happening, he focused on Nightshard. It was here with them, inside the gem embedded in the base of its blade.

The hidden figure was also here. It watched with amusement. This irritated the paladin. He would not be made a fool, not by a god or anyone. His attention drew back to Nightshard. It was as if the weapon were speaking to him. His mind roiled at the complexity of the situation.

Despite the madness, Thomas could not keep his eyes off it. He tried to focus on his enemies, but his gaze kept straying back to Nightshard. And he was full of fear, so much fear. There was no fear of failure. He feared that Nightshard would live up to its promise but be so much more terrible. There was a drumming noise in his head. Thomas did not know if it was his heart beating in anticipation or if the noise was occurring outside his head.

The runes on it pulsed, and Nightshard let out a hideous moan. The pulsing synced to the drumming in his head. Then a voice spoke. *Strike two down to become one. Choose.* It was the weapon commanding them to slay one another. Thomas considered the implications of that. His throat was parched. The mysterious figure rubbed its hands in anticipation. The armored beings didn't move, focusing on Nightshard.

When the incessant noise could no longer be tolerated, Thomas lunged for it. The two other men reached for it. He grasped it first, the scythe morphing into a longsword. He swung at Eldric. Thomas cackled as he embraced the power of the sword. He no longer feared. Glee coursed through his body. The weapon was even more potent than its legend. He needed to kill Eldric and Kendrick. The sword promised revelations if he allowed it to drink their blood and consume their souls.

Eldric killed your mother. He did not know if Nightshard told the truth and did not care. Eldric was in league with the Lord of Tempests, and for that, he would receive a sentence of death. He swung the mighty blade through the air. Eldric countered and managed to deflect the blade.

Emboldened by his success, the baron pressed in to gain further advantage. At the same time as he swung his blade, Eldric drew on the pulsing chaos energy. Thomas drew on the reserve of holiness within, shrugging off the spell attack. Nightshard and the baron's blade clanged together in a symphony of metal.

Thomas focused on Nightshard, for he no longer controlled his arm and watched helplessly as the blade manipulated him.

Eldric was a formidable warrior. His use of the sword would have been a match for Thomas, but he was no match for whatever entity Nightshard was. Together, the two men wove a wicked and sharp orb of thrusts and parries. It became a blur, and Thomas no longer experienced the passage of time. He could feel the numerous nicks and cuts on his body, but was unable to do more than witness them happening.

Eldric, too, was aware that this was more than a fair battle between men. The look on his face suggested defeat was inevitable. His posture turned entirely defensive. Nightshard connected more and more times. Each nick sent a surge of strength through Thomas as Eldric's essence flowed from Nightshard into him. Eldric called out to Kendrick for help, and Nightshard slipped past his defenses.

Eldric realized the mistake and tried to bring his blade to parry. He was too slow, and Nightshard pierced his armor like paper. Energy surged into him as the blade grabbed at Eldric's life force. Eldric dropped to his knees, pleading wordlessly until he was dead. Thomas pulled the blade free, rounding on his half-brother. Kendrick stood there with his sword at the ready. When Thomas asked who killed his mother, Kendrick only shrugged.

"She's dead. Does it matter?"

Thomas snarled. He said, "You die today, Kendrick. Here, where no one will ever know."

"Kill me if you can," Kendrick said, "but not with that."

Thomas said nothing, launching into a furious attack. Sparks flew as their blades connected. Eldric had been on the throne at Ceylon for many years, but Kendrick spent that time with a sword in hand. He would be harder to kill. As if to drive that point home, Kendrick struck first, a glancing blow that buckled the breastplate Thomas was wearing, breaking ribs. Kendrick snarled in glee and struck again, the blade slipping through to open the breastplate where it had been damaged and slicing into Thomas. Though it could do nothing about the rent in his armor, Nightshard sent more energy into Thomas, and the paladin channeled it into healing himself.

It did more, and Thomas responded by slashing at Kendrick, missing the man but striking an antler from his helm. Nightshard retook control, and a flurry of blows was launched at Kendrick before Thomas could exert his will. Kill Kendrick, he would, but not as a puppet. Thomas was now engaged in two battles. One against his half-brother and the other against Nightshard itself. The sword surged toward Kendrick's chest, and Thomas used every bit of his strength to cause the blow to miss.

"If you wish to leave this dusty place," Thomas said, "you will offer your power to me. Otherwise, I will leave you here to beg the goats to take you up."

Nightshard answered by withdrawing its supporting flow of energy, and Thomas grew fatigued from his battle with Eldric and the continued drain from deflecting Kendrick's blows. What use was there to kill Kendrick only to become the servant of whatever thing Nightshard was? The battle wore on. Thomas began to take more wounds, causing Kendrick to redouble his efforts. It would not be much longer. Better death than to lose his way.

A blow came his way, and Thomas knew that it would be a mortal wound. He no longer had the strength. In a blink, Nightshard yielded, and fresh energy poured up his left arm. Invigorated, Thomas caught the blow and forced Kendrick back. The battle shifted. It was Kendrick who now fought in a frantic way. Thomas laughed maniacally, not sure whether he won the internal struggle or would still have to exert his will upon Nightshard. Regardless, he was in control of his arm, and he intended to bring Kendrick down while that lasted.

Thomas traded blow after blow until he sensed his brother tiring. Earlier, his brother changed strategies while Thomas struggled with the blade. He faked that moment, gasped, and shrugged his shoulders, faking exhaustion as well. Kendrick smiled, falling for the ruse. He stepped in for a killing blow, and Thomas reacted. Nightshard lodged in Kendrick's throat, with a wet gurgle, the man's only response. A surge of energy ran from the dying man into Thomas.

He laughed as Kendrick succumbed to his fate, and suddenly, voices began to appear in his head. At first, it was a chorus so out of tune that it was impossible to understand the words, and then two voices separated from the clamor.

"*You killed us,*" Kendrick and Eldric spoke in his head. "*We are yours to command.*"

Suddenly, he was no longer within the gem but standing next to his companions, holding the blade. Thomas tried to ignore it, but the blade kept speaking to him in his head. It promised to show him innumerable worlds ripe for destruction. With every soul taken, Nightshard proclaimed, Thomas would become the most powerful being ever to exist. His companions rushed toward him, but he held up his free hand for them to stop.

Another voice spoke in his head. It was his mother. Thomas cried, hearing her voice. She, too, was a victim of Nightshard.

"Do not intervene," he said to his companions, "no matter what happens."

Another knight appeared, this one emerging from an inky black portal much like those conjured by the Grey Wizards of Sambor. There was little doubt in his mind what the knight came for, and he readied Nightshard to cull another enemy of Binsmuth. There was no need for conversation. He would settle once and for all the ownership of the blade.

Thomas engaged with the knight, dancing around the room, keeping clear of his companions. The blade was hungry, and

Thomas was not sure whether it would recognize friend or foe. The hidden figure did not attempt to intervene. If Thomas was its chosen champion, they were leaving it to him to prevail. Thomas knew that he had to find a way to do that.

He fought the knight to a standstill, mirroring its movements, anticipating every swing and parry. It reminded him of his time with Sir Gavrel. He knew the motion before it occurred. Some were unanticipated, but those lessons came back to him. The knight growled and fumed. Thomas realized that the biggest weakness of the knight was his brash attempts. They were reckless. It dawned on him who his opponent was. His mind reeled, nearing total insanity, as he tried to comprehend how this was possible. He tightened up his moves, scoring blow after blow as the glowing sword came near but never connected. Somehow, the knight connected, and Nightshard tumbled from his hand to be caught by the knight.

The knight pushed him away and conjured a portal. Thomas screamed, drawing his mother's attention. Inside the opening was a familiar scene. It was the room where his mother awaited him on that fateful night. Thomas saw his mother in the portal, her face shocked by what she was seeing. She responded by shooting icy blue bolts from her fingers, but they never reached him. Instead, Nightshard drew them within itself. The knight stepped through, and the portal closed behind it. Thomas screamed again, realizing the knight had somehow gone into the past. He fell to his knees. A moment later, the portal opened, and the knight stepped back through. Thomas did not have to look to know what lay on the other side of the portal, but he looked anyway and saw the pool of blood spreading out from under his mother.

He stood and advanced on the knight. Fury boiled within him, but he remained calm. The answer was in the actions. He traded thrusts with the knight, drawing on Aleara and raining blows of force on the knight. The knight backed away and then rushed forward. Thomas smiled and threw himself at the knight, smacking his blade on the knight's helm. The knight slumped forward, and Nightshard fell, only to be caught by Thomas.

CHAPTER

20

The ancient stone walls of the temple faded away, replaced by a void. He could feel chaos swirling around him. Nightshard, the cursed and sentient sword, threatened to consume his mind and take control of his body. He fought against the blade in his hand, pushing back against the entity, trying to take control. The voices of his companions came to him as an echo in his mind, urging him to hold on. He knew that Nightshard was powerful, but without him, it was a useless hunk of metal. He also knew that rather than lose control of himself, he would plunge his dagger into his own chest.

He reached out and called on Aleara, bracing himself for the worst. However, this quieted the sword. Nightshard retreated from its assault on his mind, leaving Thomas gasping as he was released from its mental grip. As the sword retreated, a multitude of voices began to clamor for his attention, each one demanding to be heard. These disembodied beings were wailing and pleading for him to command them. He tried to separate them but failed. He persisted until finally, he could focus on a single voice, only to have it fall silent. Thomas felt rather than heard the remaining voice.

"Who dares hold me?"

Thomas clenched his jaw, and the veins in his forehead stood out, straining against the incorporeal force that threatened to overpower him. The sword moved of its own volition, forcing itself upward towards his throat. Beads of sweat formed on his brow as he struggled against the unseen power.

"Foolish mortal," the sword sneered, its voice echoing inside his head. "I have existed before all things."

"Klydos?"

"You would invoke that bastard," the sword said. Its disdain for Klydos pounded in his head, leaving behind a headache.

Desperate for a way to end this contest of wills, Thomas focused on all the sacrifices made and the loved ones lost in his opposition to Klydos. His determination solidified into resolve, drawing strength from the faces of those who had suffered or died. Brontë, Janelle, Avery, and his mother. They were all there, along with countless others whose lives flickered out throughout his life. Even his brother and Eldric stood among them, adding to the turmoil within him.

Despite all of the reasons there were to give in and let his pain end, Thomas refused to give up. With fierce resolve, he said, "No. I have come too far to fail now."

With a massive effort, Thomas pushed the entity away from the precious memories of those affected by his failures. Aleara's light flooded into his mind, forcing the being into the darkest recesses of his head. He could feel its fury as he brought it under his command. Chaos magic mixed with the light of Aleara, and Thomas saw a spindly creature in his mind. It shied away from the combined force of Order and Chaos.

"Impossible," it snarled. "This should not be possible."

Thomas grinned at winning this battle. His will triumphed over the sword. As its influence receded, a terrible realization filled the void it left behind. Nightshard was his, with only the price left to pay. The horrible reality of the decision ahead washed over him.

"No," he said. "It cannot be."

But deep down, he knew it was true. To claim Nightshard, he would have to sacrifice someone he loved to its blade. Images of friends, family, and loved ones flashed through his mind, but there was only one choice. One that should be impossible, but Thomas knew it to be true.

"Mother," Thomas said.

In an instant, cold metal encased his body, and he found himself in the suit of black armor. A hundred thousand lives will flicker out forever to do this, Nightshard droned inside his head.

"We will kill a hundred thousand more," Thomas said.

A portal opened into the past before him. On the other side were the stone walls of the keep in Ceylon. Tapestries fluttered as a chill wind blew through the portal. With slow and deliberate movements, Thomas stepped through the portal, knowing what he had to do. He lifted the visor. If he had to do it, he wanted her to know it was him. He wanted her to see that she was the key to saving the world. She stood before him, her eyes wide with fear and confusion. He lifted the sword, its promise of victory held back by the blood of someone he loved.

"Why?" she asked.

"To save the world," Thomas said. "For your people, for the Fada, and the humans. I love you."

Tears streamed down his face. Thomas hated himself for the choice, but he could think of no other way of fulfilling the vow. The hidden figure appeared, and the Threshold materialized around Thomas. He no longer wore the armor.

As Thomas drew closer to the hidden figure, he noticed the faint scent of burning incense and could make out the silhouette of a man with piercing blue eyes. When he spoke, his voice had a hint of amusement.

"You chose," the figure said. "We may get to see the best version after all."

None of this made sense. Drained from the mental battle with the weapon, Thomas was even more tired of the games being played.

"Who are you?" he asked.

"After a test like that, you deserve an answer," the man replied with a sly smile. "For now, we will call me Oldiren, brother of Klydos."

"You are Oldiren? Selvus mentioned you."

"Yes, my guard dog has been on watch for some years now. You'll meet again, at least I hope you will. It gets confusing."

Thomas took a step back in shock. "Brother? But there is nothing in our religion that speaks of a brother."

Oldiren chuckled. "A convenient omission, I assure you. You may also call me the God of Chance or The Enigma, as my niece and nephew do."

"The Enigma?" Thomas repeated, trying to process this newfound information.

"Yes," Oldiren confirmed. "I'm sure you have many questions, but we must act if we are to defeat Klydos and save your world."

"How can I trust you?" Thomas asked.

"You have no choice," Oldiren replied matter-of-factly. "Like my brother, I can be fickle. But unlike him, I know that some things are better left alone. For now, our fates are bound together."

A wave of guilt washed over him as he remembered his recent actions. As they spoke, two other beings appeared. It was Aleara and Donegal, now human-sized. Standing behind them was another familiar figure. Klydos himself. Aleara and Donegal bowed before their father. Thomas looked at Oldiren and joined the God of Chance in choosing not to bow. Klydos would soon bow right before Thomas broke him. The God of Chaos looked at the two rebels with a sneer on his handsome face.

"Oldiren," Klydos sneered, "what are you plotting now?"

"Just sprinkling a little chance along the path," Oldiren said.

"Prepare to pay for your heinous acts," Thomas declared, his hand instinctively reaching for Nightshard. To his surprise, the blade refused to move. *Not here.*

"You'll do nothing, mortal. Give me the sword," Klydos demanded, "and you can have them all back. I'll leave this world alone until you're dead. You can live your life with all these precious people."

Thomas looked to Oldiren for guidance, but the god only shook his head with a knowing smile. Klydos did not act. He could feel himself sweating. The foolishness of standing up to beings capable of creating worlds was dawning on him. It was too late. He was going to make them pay for treating his world as a gaming board. It would be better never to exist than to be used in this way. He glanced at Aleara and Donegal, then back at Oldiren. Those who opposed Binsmuth were his enemies.

"Don't look to him for help," Klydos taunted. "He can give you a chance, but I can guarantee you live your life with all your precious people around you."

Thomas admitted that it was tempting. With this offer, he could rectify all his mistakes and reunite with his loved ones. Even if his Valkrunian parentage granted him a longer-than-human lifespan, he would not betray the people of his realm. He started to respond to the Lord of Tempests, but the Threshold faded away. He found himself in the temple with Oldiren. His companions were no longer present.

"Where did they go?" Thomas asked.

He looked around the empty temple chamber, a sense of unease settling over him. His companions' absence was jarring after everything they had just experienced together. This was his greatest fear. He did not want to do all this and end up alone.

"They are safe for now," Oldiren replied cryptically. "They went back to Brindall. You have a different path ahead."

Thomas gripped Nightshard tightly, still coming to terms with the terrible price of wielding it. "What path is that? Haven't I sacrificed enough already?"

Oldiren's expression softened slightly. He said, "The road ahead will not be easy, Thomas. But you now possess the power to challenge Klydos. The choice of how to use that power rests with you."

"And what about you?" Thomas asked. "Are you on our side in this fight?"

The god chuckled. "I am on the side of chance, of possibility. Klydos seeks to destroy all potential, to reduce everything to chaos. I prefer...options."

Thomas frowned, trying to parse the cryptic words. "So you will not help us defeat him?"

"I've already helped more than I should," Oldiren replied. "But I can offer you one last bit of guidance. Seek to do more than have a truce with that blade. If you cannot control it, you will lose yourself. I lost myself to it once and created a monstrosity."

"How do I control it?" Thomas asked.

Thomas watched as Oldiren faded from view. "Follow your training. It will guide you when the time is right."

Without the deity, silence surrounded him like a thick woolen coat, broken only by the sound of his breathing. He stood alone in the chamber, questions on his mind. The weight of Nightshard in his hand compounded his hesitation. He took a deep breath and looked around. He noticed that other passages were leading off from the circular chamber.

Aleara's blessing no longer lit his shield, but he could still make out the dim shapes and outlines of the surrounding objects. With hesitant steps, Thomas moved toward one of the adjoining rooms, his eyes scanning the shelves and tables lined with scrolls and books. The sheer amount of knowledge before him was staggering, and he cursed the lack of time to explore it all.

A voice echoed through his mind as if responding to his thoughts. I can give you all the time you need.

A shiver ran down his spine. He considered the possibility that Nightshard was using this as a ploy to regain control. Even if it was not, what was the price to be paid for such an offer?

"Feed me," it demanded.

A chill wind blew through the room as a portal opened into a dark place. As his eyes adjusted, he realized that it was not dark. He stood on a peak overlooking two inhuman armies camped near each other.

"Where are we?" Thomas asked.

Another world was the response he received. The voice explained that these creatures would provide him with vitality. The energy that would aid their success on Binsmuth. Thomas had no idea which army was the aggressor and said so. Nightshard laughed at his question. Did it even matter? Kill them all. If you do not take their souls, Klydos will, and he will send them back to chaos. We have much better plans for them.

As Thomas stood atop the mountain, determining how to get down to the plain, he heard a voice calling out from within Nightshard. It was a deep, resonant voice that seemed to emanate from all directions at once.

"Pick me," it said. "I will carry you into battle."

Nightshard agreed that this was a good choice, though the sword lamented the loss of that particular soul. Thomas agreed, and a form solidified before him. It was a being like none he had ever encountered. It stood twice his height, with vast leathery wings sprouting from its shoulders. Five glowing red eyes stared back at him, and long, ram-like horns curled from its shaggy head. Despite these intimidating features, its face retained a human-like shape.

"I'm Denyrus," the creature said. "I will serve you in this battle in exchange for my freedom."

"I will grant you freedom," Thomas said, "you have my promise."

The creature gracefully lifted Thomas onto its back. Sharp protrusions lined its strong, muscular spine, and Thomas found a comfortable spot between the two of them to hold on. With a powerful thrust of its wings, Denyrus took flight. The wind rushed past his face as they soared higher into the sky, the ground shrinking below them. It was like nothing he had ever experienced before, more exhilarating than any horseback ride or game with his brother James.

As they descended towards the ground, Thomas spotted the army below and pointed it out to Denyrus. In one swift motion, the creature landed in their camp, causing the shaggy creatures to jump up in surprise. Thomas did not wait. We waded in, brandishing his hellish weapon.

Amid the chaos, Nightshard howled an eerie tune that echoed through the night. Thomas could not help but join in, adding his voice to the unnerving melody that filled the air. Despite being surrounded by strange creatures and caught in the middle of the army camp, a sense of exhilaration and freedom coursed through him. He battled long past what his mortal body was capable of doing.

Thomas lost track of the number of soldiers who fell to Nightshard, but he kept fighting until the sun arose on that foreign world. When he dispatched the last, he looked across the open plain and saw that the opposing army had hastily retreated, leaving behind their equipment and tents. Denyrus approached him.

"I have fulfilled my part of the bargain," Denyrus said.

Thomas nodded, saying, "You have. Thank you."

"Good luck," Denyrus said, then his form faded away.

Thomas shut his eyes tightly, acknowledging the presence of new souls waiting there to serve one last time before being released from the horrific prison that was Nightshard. He searched and found his mother. Kendrick and Eldric were there as well, but he ignored them. Carina appeared before him. A sorrowful look was on her face until she recognized Thomas.

"Will you free me?" his mother asked.

"Tell me about your life first," he said.

"And then I will be free?"

He knew that simply hearing her story would not be enough to free her from Nightshard's grasp. Despite not wanting to cause her any more pain, he took some comfort in having her spirit close by. He shrugged in uncertainty, pretending he was not sure if he could grant her freedom. It was a lie, but it served as a small reward for all the sacrifices made as a child. Like Denyrus before her, she would have an opportunity to break free from Nightshard, but it would not happen today.

Carina's voice trembled as she recounted her painful past, and Thomas listened intently, his heart breaking with every detail. Lyrei had spoken truthfully. His mother suffered harshly at the hands of Duke Kendrick and his grandfather, and it filled him with a determination to seek justice for her. His anger served to keep in check the irony of his murdering her.

As she finished speaking, Carina's form blurred and dissipated, leaving only a faint trace of her presence in the air. Thomas found that he could still communicate with her, even though she was no longer in her physical form. Resigned to her fate as a trapped spirit within the sword, Carina began to teach Thomas about the ways of Valkrunian magic and how they harnessed chaos itself to fuel their spells. As he learned, he began to see chaos everywhere, hidden amidst order.

He saw it in the leaves of trees, causing branches to grow in unpredictable directions. He saw it in the random way shoots sprouted from the ground, defying nature's structured patterns. Under his mother's guidance, he even learned how to open portals on his own, though he could not always control where they led.

Despite his growing mastery of manipulating chaos, Thomas still relied on Nightshard for the energy to travel through time. Although he believed he could achieve this level of skill, it was beyond his reach. When they opened a portal to a beautiful world filled with lush forests, he allowed his mother to materialize.

"This place reminds me of my world," she said.

"Is it where you are from?" Thomas asked.

"No," she replied, "the sun is different here, and there are three moons."

Beings emerged from the trees with weapons drawn and shouting in a language he could not understand. Nightshard howled in fury when he refused to cut them down. It was tempting to give in to that kind of destructive force, but Thomas knew he had to resist it if he wanted to defeat the Lord of Tempests without becoming like him. Oldiren said there was the best version of him. He was still trying to be it.

Carina came to his aid, teaching him how to warp the chaos so that he could understand them. They were the Myshikl. Thomas thought they were like apes, but their bodies were different, allowing them to take to the trees and elude their enemies. Thomas learned about their society, which was also facing an invasion from Klydos, although they called him by a different and unpronounceable name here. They worshipped a god, although male, who sounded like Aleara. He prayed, hoping to sense his patroness.

His prayer caught the attention of the tribe's shaman, who came forward to speak on Aleara's behalf. She did exist here, and she was glad that Thomas was going to help her people. He still had no idea how he would save them, but her reassurance comforted him.

They journeyed to the treetop village like old friends, even though they must have seemed as alien as the Myshikl did to him. The shaman's eyes gleamed as he spoke of prophecies and ancient rituals that they followed. Thomas shivered at the expectation settling on his shoulders. He glanced at his mother's spirit, her face a mask of concern and resignation.

"How am I to save them?" Thomas said.

Carina made as if to touch him, then drew back. "Perhaps this is not your burden to bear, my son."

Thomas knew it was futile. He could not allow Klydos to destroy this world any more than he could his own. This world was another tendril ensnaring him and pulling him deeper into the cosmic machinations that he struggled to understand. Nightshard pulsed at his side, a dark reminder of the power he wielded and the price it demanded. The sword was an enigma, though Thomas was sure that the truth of it was worse than not knowing.

The following day, the Myshikl led them through the dense forest. Their unusual knuckle-walking movement forced Thomas to sprint and rely upon chaos to keep up with their pace. He could not shake the sense of being watched, not just by the strange inhabitants of this world but by unseen forces that lurked beyond their reality.

The Myshikl stopped to drink water, and Thomas was curious about what their enemy was planning. He impulsively drew upon chaos once more, attempting to peer into the Threshold. He remembered the place and tried to connect to a portal. Nightshard reacted, warning him not to disturb the veil between worlds. He stopped and questioned the blade.

"Do not break the veil," Nightshard said. "You cannot close that one."

Thomas wanted to understand more, but the shaman called for them to resume their trek. As they journeyed, he tried to piece together the fragments of information he gathered from his adventures. Klydos' influence stretched far beyond the boundaries of their world, but here in this alien forest, Aleara's presence offered a glimmer of hope. However, Nightshard adamantly refused to explain the consequences of opening a portal into the Threshold.

The shaman stopped abruptly, gesturing toward a clearing bathed in soft light.

"The sacred grove," he said. "Here, you will commune with the goddess and learn what you must."

Thomas cautiously approached the grove, his hand resting on the hilt of Nightshard. The Myshikl watched him, their expressions hopeful but tinged with fear and distrust. He knew he could not risk taking the cursed sword into their sacred space.

Desperate for guidance, he turned to Aleara. "Please," he said, "help me protect these people from Nightshard."

In response, vines burst forth from the ground, weaving together to form a tall column filled with sharp thorns. Thomas placed Nightshard inside the column and watched as it continued to grow, completely enveloping the sword. He breathed a sigh of relief that the Myshikl were safe from the powerful weapon.

Thomas stepped into the sacred grove as the air shifted around him. The light shimmered, casting shadows across the forest floor. The trees were different than those protecting the groves of his world. They formed a living cathedral, their gnarled branches intertwining. As he moved deeper into the grove, A tingling sensation came over him. The veil between worlds was thin here.

A scream shattered the peaceful calm of the grove. Thomas whirled to see chaos erupting at the edge of the grove. Grotesque, misshapen creatures were pouring from shimmering portals, their bodies twisting and reforming, and they crossed over. The warriors sprang into action, their powerful bodies a blur as they engaged the invaders.

Thomas reached instinctively for Nightshard, only to remember he left it behind. Panic gripped him for a moment before he steadied himself. He had to get the sword before something or someone else did.

Drawing on the chaos swirling around him, Thomas drew upon the power building within. With a shout, he thrust his hands outward, a wave of force flowing from them. The force sent the nearest creatures flying back through their portals, but more continued to arrive. Worse still, the veil within the grove weakened and gave way.

Chaos leaked through, eating the grove. Aleara screamed and appeared to glance momentarily at the damage Thomas had caused, then disappeared. Thomas saw the shaman drop to the ground, his spell having warped, tearing the flesh from his hairy arms.

The Myshikl fought valiantly, their crude weapons proving effective against the horrors emerging from the portals. However, they were vastly outnumbered. Thomas saw a group of Myshikl children cowering behind a massive tree root. A tentacled monstrosity loomed over them, its gaping maw snapping in anticipation of its feast.

Without thinking, Thomas leaped forward. He channeled chaos energy into his legs, propelling himself onto the thorny column. The sharp thorns pierced his hands and boots. He groaned in pain while reaching within for the sword. When he grasped Nightshard, the column withered and fell, dropping Thomas to the ground.

He ran to the children, thrusting his sword into the mass before them. It shrieked and fought against its soul being drawn into Nightshard. He turned, gleefully looking for his next battle, only to witness chaos consuming the grove and spreading beyond. He had inevitably doomed this world.

The onslaught was relentless, and the Myshikl were being overwhelmed. Thomas reached out with his mind, seeking to connect with Aleara. With a howl, he raised his arms to the sky. Light exploded out in all directions. The invaders roared in agony as the holy fire consumed them. In moments, the grove was clear.

Thomas sank to his knees, exhausted. Nightshard told him to move, and he saw that entropy was steadily approaching to reclaim this world. The remaining Mishikl gathered around him, awe and gratitude in their eyes, though they did not know he caused more destruction than the forces of the Lord of Tempests.

With Nightshard's help, Thomas opened a portal, ushering the Myshikl through into his world. He failed to save their world, but they could at least survive on Binsmuth.

CHAPTER

21

T homas made his way back to the temple, where he had previously discovered Nightshard, with the Myshikl in tow. He was
still trying to make sense of the events that had transpired in
their world. His companions were talking excitedly around him,
but he had no answers for them. He was not yet ready to reveal
the truth. Seeking solitude, he retreated to the circular chamber
within the temple to reflect on his failure.

The ruin of the Myshikl world haunted him. Thomas huddled
in the damp, stale air of the underground chamber, taunted by
the carvings on the walls. Nightshard cajoled and threatened as
the days passed, telling Thomas to forget the Myshikl and set out
to complete his quest. His mother appeared, begging him to snap
out of his depression. It was pointless. Thomas could not shake
the weight of his failure and the burden of centuries-old secrets
that lingered in this place.

Instead, he just stared at his feet, boring imaginary holes in
the stones below them. In the heart of his forsaken sanctuary,
Thomas grappled with the heavy weight of his troubled con-
science. Aleara consumed his every thought. He called upon her,
but her presence was distant. For the first time since he was sixteen, Thomas could not feel her power coursing through him.
Then suddenly, like a gentle breeze on a still night, a whisper in
the gloom brushed against his senses.

"Show yourself," he begged.

Aleara's rejection was worse than being wounded in battle. She did not need to say anything, for her disapproval was evident. As the keeper of the woods, the guardian of all living things, her paladin prayed even though she remained silent. He continued to beseech, not for himself, but for the Myshikl, who deserved a better fate than residing in this dusty cavern. Aleara remained silent, but a gesture of mercy was evident. She created a refuge for the Myshikl, nestled within the deep forest that surrounded the temple.

"Let them find peace," the rustling leaves on the chamber floor seemed to convey. This decree was not meant to absolve Thomas of his guilt but rather to provide solace for those weary souls from the destruction their supposed savior brought upon them. Every action he took left him feeling as if he were doomed to fail.

He nodded, though no one was around to witness the gesture. It seemed ironic that they would dwell just outside the temple, where Nightshard and Thomas sat in the shadows. The sword had only brought Thomas sorrow and temptation. Would they sense the tragedy that seeped from the very mountain of the temple, he wondered?

Thirst won over melancholy. He emerged from the temple to find twilight settling over Binsmuth. The Myshikl chattered amongst themselves in the nearby trees. Thomas slaked his thirst in a nearby stream, sitting on his haunches and listening to their guttural language. He listened until his guilt became too much, and he retreated into the safety of the temple.

He drew upon chaos, his powers reshaping the dais where Nightshard lay for countless years into a throne of sorts. The sword protested at first, its voice ringing out before falling silent. In the stillness that followed, he could hear the murmurs of the Myshikl outside the temple. They were sending prayers, mostly to Aleara, which he echoed, hoping that Aleara might answer them.

Some began to call for the Veilbreaker to aid them just as he had done on their world.

Thomas traced his fingers over the frayed spines of ancient tomes, each one containing knowledge that might otherwise be lost from memory. The dust of ages thickened upon the air, each mote a silent witness to forgotten tragedies. The temple library, a mausoleum of history and wisdom, loomed around him. Its cavernous shelves towered like the trees of Aleara's sacred groves. Here, amidst the relics of bygone days, he sought to unravel the tapestry of the cosmic war that had somehow ensnared him.

The weight of the volumes served as a constant reminder of his existence. He spent endless hours poring over their pages, diving deeper into the abyss of history. He pored over cryptic texts, the script as elusive as shadows on the walls. The words spoke of cycles unbroken. This temple told a never-ending tale of attempts to supplant Klydos, with no happy endings among them.

As he delved deeper into the library, whispers in his head disrupted his studies. They were faint at first, like leaves rustling in the nearby forest. They steadily grew in number and fervor, a litany of voices that brushed against his mind like a rising tide. The Myshikl, their prayers seeped in, invading his solitude. They reached out to him, the one they believed their savior, by tearing open the veil between this world and their own to save them.

"Veilbreaker," they called.

Thomas winced, rejecting the title that was like a crown of thorns upon his head. He had initially dismissed the whispers as products of his imagination or exhaustion. Time lost all meaning within the temple. As the hours dragged on and the chill of the night descended upon Binsmuth, the voices persisted. They grew louder and more insistent, filling him with suspicion. Nightshard was strangely silent through it all. Could this be another trick by the sword, thirsting for conquest? Was it serving him this song of sorrow to ensnare him further?

He found the sword in a corner of the library, covered in dust. He grabbed it, cursing the blade. It was cool and unresponsive to him. Nightshard, dormant yet never silent, seemed to pulse with malice as if it relished in tormenting its wielder. The spindly presence bounced around in his mind. It withered through disuse, but it stepped forward, ready to add its wail to the despair he could hear.

"Silence your lies," he said.

The blade was deaf to his plea for mercy, but the prayers did not cease. In the ensuing days, a chorus of souls clung to him like an anchor in a sea of uncertainty. Their words, not the sword, weighed heavily upon him. They were a chain, a duty he could neither accept nor escape. They called him a savior, but the truth was that he was a destroyer. He stalked through the rooms of the temple, trying to find peace in them. Thomas Grimhorn, once a child of innocence, was now Veilbreaker. In the darkness of the temple, his heart beat in time with the prayers of the Myshikl.

The straps on his armor rotted away over time. He no longer ventured out into the woods for fear of stumbling across a Myshikl. Walking to the entrance of the temple, he grimaced at the offerings left there. Absentmindedly, he picked up a fruit and bit into it. He flinched as another whispering plea found its way to his ears. They came in a ceaseless stream now, Myshikl voices that curled around the pillars like clinging vines, seeking him out in the temple's dimness.

"Veilbreaker," they pleaded.

Thomas heard their prayers. The name caused him to flinch. It was a title unasked for and undeserved.

"Water... we thirst," came another prayer. It was a frail plea.

Thomas gazed at Nightshard. The blade, sheathed in a rotting leather scabbard and propped against the wall of the circular chamber, offered no support. Thomas caught a glimpse of his tattered visage in the reflection in the gem inset into the hilt. He could not bear to look at it for long as the cries and screams that echoed through his mind were too much to handle.

Turning his attention to the ragged man in the gem, Thomas saw a bearded figure with unkempt hair cascading down his back. The robe he wore was more tattered than a moth-eaten blanket clinging to his emaciated frame. With a sigh, Thomas reached out and used the aether to fashion himself some new clothes.

With a sigh that sent dust flying about the room, Thomas picked up the blade, giving it a new sheath in the process. His footsteps were mere whispers in the vast chamber as he made his way to the doorway, pausing at the threshold. There, he noticed a single trail of hoofprints leading down the hallway. A brave goat must have decided that the offerings outside were mere temptations for something better inside. The thought of fresh goat meat made his mouth water. It had been a long time since he last tasted meat.

Casting a glance around, Thomas stepped over the offerings lining the hallway. Fresh fruits and other delicacies lay scattered about, tended to by devoted Myshikl followers. The air was chilly, signaling the arrival or departure of winter. He was unsure. He made his way through the snow-covered trails and found the village of the Myshikl high in the towering oaks. He put his hand to the ground.

"Water," he promised his unseen supplicants.

Where he touched the ground, water sprang forth. Thomas stood there feeling hollow and fake. After all, it was his actions that destroyed the Myshikl world. Their words of gratitude echoed through his mind, making him more conflicted. They climbed down from the trees and waved back at one curious child. When they gathered around him, he explained that he had used the power of Aleara to provide them with a new source of water. He raised his eyes to the sky.

"I did it for you, goddess," he said. "To show them that Aleara is the true power."

She did not respond. With a heavy heart, Thomas started walking back along the path. Suddenly, a young Myshikl jumped up into his arms and hugged him.

"Thank you, Veilbreaker."

He muttered the word under his breath, the word bitter on his tongue. A chorus of thank yous spoke and mentally assaulted him. He put the child on the ground, and it bounded away. The moniker clung to him even after all this time. It was the specter he could not flee. The Veilbreaker ripped their world asunder and saved them, only to cast them adrift in his world. Each step he took back to the temple echoed that name, miring him in failure. He was both guardian and reaper. He repeated the word often until he was back in the sanctuary of the temple.

"How long have I sat there?" he asked.

"Years," Nightshard said. "I was hoping that someone would stumble in and relieve me of you, but I hoped for naught."

"Do you know anything of the outside world?" Thomas asked.

"Without you to take me, I cannot see anything. Venture out. Let's find some sport to shake off this pity that shrouds you."

Thomas stood up from the throne. He rubbed his stiff muscles and gazed at Nightshard. He agreed with its silent urging to leave this place and find some answers. He was tired of sitting there. His world still existed. Therefore, someone managed to keep Klydos at bay. Perhaps he would stumble upon some good news.

He walked for a day, briefly picking up a Myshikl escort. As he traveled past their known area, they waved and turned back. He could hear their prayers in his head. Thomas continued alone until he reached Brindall, which appeared vastly different from how he remembered.

The wooden buildings were not present, and the stone buildings of Donegal's worshippers were in disrepair. At first, he guessed that after the battle with the ogres, the inhabitants fled, but he changed his mind. There was no wall. No remnants of fire. Even if he sat in the temple for years, he should have seen the remnants of that battle. He continued. It would be a long walk to Ceylon, but it was refreshing to move about after sitting for so long. It was not long, though, before the forces of Ceylon found him.

The rhythmic thud of hooves on the dirt road grew louder as the troops came into view. The leader pulled back on his reins and brought his horse to a stop just in front of Thomas.

"Where are you headed?" the captain asked.

"I am on my way to Ceylon," Thomas said.

Thomas knew the soldier was wondering how such a dirty man managed nice clothes and a fine sword. He would have questioned it himself.

"Harold, the Master of Finance, employs me," Thomas said.

"Never heard of him," the captain replied. "Ceylon doesn't have a master of finance."

Nightshard chuckled, its raspy voice accosting his mind. Thomas was accustomed to treachery by the sword, so he put little faith in the notion that the sword knew what was going on. The soldiers fanned out, their horses prancing sideways as they worked to prevent him from running away. A keening sound rose as Nightshard slithered from its sheath.

"You do not want to do this," Thomas said.

They ignored his words and stepped forward, weapons drawn, to subdue him. He spared the captain's life long enough for him to realize that he had been sent far back in time. Even farther than he expected. Nightshard chuckled at his frustration.

Realizing it was pointless to continue to Ceylon, Thomas made his way back to the Temple of Nightshard, with Myshikl guards bowing deeply and offering prayers as he passed by. The temple loomed ahead. As the day grew darker, shadows engulfed the entrance. Thomas could not help but feel darkness consume him as well, one that matched the terrible deeds he committed against those people.

He sat upon the throne, contemplating what he should do next. He pulled Nightshard free of its scabbard to interrogate the foul blade.

"What did you do?" Thomas asked.

The gem pulsed with an evil light. The raspy voice spoke to him in his head.

"There are consequences to resisting me. Though I did not expect us to get flung this far into the past," Nightshard said.

"Do I dare ask the price to return us to my time?"

"One hundred thousand souls should do it," Nightshard said.

As he entered, he could hear faint noises coming from the circular chamber. His appearance in the room startled its occupants. He immediately recognized the Fada, Scherie's folk, and could not help but smile. They looked weary and exhausted, as if they had been running for a long time. Some of them shifted away from him, their elegant movements reminding him of his companion. They looked at him with trepidation and awe in their eyes. One brave male stepped forward and bowed deeply.

"We have spoken with the Myshikl, Veilbreaker," he said.

"My name is Thomas. Nothing more," Thomas said.

The man winced at his response but accepted it. These Fada found a way to escape service to Klydos and were here seeking refuge. Thomas remembered what Harold and Scherie had mentioned to him about the Fada seeking refuge in Ceylon. He chastised Nightshard for its evil ways. His father would not even be sitting on the throne at Grimhorn. It would be his grandfather. This situation was entirely due to Nightshard's meddling. Shaking off those thoughts, Thomas turned his attention to the Fada standing before him.

"What is your name?" he asked.

"Vyjulis, milord," the man said.

"What do you need from me?"

Vyjulis pleaded with Thomas for a place to call home. Exhausted from constantly being on the run, they all longed for safety and stability. When they stumbled upon the Myshikl, it was the miracle they had hoped for. To hear that the Lord of Tempests descended upon their world and the Myshikl had been rescued was a sign to the Fada. When they learned that Thomas had saved the Myshikl from Klydos, the remaining Fada wanted the same thing. Seeing the exhaustion and desperation in their eyes, Thomas offered them refuge within the walls of his temple in exchange for their help in restoring it from years of neglect and dust. Thomas saw relief on their faces as they excitedly agreed. He knew it was temporary. For one reason or another, the Fada would relocate to Ceylon, and Vyjulis would give birth to a daughter.

The nature of the Myshikl was to stay in the forest, building their homes in the trees. The Fada, however, wanted nothing to do with the heights. Thomas wandered around, watching them develop their respective homes, but coming together to create familiar places for the two races to intermingle. The Fada had learned a hard lesson in their service to Klydos. Building a community required the involvement of everyone. Their incisive leanings would eventually help them fit in with the people of Ceylon.

Determined to make the most of his time in the past, he returned to his studies. Attempts were made to engage Nightshard in conversation, but the sword remained stubborn. Fresh souls were its only exchange with him. Thomas reminded the infernal sword that they had recently killed the soldiers of Ceylon. The sword dismissed this as insignificant and made it clear that it would not reveal any information until its demands were met. He soon tired of carrying the brooding weapon around and placed it gently upon the throne in the circular chamber. Then he brought Vyjulis into the chamber.

"Remember, my sword is never to be touched," Thomas warned.

"Never, milord," Vyjulis replied.

The Fada upheld their promise, consistently showing their diligence in maintaining the temple. They stayed out of his way but managed to keep the place clean and orderly, allowing him to focus on his research. He was so engrossed in his work that he accidentally startled a Fada woman who had brought him food. She gasped as he rounded a corner unexpectedly and quickly bowed before him, tray extended in supplication.

"My apologies," he said, helping her up.

The Fada woman blushed. "It was my fault, Veilbreaker. I should have announced myself."

"Good grief, woman, do not act like that. What is your name?"

She bowed again, then said, "Julie, Veilbreaker."

"Can we skip the Veilbreaker part of the conversation?"

Julie blushed again. He looked her over and then smiled. The Fada were as varied as humans. Something about her kept tugging at his mind. Then it dawned on him.

"Is there enough for both of us to eat?" he asked. "It has been many days since I have had a simple conversation."

Julie said, "I ate before I brought this, but if you want me to sit and talk with you, I would be honored."

"I am just a man. You honor me by conversing with me."

"You are the Veilbreaker. Man or god, or something in between. All I know is that we have found safety with you, and that makes me grateful," said Julie.

That conversation would get them nowhere, so he abandoned it. Instead, he asked her questions about their growing village and how they were getting along with the Myshikl. Once he got her past her nerves, Julie began to talk without hesitation. She reminded him so much of Scherie. He had taken the Fada woman for granted, never really getting to know her. Now that he was separated from her by many years, it pained him to have taken Scherie and others for granted. It was something that his father had excelled at. Thomas made a vow to change that about himself.

"There was a fight, though," Julie said, rousing him from his reverie.

"Oh," Thomas asked, "between Myshikl and Fada?"

"Nothing much. A group of Myshikl children had wandered away. Vyjulis wanted to help look for them. He had quite the time convincing the Myshikl that it was an honest intention."

"I like Vyjulis," Thomas said.

She gushed about the Fada leader and the things he was accomplishing for both races. Thomas suspected that Vyjulis had an admirer and resolved to tease his new friend about it. When Julie left, he resumed his research with a lighter heart and made plans to see what the two races were building outside the temple. He forgot about that for a while when he stumbled across some passages in a dusty scroll that piqued his curiosity. That kept him busy for a time. His musings also stirred Nightshard, though he ignored the attempts at conversation. He did find it interesting that one word agitated the sword whenever he mentioned it. Larisella.

One day, as Thomas left the library, he stumbled upon a joint prayer service between the Myshikl and Fada in front of Nightshard. Frustrated by their false worship, he shooed them from the temple and brooded over the event. Confused, he called Vyjulis later that day to meet with him.

"What is happening?" Thomas asked. "I told you I would teach you about Aleara. Do not encourage that foul weapon with your prayers."

"There was no worship of your sword. Our prayers go out to you, even though you walk amongst us. We are loyal to you, Veil-breaker," Vyjulis replied with conviction.

A grin appeared on the Fada's face when Thomas did not scold him for using his title. It was not necessarily that Thomas grew to enjoy it, but the weight of the combined prayers of the Myshikl and Fada seemed to be a force he could not resist. Sometimes, his presence alone was enough to fulfill their prayers. One such instance was when Julie begged for Vyjulis to fall in love with her. Instead of granting her prayer, Thomas told her to go and tell him herself. This led to their marriage.

He finally relented and allowed the Fada and Myshikl into the circular chamber for their worship. Vyjulis asked Thomas to attend so they could praise him, a request that both flattered and frustrated him. Aleara worked in mysterious ways, and Thomas was beginning to understand why. The constant attention and adoration of the two races were enough to make him want to disappear into the shadows.

Once again, they wore him down with their persistent requests, and he reluctantly agreed to be present on the anniversary of each race's arrival. Today, it was the ceremony for the Fada.

Thomas stood tall and still, a sentinel amidst the encroaching gloom of the chamber. The Fada approached him, their steps hesitant yet reverent. They bore no grand offerings or gifts, only the simplicity of their presence. Their weathered hands were ready to toil, and humble hearts prepared to serve. In silence, they pledged their fealty to Thomas, not with words but with an unspoken devotion revealed through bowed heads and quiet surrender to a fate entwined with that of their newfound deity. He looked out at them, finding a sense of gratitude and purpose wash over him. Accompanying them were the Myshikl, joining the Fada in praise of the Veilbreaker. Their apelike bodies lined the walls of the chamber, quietly praying and swaying in rhythm with the chants and songs of the Fada.

While the Myshikl would come and worship, they quickly adjourned back to their domain in the crowns of the trees. The temple, once a peaceful sanctuary for deep contemplation, now hummed with the quiet buzz of the Fada's industriousness. They glided through its halls like shadows, their nimble fingers restoring order where neglect reigned previously. Their laughter provided a subtle undercurrent, contrasting with the solemnity that once was present. The scent of incense and polished wood lingered, blending with the sound of gentle footsteps and the rustling of robes. The temple was alive with the energy of the Fada and Myshikl.

Thomas returned to the temple, his footsteps heavy with purpose. The weight of his actions and their potential consequences was a burden he bore out of necessity. His actions would set events in motion that would lead Lyrei to the role of baroness and bring about integration between humans and ihuaj. He hated the word, but it was necessary to describe the alien races he had somehow influenced in this world. Now, he needed to put the Fada on that same path.

As he entered his inner sanctum, he called upon Vyjulis to join him. Since their arrival, the Fada man had proven himself to be a kind and caring leader of the diaspora. He bowed deeply to Thomas. The paladin waved at him to stop and motioned for him to sit. They settled onto cushions scattered around his makeshift home within the temple walls.

"Yes, Veilbreaker," Vyjulis said. "How may I be of assistance?"

Thomas couldn't help but cringe at the title bestowed upon him by the Fada. It only reminded him of Nightshard, his sentient sword, feeding off their prayers and beliefs in him. Though many of their prayers were minor, Thomas could not help but feel regret at their mistaken belief in him. They needed to seek Aleara. She was the true deity. No manner of explanation had steered them from their false worship of him.

Setting aside these thoughts, Thomas explained his plan to Vyjulis, omitting the part where he came from the future. Instead, he drew from the details of his conversations with Scherie and reassured Vyjulis that by the time his daughter grew to adulthood, humans would accept their kind. This caused Vyjulis to bow before him in gratitude, thanking him for the gift of a daughter.

"A daughter," Vyjulis repeated with wonder. "I never thought I would live long enough to see a Fada child of my own. If it is your will, Veilbreaker," he said with reverence, "we will make the journey to Ceylon."

Thomas shook his head slightly. "It has nothing to do with my will, Vyjulis. It is about opportunity. Your people can have a true home again and no longer have to eke out a life in this musty temple. You deserve so much more."

He saw the uncertainty in Vyjulis' eyes, and he knew all too well what it felt like to face an uncertain future. Lately, every action he took was one of doubt and uncertainty. It was those feelings that kept him trapped within the temple.

"If you do decide to go, I will not be joining you," Thomas stated. "My journey takes me in a different direction. But I will stay with you long enough to teach you about Aleara and her ways."

"We owe you our lives," Vyjulis said. "You are a better god than what we had."

Thomas shook his head again.

"I am no god," Thomas said. "My powers come from Aleara, the goddess of Nature."

"Forgive me, Veilbreaker, but you do more than command the forces of nature. We have heard the stories of the Myshikl."

"It is not easy to explain," Thomas said. "Sometimes stories grow beyond the simple truth."

Vyjulis replied, "We respect the mysteries of your existence, Veilbreaker. We are forever grateful for your protection."

Thomas threw a pillow in frustration. Were there no words that would get them to accept the truth? Vyjulis was not an ignorant person. This was not blind faith. He fumed at his inability to get them to understand. He took a deep breath, apologized, and looked at the Fada, who was mustering the courage to speak.

"It is difficult for us," Vyjulis said. "You brought us freedom, for which we are eternally grateful. However, we now face uncertainty in ways we have never faced before. We are not accustomed to guiding our own lives. For generations, we served at the whim of the Lord of Tempests."

Thomas had not expected that. Though longer-lived than humans, the Fada had been controlled by Klydos for a very long time. Free will was an unexplored concept to them. A heavy silence fell between them as each grappled with the problems before them. Thomas had always known that there would be strife with Klydos, and as a soldier of Aleara, his life was committed to combating chaos. In that moment with Vyjulis, a kinship formed. The Fada was desperate to prove his worth, but he was burdened by doubt. Thomas understood that all too well.

"You will be tested," Thomas said. "But one day, you will work alongside humans with pride."

Vyjulis's eyes widened at the thought, hope rising in that look. It would take a strong constitution to take the harassment. The Fada would be treated poorly for many years before they would be accepted, and even then, it would only be in the backwater province of Ceylon.

"You claim to be no god," he said, "but your actions suggest otherwise."

"I have seen glimpses of the future," Thomas said. "Prepare for a trip. Remember, it will be hard, but it will be worth it."

He enjoyed their laughter one last time before leading Vyjulis and his people to Ceylon.

As he made his way back to the temple, Thomas couldn't help but question if he was making the right decisions. Did he have the right to influence the futures of both Valkrunians and Fada? Though he now respected Scherie, he couldn't help but wonder if she would approve of his actions. If she knew he could have prevented her people's suffering, would she still look at him in the same way?

And soon, Lyrei would cross paths with both him and the Fada again. The fierce warrior-queen would face yet another test of her strength.

***

He left the Fada on the outskirts of Ceylon, not wanting to mingle amongst its people. Julie and Vyjulis lingered the longest. He would miss them, almost as much as he missed those he had left behind in the future. They promised to pray to him many times a day to remind him of what he meant to them. He promised to do his best to answer their prayers, but deep down, he knew that they would turn to Aleara and forget about the Veilbreaker. Despite this, a small part of him longed for their voices in his head, reminding him of his purpose.

"You still have me," Nightshard reminded him, "and the Myshikl. I can talk to you as much as you want."

Thomas tried to fight off the loneliness as he replied, "But you are not the same as having human companionship. Aleara, please do not leave me with this as my only source of companionship."

That night, Aleara fulfilled his prayer by taking him to the Threshold. As the landscape changed around them, Thomas couldn't shake the notion that this was where the gods plotted their games and made pawns out of mortals like himself. With newfound knowledge and power, Thomas was able to stabilize a larger portion of the shifting realm. Whether it was a real place or not, it was responding to his will.

Aleara appeared before him, accompanied by her brother and uncle. The goddess was impressed by how Thomas suppressed the changes to the Threshold.

"You've come a long way, my precious knight," Aleara said.

Thomas laughed and said, "Living beyond one mortal lifetime has that effect. I am tired of waiting for you and Donegal to contain the Lord of Tempests. I have decided to throw some chaos of my own into your game."

"Your followers see you as a god," Oldiren replied. "Use their faith to your advantage."

"No, they need to have faith in Aleara," Thomas said.

"While you've been playing godling," Donegal interjected, "Klydos brings a new player onto the board. One that won't be so easily defeated."

"Klydos turned to dark magic, something we once agreed not to do," Oldiren added gravely. "There is a new force growing, one that could undo everything we have worked for on Binsmuth."

The gods exchanged troubled looks before Aleara spoke, her voice filled with sorrow.

"Thomas, what my brother speaks of is far more dire than you can imagine," she said. "Klydos opens rifts between realms, unleashing monstrous beings and unknown races into this world."

Oldiren said, "Picture armies of creatures we have never seen before on Binsmuth. Beings with multiple limbs and eyes that glow with otherworldly power, humanoids with skin like bark and blood like sap, beasts that defy all logic and description."

"These invaders pour through portals that scar the very fabric of our world," Donegal said. "They bring with them magics foreign to this realm."

A chill ran down his spine as he tried to comprehend the scale of this new threat. He did not have much faith in Donegal. Even as he saw the God of the Land and Sea before him, he could not remember the last time that the god or his followers had actively opposed the Lord of Tempests. They offered their crops and products of the smithies, but they were not evident on the battlefield.

"We must act now! Could you take me to the battlefield? With Nightshard's help, I can stop this invasion before it consumes us all."

Aleara shook her head, her eyes filled with a mixture of compassion and sadness.

"We cannot, Thomas. Your presence there would only drive Klydos to even more desperate measures. Already, he threatens to collapse entire planes of existence to fuel his conquest."

Oldiren weighed their options, a grave expression on his face.

"Yes," the God of Chance said. "My brother's madness knows no bounds. If pushed too far, he may attempt to merge entire realms...a cataclysm that could erase everything we know about reality."

Donegal said, "Is he the champion we need in this darkest hour? Even now, I'm reminded of Grand Commander Marla's doubts. She saw you as reckless and impulsive. Qualities that could spell doom for us all in this delicate game of cosmic strategy."

"How do you know of that?" Thomas yelled.

As Donegal turned his gaze from Oldiren to Thomas, a knot formed in the pit of his stomach.

"We have been watching your entire life, boy."

Thomas bristled at the reminder, but before he could retort, Aleara stepped in.

"Peace, brother," she said. "His recent actions, while unorthodox, have shifted the tides in ways we could not have predicted."

The gods debated while the paladin's mind raced with visions of the horrors being unleashed upon Binsmuth. He imagined cities crumbling under the assault of impossible siege engines, forests withering as alien spores took root, and the very sky itself tearing apart to reveal nightmare realms beyond. The weight of responsibility pressed down upon him like a physical force. Each thought was heavier than the last.

His hand strayed to the hilt of Nightshard. He had discovered much in the temple, but nothing about the nature of that infernal blade. Hints that he feared to say aloud should they be actual. Aleara cleared her throat, drawing his attention. Despite his contact with the goddess, he remained in awe of her, amazed that she had chosen him to channel her powers through.

"What are you that Klydos could fall to you?" Aleara asked. "Is it you or that weapon you wield? I am afraid to know the truth either way."

"It is not me," Nightshard spoke confidently. "It is you, backed by your worshippers. They call you Veilbreaker. You should believe them."

Thomas could feel the overwhelming power and confidence radiating from Nightshard's words, and his doubts began to fade away. But before he could embrace this new path, Donegal's booming voice pierced through the air and shook him out of his thoughts. The god's hand was outstretched towards Thomas, demanding the blade.

The order came from a god, but Thomas only heard his father speaking. His lip curled into a snarl. He was no longer a child who could be bullied. Nightshard howled, causing the three gods to take a step back. It was too late for Donegal as Thomas pulled the sword free from its scabbard and plunged it into the neck of the god. Whatever admonition Donegal tried to utter ended as the width of the blade severed vocal cords.

Thomas expected the head to fall from his shoulders, but somehow, Donegal managed to stay upright. He pulled at the sword, trying to free himself from it. Fear became visible on the god's face. Thomas drank in the energy, wondering why the being felt any different than when other avatars fell to Klydos.

"He falls to us. Everything changes now," Nightshard howled.

Energy surged up the sword and into his body, overwhelming him with powerful sensations and information. But during this chaos, a calming presence joined him. Aleara came to his side, her expression concerned yet determined. Thomas stared at Donegal's crumpled form, blood pooling around the god's body. The sword pulsed in his hand, radiating dark satisfaction.

"What have you done?" Aleara asked.

"I...I didn't mean to," Thomas said. "The sword..."

Oldiren's eyes narrowed. "Did it? Or did you give in to its whispers of power?"

Thomas opened his mouth to protest, but found he couldn't deny it. Part of him wanted this, craved the rush of godly energy flowing into him as Donegal fell. Mortal lives fed him like a fine court meal. Donegal's life force was intoxicating, and he could feel his mind and body evolving. For a second, he considered letting Nightshard drink of the god, then pulled the blade free. The sword twisted in his grip.

Even now, his mind was processing things that he had never understood before. He looked out at the ever-changing landscape of the Threshold, demanding that it stop. The dance between entropy and order slowed, then came to a halt. Aleara looked up. Like Oldiren, the latest turn of events shocked her. Thomas ignored their shocked faces. He had not asked for this, but since it had been thrust upon him, he would not shirk the duty.

"He's not dead," She said. "Return his life force to him."

"Goddess," Thomas said. "I will return when I have forced your father to leave my world alone."

"Take them both," Nightshard howled, "and finish Donegal. Here in this place, let me show you my true power."

"No!" Thomas said, causing Aleara and Oldiren to flinch.

Oldiren laughed. Thomas and Aleara both focused their gaze on him.

"You fool," Oldiren said. "Do you realize what you've set in motion?"

The Threshold seemed firmer to Thomas. The slight vibration of the place stilled, at least for the moment. As he looked out, a large green man, perhaps a god, materialized. In its large hands was a giant club. There was no time for contemplation or fear. Nightshard's voice roared in his head, urging him to act.

His hand tightened around the sword's hilt, its insatiable hunger for blood and destruction beckoning to him. As if on cue, the god tore through the fabric of the Threshold and disappeared into the unknown beyond. Then Nightshard let out a blood-curdling battle cry, causing Oldiren and Aleara both to cover their ears. Other beings emerged from hidden spaces within the Threshold. Many were alien to him, monstrous though humanoid.

Thomas stood frozen as the monstrous beings emerged into the Threshold. His mind reeled, trying to process the chaos unfolding around him. The sword pulsed eagerly in his grip, hungry for more blood and power. Donegal climbed to his feet and stepped away from the paladin. The gods were smaller, and Thomas no longer feared them. They should fear him. He was the Veilbreaker. Even gods would fall at his feet.

"What have I done?" Thomas said.

"Thomas, you must stay in control of yourself. Give Donegal his life force back."

He looked at her, seeing the fear and desperation in her eyes. For the first time, the goddess seemed vulnerable.

"No!"

Oldiren's laughter echoed around them. His hood fell back, and Thomas flinched at the mirror image of Klydos.

"Perhaps my brother had the right idea after all. You may have doomed all the mortal realms. Put that blade away, Thomas Veilbreaker. It cannot be used in the Threshold."

Thomas stared at the god. He understood that Oldiren, like Klydos, was a creature of chaos, but what gain could such a flippant response elicit? Or perhaps he knew more than he was letting on. Either way, it was not a pleasant experience. First, he would deal with Nightshard. Off in the distance, a castle or a temple, long ruined, was slowly returning to its former grandeur. He was tempted to go to that place. It called to him. Perhaps within it, there were answers to the questions that arose in his evolving mind.

"Enough!" Thomas said.

Nightshard would not relent, and the feeling that he should go to that dark castle increased with every moment. He tried to push the thoughts away. Nightshard shrieked within his head. He could feel it resisting, trying to draw him further into madness. But he thought of all he had sacrificed to reach this moment. He would not let their deaths be in vain. The sword alternated between promises and threats. Energy surged out of the sword, surrounding him. His body strained as if it would crack and burst apart from the turmoil he was facing. He was able to clear his mind and force the sword from his head.

"You will do my will," Thomas said, "or I will cast you into the deepest part of the ocean, and you can manipulate crabs for eternity."

Even as he said it, Thomas was unsure whether he truly had the strength to cast away the weapon. So much depended on him clinging to its power. A debate raged within his mind, and eventually he decided that it was not worth it. He would choke Klydos with his bare hands before he would become a pawn to whatever Nightshard truly was.

The sword became quiet, seething like a petulant child. With tremendous effort, Thomas drove the blade into the ground. Light exploded outward as he channeled every ounce of his power and faith. The alien entities screamed, sucked into the rifts from which they came.

When the light faded, Thomas found himself alone with Aleara and Oldiren once more. The Threshold was stable, though cracks still lingered at its edges. No sign remained of Donegal. Off in the distance, the once crumbling building now stood complete and new-looking. It was terrible to look upon. Something said that was a place he was not ready to tread. Nightshard attempted to convince him to go to it, but he held his ground. Both gods gasped when they saw it. Thomas fell to his knees, utterly drained.

"Is it over?" he asked.

Aleara placed a comforting hand on his shoulder.

"For now. But the damage is done. The walls between worlds have been weakened. Klydos will surely exploit this. Worse still, you may have set events in motion for something far worse."

Oldiren said, "Do not speak of it. We already tread very carefully here. When my brother learns of today's events, his intentions will grow."

"Then what do we do?" Thomas asked.

"We adapt. We evolve. The game changes, Thomas. Are you prepared to change with it?"

Oldiren was enjoying the discord of these events. A sadistic look decorated his visage, and the paladin wondered if Klydos was the true evil amongst these gods. He looked down at Nightshard, still vibrating with restrained power. Thomas knew the choice before him. It was either to embrace the sword's power and risk losing himself, or find another way forward. With grim resolve, he stood and faced the deities.

"I am the Veilbreaker," he said. "And I will do whatever it takes to save Binsmuth. Even if it means becoming something more than human."

Aleara and Oldiren exchanged a significant look. The god of Chance lost his insane look, and what replaced it seemed to be relief, as if a crossroads had occurred with Thomas making the right choice. The die had been cast. Thomas could feel Donegal's power within him. Nightshard retained some as well, though the sword was sulking. Its inky black presence remained in his head, though it remained subdued.

"You have broken your oath to me, Thomas," Aleara said. "I am not sure what you are, but you are no longer one of mine. I hope that we do not find ourselves on the opposite side of a battlefield."

"I would never raise my sword against you, goddess," Thomas said. "All my life, I have served you faithfully."

"You believe that," Aleara said. "But all lives are precious to me, even that of my brother, though his actions against you are what caused you to stray from me."

He mulled that over. Finally, he shrugged his shoulders and turned away. She might be right. However, Aleara and Donegal betrayed their oath to their creations every time a world fell to Klydos. It was their inability to stabilize the situation that brought them to this point. It was not Nightshard's fault. The sword, for all its sentience, had to be wielded. Thomas was like Nightshard. Aleara wielded him once to enact her will. It was not his fault if she lacked the stomach to do what it took.

"Veilbreaker," Oldiren said. "What will you do?"

Thomas ignored the god. He was now immune to their machinations. When he had a plan, he would enlist them if he could. They would either fight alongside him or they would feel the cold steel embrace of Nightshard. There were only two sides of the coin, that of him or Klydos. If they were not for him, they were enemies.

"Thomas, I am not your enemy," Oldiren said. "There are things we could not tell you before. If you will listen to me, I will try to explain."

The last words were not spoken, but echoed in his head. Having Nightshard creeping around was enough.

"Get out of my head," Thomas growled, turning back to the god.

Aleara was nowhere to be seen. As if sensing a changing of the tide, Nightshard stirred in his mind. Take him now while we are alone, the sword whispered in his mind. It was tempting. Oldiren was an enigma, but Thomas was sure that whatever power the God of Chance had would be useful. Oldiren sighed and disappeared. Thomas would give them time to reconcile their place in the coming battle. He looked about the Threshold.

It had been a mystical place the first time he had been there. Now, his mind conceived the truth of it. It was like the long castle hallways of Grimhorn. Doorways that opened into worlds instead of rooms. With that knowledge also came the understanding that he could utilize the Threshold for his benefit. Where Klydos could enslave and cajole, the Veilbreaker could liberate and inspire.

He would look for and bring back any creature that wished to stand against the Lord of Tempests. However, before he sought allies elsewhere, it was time to secure the commitment of his allies on Binsmuth.

Thomas opened the veil between the Threshold and Binsmuth, laughing as he passed back into his world. He could feel the cold of his world chilling the damp mist of the Threshold into icy crystals on his skin. He shivered at the feel of it and wanted to be warmer. His smile widened as the energy within him responded to his thoughts. All his life, he longed for love and respect. The power of a god surpassed those desires. He embraced it.

Donegal's power flowed through him. The capabilities now at his fingertips shattered his limited understanding. As his mind grappled with the knowledge, his viewpoint changed. He recognized how all things connected to the raw stuff of chaos. As he looked at the flora and fauna of Binsmuth, tiny streamers flowed from them where the order decayed, turning back to chaos. He could understand the futility that Aleara and Donegal, in all their many incarnations and avatars, felt. Despite their best efforts, creation turned back to look at Klydos and ran back to him. Everything was temporary. Even the ground beneath his feet was crumbling, disintegrating into grains that stretched into the tendrils connecting back to the Threshold.

Unchecked by the nurturing of Donegal and Aleara, things began to decay. Klydos either knew this and did not care or was unaware that his children had to actively prevent things from slipping back to their primal state of chaos. Worse still, they created things intentionally, putting them at odds with the Lord of Tempests. Thomas thought of all the lives lost in the struggle against the forces of Klydos. Would it have been better not to exist than to face a life of strife? They never had a chance.

Not only could they nurture what existed, but they also understood that they drew upon entropy to mold it into new things. Deer, rivers, and even entire ecosystems. With the knowledge gained from Donegal, he could tap into it and make things of his choosing. He understood the immense capabilities Aleara and Donegal wielded. What he did not understand was why Klydos lashed out. He would always win in the end.

When he absorbed Donegal's godhood, Thomas gained the deity's knowledge and power. His evolving brain was absorbing the concepts. It was fantastical to his mortal understanding, but with each iteration of harmonizing Donegal's memories with his own, things were becoming clearer.

"And now you," Nightshard said, "have transcended mortality. What do you intend to do with this new power?"

He could feel the prayers of the Fada and Myshikl. He intended to return to his own time, but with them still praying to him, he must have misjudged. He should not hear them in his original timeframe. Their connection to him should have been severed across the intervening years. He shared his thoughts with his sword.

"No," Nightshard said, "we are very much back to where this all started. They must have ignored your plea to worship Aleara."

"Then why did I not hear their prayers before this?" Thomas asked.

"You are no longer Thomas Grimhorn," Nightshard said. "As a mortal, you would not hear them. That doesn't mean they were not praying to their savior."

"Is there a Thomas Grimhorn," Thomas said, "going about his life, oblivious to the reality of things?"

"No," Nightshard said. "You made a choice. You, for better or worse, are Thomas Grimhorn, but you are also the Veilbreaker."

What Nightshard said was true. While he bore a resemblance to Thomas Grimhorn, several aspects of him differed. He saw Binsmuth in a different light. If he looked hard enough, he could view the Threshold. Within there, a multitude of deities waited for a chance to emerge from their exile to become active in the affairs of the mortal creations. He was as much one of them as he was anything else. Lingering in the distance, he could still see the building that had emerged during his visit there. Something about it warned him that as much as he knew, there were still mysteries surrounding this celestial game. With Donegal's energy within him, he might eventually understand.

He tested his new powers. His first attempts were laughable. He created a lump of stone that resembled a child attempting to form a horse from clay. A child who had never seen a horse. He dismissed the attempt, and it dissipated before him. Though he was angry with the goddess for rejecting him, he had a greater appreciation for the efforts she underwent to create all the things that populated Binsmuth. His brow furrowed in concentration, drawing on all his years around horses to guide him. He worked on the design in his mind, refining it until he was satisfied.

Thomas was not sure whether the exercise took moments or centuries. With his design clear in his mind, he drew upon the aether. He reached out with it, willing the horse into existence, and screamed as his hand warped into something gruesome to behold. The chaos magic resisted him, altering him instead. Out of old habit, he started to pray to Aleara. He laughed, realizing she would not answer and he did not need her, then drew upon even more aether to fix his hand. Nightshard cautioned him about wasting his energy reserves. Without knowing how to replenish himself from the aether, he would need to wield the terrible blade once again.

Despite his reluctance to rely on the sword any more than he had to, he drew upon chaos to create a steed. The aether swirled around, forming a pitch-black destrier with rippling muscles. He reveled in what he had made. It did not exist, then it did, reshaped from the aether for him to use. The horse looked at him and pawed the ground beneath its forehooves.

He fashioned a saddle and blanket but skipped the reins. The horse let him approach, but did nothing as he saddled and mounted it. It was a fine warhorse, like his destrier, but better and more intelligent. It was the horse of a god. The animal bolted at his laughter, and he sat astride it, amused as the wind blew through his long black hair. Thomas laughed once more, this time from genuine joy at riding a horse again.

The distance flew by until, at last, he sat in front of the Brindall gates. The horse was sweating but had easily crossed the distance between the temple of Nightshard and Brindall. He was not surprised at the sturdy timber between him and the town. There were significant signs that more creatures had attacked the town since he was last here. His Valkrunian kin triumphed over the opposition. He could hear the sounds of afternoon traffic within the walls.

"Who goes there?" the soldier asked.

"It is Thomas Grimhorn," he replied. "I have come to ask the Valkrunians for aid."

There was no immediate recognition. He waited, listening as someone descended the ladder and scurried away from the gate. He was not sure that Lyrei returned to Brindall after leaving the temple, but as it was the closest place she might have gone, he would cross it off his list. He heard the person returning and then the sounds of the crossbar being removed. Someone remembered him.

"Fools," Nightshard said. "You should show them who you are."

"I am," Thomas said. "Just not in the way you mean."

When the gate was open enough, the horse pranced through the space. The tall Valkrunian, Kemith, stood there. Armed Valkrunians surrounded him.

"Good day, Thomas Grimhorn," Kemith said. "Our lady worries about you. She will be pleased when we escort you to her."

"No need to send all these people," Thomas said. "If you tell me where she is, I can make my way there."

Kemith bowed, "As you wish. She is occupying the village hall."

Thomas thanked them. He rode through the group, sensing something was not right. Two soldiers were standing on either side of the door. They said nothing as he mounted the steps and pushed his way through the door.

The scene he entered brought a grin to his face. Lyrei was sitting on a couch, sewing. It was as if he walked into a farmstead to find the farmer's wife hard at her chores while waiting for her husband to come in from the fields. A shocked look crossed her face, then she jumped up and ran to him.

"Where have you been?" Lyrei asked.

"It is a long story," he replied.

She looked at the sword sheathed at his side. Thomas nodded at her unasked question. There was a look that Thomas could only imagine as a mixture of fear and awe. She dragged him to the couch, pushing off her sewing supplies to make room. A Valkrunian woman emerged from the next room, bowed to Thomas, and picked up the threads and cloth before leaving again. For a long moment, Lyrei clung to him, and Thomas, who had never been touched much in his life, awkwardly embraced the feelings of being missed by someone. He decided to end the moment, not knowing if he could respond in the way she wanted.

"Why is Kemith acting strangely?" Thomas asked.

Lyrei said, "A doppelganger visited us. It killed two before we realized it was not you."

He swore under his breath. Duke Kendrick must be behind the attempt. Regardless of the dilemma regarding Klydos, that was one enemy that he could dispatch without worrying about the ramifications. Even if he had to tear Castle Grimhorn down stone by stone, Kendrick would no longer occupy its throne. He pondered the look on his father's face when he returned to unseat him. Hopefully, the man still ruled, if only so Thomas could end that reign.

Thomas asked, "How long have I been gone?"

"It has been days. What do you mean by that question?"

"Nightshard took me into the past," Thomas said.

He wept when he recounted the tale of choosing his mother as the sacrifice that bound him to Nightshard. Sharing the tale of his past drew some strange looks from Lyrei. When he told her of his role in sending her to the duchy, she covered her face with her hands.

"I had no choice," Thomas said. "It all had to happen for this to come to pass."

"It was you?" she asked. "You who sent me to the duchy?"

"I tried to think of a way to avoid it," Thomas pleaded with her. "If I had chosen another path, I might not have been born. Can you imagine Nightshard falling into someone else's hands?"

"You allowed me and your mother to be terrorized so you could control that sword? You are no better than your father. Surely you do not expect me to accept such a rationalization?"

"I did it so we can have a better life. One without Klydos."

"Klydos is a god. You are a fool to believe that you can prevail."

Silent tears streamed down her beautiful face. Thomas willed his armor to disappear and placed a gentle hand on her face to wipe away the tears. She gasped as she recognized the signature of chaos magic in use.

"Donegal attacked me in that place between worlds. I had no choice but to defend myself."

That was not entirely true, but explaining it would not mollify her. The look she gave him said it all. She was appalled by his choices.

"With Nightshard and the allies I have found, we can free this world from the Lord of Tempests," Thomas said. "Is that not worth the pain we each have suffered?"

Lyrei stiffened and said, "Do not compare your suffering with mine. Yours were the result of your choices. Mine was not of my making. It seems that you are just as responsible for my suffering as the father you hate so much."

"I only did it so we would meet and find a way to be together."

Despite that revelation, Lyrei remained distraught over his part in the terror she lived through because of his choices. Even worse, it had been Thomas who allowed Carina to be abused by her husband. Not only was he responsible for her death, but his mother's suffering as well.

Thomas was angry that she blamed him, but it was true. All of it had been done to ensure that events would transpire to put Nightshard in his hand. Perhaps it was the wrong decision, but he could not take the chance that Oldiren would let it play out differently, knowing that Thomas would wound Donegal.

"I knew that you would suffer," Thomas said. "I am sorry for that. It was the only way to ensure that events would unfold to place us together here and now."

Lyrei broke down, unwilling to listen to his explanation. He explained his rationale, but the words sounded hollow, even to him. When he realized that he could not console her, he kissed her gently on the forehead. As he watched her pain unfold, he realized something about himself. He had always believed himself to be a loner, but with Lyrei, he found someone who made his life better. Though he feared for what might happen to her, he knew he needed her in his life.

"For you, it has been days," he said, "but I have missed you for hundreds of years. I hope you can forgive me."

She did not look up, nor did she acknowledge his words. Though it hurt, he understood that apologies could not instantly heal wounds delivered by a loved one. His own life was a testament to that. When he failed to find words that might soften what he had told her, he decided to give her space. He turned and headed for the door.

As he was opening it, Lyrei said, "Tell me it was for a good reason. Tell me you can stop Klydos."

"I can," Thomas said.

There was no more to be said, so he strode from the room. He closed the door behind him. His steed stood there. In the quiet of the late afternoon, Thomas heard voices in the wind. At first, he thought it was just a trick, some acoustical property channeling voices from around the village to where he could hear them. Then he heard them saying 'Veilbreaker,' and he knew it was not Valkrunian villagers but something else.

Myshikl and Fada voices came from Ceylon and the forest near the temple. They were imploring, calling on him to return to them and answer their prayers.

While most were distant, one lone prayer sounded closer. One singular voice stood out. At first, he thought it was his imagination or some desperate attempt to put the pain he had caused behind him. The prayers did not cease. He could hear Scherie imploring him to return. Motioning to Wilhelm, he followed the sound of her plea. The prayer was repeated until he found his steps pacing in time with the words.

Thomas looked up, and he was standing in front of the village inn. He could hear the music and the gentle laughter of the folks inside. Despite the noise, over it was her prayer, asking for the Veilbreaker to return. He reached out to her.

"Come to me," he said.

The door opened, and she stood looking out through it with a smile on her face. The Fada were joyous people, but Sherie was beaming. She came running to him and hugged him. To the casual observer, it might have appeared that she was trying to strangle his thighs, but Thomas patted her on the back until she broke free and looked up at him. Her straw-blonde hair framed the impish smile.

"You knew?" he asked.

"My father told me the story of the Veilbreaker every day since birth," she said. "Our flawed god who graced him with me."

"Why did you not say anything?"

"Thomas Grimhorn was not who my father was talking about," she said. "But you have become what he believed in."

"Nightshard said as much to me. I tried for years to convince the Fada and the Myshikl that I was not something to believe in," Thomas said.

Her father, Vyjulis, preached to his people the evolution from Thomas Grimhorn to Veilbreaker. Doubt and isolation faded away as the Myshikl and Fada built their lives around the temple. In that haven, Vyjulis realized that the Veilbreaker was not a distant and uncaring god. He experienced the same emotions as those who worshiped him. Scherie's father had painted a mental picture that she held tightly in her mind. Thomas chuckled at her ability to rationalize meeting her father's god and keeping it to herself.

"Is this the first time you have heard my prayers?"

"Yes," he said, "but I have been far away. Lost in time until recently."

Thomas explained the situation. He left nothing out, including how he chose to send the Fada to Ceylon, knowing the hardship they would face. He expected to receive the same response as

Lyrei had given him, but instead, Scherie thanked him. The Fada were ready for the Veilbreaker to return, and Vyjulis was prepared to be at his side.

This was not the place for that. It would only serve to reopen the wounds Lyrei had thought healed. He let her know that he would be at the temple of Nightshard, planning his battle to topple Duke Kendrick and Klydos, ending the strife on Binsmuth. As they talked, another face opened the door to the inn. It was Harold. He looked rough.

The spymaster hobbled from the inn. His normally well-kempt locks hung limply, matted, and drab. The man wore a simple linen shirt and breeches. The stick he leaned upon was freshly cut and still rough in places. Thomas frowned as Harold approached, though he was glad that the man had not perished.

Before the man reached them, Scherie assured Thomas that Harold had no clue about the Veilbreaker. His physical wounds no longer plagued him, but something was not right, even though the best healers of the Valkrunians tried.

"Were they not able to heal you?"

"No, lad," Harold said. "They did as much as they could."

"I am more than they. Let me heal you."

Harold said nothing but stared at the taller man with amusement. Thomas grabbed his shoulder and let the energy wash over the man. Aleara was not there. It was the Veilbreaker who examined the thread of chaos emanating from Harold. The tendrils of chaos were different than those around him. Thomas surmised that Harold weakened, perhaps close to expiring.

The wounds inside Harold's body leaked blood from the trauma caused by the battle outside Brindall. He drew upon the aether, sending it through him into Harold. As the energy knitted together the wounds, Harold's connection to chaos shrank, becoming a tiny thread that reached back to the Threshold. It took a moment, but Harold straightened, the color returning to his face.

"Aleara be praised," Harold said.

"Yes," Thomas agreed sarcastically, "Aleara be praised."

Scherie smirked and hugged Harold. She led the man inside, heeding his earlier words. Thomas mounted his horse. The ebony stallion knickered softly. Where do we go? Home was his answer. The horse let out a whinny and kicked up dust as it sped away from the inn.

Thomas heard Scherie shouting at him. He did not look back. He knew that she and her fellow Fada would find their way to him. The Myshikl would gather at the temple. Perhaps, if Lyrei could forgive him, the Valkrunian diaspora would find their way there as well. The choice was made. With or without them, he would see this through. Binsmuth needed him to stay true and not shirk this task, regardless of the personal consequences it might have for him as a man.

As he charged for the gate, the soldiers moved out of the way, letting him through. He poured energy into the horse. Unbidden, a name came into his mind. His creation shared its name. Bolstered by the chaos, Wilhelm churned the distance away. The forest between Brindall and Nightshard's Temple was a blur.

Wilhelm pulled up as they got close. The horse panted but was not exhausted. His head swiveled around, looking off into the forest. Thomas sensed what the horse was sensing. It was his worshippers emerging from their treetop homes to bear witness to the return of the Veilbreaker.

They drew close and then prostrated themselves around him. Thomas slid out of the saddle onto the ground. He loosened the saddle and pulled it from Wilhelm's back. The horse let out a whinny, then bounded over the Myshikl and trotted up the path to the temple.

"I have returned," he said. "I am sorry for neglecting your prayers. The time comes for us to thwart Klydos. Together, we will free this world of its menace."

And a chorus of other prayers began flooding into him. He thought at first that the Myshikl and the Fada diaspora were the only ones, but he began to hear the prayers of farmers and other worshipers of Donegal. The people of Binsmuth were calling upon their god, and their prayers were coming to him. Thomas laughed, and those around him joined in with amusement. He started to explain, but thought better of it. He needed some mystery to give him some space from those who sought answers from him.

Instead, he turned and marched up the trail into the temple. It was brightly lit, with colorful paintings adorning the cave walls. The Myshikl had been working hard. He stopped before a scene, and guilt flooded him. Some artists had carved a very flattering portrayal of the salvation of the Myshikl. He wondered if Aleara experienced these same feelings, or was it his mortal nature that led him to feel guilt and doubt?

The hours turned to days, and Thomas reached out to the strongest of prayers, calling on this new group of faithful to come and join him. He hoped Donegal reflected upon the impact of this and regretted looking down upon the mortal-turned-god.

CHAPTER

24

S hadows flickered across the obsidian walls of the Temple of Nightshard, cast by the guttering flames of braziers that never went out. Myshikl priests, with their apelike gait, moved in and out of the room, anticipating the needs of their god. He smiled at them, grateful for their kindness, knowing that he was relying on the energy stolen from Donegal to meet their expectations. Much of it he held in reserve, hoping to use it to strike down Klydos and whatever champion he might send to do his bidding.

Thomas looked up from his brooding over the map, one hand resting on the hilt of the sentient sword Nightshard. The weapon pulsed with dark energy, its angry heartbeat a reminder of its thirst for blood and ruin. Around the room were friends and allies. Unseen by them was the ghost of his mother, whom he conversed with, trying to make up for the lost years away from her. Had anyone seen her, they would have thought it ironic that their relationship was better since he used Nightshard to slay her.

Around him, the Myshikl acolytes moved with reverent purpose, their furred hands polishing the altar and laying out offerings from the forest. They worshipped him now, the Veilbreaker, their savior and destroyer. Outside, he could hear the thud of hammers and the scrape of whetstones as they prepared for the war to come. A war against the Lord of Tempests and his monstrous hordes.

The heavy doors groaned open, and a familiar figure strode in. It was Sir Silas, his mentor, his father in all but blood. The old knight's armor, emblazoned with the sigil of Aleara, showed the wear and tear of many battles. Thomas flinched at the symbol, a reminder of his falling out of favor with her. Despite the sadness, he remained committed to using the power of Donegal to thwart Klydos. He welcomed the paladin with a mighty hug.

"Thomas," Silas said. "I bring word from Aleara and dire news."

Thomas stepped back. Inside his head, Nightshard was verbally drooling over the thought of being plunged into the older paladin. It scoffed at the mention of Aleara. Thomas mentally chastised the blade, but his hand tightened on the hilt at the mental image of draining Silas of his life force. Thomas knew the allure. Having Silas by his side forever might satisfy his loneliness, but it would be unfair to the man. He looked over at the ghost of his mother, and the sadness in her eyes stilled his blood lust at least for the moment.

Nightshard whispered a parting thought in his head, "Let him come to you. You are as much a god as Aleara now. Don't be the mewing boy who held onto his pant leg."

He hated that the sword was right. In this moment, he needed an ally, not a father figure. What Silas might offer on another day was not what he needed at that moment. The elder paladin solved the dilemma for him, stopping before the dais and bowing his head. The urge to jump down and clutch the man to him was still there, muted by the admonition of his fiendish, sentient blade.

"Aleara sends her blessing and her regret in not being able to join you. The enemy is gathering on the eastern plains. Their numbers are vast, and their leaders are cruel. We must prepare," said Silas.

Too late for blessings. Too late for regrets. Nightshard slithered out of the recesses of his mind and whispered these things in his head. He ignored it and descended the steps, his boots ringing on the basalt.

"Then we shall meet them on those plains. Think of it, Silas, we can finally be free of the influence of Klydos."

Nightshard purred in his mind, thinking of the battle ahead, hungry for slaughter. Images flashed through Thomas' mind. The piles of the dead and the pyres burning high into the sky. Klydos, Aleara, Donegal, and Oldiren kneeled before him, or was it him? The shadows on his face left Thomas wondering who was standing there before the Gods.

Thomas gazed down at the Knight Commander. Either he grew, or Silas shrank. The elder paladin met his gaze, and for a moment, Thomas recognized grief and fear in that gaze. He looked at me and saw a stranger or a monster, perhaps. The thought left a bitter taste in his mouth. Almost as bitter as turning away from the opportunity to end the strife on Binsmuth.

"Thomas...I know the burden you bear. I know the price that you paid." Silas said. "Know that you are not alone. Aleara's host rides with you, as do I."

Not alone. Never alone, with the souls in Nightshard clamoring for an audience or the prayers of those worshipping him in his head. Thomas clasped the outstretched hand, touching the calluses of a life spent wielding a sword.

"If Aleara's host is here," Thomas said, "why is the Grand Commander not delivering this message?"

"Marla thought you would receive us better if I came to see you," Silas replied.

"Hard to look down on me now," Thomas said.

He debated gloating about taking Donegal's life force but resisted. Acting childish would get him nowhere. Despite his awakening, every ally was an important one. He also wanted to restore his relationship with the goddess. When this was all over, he would need her forgiveness to serve her again. She had been his guiding purpose for far too long.

"Nobody has ever looked down on you, lad. I've always believed you embodied our beliefs."

"I know, Silas. Forgive me. The temple walls press close some days, and Nightshard is eager to whisper treason."

"All is forgiven," Silas said. "We will speak more of the war to come. For now, know you have allies."

He turned to go, pausing at the threshold to glance at the sword Thomas held.

"And Thomas? Remember, no fate is sealed, and no man is beyond redemption. Not even the Veilbreaker."

Then he left without another word, the doors closing behind him with a whisper. Thomas stared after him, Nightshard's voice coiling around his heart. Thomas debated whether to leave the blade there in the temple and walk Silas back to his encampment. His biggest fear was that the link between him and Nightshard did not need that physical connection. In response, Nightshard chuckled, a cold and terrible sound that was its joyous response to that revelation. Redemption? Oh, my sweet knight, that is a dream, dead and buried.

He turned back to the shadows and waited for the war drums to begin. His life was on hold, waiting for the moment that he could free his world and let go of his role as Veilbreaker. At least he hoped to free himself of that duty. It was not clear whether he would even prevail against the God of Chaos. Thomas did not fear death. He only hoped that it would free Binsmuth from this constant war.

The shadows lengthened as the day waned, and with them came a whisper on the wind, a rustling of leaves that heralded a new arrival. Even deep within the temple, Thomas could feel the approach. He stepped out into the courtyard, Nightshard at his hip, a procession emerging from the treeline. At their head strode Jaxxon, his weathered face creased in a frown. The scurrilous druid looked as irreverent as ever.

"Hail, Thomas," Jaxxon said, "I bring tidings and a warning."

Thomas inclined his head, calming the Myshikl, ready to respond if this was a foe. He spread his arms and embraced the druid as he got close.

"It is good to see you, Jaxxon. What wisdom do you bring to the Temple of Nightshard?"

"Can't stand the place."

"Let me get my horse," Thomas said with a smile. "We can disappear into the woods."

Jaxxon's frown deepened, his eyes meeting Thomas' unflinchingly. Thomas knew the words were hollow and regretted them instantly. The druid was unusually somber, and it wasn't reassuring. Thomas thought back wistfully to the days when he, Avery, and Jaxxon operated on the fringes. With Avery dead and the burden of leading the fight against Klydos squarely on Thomas' shoulders, it was little wonder the druid was serious.

"If only we could, my boy, if only we could. I may have some wisdom, but it will bring little comfort. Nemordia marches for the eastern plains."

Let them come, Nightshard whispered a sibilant caress. Let them break upon our walls like waves upon the shore. Thomas shook his head, pushing the voice away.

"And what counsel would you offer, Jaxxon? What strategy might win the day?"

Before Jaxxon could answer, a murmur ran through the gathered Myshikl, and Thomas turned to see a new group approaching. They were small in stature, reaching his chest, but they moved with a grace that belied their size. The Fada arrived. Vyjulis stepped forward and bowed.

Scherie joined her father, winking at Thomas, and bowing her head. He told them to rise. Time was growing short, and he needed confident allies, not bowing worshippers. The Fada would realize the need to worship Aleara. However, they wanted to bow to him. He would have to take Scherie aside and understand that.

"Veilbreaker," she said, "we offer our blades and our magic to your cause. The Lord of Tempests is an enemy to all, and we would see him fall."

Thomas smiled at Scherie's confidence. He looked at Jaxxon, and the druid was staring at the Fada woman. Thomas would be grateful if they could ride together and trade verbal barbs with one another as they traveled to meet the amassed armies of Klydos. If only Avery were there. He considered using Nightshard to return him to that battle and prevent Avery from dying, but the sheer number of souls the blade would demand ended that thought.

As if reading his thoughts, the Fada leader smiled and said, "The winds change, Veilbreaker, and we change with them. Aleara's light fades, and yours rises. We would be on the right side of history."

What they could not know was that he, too, would fade once he released Donegal's power during the battle. All the things Thomas was experiencing would be but memories. It was immaterial. Despite the urgings of the sentient sword, Thomas did not crave power. He only craved safety for Binsmuth.

They pledged their loyalty as he mused on these things. Once they were done, the Fada melted into the shadows. Jaxxon turned to speak with Silas, leaving Thomas to ponder his thoughts further on his own. If Aleara and Donegal did not materialize on the battlefield, would Klydos even be there, or would he have to chase the god into the Threshold to conclude their business?

Klydos might control the tempests that plagued the seas, but Thomas was lightning. Where he struck, nothing would survive. But even as the thought formed, a flicker of doubt joined it, a whisper of the man he had once been.

"What if I am not the lightning," he wondered, "but the tree that burns beneath it?"

"Did you say something?" Silas asked.

Before Thomas could respond, a distant horn pierced the air, a plaintive cry that sent a shiver down Thomas' spine. He turned, hand instinctively reaching for Nightshard's hilt, as a procession emerged from the treeline. At their head rode a figure achingly familiar, her black hair braided and ready for battle.

Lyrei. The name caught in his throat, a prayer and a curse intertwined. She was resplendent in polished silver armor, the crest of the Valkrunians gleaming upon her breastplate. Those eyes, once soft with love, now glinted with a hardness that spoke of betrayal and sorrow. Like everything else he touched since picking up Nightshard, his actions tainted her feelings for him.

Behind her, the Valkrunians marched in perfect formation, their tall frames towering over the assembled Myshikl and Fada. They moved with a fluidity that spoke of centuries of martial tradition, their steps perfectly synchronized as if they were one entity rather than many. Kemith rode alongside her. Despite his advanced age, the man carried himself with the confidence of a proven warrior.

As they drew closer, Thomas could feel the crackle of their magic in the air, a wild and untamed force that set his teeth on edge. They were drawing upon chaos itself, manipulating it to reveal the power wielded in that small but deadly force to their allies. He caught the gaze of a Myshikl shaman and held up his hands for them to remain calm. This was a show of strength, but it was an ally, even if Lyrei hated what he allowed to happen to her.

Lyrei reined in her steed before him, her gaze boring into his with an intensity that made him want to look away.

"Husband," she said, "I see you have been busy in my absence."

Thomas inclined his head, fighting to keep his expression neutral. The tone was the message. Allied and bonded, they might be, but the marriage bed would be cold and lonely until her feelings resolved themselves. Her anger at his choices surely rivaled the feelings Aleara exhibited in the Threshold. He altered that thought. Donegal had a stronger claim than they did.

"Wife," he replied, "I did what I had to do. For our people. For our future."

Her laugh was sharp and bitter. Then she said, "Our future? What future is there for us now, Thomas? You have embraced a power that will consume you, that will leave nothing but ashes in its wake."

"She fears you," Nightshard whispered, "she fears what you have become."

Thomas shook his head, pushing the sword's voice away. He nodded to Lyrei, ignoring what she said, instead directing his comments to Nightshard.

"I have become what I must to protect those I love," he said softly, "even if they cannot understand it."

Though he meant it to be nothing but a whisper, his wife's regal head tilted down in response. For a moment, Lyrei's façade cracked, and the pain that lurked beneath came to the surface. He set her up for abuse, physically and mentally. He allowed his own mother to be abused at the whim of his father. It was easy to understand that his good intentions were not easily understood.

"I want to understand," she whispered, "I want to believe in the man I married. But I look at you now, and I see a stranger wearing my husband's face."

Thomas reached out, his fingers brushing against her armored hand.

"I am still here," he replied, "beneath the power, beneath the duty. I am still the man who loves you, Lyrei."

She held his gaze for a long moment, and he recognized the war raging behind her eyes.

"Prove it," she said, "prove that there is still a shred of Thomas left in you."

He struggled to find the words. Lyrei waved to Kemith, and the Valkrunians began to disperse, setting up camp around the temple's perimeter, next to the human army and the Fada. He worried that the groups would keep their distance, but despite old grievances, they intermingled. Less than a hundred Fada. Nearly three hundred Valkrunians. Nine thousand human paladins and retainers. The army of Binsmuth was coming together.

It was Lyrei and her kin that broke down the barriers. He imagined that chaos magic had been used to soothe the worst of the human responses. Thomas envied those men and women who touched Lyrei's hand as she meandered through the camp. They moved among the Myshikl and Fada, their hands glowing with arcane energy as they reinforced weapons and armor.

"They seek to make us strong," Nightshard said, "to make us worthy of the battles to come."

Thomas nodded. The burden weighed upon him. Having the support of those answering his call helped him shoulder it. These disparate peoples responded to his call to be forged into an army to withstand the Lord of Tempests. He called upon his brother and Baron Eldric. Their ethereal forms stood on either side of him.

"Look upon the destruction of your god," Thomas said.

Let us serve you, too, was their plea. Thomas looked at them and questioned Nightshard. When asked if this could be done, the sword hemmed and hawed before acknowledging he could release their souls. It was foul magic, Thomas thought, for what Nightshard described was a necromancy of sorts, allowing the consumed spirits to occupy bodies fallen on the field. He disagreed, but held that it was a last resort.

But at what cost? He looked down on the encampment, re-membering the sorrow in Lyrei's eyes. What if I lose myself in the process? What if I become the very thing I seek to destroy?

"You are the Veilbreaker," Nightshard insisted, "you are beyond such petty concerns. Embrace your destiny, and let nothing stand in your way. The Valkrunian is mortal. Finish Klydos, and I will present you with a bride worthy of the Veilbreaker."

The voice was even more seductive than usual. It tugged at him. He was deserving of affection, though the weapon was dan-gerous beyond comprehension. Thomas closed his eyes, embrac-ing the pull of the sword's power, the seductive whisper of its voice. I am the Veilbreaker, he thought, and I will do what I must, no matter the cost. He would make sacrifices to tear this world away from Klydos. What Aleara and Donegal failed to do on countless worlds, he would do here. It would be worth it.

Later, in the shadowed halls of the Temple of Nightshard, Thomas gathered his war council. The air was thick with tension, the weight of impending battle heavy on every brow. Vyjulis and Scherie of the Fada sat to his left, their mischievous eyes glinting in the candlelight. Lyrei and Kemith of the Valkrunians flanked his right, their powerful frames poised for action. Marla and Silas represented the human contingent. Gyrok and Fulsa of the Myshikl completed the circle, their ancient wisdom etched into every line of their faces.

"The Grey Wizards of Sambor pose the greatest threat," Thomas said. "Their destructive capabilities could tip the balance in favor of the Lord of Tempests."

Vyjulis leaned forward, his pointed ears twitching. All eyes turned to the man. There was no respect yet, but they were sure that if the Veilbreaker sought his counsel, they should listen as well.

"We have faced their kind before," he said. "They are formida-ble but not invincible."

Scherie nodded in agreement, saying, "With the right strategy, we can neutralize their power."

Lyrei spoke up, her voice clear and strong. Thomas looked across the chamber at her, saddened by the distance between them, but he respected her decision. If he chose, he could enforce their bond, but giving in meant being like his father.

"The Valkrunians stand ready to face any foe," she said. "We will not falter in the face of their magic."

Jaxxon, who had been silent until now, rose to his feet. He looked the same. His words suggested otherwise.

"I will lead the ambush against the wizards," he said. "My knowledge of their ways will give us an edge."

Thomas met his mentor's gaze, seeing the determination that burned there. They had a history with those chaos-wielding humans, and it was not a good one. Jaxxon was not the most level-headed man. However, this was not the time for that. He needed a vicious response. The few druids that arrived with Jaxxon would use their varied gifts to counter the wizards. Jaxxon smiled, a grim twist of his lips.

"I have faced worse odds," he said, "and emerged victorious. This time will be no different."

Hopefully, he was better prepared now and would not lose himself in whatever form he took. If Thomas fell, he would not know what became of Jaxxon. He pushed the thought aside, focusing on the task at hand. There was also the rune that would call upon Selvus and whatever forces that mighty being could muster. Knowing Jaxxon was on the battlefield, Selvus would fight to see his son live another day. Oldiren had placed a debt on the man turned owlbear and Selvus would repay it with the blood of Klydos' minions.

"Then it is settled," he said. "Jaxxon will lead the ambush while the rest of us prepare for the battle to come."

The council dispersed. Hoping to catch his wife, Thomas stood, pushing his way past those trying to get words with him. Lyrei took her leave before Thomas could reach her. He sighed and retreated to his chamber, brooding on the throne until the dawn came.

When the sun rose again, Thomas walked out of the temple, unsure if he would ever see it again. He walked out to see his army breaking down their tents and preparing for the trek to the western plain near the coast. In the intervening days before they arrived, Thomas hoped to apologize and restore his connection with Lyrei. There was much to discuss about the future of Grimhorn and its subject territories.

The combined army moved out, a sea of glinting armor and fluttering banners beneath the dappled light of the forest canopy. Thomas rode at the head of the column, Nightshard strapped to his back, its presence a constant reminder of the burden he bore. Beside him, Scherie, Harold, and Jaxxon sat astride their mounts, their faces grim with determination.

As they trekked through the forest, Thomas' thoughts turned to Lyrei, who insisted on accompanying them despite his protests. She rode a few paces behind, her black hair gleaming in the filtered sunlight. No one said anything, but Thomas worried about regaining her trust in time. He knew there was no dissuading her, not when the fate of their people hung in the balance. Lyrei was a warrior, a queen in her own right, and she would not be left behind while others fought and died in her name.

They reached the edge of the forest as the sun began to set, painting the sky in shades of orange and red. Thomas called a halt, signaling for the army to make camp for the night. As the soldiers pitched tents and lit fires, he gathered his trusted companions around him.

"We must know what we are facing," he said. "Jaxxon, Scherie, Lyrei, and Harold, come with me. We will scout ahead and see what the Lord of Tempests sends against us."

"It is days before we reach the perimeter of their camp," Lyrei said.

"Witness the power of the Veilbreaker."

They slipped out of the camp under the cover of darkness, stopping only when Thomas was confident they were beyond the sentries. He drew upon chaos, conjuring a portal. When it formed, he motioned for the group to step through. Jaxxon hesitated, but Scherie and Lyrei strode through confidently. Lyrei made this journey to many worlds while serving the Lord of Tempests. Scherie must have heard her father's tales.

Finally, Jaxxon went through, and Thomas followed, closing the portal behind them. If things went wrong, he did not want to lead Klydos to the army. Once through, they began moving through the tall grass of the plains with the silence of ghosts. Thomas led the way, his senses heightened by the power that thrummed through his veins.

He could feel the enemy's presence, a dark weight on the horizon that seemed to swallow the stars. As they drew closer, Lyrei let out a sharp intake of breath.

"Those banners," she whispered, "I know them. They belong to the Valkrunian forces that remained loyal to Klydos."

Thomas followed her gaze, his heart sinking at the familiar emblems fluttering in the breeze. The army of Grimhorn camped among the forces of Klydos. He doubted the soldiers understood. They were loyal and would follow Kendrick into battle without comprehending that they served with those who sought to destroy Binsmuth. It was a flaw in the system. While the paladins, priests, and druids of Aleara were fully aware of what they faced, the ordinary people were more confused.

"General Caelis leads those soldiers," Lyrei said, her voice tight with tension. "He is my kin, a brutal warrior. We must be wary of him. He is more dangerous than Duke Kendrick."

"I will find him," Thomas said, "and he will pay for what he did to her, for what he did to all of us."

A gentle presence stirred within the depths of Nightshard. A soft, ethereal glow emanated from the blade, and suddenly, his mother's voice echoed in his mind.

"My son," she said. You must let go of this hatred, this desire for revenge. It will only consume you and lead you astray from your true purpose."

Thomas shook his head, tears stinging his eyes. Nightshard was nefarious, but he doubted the sword would foist this on him. The sword embraced vengeance. It must be his mother reaching out from her prison.

"How can I let it go?" he asked. "How can I forgive him for what he did to you?"

Taking a deep, shuddering breath, Thomas forced himself to look away from the Grimhorn banner. She was right. His true purpose was to defeat Klydos. As one pledged to serving the Lord of Tempests, his father would fall with the rest of those minions.

As he turned back to his companions, a sense of grim resolve settled over him. The enemy easily outnumbered them, but they had come too far to turn back now and sacrificed too much to give in to despair. They needed allies. He fumbled with an idea, more like an insane suggestion, and then decided he would seek the help of those within the Threshold.

He shared this idea with his friends. He trailed off, the enormity of what he was suggesting hanging heavy in the air. To enter the Threshold was no small feat, and there was no guarantee of what they might find on the other side. Thomas looked out over the sea of enemy forces. They had no other choice.

"It's a risk," Lyrei said. "It may be our only chance. We are with you, Thomas, whatever you decide."

Thomas nodded, his heart swelling at the touch of his estranged wife. Jaxxon, too, agreed that they needed whatever help they could get. They had been through so much together, faced impossible odds, and emerged stronger for it. Whatever lay ahead, he knew they would face it as one. If it came to it, he would find a way for Aleara to wield the sword.

Thomas took them back to their camp. Unless he secured additional allies, they would be sorely outnumbered. Lyrei kissed him on the cheek and disappeared into the night. Hope. Thomas bathed in it. Perhaps he might not lose her after all. He left instructions with Jaxxon on what to do if he did not return. The druid scowled at his words but left after swearing he would follow through.

As the sun began to rise, casting long shadows over the camp, Thomas turned his gaze to the shimmering veil that marked the threshold. Oldiren brought him there in dreams, and once before, he had emerged on his own in Binsmuth after being there. Although he was unsure of how to do it, he had to do it. Surely that was enough. With a deep breath, Thomas stepped forward. There had to be answers in the Threshold.

CHAPTER

25

The Veilbreaker emerged from the magical barrier known as the Threshold. His sudden appearance caused the Myshikl sentry to jump in surprise, his hand reaching for his club. The creature's jaw dropped in shock as he tried to process the sight of Thomas standing before him. Thomas surveyed their location, his eyes scanning the tall grasses that surrounded them, a sign they were nearing the plains. As he took in the camp, a sense of pride swelled within him. Jaxxon took command in his absence, pushing their troops and preparing them for the upcoming battle.

They were only a day's march away from their enemy, and Thomas couldn't help but smile at the thought. He helped the warrior to his feet, accepting his grateful bow with a nod. Thomas made his way into the camp, his gaze fixed on the flags that danced in the wind. His tent came into view, adorned with a familiar Grimhorn stag encircled by a black square against a deep green background.

As he made his way through the camp, the sentries immediately saluted upon his arrival, their gazes a mix of reverence and awe. He paid them no attention, his mind consumed with the upcoming battle and the news he had to share with the leaders.

Thomas strode through rows of devoted worshippers from both Fada and Myshikl races, who knelt or lay prostrate on the ground in solemn reverence. The human and Valkrunian soldiers could not help but watch in mild amusement as they passed, but Thomas paid them no mind. He knew that their loyalty had to come from a deep-seated desire to rid the world of Klydos's evil influence. Anything else was secondary.

When he finally reached his tent, the assembled leaders were waiting for him. He gazed at them with a sense of urgency, knowing that his news could make or break their morale. He hoped they viewed the news as positively as he did.

"I have secured us some powerful allies," Thomas said.

A cheer erupted from those closest to him, spreading throughout the entire army as they took up the chant. The various leaders called for silence, and soon, a hush fell over the crowd. Drawing on chaos, Thomas's voice carried to every corner of the camp.

"These are beings whose worlds have also fallen under Klydos' control," he declared. "But they are willing to join our cause if we offer our aid in return. We must vow to answer their call should it ever come, even if we cannot be there ourselves. This vow extends beyond us. It is a promise for our children and future generations to uphold. What say you?"

The soldiers cheered as Thomas stood before them, his armor glinting in the torchlight. He raised his hand for silence and gave out orders to disperse the men back to their duties or revelry. It was their last night of freedom before they would face the enemy across the field.

Thomas and his generals stepped into his tent adorned with extravagant tapestries from Ceylon. A great wooden chair stood ready for him, but he scowled at the thought of sitting in it. Pages and squires helped him out of his heavy armor while he poured himself a flagon of ale.

"We may have another thousand joining our ranks," Thomas announced to his assembled leaders. "It is not the horde I hoped for, but it will make a difference."

The plan was to open portals under the cover of darkness, allowing them to emerge quietly and catch the enemy off guard. Jaxxon and his group of druids and paladins would flank the battlefield, searching for the Grey Wizards of Sambor. If they could neutralize them, their chances of victory increased. It was a risky move, but it was their best option.

After revealing the plan, the leaders dispersed to relay it to their subordinates. Thomas sat back in his chair, grateful for a moment of peace. However, Lyrei stood on the other side of the table, twirling a figurine between her fingertips before setting it down with a flourish. He sensed the flare of chaos magic. The animated thing wandered across their armies, smashing everything it encountered.

"Am I to assume you are skeptical?" he said.

Lyrei said, "Assume nothing. That is you. But that is your army."

He was not entirely sure of what she meant. Lyrei came around the table to stand before him. He looked up, sensing that he was about to find out. He prepared himself for the worst.

"Release me from my bond," she said. "I cannot truly aid you if you have power over me. If you love me, you will see that the time is past for me to be bound to the heirs of Grimhorn."

Thomas frowned and said, "Can you not see that I was trying to protect you? The only way to ensure you were there in Ceylon to meet me was to put you on a collision course with my father."

"Release me," she said. "I will fight against the Lord of Tempests because it is my duty as part of this world, not because of any spell or manipulation."

"Fine," he said. "I release you from your bond."

"If," she said, "Thomas Grimhorn survives the battle, then we will talk about a future. If it is the Veilbreaker that survives the battle, I do not know that I can follow you."

As she walked away, Thomas came up with more questions than answers. Even Oldiren expressed doubts about his true self, and now Lyrei had done the same. What had he done?

"You're not," Nightshard whispered in his head. "Go back to the Threshold and take their essence for yourself. If you destroy them there, my temple will open to you, and a true power will emerge. We will quench our thirst on a thousand worlds. You can rival Klydos yourself."

Thomas stood in front of the foul blade, his eyes searching for an answer. He could feel its hatred toward the gods and wondered why it was so bitter. All he got in return was a deafening silence. The sword never stopped whispering dark thoughts and twisted plans to him, and its sudden silence left him wondering.

He longed for some company. He called out to Carina and Kendrick, and with a wave of his hand, they appeared beside him in their ethereal forms.

"Do you have any wisdom to share?" Thomas asked.

His mother's ghostly form spoke first, "Lyrei is wiser than you. She knows what tomorrow will bring. There will be challenges that will test your determination. Do not succumb to the easy path to victory, for there is no true gain if we trade Klydos for a twisted version of yourself."

"Your mother speaks the truth," Kendrick added. "Defeating Father and Klydos will be no easy feat. The Lord of Tempests craves this world and will stop at nothing to consume it. You must be prepared to push yourself beyond your limits."

Their words brought no comfort. With another wave of his hand, the ghosts disappeared. Trepidation made his heart pound, though seeing it through was the only possible path. This battle would shape the future of Binsmuth, not just for himself but for every creature fighting alongside him. The decisions made here would forever alter the landscape of their world.

Just then, a page burst into the tent. The boy bent over, gasping for breath before speaking.

"Veilbreaker," he said, "the king and his army have arrived."

A small smile tugged at Thomas's lips. Two essential stops were made before returning to camp. One to ensure Faisel's freedom, and the other to seek an audience with the King of Zel'Drea. The king and his army now stood at their doorstep. It looked like the gamble had paid off. Thomas donned a long coat and strapped Nightshard to his side. This was not just about the survival of Binsmuth but the entire world. Determination and excitement coursed through him as he went to greet the arriving king. This was a battle they could not afford to lose.

The camp was a madhouse. Humans mingled with the other races, and if the impromptu celebrations were any indication, they were dealing with it well. Once the introductions concluded, the army assembled, prepared to march the remaining distance, and battle with their enemies. Though the assembled leaders lobbied to lead, all deferred to Thomas. He did not relish what was about to occur. Despite his determination to end the influence of Klydos on this world, he did not seek the mantle of leader.

He prayed to Aleara, but he received no response. It did not matter. He did this because it was his duty to her. He would be faithful to that oath until the end of his days.

The sight of the enemy caused him to draw in his breath. Arrayed on the other side of the plain was a score of giants lounging against the slopes of the foothills. Below them milled various monstrosities. A ring of Grey Wizards of Sambor held them in check. Thomas sensed the aether being used by them. This was the moment. Here, he would finally realize his purpose. He would lead this army to victory over the Lord of Tempests.

The leaders gathered around him. He had few words, instead getting them to focus on what lay across the open stretch of field. The moment served two purposes. It rallied the troops, and it gave

Jaxxon's motley band a chance to slip around to neutralize the Grey Wizards. He ordered the banners struck to prepare for formation. A noise arose as the combined forces took their places.

Sir Silas nodded to him. He returned the nod. Nightshard sat comfortably in his hand, and the shield, given to him by Aleara, was in place across his right forearm. He grabbed his banner from the Myshikl standing nearby and walked out ahead. He told them he would advance just a few paces, but that was a lie. It was for them that he did it. The distance grew, and then his magnificent destrier, created from pure chaos and gifted with speed, raced out to meet him. Shouts went up from behind him as the soldiers realized something was not right. He ignored them and mounted his steed.

"Are you ready?" he asked Nightshard.

The sentient weapon laughed in his head. He launched the horse forward, but the pounding of hooves could not drown out the glee of his sword. As he raced forward, giants stood and took note. A horn went up, and the army of Klydos responded by lurching forward. He did not look back. Thomas knew that by now, his generals were spurring their units forward. Thomas hoped they were too late. Nightshard agreed.

He drew closest to a frost giant, whose breath rained frosty shards at him. The horse dodged as best it could. Thomas called upon the aether and erected a barrier to keep it from being injured. Shards of ice rained down, glancing off the barrier or shattering from contact. The giant roared as its icicle breath became ineffective. He drove Nightshard into its foot, and the sword drank. A howl went up from the sword, and by the look on the faces of the creatures running toward him, they heard it, too.

The giant fell, and Thomas pulled energy from the sword, sending an icy blast back at his enemies. He wove a furious screen of death with his blade. It mowed down everyone close to him, and the cacophony of his sword broke the enemy's morale. The

Valkrunian general charged toward him, and then his army arrived, cutting off General Caelis. A wave of soldiers washed between him and the general. Thomas snarled.

Whether it was the malevolent energy of Nightshard or the battle, he could not tell. All he saw and felt were the living before him and how they needed to be brought down. He remembered his allies and paused, drawing on the aether to create giant portals that broke the veil between his world and theirs. The diaspora of a dozen worlds vaulted through the portals. In the ensuing chaos, some of his allies mistook them for the enemy.

Thomas waded through body after body, striking down whoever got close enough. Nightshard emanated chaos as it found throat, chest, or appendage. Each blow was mortal. The blade shrieked louder with each soul it devoured, becoming stronger and stronger so that just a slice or the piercing of flesh was enough to draw the soul from the creature. His soldiers began to give him a wide berth, saving their efforts for whatever managed to slip through.

The ground shook with the heavy footsteps and hooves of both armies. Thomas could hear the clash of metal and screams of pain. So far, they had not encountered much magical opposition, but the Valkrunian forces allied with Klydos disengaged and batted away whatever attempts came at attacking them. The vainglorious general with his golden armor. He was a pale imitation of Lyrei's regality.

Dispatching two ogres earned him a crushed breastplate. He abandoned the armor, cutting through the straps with his long knife, even though he injured himself in the process. He drew on even more chaos to staunch his wounds and heal the ribs. His greaves creaked and finally gave way as his body grew enough to burst free of them. Thomas looked around. He had somehow grown. He conjured armor to replace the one he had lost. The black plate mail enveloped him once again.

He sensed the blow but was unable to dodge it. A green giant, one from the Threshold, struck him with its club. This was an avatar of Aleara, and that confused Thomas. The giant rumbled forward only to find Nightshard in its chest.

"Forgive me," Thomas said.

The power of the destroyed god surged into him, spilling out of Nightshard. He looked around, and some of the less intelligent creatures Klydos summoned to the battlefield were escaping through the portals Thomas created. He closed them. It would be decided here and now. He looked back at the army. Humans, Valkrunians, Fada, and Myshikl worked together. Their banners flew proudly over the field.

"Do not stop now, Veilbreaker," Nightshard whispered. "We are on the verge."

"The verge of what?" Thomas asked.

The sword resumed howling, ignoring his question. Thomas would have pressed the matter, but trolls surrounded him. Before focusing on the creatures, arcs of magic flew from behind the Valkrunians. The druid kept his promise. He hoped Jaxxon was okay. Finding out would have to wait. He swung Nightshard. They would not recover from Nightshard. Thomas feared for those of his army who faced these creatures, for they would reassemble and rise again if not burned.

The battle raged all around him, a symphony of destruction and mayhem. The paladins of Aleara pressed through the hordes of creatures, employing their power along with their mighty weapons. Thomas hoped to see Lyrei, but he was unable to find her. There were too many monsters around him. He smiled at a giant ensnared by the ropy vines emerging from the earth. That meant that at least one of the druids survived.

There was a lull in the creatures around him. He raised Night-shard and bellowed for his comrades to hold the line. It was a mis-take, as a large spear slammed into him, causing Nightshard to fly from his hand and pinning him to the ground. Pain wracked his body. He tried to pull it from his body, but he weakened as he struggled with it. A golden image materialized next to him, and with a mighty tug, Aleara freed him of the spear.

"Better win, Veilbreaker," Aleara said. "I have emerged into this world, and my father will raise the stakes."

A rumble of thunder echoed across the battlefield in response to her ominous words. The goddess blinked out. Thomas went into shock. Despite being infused with the energy of gods and lost souls, his mortal body had reached its limits. He drew upon aether once again, and the gaping wound in his chest began to close. Ribs crushed and blown free of his body rose from the muddied ground.

Oldiren emerged. The god said nothing, but he pointed to where Nightshard stood stuck in the ground. So far, no creature has chosen to pick up the mighty blade, but they were all around it. Thomas found the strength to stand, then drew on chaos again. The sword seemed smaller. He looked at himself. The plate mail was healing itself. Thomas fought his way to his weapon. Tentacled creatures surged forward, and he sprayed chaos, turning it into tiny bolts of fire that peppered the beast. It reared up in anger, and Thomas grasped Nightshard, plunging it into the toothy maw as it crashed down to devour him. He shrugged and pushed the corpse off to the side. He looked up to see his father off to his left, clashing with Aleara's knights.

He concentrated and forced his body back to its human-sized form. He whistled and waited for his steed to find him. Wilhelm came. He mounted the horse and spurred it toward the Duke. The storm clouds continued to roil and draw closer, promising a miserable battlefield or worse. His need for revenge consumed him. Nightshard had been wailing nonstop, but since he retrieved it, the sword was silent. He called, and his ghostly mother and brother came forth from the sword, their incorporeal forms bouncing along beside the charging horse.

Thomas remembered the mighty owlbear Selvus. He looked down. The rune appeared on his gauntlet, and he touched it. A roar escaped as the rune vanished. When or how Selvus would aid him remained a mystery, but they definitely could use the help.

"This is for you, mother," Thomas said.

He pulled up, drawing upon the chaos until his voice could be heard across the battlefield. With a mighty roar, Thomas got the attention of his father, and the duke turned his horse, spurring it toward him. The black horse, formed from chaos, snorted and resisted the order to halt. Thomas finally relented, and the destrier ran forward. The horses came close, hooves flashing as they went by. The Duke tumbled from his saddle as his horse went down from the kick it received. Thomas vaulted from the saddle, the weight of his armor a mere nuisance as he channeled chaos more and more.

"I'm going to teach you a trick," Nightshard said in his head. "See those fresh bodies. Command them to rise."

Thomas looked around at fallen soldiers everywhere. He chose two intact ones and ordered them as Nightshard said. Screaming came from the dead bodies, but Thomas did not see what happened as his father was upon him. He looked down at his father. Nightshard got there before the Duke's blade could make contact, and sparks flew where the blades connected. He pushed the Duke back and threw his helm on the ground.

"I want you to see the look on my face when you die," Thomas said. "Let there be no doubt that it will be a joyous one."

He slashed, and Kendrick parried. The paladin spun around, rocking his opponent backward with a blast of energy. His father fell, struggling to his feet. Thomas stepped forward, and a slash at his knees made contact. His left leg buckled, causing his attack to glance off the other's armor. Thomas tried to stand, but the leg would not respond. The duke rose, and he pulled his sword backward, ready to strike his killing blow. Something ran past him, and the two fallen soldiers fell upon Thomas' foe. The dead man's head lolled to the side, its neck broken. The other bristled with arrows. The duke recoiled at the sight of his soldiers rising from the dead.

They pinned him down. Thomas grimaced but forced himself to stand, using Nightshard as a crutch. He drew upon the aether, and the leg healed, but something went wrong. The leg burst from the armor, black, scaly flesh growing over the broken greave.

He ignored the sight of his perverted flesh and strode forward. The two soldiers released the duke. The elder man circled away from the soldiers, watching his son. Thomas waited. The temptation to use the aether again gnawed at him. His leg told him that it might be a bad idea. Instead, he readied Nightshard.

He didn't have to wait long. The duke yelled, cursing the thirdborn and charging forward. His sword cut multiple arcs, causing Thomas to step back. Up the duke's arms went, and he drove down for a final blow. Thomas ignored it and plunged his sword into his father, staring into the man's unbelieving eyes. The armor parted like paper, and Nightshard sucked his spirit from him. The duke fell to his knees, clutching at Nightshard, and Thomas leered into his face before pulling his blade free and striking his father's head from his body.

"Release us," one soldier said. "Let us have a clean death."

"What do they mean?" Thomas asked.

"You just exposed one of the greatest lies Aleara has allowed to exist," Nightshard said. "The dead never return to Aleara. They are doomed to be trapped in their bodies until they turn to dust. Even then, their spirits do not return to her."

"That cannot be true," Thomas growled. "Aleara would never do that."

"Believe what you will," Nightshard said.

Both soldiers collapsed. Klydos' army no longer outnumbered them, and that meant the battle was even, perhaps even turning in their favor. He heard a roar and raised his sword in joy at the sight of the ancient owlbear crashing from the woods, wading through the forces of Klydos. Jaxxon saw his father and sprinted to join him in the chaotic carnage unfolding. A smile creased Thomas' lip. If Klydos hated Binsmuth before today, he would find new levels of animosity after this loss. A noise brought his attention back to the battlefield.

As he turned, another portal opened. An army waited beyond. He called to his horse and mounted. The destrier burst into motion, heading for the portal. This would have broken their ranks if he had done nothing. He looked around, hoping to find Lyrei. He glimpsed the Valkrunian banner but could not find her. Insect-like soldiers began to pour from the portal, and Thomas realized he was out of time. He spurred the horse onward.

Faisel rode toward him. Though Wilhelm was fashioned from the aether itself, his uncle's horse came alongside. The man was using chaos to aid his steed. There was no time to stop him. Whatever happened, the die was cast. His steed leaped, and as they passed through the portal, Thomas drew upon as much chaos as would respond and sealed it behind him. Where he was, he did not know, but at least his friends stood a chance without this latest threat. He landed amongst the insect men, and he poured his frustration into killing everyone who got close to him. Nightshard drank of them willingly, and Faisel held his own. Once the insect men were dispatched, he looked around at the strange sight before him. Faisel and he might die on a peculiar world, but at least their world could prevail. Would he ever know?

EPILOGUE

K lydos materialized in the clearing. His kilt billowed out around him, blown about by a breeze that only affected Him. He was beautiful to behold. Long black hair was pleated into a single braid. His eyes were a piercing, ice-blue. When Klydos took a step, the land beneath his feet changed, transforming from sand to molten lava, then to green grass, and finally to barren rock. Nearby trees wilted and shriveled as chaos swirled about the being. He knelt before the cairn, reached out his armored, clawed hand, and the blue-black energy of chaos poured forth down into the grave. Donegal appeared nearby.

"You look like you had your ass kicked," Klydos said.

"Heal me, father," Donegal said. "Help me to fight that upstart. I will join forces with you. I will make the very land itself rise against these humans."

Klydos said nothing, instead focusing on the ground below the rocky cairn. Donegal gasped as he sensed what Klydos was doing. This was the grave of the priest so beloved by Thomas Grimhorn, the Veilbreaker. The Lord of Tempests stopped for a moment regarding his son.

"They have done well against the living," Klydos said. "My pesky brother made a move, though his puppet does not know it. We must fight to prevent Larisella's return. The humans think I hate them. Little do they know that I save them from a worse fate."

"You could tell them or ask Aleara and me to spread the word through our clergy," Donegal said.

The god of chaos snorted. Off in the distance, thunder rumbled. Klydos resumed his digging.

"Let's see if they can fight against the dead."

A shriveled arm pushed through the ground and knocked rocks away from the cairn. Klydos threw back his head and laughed as lightning raced across the sky. Donegal gasped as the figure rose from the grave. He joined his father in laughter as he realized the irony of choosing Avery as his newest general. Together, they gloated, knowing Avery would be a millstone around the neck of Thomas Grimhorn.

The dead man opened his eyes. His shattered bones poked through the tight, leathery skin. He looked from Klydos to Donegal, settling finally on the Lord of Tempests. He stretched as if the grave were no more than a cozy corner of a library where he dozed, awaiting the call to supper.

"Aleara," Avery said, "I have returned to you."

"My daughter cannot help you, priest," Klydos said, "but I can. Swear your allegiance to me, and you shall have a chance to repay Aleara for failing you when you needed her the most."

"Give me life," Avery said.

His voice sounded like a desert breeze fluttering through a sheaf of old parchment.

"I'll give you something better than life," Klydos said.

Before Donegal could react, Klydos plunged one clawed hand into his son's chest and, with the other, streamed the remaining life force of the god into Avery. A dry, dusty laugh came from the emaciated corpse, but flesh knit itself together. Muscles and sinew reappeared. Avery's body filled out. It was not life but a cruel mimicry of it. Better still, with the lifeforce of the god flowing into him came answers. Ones he had spent a lifetime asking Aleara.

"I'm not breathing," Avery said.

"Nor will you," Klydos said.

Donegal disappeared, his remaining life force humming inside Avery. Dirt tumbled away from his body as he rose from the cairn. The former priest looked down and saw his heart pulsing with a blue light. He looked at the tattered robes hanging from his body. A thunderclap resounded, and black armor replaced them. Avery looked at the helm in his hand. On the forehead was the symbol of the strangler tree, its vines and roots curling to form an A.

"Come," Klydos said, "we have an army to build. We will finish this world and go on to destroy others."

EPILOGUE

Klydos materialized in the clearing. His kilt billowed out around him, blown about by a breeze that only affected Him. He was beautiful to behold. Long black hair was pleated into a single braid. His eyes were a piercing, ice-blue. When Klydos took a step, the land beneath his feet changed, transforming from sand to molten lava, then to green grass, and finally to barren rock. Nearby trees wilted and shriveled as chaos swirled about the being. He knelt before the cairn, reached out his armored, clawed hand, and the blue-black energy of chaos poured forth down into the grave. Donegal appeared nearby.

"You look like you had your ass kicked," Klydos said.

"Heal me, father," Donegal said. "Help me to fight that upstart. I will join forces with you. I will make the very land itself rise against these humans."

Klydos said nothing, instead focusing on the ground below the rocky cairn. Donegal gasped as he sensed what Klydos was doing. This was the grave of the priest so beloved by Thomas Grimhorn, the Veilbreaker. The Lord of Tempests stopped for a moment regarding his son.

"They have done well against the living," Klydos said. "My pesky brother made a move, though his puppet does not know it. We must fight to prevent Larisella's return. The humans think I hate them. Little do they know that I save them from a worse fate."

"You could tell them or ask Aleara and me to spread the word through our clergy," Donegal said.

The god of chaos snorted. Off in the distance, thunder rumbled. Klydos resumed his digging.

"Let's see if they can fight against the dead."

A shriveled arm pushed through the ground and knocked rocks away from the cairn. Klydos threw back his head and laughed as lightning raced across the sky. Donegal gasped as the figure rose from the grave. He joined his father in laughter as he realized the irony of choosing Avery as his newest general. Together, they gloated, knowing Avery would be a millstone around the neck of Thomas Grimhorn.

The dead man opened his eyes. His shattered bones poked through the tight, leathery skin. He looked from Klydos to Donegal, settling finally on the Lord of Tempests. He stretched as if the grave were no more than a cozy corner of a library where he dozed, awaiting the call to supper.

"Aleara," Avery said, "I have returned to you."

"My daughter cannot help you, priest," Klydos said, "but I can. Swear your allegiance to me, and you shall have a chance to repay Aleara for failing you when you needed her the most."

"Give me life," Avery said.

His voice sounded like a desert breeze fluttering through a sheaf of old parchment.

"I'll give you something better than life," Klydos said.

Before Donegal could react, Klydos plunged one clawed hand into his son's chest and, with the other, streamed the remaining life force of the god into Avery. A dry, dusty laugh came from the emaciated corpse, but flesh knit itself together. Muscles and sinew reappeared. Avery's body filled out. It was not life but a cruel mimicry of it. Better still, with the lifeforce of the god flowing into him came answers. Ones he had spent a lifetime asking Aleara.

"I'm not breathing," Avery said.

"Nor will you," Klydos said.

Donegal disappeared, his remaining life force humming inside Avery. Dirt tumbled away from his body as he rose from the cairn. The former priest looked down and saw his heart pulsing with a blue light. He looked at the tattered robes hanging from his body. A thunderclap resounded, and black armor replaced them. Avery looked at the helm in his hand. On the forehead was the symbol of the strangler tree, its vines and roots curling to form an A.

"Come," Klydos said, "we have an army to build. We will finish this world and go on to destroy others."